It was exactly twelve thirty when the three figures emerged from the shadows at the side of the super-market. Pasha's nephews. Or 'The Goons' as Lee called them. They were illuminated for a split-second by the street lamp before disappearing around the gate into the rear yard.

'And they're off,' hissed Lee excitedly. Slouching down in his seat he pulled his mask over his head.

A jolt of electricity charged the air. The windows fogged over as their body heat surged . . . Mal rubbed a small hole in the condensation to watch the van drive away. 'Let's go!' he yelled as soon as it disappeared around the corner. Grinning, he pulled his mask on and reached for the door handle.

About the author

Mandasue Heller was born in Cheshire and moved to Manchester in 1982. She spent ten years living in the notorious Hulme Crescents, which have since become the background to *The Front*, her first novel. She has sung in cabaret and rock groups, seventies soul cover bands and blues jam bands. She shares a house with her partner, three children, a tarty squirrel-tailed cat and a fearless hamster.

THE FRONT

Mandasue Heller

CORONET BOOKS
Hodder & Stoughton

A CIP catalogue record for this title
is available from the British Library

ISBN 0 340 82024 1

Typeset in Sabon by Hewer Text Ltd, Edinburgh
Printed and bound in Great Britain by
Mackays of Chatham plc, Chatham, Kent

Hodder and Stoughton
A division of Hodder Headline
338 Euston Road
London NW1 3BH

To my amazing family

ACKNOWLEDGEMENTS

I would like to thank the following for their support and encouragement:

My beautiful mother – JEAN HELLER – for everything.
My gorgeous partner – WINGROVE WARD – for endless love & support.
My fantastic children – MICHAEL, ANDREW, & AZZURA – for being who they are.
Special thanks to my family – AVA, AMBER, MARTIN, JADE, REECE & KYRO.
NANA, DOREEN & Co.
DANIEL & NATALIE.
KAINE BROWN – for opening the windows.
Many thanks to my agents – CAT LEDGER & FAYE WEBBER. (Talkback) for help and belief.
NICK AUSTIN.
Every-lovely-one at HODDER, especially:
  BETTY SCHWARTZ – my guardian angel . . . need I say more?
And lastly – but by no means least . . .
  My fabulous editor – WAYNE BROOKES (it was meant to be!)

1

Mal woke with a start to the shrill ringing of the phone on the bedside table. He raised his head, but dropped it back when a sickening flash of pain tore through it. His stomach lurched in sympathy. Too much lager the night before. *Never again*! Groaning, he pulled his pillow up around his ears and waited for Suzie to pick the phone up. She didn't.

'Oi!' he croaked, lashing an arm across the bed to wake her. Hitting empty space instead of the expected shoulder, he forced his eyes open, clamping them shut again as a stream of sunlight struck them like a hammer blow. Why had the stupid bitch opened the curtains when he was still asleep? And where was she, anyway?

Annoyed as much by Suzie sneaking off as by the still-ringing phone, he rolled across the bed and snatched it up. An unmistakable snigger flooded his ear. *Lee*! He might have known it'd be that little dickhead. Who else would bother him at this time?

'Whaddya want?' he grunted.

'You still in bed, you lazy cunt?' Lee yelled.

Mal peered at the small bedside clock but couldn't focus. It could have been six in the morning for all he knew. It sure as hell felt like it.

'Why, what time is it?' Pushing himself upright, he reached for an urgent hit of nicotine.

'Near enough two!' Lee was still yelling. 'Time you was up and about, matey. What you doin', anyhow?'

'Getting a fucking headache, thanks to you!' Mal yelled back. 'Keep your bleeding gob down, will you!' Lighting the cigarette, he sucked on it hard, exhaling noisily.

'Fine way to greet a mate who's about to do you a favour,' Lee said.

'You'd have done me a favour by letting me kip in peace,' Mal retorted grumpily.

'You'll thank me when you know what it is.'

'I bleedin' won't!'

'You will, mate,' insisted Lee. Then, with another irritating snigger, he began to sing: 'Money, money, money!'

Despite his mood, Mal's ears pricked up. 'What money?' he demanded. 'What you on about?'

'You'll see,' Lee told him archly. 'All's I'm saying is it's a biggie! I'll be outside in twenty, yeah?'

'Piss off. I ain't getting up yet.'

'If you wanna earn top dollar you will. Anyhow, I've gotta give you a ride in me new babe-mobile! Man, you'll wanna shag it when you see it, it's so gorgeous!'

'Where did you get the sponds for a new motor?' Mal asked grumpily. 'You're always skint.'

'Bit a this, bit a that,' said Lee. 'You know the score, man. Anyway, look, I gotta go, so I'll see you in twenty, yeah? And don't be late 'cos we're going to Sam's.' And with that, he hung up.

Mal slammed the receiver down hard. He hated it when people did that: hung up before he had a chance to tell them to piss off. Still, Lee had mentioned money, and if anything was guaranteed to get him out of bed it was

2

the ever-elusive dollar. Needs must, and all that – and Charlie was becoming a very greedy lover these days!

Stabbing the cigarette out, Mal pushed the quilt aside and staggered to the bathroom for a cold shower.

Twenty minutes later he heard a series of rapid horn-blasts down below signalling Lee's arrival. Giving himself a last look-over in the mirror he headed out – feeling much more on form than earlier, thanks to two nice lines of premium-white.

Strolling along the fifth-floor balcony, whistling as he walked, he breathed in the crisp April air and looked down on the great sprawl of grass separating Robert Adam Crescent from William Kent. It was a pale greeny-yellow in the weak afternoon sun, heralding spring – his favourite time of year. And today was a particularly fine specimen. Bright enough for shades – nippy enough for his new black leather jacket. The perfect posing day. A Stallone kind of a day.

In the car park down below, Lee was happily revving the balls off his new car: a metallic grey Mark II Escort, with blacked-out windows, alloy wheels, chrome trim, and a full body kit, including state-of-the-art tail fin. He couldn't wait to see Mal's face when he saw the motor. He'd be green.

It was the flashiest car Lee had ever owned – and, at two and a half gees, the most expensive. Still, he hadn't paid a penny yet – and maybe never would. He hadn't made his mind up yet. It would teach the bloke a lesson if he didn't. What kind of idiot must he be to hand his car to a complete stranger and seriously expect him to turn up with fifty quid a week just because he'd said he would? The bloke had to be a candidate for Prestwich.

Running his hands around the worn leather steering wheel, he felt a thrill of pride. It was a little beauty, there was no denying that. Maybe he'd bung the bloke a couple of tons for good-will – if he got the wedge he expected tonight. But then again . . . maybe not. The bloke had said everything was in perfect working order, when in fact, the cassette player didn't work. The radio did, but that wasn't the same. And maybe it was a tiny blip in the greater scheme of things, but to Lee it was a blatant lie, and he didn't see why he should honour his side of the bargain, given that.

Spotting Mal striding towards him through the tunnel beneath the flats, Lee lowered his window and stuck his greasy blond head out, already grinning in anticipation of Mal's envy. Then he saw what he was wearing and shook his head. What did the cunt think he looked like? Gel-slicked hair, leather jacket – collar up – and ironed jeans – *ironed*, for fuck's sake! Nobody ironed their jeans!

' 'Ere,' he jeered, squinting against the sun as he looked Mal up and down. 'What you ponced up for? You look like a right batty boy!'

'Nothing wrong with looking good,' Mal retorted, pointedly returning the look. 'You want to try it yourself, mate. You could start by buying yourself a toothbrush. And a shower once in a while wouldn't go amiss, know what I mean?'

Too thick-skinned to take this personally, Lee grinned, his cheeks creasing into deep, dirty lines around a mouthful of partially rotted teeth. 'Nah, I'm handsome enough as I am, me. And birds go for the natural smell, innit?'

'If you say so!' Mal snorted, wondering exactly what

4

kind of bird would go for the scent of week-dead donkey? Certainly none he'd care to meet.

Lighting a cigarette, he dangled it from the corner of his mouth and dipped down to check his immaculate black hair in the wing mirror, then slipped his shades on. A Latin James Dean now, he sucked on the cigarette, letting the smoke swirl out from his nose.

Lee laughed. 'You're a right poser, you!'

'You're calling me a poser?' Mal drawled. 'Sitting there like the dog's bollocks on wheels!'

'Yeah, but ain't she gorgeous?' Lee said, giving his door a proud pat.

Mal flicked his eyes over the car with studied detachment. It looked shit-hot, but he was buggered if he was going to tell Lee that. Giving him the slightest hint of approval gave him licence to go on and on until you had to slap him to shut him up. Anyway, he didn't deserve praise after his snide cracks.

'It's all right, I suppose,' he said after a minute.

'All right?' squawked Lee. 'It's a pure babe-magnet, this!'

'Put a magnet near this, it's a goner, mate,' Mal snorted. 'It's bogged up all over the show.'

'Leave it out!' Lee protested. 'It's in top nick, this. The bloke told me—'

'A load of old bollocks!' Mal cut him off with a smirk. 'Now how many times have I told you not to believe everything you're told, eh? Anyhow, you should have asked me to go with you if you were shelling out for wheels – you know you ain't got a clue.'

'Thanks,' muttered Lee, deflating fast.

Mal shrugged. 'Hey, man. What are mates for?' Hopping in the passenger side, he slapped a hand down on the dash. 'Come on, then. What you waiting for? Let's go!'

Lee brightened immediately, more than happy to demonstrate what his new baby could do. Mal wouldn't be so quick to criticize when he got a taste of the action. Throwing it into first gear, he rammed his foot to the floor and rocketed out of the car park with a tyre-burning screech.

Mal gripped the edge of his seat with as much cool as he could muster as they careered onto the main road on two wheels and hurtled towards the traffic lights ahead. The car had balls, he'd give it that. He just hoped Lee could handle it. It was too nice a day to end in a hearse.

When all four wheels were back on solid ground, he relaxed enough to unhook his nails from the seat. 'So what's this "money, money, money" business?' he asked. 'And it better be good, dragging me out of me pit at this time of day.'

Lee smiled. 'Oh, it is, mate, it is. Remember that job I said I was working on?'

Mal rolled his eyes. For a minute there, he'd actually thought Lee might have stumbled onto something that didn't require his doing anything. Like a mislaid Securicor case stuffed full of cash, or something. But no – he was on with one of his crap schemes again.

Leaning forward, he fiddled with the radio, flooding the air with The Smiths' latest dirge. He sighed exaggeratedly. 'Go on, then. What's it gonna be this time? Taj Mahal? Crown Jewels? Hi-jacking a jumbo?'

Lee shot him a sulky side glance. 'Take the piss all you want,' he said, his voice matching Morrisey's for petulance. 'But it's right this time, and I've worked everything out proper like. Still, if you don't wanna come in on it, I'll just—'

'D'y' have to whine?' Mal interrupted in a bored voice. 'I ain't said no, have I? I'm just saying it depends. Try clueing me up and I'll let you know. What, when and where?'

'Only if you stop taking the piss?'

'Stop fannying around and tell me if you're gonna.' Mal lit another cigarette off the butt of his last and waited.

Lee wanted to keep him guessing as a punishment, but managed all of three seconds before blurting out: 'All right. It's Pasha's place. And it's going off tonight.'

Sure it must be a wind-up, Mal twisted around in his seat to look at Lee fully. 'Pasha's?' he spat. 'You're having a laugh! That's the poxiest shite-hole in Manchester! What d'y' reckon we're gonna pull from there? A pack of bleedin' nappies and some fanny plugs? Jeezus!'

'Nah, man, it's perfect,' said Lee, quite seriously. 'I've been casing it for weeks and he is *raking* it in. Just think about it.' He held up his hand and began to count off on his fingers: 'Look at the threads he's strolling about in – they've got to be worth a fair few bob, yeah? And that big fuck-off jeep he's driving is twenty-five grand's worth at least. And look at all them new security cameras and shit he's had put in. How much d'y' reckon that lot's setting him back, eh?' He raised a questioning eyebrow but didn't wait for Mal to answer before continuing: 'A fucking mint, that's what!' He shook his head, his lip twisting with contempt. 'The cunt's flashing it about something rotten, and by my reckoning, it's time someone relieved him of some, know what I mean?'

Gripping tight to his seat again as they sailed through a

red light, narrowly avoiding a van, Mal considered what Lee had said and grudgingly agreed that he might just have a point. Pasha Singh, owner of the local supermarket, had been acquiring some heavy-duty goods recently, and to do that he must be making serious profits. And now that he thought about it, it also occurred to him that Pasha's shop was virgin territory in the blagging stakes. All the other shops in the row had been done over numerous times, but never Pasha's.

It didn't occur to him to wonder why.

Lee saw the thoughts ticking over on Mal's face and knew he was interested. 'Well?' he asked eagerly. 'You up for it, or what?'

Mal shrugged casually. It sounded just the boost his depleted funds needed, but he didn't want to appear too eager – didn't want Lee to get ahead of himself and start acting the great I Am.

'Sounds all right,' he said at last. 'So long as you've worked it out right, 'cos I know what you're like for ballsing things up.'

Lee grinned confidently. 'Nah, not this time, man. It's a dead cert, this. I've worked everything out to a T – all the times and shit. It'll be right, you'll see. Especially with Sam and Ged in on it. The four of us together, man, we'd be like a bleedin' army!'

'They said they'll do it, then?' Mal asked.

Lee shook his head. 'Haven't told 'em yet. But if Sam says yeah, Ged'll do it and all. You know what them two are like. Anyhow,' he went on with a grin. 'I wanted to make sure you were in first. You're me number one, ain't you?'

Mal allowed him a small smile for his loyalty, then asked, 'So what we looking at?' He just hoped Lee wasn't planning on loading the car with fags and booze. He needed hard cash, not shopping.

Lee shrugged. 'Can't be sure exactly, but I reckon it should be a fair few grand.'

Mal frowned. 'Won't come to much, split four ways.'

Lee pulled his head back. 'Who said anything about a four-way split? Do I look a complete numpty?'

'You don't want me to answer that!'

'Ah, shaddup!' Lee grinned, then said more seriously: 'Look, I've got it sorted in me head. If we drop them at Sam's straight after and take the dosh back to yours to count, they won't know how much we've got, so they'll be none the wiser when we give them a third between them and split the rest between us, will they?'

Mal pursed his mouth. 'Oh, I dunno, mate. It still won't come to that much. It ain't really worth the hassle, is it?'

'Come off it,' Lee spluttered, taking his eyes off the road for a full five seconds. 'Even if it's only a couple of gees, it's gotta be worth it for ten minutes' graft!' He grinned hopefully. 'You're just messing about, ain't you?'

Mal laughed out loud. 'Course I am, you plank! Think I'm stupid or something?'

'Yes!' Lee yelled excitedly. 'I knew I could count on you, mate. And here, seeing as you're in . . .' Reaching under his seat, he pulled out a crinkled plastic bag and tipped it up onto his knee. 'Cop a load of this little beauty!'

Mal's eyes widened. 'Holy shit!' he gasped. 'Where d'y' get that? Giz a look.'

Reaching across, he snatched up the gun and gazed at it in reverent wonder. He didn't have a clue what make it

was, but he knew a dangerous piece when he saw one –
and this was deadly. A thrill ran through his groin as he
stroked his fingers along the smooth matt-black finish.
Guns were the ultimate turn-on – the ultimate frightener.
And this one, as Lee had rightly said, was a little beauty.

He whistled through his teeth respectfully. 'Very nice!'
Turning it around, he squinted down into the barrel.
'Loaded?'

'Course!' Lee said, his voice thick with pride. 'It ain't a
toy, you know. That's the real McCoy, that is!'

Turning it streetward, Mal closed an eye and peered
along the barrel, setting his sights on a young mother
pushing a pram along the pavement. His finger quivered
on the trigger, the urge to squeeze almost overwhelming.

Kaboom . . . Kaboom!

Blowing imaginary smoke away as the girl and her
unseen sprog mentally hit the deck in a pool of blood and
gore, he asked again where Lee had got it.

'Jamie Wotsisface from the Eagle,' Lee told him,
jealously reclaiming the gun. Slipping it back into the
bag, he stashed it safely back under the seat.

'Junkie Jamie?' Mal sneered, rubbing his tingling
fingers on his thighs. 'That rip-off merchant? How much
did he rush you?'

'A tenner,' said Lee smugly. 'He wanted fifty, but I
bunged him a brownie and promised the rest later. Yeah,
like he's ever gonna see it,' he cackled. 'Suck-er! Anyhow,
he wasn't gonna say no, the state he was in, snottin' and
shakin'.' He wrinkled his nose in disgust. 'Bleeding
junkies, man. They've got no sense.'

Mal nodded, totally agreeing with this sentiment.
Smack was a mug's game, in his opinion: it took a man's
pride, ate it up and spat it out. Now Charlie – that was

the stuff. The essence of life. Mother of recreation. Charlie was the main man!

'It's only in case,' Lee was saying now. 'Just to shut him up if he gets lippy, like.'

Mal pictured Pasha on his knees behind the counter, begging for mercy as Lee thrust the gun into his face, demanding all the dosh from the till. He shook his head. 'Nah, he's a pussy. You won't need it.'

Looking out of his window as they turned on to Barlow Moor Road, Mal's forehead tightened into a frown. South Manchester sucked the big one. All twitching net curtains and 999 on permanent redial. You couldn't blend into the background in places like this. Load of creepy bastards! He didn't care how posh it was, he didn't want to be here, and he'd make damn' sure they didn't stay too long. He didn't know why Sam and Wendy had wanted to move up here in the first place – or how. It was supposed to have something like a ten-year waiting list.

As if reading Mal's thoughts, Lee said, 'I think they were dead lucky getting a gaff up here. You seen it yet?'

Mal grunted, 'Nah. I ain't had me invitation yet. Must've got lost in the post, eh? Anyhow, it's a bit toffee for me. And I thought Sam would've had more sense and all. What's he want to get stuck up here for?'

Lee shrugged. 'You know what Wendy's like once she's made her mind up about something. Remember how bad she kicked off when they offered her that dump in Sharston?'

'Yeah.' Mal smirked, remembering only too well. Wendy had an evil temper, and a tongue that could slice you in half.

'I reckon they shoved her here to keep her quiet,' Lee

went on. 'Her threatening to go to the news if they didn't give her somewhere decent. They couldn't exactly risk that with her fit to pop, could they? Ah, here it is.'

Swinging through the gateway of a neat, pebble-dashed semi with a tidy gravel drive and a well-tended garden, he screeched to a stop, sending a spray of small stones across the lawn.

'All right, isn't it?' He nodded towards the house, as proud as if it were his own. 'And Sam's well made up, being this far out, especially with that posse after his arse an'—'

'You what?' Mal cut him off with a frown. 'I thought he'd sorted that?'

Lee shrugged, opening his door. 'So did he, but Jimmy Feeley give him the tip-off the other week that they ain't too happy with his attitude now. They reckon he's been dissing 'em, or something. Load of bollocks, but what can you do?'

Mal was not happy about this last piece of information. The City Road Posse were an evil bunch of bastards, and Pasha's shop was smack in the middle of their turf. Being seen with a marked man would be very dangerous, and he wasn't sure he wanted to take that chance.

'Hang about a minute,' he said. 'You reckon we should let Sam in on this? You know what that crew are like, man. It won't just be him who cops it if they see him. We'll all get it.'

Lee shook his head, dismissing Mal's concerns with a wave of his hand. 'It's cool, man, I've got it covered. I've got us some masks. And wait till you see 'em. They're the works, man!' With that, he got out and marched up to Sam's front door.

Mal followed reluctantly, unable to share Lee's confidence. If Lee was wrong – which was extremely likely – bringing Sam along could seriously damage Mal's health.

Sam frowned when he peeped out through the net curtain and saw Lee and Mal standing on his step. He was already having a crap day, thanks to Wendy making him look a complete bastard in front of his kids that morning, and these clowns turning up unannounced did nothing to raise his spirits. He was just glad she was out now or there'd have been hell to pay. It wasn't Mal so much – she didn't seem to mind him, for some reason Sam had never quite fathomed. It was Lee. She hated him with a passion, and had fully expected him to vanish off the face of the earth after they moved. She wouldn't be too pleased if she came home and found him here now.

With that thought in mind, he crept away from the window, hoping they'd think he was out and go away. But it was too late. Lee had already spotted him. With another glass-rattling hammering on the door, he lifted the letter-box flap and shouted: 'I know you're in! I saw the curtain move!'

Sam cursed under his breath, knowing he couldn't blatantly ignore them after that. It was Wendy's fault, the bitch! She'd nagged him into submission – turned him into a pushover. She'd always been headstrong and opinionated, but these last few months, she'd turned into a Grade A ball-breaker. And there was nothing he could do about it, apart from belting her – and there was no way he was starting any of that shit, no matter how bad it got.

Under this cloud of despondency, Sam opened the door without a word, then turned and sloped away, leaving Lee and Mal to make up their own minds if they were going to come in or not.

Picking up on the atmosphere, Mal hesitated. But Lee had no such qualms. Hopping over the step, he followed Sam through to the showpiece lounge and threw himself into one of Wendy's new chairs, jeering: 'What's up with you, you sad bastard? You look like you've had shit for breakfast!'

Sam rolled his eyes and muttered, 'It might come to that yet.' Slumping even further down in his chair he stared at the floor, hoping they'd get the hint and leave in less than two minutes.

Mal perched on the arm of the couch with a frown. Seeing Sam like this made him even more certain that they shouldn't involve him in the job. The miserable shit would only put a damper on everything – if he didn't get them wasted first!

'Where's the missus?' Lee asked, helping himself to one of Sam's cigarettes.

'Out spending what we haven't got,' Sam told him glumly. 'And don't smoke that in here, she'll have a fit. Take it out the back.'

Lee laughed. 'Piss off, I'll open a window.'

'I'm not joking!' Sam snapped. 'Take it outside!'

'Behave yourself!' Lee snapped back. 'I ain't a dog you can shove in the yard.' Standing, he opened the window and parked himself on the sill, defiantly blowing his smoke outside.

Sam gritted his teeth as a familiar wave of nausea signalled an impending migraine. He had to get rid of them ASAP. 'Look, what you here for?' he asked, looking pointedly at his watch. 'Only I've got to go out in a bit . . .'

Mal's hackles rose at the obvious brush-off. He fought down an impulse to jump up and kick Sam's head in. The bastard knew how far they'd come – the least he could do was act pleased to see them. Pushing himself to his feet, he looked down on Sam with contempt, saying icily, 'Don't worry, we weren't planning to stick around. You're obviously too good for the likes of us now you're living up here, eh?' Still glaring at Sam, he motioned Lee to the door with a nod. 'Come on, mate, we obviously ain't welcome in his poncey new gaff.'

Blushing at the partial truth of the words, Sam looked down at his feet. If they did but know it, Wendy had in fact said just that – about Lee, anyway. Still, he shouldn't let her bully him into treating his mates like dirt.

'Look, don't go,' he said as Mal made for the door. 'Stay for a brew at least. I'm sorry for being such a git, but I've got a lot on my plate right now.'

'We've all got shit to deal with,' Mal snapped unsympathetically. 'But you don't see us moaning about it, do you? You want to sort your head out, mate.'

Sam nodded contritely. 'I know . . . I know, and I'm sorry. I'll make that brew, eh?'

'Four sugars,' called Lee from behind the net, then: ''Ere! Who's the bird with big tits going in next door?

'E' yar darlin'!' he yelled out through the window. 'What's your name, then? You got a fella? Fancy a sha—'

'Pack it in!' hissed Sam, running across the room to drag Lee away from the window. 'She'll tell Wendy!'

Mal and Lee exchanged an amused glance as Sam hurriedly slammed the window shut. Scared shitless of his own wife. How sad was that? The bloke needed a bollock transplant to remind himself who wore the kecks in the house.

'I'll put the kettle on,' Sam muttered, heading out of the room with his gaze cast down.

Mal followed, all set to hammer a few more nails into the coffin of Sam's manhood. Stepping into the kitchen, however, he was knocked back a step by the fluorescent yellow walls.

'Fuck me!' he exclaimed, throwing his hands up to shield his eyes. 'Jesus wants me for a sunbeam or what!'

Sam grinned sheepishly. 'It is a bit, isn't it? And if you think this is bad, you want to see what's she's planning for the conservatory!'

'You ain't got one of them, have you?' Mal jumped up at the sink and peered out of the window to see for himself.

'No,' said Sam, 'but it's on her never-ending list, second only to the royal nursery!' He shrugged dejectedly. 'I've told her we haven't got the money, but what Wendy wants, Wendy gets.'

Lee popped his head around the door. 'Does she want me?' he asked hopefully. ' 'Cos she can have me anytime!'

'In your dreams, you plonker!' Mal snorted. Then, turning to Sam, he asked: 'Is that what's up with you? Dosh?'

Sam nodded and ran his fingers through his hair. 'Man, I'm so far up shit creek I'm gonna need a passport to get back home!'

Lee came in and jumped up onto the ledge. 'Might be able to help you out there.'

'I doubt that,' Sam muttered, moving him out of the way to reach for the kettle. 'Not unless you've got a couple of grand going spare?'

Lee grinned. 'And if I did . . .?'

Sam narrowed his eyes. 'Come off it. Where you going to get money like that?'

16

'Where are *we* going to get it, you mean,' said Lee, opening the cupboard behind him and helping himself to a chocolate biscuit.

'Eh?' Sam looked at him quizzically. 'I don't get you.'

Lee looked at Mal. Mal hesitated, then nodded. It looked like Sam needed this even more than he did. The least he could do was let him in on it.

Lee grinned and puffed himself up to play Santa Claus. 'Right then . . .' he began. 'I've got this plan, see . . .'

An hour later, Wendy and the kids arrived home, complete with the latest Sega games console and four brand new games. The console had cost a bomb, but Wendy didn't care. It would serve Sam right for being too mean to buy the knock-off one they'd been offered that morning. She'd also treated herself to a couple of new dresses and a jacket. They'd cost almost as much as the kids' stuff, but again she didn't care a jot. Let Sam dare to complain – she'd soon set him straight. Anyway, he'd better get used to it, because she planned to buy lots more when she dropped this third – unplanned, unwanted – sprog he'd landed her with. She'd like to see him cart this monstrosity around for nine months without reward!

Finding the driveway blocked by a car she had never seen before, she had no option but to park on the pavement, and she was not amused. After traipsing around the Arndale Centre all day, the last thing she needed was a further walk to get into her own house. And her with her swollen feet! Sam was such an inconsiderate shit!

Marching up the path, she slammed the front door open and hustled the kids in, sending them straight upstairs to set the new game up on their week-old portable. Dumping her own bags in the hall, she stalked into the living room in fighting mood.

'What's that heap of shit doing up my path?' she demanded, glaring at Sam. 'It's a fucking eyesore, and I want it moved right no—' Her voice trailed off as she spotted Lee lounging in her chair with his filthy trainers on her new carpet and one of her china saucers on his knee catching his ash.

'What the fuck is he doing here?' she yelled. 'And why is he grinning at me like a dog on fucking heat?'

Mal suppressed a laugh as Sam's face drained of colour. He had a lot of time for Wendy. She was feisty as hell, and gorgeous to boot. And today, she looked amazing. Her thick black hair longer and glossier than usual, her huge breasts straining at the soft material of her dress. But best of all were her eyes. Usually a sultry violet, they were now alive and blazing with vim and fire. Very horny! Feeling the stirrings of a hard-on, he stood up.

'Hi, babe,' he crooned, pulling her into a hug and breathing in the heady scent of musk oil. 'You're looking particularly sexy today.'

'Thanks,' she sniffed, knocked off balance by the compliment – despite feeling about as sexy as a walrus right now. 'Look, no offence, Mal,' she went on. 'It's not you I'm pissed off with, it's that nonce!' She jabbed a finger towards Lee. 'I don't want him in my house!'

Mal laughed softly. 'No offence taken, babe, but you don't need to go upsetting yourself in your condition, so we'll get off. Come on, Lee. On your feet.'

'How come we had to go?' Lee pouted as they pulled out of the drive minutes later. 'I haven't seen Wendy for ages.

I could have stayed all day just lookin' at her tits!' He groaned lustfully. 'Man, did you see 'em? They're gi-fuckin'-gantic! One of these days I'm gonna—'

'Are you thick or what?' Mal cut him off sharply. 'She can't fucking stand you. She ain't gonna let you nowhere near her tits. She doesn't even want you in her house.'

'She does!'

'She just said she don't, you dense bastard!'

Lee sniffed sulkily. 'She's just playing hard to get.'

Mal shook his head in despair. 'Shut the fuck up, man. You're doing me head in.'

'Be like that!' Lee muttered. 'But I know what I know.'

Settling back in his seat, Mal closed his eyes and tuned Lee out, thinking instead about what he was going to do with his dosh. After tonight, all being well – which was a long shot, considering whose idea it was! – he'd be rolling in it. And just think how much Charlie he'd get with a few grand in his pocket!

As soon as he thought of Charlie, his stomach tigh-tened, as though an invisible hand were in there, squeez-ing his guts. Recognizing the signs, he groaned. *Come-down city! Bummer!*

Back at the house, Sam sighed heavily as Wendy sprayed air freshener all over the chair Lee had been sitting on. She was fuming, hissing her tirade at him through gritted teeth.

'I'm telling you now, Sam, I ever catch that dirty little bastard in my house again you'll know about it! It bloody stinks in here now! And look at that filth!' She pointed at a faint scuff on the carpet. 'Well, that's it! I'll have to get a new bleeding carpet now!'

'That's going a bit far, isn't it?' Sam said. 'It'll wash off. It's only dust.'

'Dust!' Wendy screeched. 'It's shite! It'll never come off.'

'I'll do it,' Sam said, pushing himself to his feet wearily. 'And keep your voice down, will you? The kids will hear.'

'Keep my bleeding voice down!' she snorted. 'Why? So the kids won't know what a stupid useless git they've got for a father? Bit late for that, mate!'

'Thanks, Wendy,' Sam muttered unhappily. 'Just leave that, I'll do it later.' Turning, he made for the door.

'That's right,' Wendy sneered. 'Slope off and leave me to sort your mess out as per!'

'I'm going to get a shower,' Sam told her. 'If that's all right with you?'

'Oh?' she raised a brow. 'Going out, are we?'

He sighed and ran a hand through his hair. 'If you must know, we've got a job on tonight.'

'A job?' Wendy demanded. 'What kind of job? And who's we?'

'Me and the lads,' Sam said. 'And I'd have thought you'd be happy. God knows we need the money.'

'Well, don't think I'm staying in,' Wendy said, viciously shaking out the cushion Lee had tainted. 'If you're going out with the lads, I'm off out to see my mates and all. In fact, I might just pay Suzie a visit, find out what you're up to when I'm not around!'

'Suit yourself,' Sam said, walking out.

Wendy glared at the closing door. 'Oh, I will, mate!' she hissed. 'Believe me, I will!'

Mal was completely pissed off by the time they reached the Crescents: itching to get a line, and ready to pick holes in anyone who crossed his path. Sensing this, Lee sensibly kept his mouth shut as he followed him up the foul-smelling stairs to his flat. Mal would be sorted once the God of White was floating up his nose.

Inside, Suzie was relaxing on the couch, watching TV. Hearing Mal's key in the lock, she jumped up guiltily. He couldn't stand it when she slobbed around in the middle of the day – as he called it. Switching the TV off, she did a frantic scan of the spotlessly clean room. Fussy to the point of obsession, Mal had a knack of spotting even the tiniest speck of dust she'd overlooked, and he could go days without speaking to her if he thought she hadn't tried hard enough.

Seconds later Mal burst through the door, and she could tell at a glance that he was on edge. She smiled, hoping to defuse the tension before it settled in. But he didn't smile back, just swivelled his eyes around the room in search of something to criticize.

'What are you doing back so soon?' she asked pleasantly. 'I didn't expect you till tonight.'

'I bet you didn't,' he muttered, taking his jacket off and flinging it onto the back of the couch. 'Catch you out, did I? Where's he gone, then? The bloke you were shagging when I came in?'

Suzie didn't answer. There was no point. She knew only too well how volatile he could be – especially when he was coming down, as he obviously was at the moment. Anything could set him off. He was like a lightly set trap waiting for a breath of air to spring him.

'And while we're at it,' he went on, his voice tense and accusing. 'Where did you slope off to this morning? You know I can't stand it when you take off without telling me.'

'I only went to the shops,' she told him quietly. 'And I *did* tell you.'

He gave her a filthy look. 'Oh, yeah? And when was that, then? When I was asleep, you dense bitch!'

'No,' she mumbled, looking down. 'You woke up for a bit and had a cig. I told you then. I had to get the chops for dinner.'

Vaguely remembering this, Mal pushed her out of the way and began to search for his paraphernalia. Sticking his hand down the side of the couch to retrieve the mirror he'd left there, he barked over his shoulder, 'I hope you got enough for Lee and all, 'cos he's staying.'

Nodding hello to Lee, Suzie said, 'I got three. He can have your extra one, if you don't mind?'

'Whatever!'

Lee's stomach rumbled at the mention of food. Hot food – cooked by a woman! 'That'd be great, that,' he grinned, rubbing his hands together. 'Better than chippy shite any day. How you doing, then, Sooze?'

'She's fine,' Mal answered for her, impatiently dragging the cushions off the couch and scattering them around the floor. 'Where've you put my fucking mirror?'

Getting it from the shelf, she handed it to him. Snatching it without thanks, he tossed it to Lee and headed for the door. 'Do the honours, mate. I'm bursting for a piss.'

When he'd gone, Suzie replaced the cushions, then perched on the arm of the couch and lit a cigarette, watching as Lee kneeled beside the coffee table and tipped a little wrap of coke onto the mirror with a look of intense concentration. She didn't understand their fascination with it at all, and wished they wouldn't do it. It just made Mal aggressive and sarcastic – and that frightened her.

Coming back into the room, still zipping his fly, Mal flopped down on the couch and eyed the mirror greedily. 'Shove the kettle on, then,' he said, nudging Suzie. 'I'm gagging here. You think you're a bleedin' ornament or something?'

Lee glanced up as she quickly disappeared into the kitchen. 'Obedient, ain't she?' he sniggered. 'Pauline would've told me to go and fuck meself if I'd talked to her like that. She was all woman, that one!' he added with a reflective sigh.

Mal shook his head, remembering Lee's last squeeze less fondly. Pauline had been a swamp goddess. Ugly as sin, with a mouth like a docker-whore. Lee was well shot of the skanky bitch, in his opinion.

Lee's memory of Pauline was very different. She was the only woman who'd ever been willing to put her mouth anywhere near his rank dick, and for that miracle alone he'd considered her a princess. It had hit him hard when she'd found a princess of her own to play with. Not because she'd cheated, but because she'd refused to let him watch them at it. She could be a selfish witch at times, but he'd have had her back in a flash.

'You see your problem?' Mal was saying now, cracking his knuckles as he joined Lee at the table. 'You just don't know how to treat birds. You should have battered Pauline the first time she opened her big gob – that would have sorted her head out.'

Lee agreed, just to save face. In fact, he was only too aware that he'd have come off worst if he'd tried that on with Pauline. Her head-butts were legendary.

Snatching the fiver Lee had rolled into a tube, Mal snorted the fattest line, sweeping over the traces until every last grain had vanished. Leaning back, eyes closed, unbreathing, he waited for the glorious rush.

'Ba-bee!' he moaned when it hit. 'Oh, shee-it, that's good!'

Lee greedily followed suit, then rocked back on his heels, groaning along ecstatically.

Opening their eyes moments later, they grinned at each other across the table. Buzzing again. Back in that high place far above the world. Gods!

'Another, Mr Kenny?' giggled Lee.

'Why, thank you, Mr Naylor,' said Mal, tweaking an imaginary moustache. 'Don't mind if I do!'

They moved in for their second lines just as Suzie came in with the cups. Mal's good mood evaporated when she went to place them on the table.

'Don't put 'em there, you fucking imbecile!' he screeched up at her. 'Can't you see what we're doing here? Jeezus!'

Shocked, she jerked the cups back. A drop of tea sloshed over the edge of one and she watched in horror as it landed with a dull splash on the corner of the mirror – nowhere near the powder, but still on the mirror. Big mistake.

'You stupid bitch!' Mal's coke-crazed eyes were ablaze as he leaped to his feet and brought the back of his hand across her cheek – so hard that she dropped the cups, sending three steaming fountains across the carpet. With a growl of fury, he seized her hair and dragged her head down to the table, smashing her mouth onto its edge, screaming, 'Lick it up, you clumsy cunt! Lick it up NOW!'

'No!' Lee squawked as a drop of blood fell from her lip and merged with the tea. 'The Charlie! The Charlie!'

A red mist fell across Mal's eyes. 'Aw, look what you done now!' he said as he yanked her head back, balled his fist and punched her. 'Look what you done!'

Oblivious to everything but the need to rescue the precious drugs, Lee dabbed at the bloodied tea with his shirt-tail. When he was satisfied that the coke was unharmed, he sat back with a relieved sigh – only then realizing what was happening. He didn't know what to do, where to look. He contemplated pretending he hadn't noticed, but that would have been impossible. Then, just as he thought he'd have to intervene, it stopped.

Tossing Suzie aside, Mal wiped his hands on his jeans and turned to Lee with an apologetic shrug. 'Sorry about that, mate. Can't trust the stupid cow to do anything right. I don't know how I control myself sometimes, I really don't!'

'It's all right,' Lee said placatingly. 'No harm done, eh? Have another line, mate. Come on . . . come and sit down, eh?'

As Mal bent his head over the mirror, Lee stole a quick glance at Suzie. The sight of her pretty face bleeding and swelling made him feel funny inside – guilty, almost. Poor kid. And at seventeen, she *was* just a kid. Too young to know how to handle a man of thirty-two, that was for sure. For a moment he felt truly sorry for her. Then Mal handed him the rolled-up fiver and he forgot all about Suzie.

Mal didn't. With narrowed eyes, he watched as she picked herself up and quietly made her way towards the door. As she reached for the handle, he called her back.

'Before you go sloping off, you'd better get that cleaned up.' He pointed at the tea stains. 'And when

25

you've finished that you can get on with me dinner. And don't be putting no green shite with them chops. Got that?'

Nodding, she moved towards the kitchen.

'And oi!' He shouted her back again. 'You'd better get that look off your face and all. Moping about like I don't know what. You want me to give you something to bleeding mope about, do you?'

'No,' she whispered.

He looked at her for a moment, then nodded, waving her away. Turning to Lee when she'd gone, he grinned. 'See what I mean, mate? It's all in the way you handle 'em!'

Suzie stayed in the kitchen until the dinner was made, and when she eventually carried the plates through she was pleased to see that Mal had settled down. He actually smiled as he took his plate from her.

'Thanks, doll. It looks good.'

'Yeah,' Lee agreed greedily. 'And it don't smell too bad, neither. God, I love chops. Me mam used to do 'em on Sundays.'

'No gravy?' Mal asked.

Suzie went back to the kitchen to fetch the jug of gravy she'd forgotten.

'*Highway to Heaven*'s on,' Lee told her when she came back. He patted the cushion beside him. 'Come and sit down and watch it.'

Frowning at the familiarity, Mal said sharply, 'We'll be getting off in a bit, Lee. Don't go getting settled.'

'Righto!' Lee saluted with his knife, then set about attacking his food with gusto. With his mouth full, he stuck his thumb up at Suzie who had sensibly chosen to sit at the far side of the couch.

'Fucking A, this is, Sooze. Didn't know you were such a good cook. And what's that funky taste?'

'Rosemary,' she told him.

'Bit weird, innit?' he said. 'But I like it. And this gravy's top. Here, what d'y' you reckon to them two?' He pointed his fork at the screen with a snigger. 'Two bleedin' bloke-angels hanging about with each other like that! Big cunt and pretty boy – bit like Ged and Sam, innit!'

As Lee cackled beside her, Suzie smiled painfully and began to eat her own dinner. Mal watched surreptitiously as she gingerly eased a tiny amount of mashed potato through her swollen lips. For a moment, he was flooded with guilt and shame, but he quickly shook it away, reminding himself that it wasn't all his fault. She knew all the buttons to push to set him off, didn't she? If she'd just think before she did things, they'd be fine. Still, he'd better say something before he left, or she'd be quiet for days and he'd end up feeling like a right cunt.

He followed her into the kitchen when she carried the empty plates out a little while later. Closing the door so Lee wouldn't see him creeping, he came up behind her at the sink and put his arms around her.

'Sorry,' he whispered, nuzzling her neck. 'I didn't mean to hurt you so bad, but I can't help it when you wind me up like that. That was good gear you nearly wasted out there.'

Suzie winced as he hugged her bruised ribs. But the tears sliding down her cheeks were not tears of pain but of relief. Relief that it was over, and that he'd forgiven her for winding him up and making a mess of things – again! Because it was her fault – he was dead right about that. He'd paid a lot of money for that coke, and she'd

27

nearly ruined it. Well, Lee had paid for it, but that wasn't the point.

When Mal and Lee headed off to Lee's flat, Suzie finished clearing up, then ran herself a bath. Lying back in the soothing bubbles, she resolved to try harder in future. Mal was a good man really. Oh sure, he was a bit quick with his fists, but that wasn't his fault – it was the coke. It was the Devil in powder form as far as she was concerned.

She just hoped Mal realized that before it was too late.

2

It was just after eight when they arrived at Lee's flat. Just a few short hours to kick-off, and Lee could hardly wait. He was so eager to get in and give Mal his mask, it took him two attempts to get his key in the lock. Mal wrinkled his nose in disgust when he finally managed it. Recoiling from the unmistakable odour of rotting feet and rancid unwashed body, he remembered exactly why he'd stopped coming round here in the first place. It was no wonder Pauline had legged it with her Lemon Dettox. She must have realized she was fighting a losing battle. It was a wonder she'd stuck it out as long as she had.

The smell was particularly overpowering in the living room, and the mess there was even worse than Mal remembered. Mouldy plates poked out from beneath the couch, cups sprouting alien life forms stood on every surface, overflowing, foul-smelling ashtrays littered the floor, suspicious-looking stains speckled the couch cushions. And everywhere else lay piles of filthy clothes and heaps upon heaps of newspapers.

Mal opened his mouth to berate Lee for his sloppy housekeeping just as Lee threw something at him. Catching it, he saw that it was a balaclava – a black woollen job, with eye, nose and mouth holes, and a new one at that! Raising a surprised eyebrow, he nodded his approval.

'I never thought I'd hear myself saying this, mate, but well done! This is the biz!'

As Lee beamed with pride at the rare compliment, Mal angled the chipped mirror on the mantelpiece, then pulled the balaclava carefully over his hair and stepped back to view the effect. It was a perfect fit – and, he decided, looked fittingly evil. Now they were cooking with gas!

Pulling his collar up around his ears, he curled his lip up through the mouth hole and turned to Lee, rasping in his best Cagney voice: 'You dirty brother . . . you killed my rat!'

Lee quickly pulled his own mask on and aimed a two-finger pistol at Mal's head, rasping back, 'Quite frankly, my dear, I don't give a fuck!'

'Wrong film, dick-wipe!' snorted Mal.

Just then, there was a knock at the front door. As Lee tore his mask off and dashed out to answer it with a whoop of excitement, Mal turned back to the mirror to practise his evil eye. Seconds later, Lee bounced back in with Sam and Ged in tow – both wearing black from the neck down.

Ged looked awesome. At six foot three and weighing a healthy fourteen stones, he always dwarfed Lee and Mal, who were five-seven and five-nine respectively, each barely topping nine stones soaking wet. But tonight, in his muscle-enhancing Puffa jacket and thigh-defining jeans, he seemed even more enormous than usual, and even Sam, who was close to six feet tall himself, seemed puny by comparison. Lee was positively ecstatic.

'Oh, this is gonna be so fucking great!' he squawked, flinging himself around the room with flailing arms. 'What a buzz, eh? Shit, man, I can taste the money already! We won't have no problem getting the cunt to roll over when he sees us heading his way! Especially you, Ged, man!' He grinned, throwing a mock punch at the big man's arm. 'You look like a fucking animal!'

With an irritated grunt, Ged swiped a pile of clothes and newspapers onto the floor and flopped, frowning, into the room's only armchair. When Sam had called that afternoon to tell him about the job, he'd said he didn't want any part of it. But Sam had pleaded, and he'd sounded so depressed about his finances that eventually Ged had relented – even managing to convince himself that it might be a laugh. Now he was actually here, with Lee hopping about like a pillock and Mal swaggering around like a Mafia reject, he wished he'd gone with his instincts and stayed away. No matter how much he fought it, these two always managed to piss him off. Always had, and probably always would. And if he'd had any doubts before, he was certain now that this blag was bound to be an absolute disaster.

As Ged silently cursed himself, Sam – looking even more troubled than usual – slumped down onto the battered couch and pulled his Rothmans and a pack of Rizla papers from his pocket. He was desperate for a calming spliff after yet another set-to with Wendy. She'd had a fit when he'd told her what he was doing tonight, and had screamed so long and loud that his ears were still ringing. If he didn't need the money so badly, he wouldn't have come. But he *did* need it – especially after totting up the damage Wendy had done to their savings today. With the monthly 'mortgage' for the new suite and carpet due next week, there was no way around it. He had to do this.

After searching his pockets several times to no avail, it finally dawned on him that his draw was missing. The small wrap of coke he'd hidden in his change pocket was still there, but the draw was definitely gone. Realizing that Wendy must have lifted it when he was in the shower, he was filled with futile rage. Why didn't she just rip his fucking heart out and be done, the selfish bitch!

'What's up with your mush?' said Mal, his voice muffled by the wool of the mask. 'Wendy give you a hard time, did she?'

'Something like that,' Sam muttered, and, lighting a straight instead, dropped his cheek onto his fist and sank deeper into the stained couch with an air of utter dejection.

'You know your problem?' Lee piped up. 'You're too soft on your Wendy. You wanna toughen up, man. Give her some licks – like Mal there,' He thumbed towards Mal. 'He's got Suzie well under control. I'd like to see her give him lip the way your Wendy does. He'd knock her for six, innit, Mal?'

Mal pulled the mask off and smoothed his hair back into place. 'Too right. No bird's gonna take the piss out of me and get away with it. Show 'em the back of yer hand before they get the idea they can open their mouths, that's what I say.'

He didn't think it necessary to mention the beating he'd inflicted on Suzie earlier – or what an absolute shit he'd felt having to look at her face during dinner. He knew he had to sort himself out if he wanted to keep her, but it was hard. He seriously wondered sometimes if he was cracking up. But making himself out to be a sap in front of his mates wouldn't help him get it sorted.

'Wendy would knife me if I tried any of that shit on her,' Sam said, flicking a crawling something off the arm of the couch with a shudder.

'That's 'cos you're a wuss!' Mal jeered, happy to shift the focus from himself. 'A pussy-whipped wuss!'

'Yeah, but she's a babe, ain't she?' said Lee lustfully. 'I wouldn't mind being whipped by her . . . Phwoar! Eh?'

'You want whipping full stop, you sad git!' Mal quipped, heading for the health-hazard kitchenette in search of alcohol. 'You wanna sort yourself out, or you'll end up hanging round that school again and get yourself nicked!'

Lee's eyes glazed over at the thought of his last little sojourn to the local high school some months before. He'd had the red Celica then, and the girls had been well impressed.

'Them schoolgirls are a right load of ravers,' he said. 'Tits out here—' he held his hands out in front of him '— all firm and ripe for the squeeze! Phwoar! What I wouldn't give to—'

'Jeezus wept!' Sam pulled the wrap of coke out and threw it at Lee to shut him up. 'They're too young, man – no matter how big their boobs are.'

'Tosh bollocks!' Lee sneered. 'They're never too young!'

Cracking his knuckles sharply, Ged said, 'You're a sick man, Lee.'

'Get out of it!' Lee snorted. 'I wasn't chasing them, they was chasing me. They're a right load of nymphos! I could have copped with loads of 'em if that teacher hadn't seen 'em flocking round me. They were gagging for it!'

'They were checking the wheels, not you, you tosser,' said Mal, coming back with a pack of beers and throwing one can to each of them. 'Why would they want a sad old fart like you with all them young lads about?'

'Me big dick!' said Lee, quite seriously. 'No school-boy's gonna satisfy them nubey babes like me.'

Mal shook his head in despair. 'Drink your ale and cool yourself down, man.'

Lee ripped the tab back and slurped at the froth bubbling over the edge of the can. Licking his lips, he turned to Ged with a glint in his eye.

'So how's your little 'un these days, Ged? I haven't seen her for years, man. How old is she now? Twelve? Thirteen? Must be getting big, eh?'

'Belt up, Lee,' Sam warned, flicking a nervous glance at Ged. The last man to disrespect his daughter had been confined to bed with a drip-feed for a month. Lee was definitely stepping into dangerous territory.

Ged didn't move. Holding his hands to his mouth, one huge mitt cupping a jaw-breaking fist, obscuring all of his face except his eyes, he pinned Lee with a glare. His voice, when it came, was low and dark. 'She's fifteen, Lee. And if you know what's good for you, you'll never mention her again.'

'I was only asking!' Lee spluttered. 'Jeez! What's it coming to if I can't ask a mate about his family?' Turning to Mal, he held his hands up innocently. 'Did I say anything wrong? Did I?'

'Pack it in,' Mal said, hoping to avert the looming disaster. Everyone knew how Ged felt about his kids. 'We're not here to talk about girls. We've got business to sort out.'

'Yeah, I know . . . I was only saying—'

'Well, don't! You can see you're pissing Ged off, so leave it, yeah?'

'What time is it?' Sam asked, anxious to get this over and done so he could get home before Wendy got back from her night out with her mates – and, he hoped, be in bed asleep, avoiding the dreaded nightly tussle. This last month she'd been like a raving schizophrenic. Bitch-queen one minute – sex-mad crazy woman the next. If she wasn't screaming at him for something he'd done wrong, she was screaming for a shag, and he was worn out trying to keep up with her.

'It's only half-eight,' said Mal. 'We've got loads of time yet. Got any new films, Lee?'

Sam groaned. 'Aw, not a bluey. That's the last thing I need!'

Ignoring him, Lee jumped up with a grin. 'Sure have!' he said, pulling three videos from a heap of rubbish beside the couch. 'New Danish imports, these,' he bragged. 'Picked 'em up down Tib Street last week, and they are capital-D Diiirty! Take your pick.'

'Any,' Mal said. 'But I'm warning you now, man – touch your dick and I'll kick your bleeding head in!'

'What about the job?' Ged reminded them. 'Shouldn't we be sorting that out first?'

'Shit, yeah.' Lee slapped a palm to his forehead. 'I forgot about that.'

Jumping to his feet again, he ran across to his jacket and pulled out the plan he'd spent the whole of the previous night drawing. Smoothing it out, he put it on the table and turned it towards them, then perched himself on the edge of the couch to explain it.

'Right,' he began, rubbing his hands together importantly. 'This is the plan of the shop. These—' he pointed out the relevant bits '—are the counter, aisles, fridges, and what-not. And these are the doors front and back. These—' three little stick-men '—are the goons. And the "X" is himself counting up.

'Now the goons go first,' he went on with authority. 'And that's never later than ten past twelve. They come out the front, go round the side into the yard, into the van and off. Pasha stays behind and bags up, then he comes out the back way at half past. And that,' he beamed around at his friends, 'is where we come in. Good, innit?'

Mal picked up the sketch for a closer look. 'You get a wanking chimp to draw this, or what?' he asked with a derisive snort.

'Piss off!' Lee snatched his masterpiece back. 'Look, never mind that. The point is the place is way overdue for a seeing-to. They're making too much dosh for my liking, an'—'

'And most of it's mine,' Mal cut in. 'Suzie spends a bleedin' fortune in there!'

'Exactly!' Lee slapped an emphatic hand down on his knee. 'It's our dosh, anyway, so it's only right we take it back, innit?'

'That's not exactly logical,' Ged pointed out. 'You've had stuff for your money, so technically it's his.'

'Fuck me, man,' Mal laughed. 'Anyone'd think you'd never blagged nothing! Correct me if I'm wrong, but did you or did you not nearly blind that poor fucker just 'cos he wouldn't—'

'Yeah, well, anyway,' Lee cut in quickly before Mal pissed Ged off even more than he already seemed to be – though why he should be pissed off, Lee had no idea! Still, the last thing they needed was to lose the only real muscle in the team. 'Let's get this finished, yeah?' He waited until he had their attention before continuing.

'Right, then. I've been keeping watch for the past few weeks, and Pasha's routine is regular as clockwork. Now, the plan is to get round the back after the goons leave, and hide in the bushes till he's locked up. Then we jump him and mash him up, and all that lovely dosh will be ours!'

'And it's dead cert the goons leave by ten past?' Sam asked.

'Dead cert,' Lee assured him. 'Like I said, I've been watching for weeks, an' that's how they do it every time. It's safe, man.'

'What if someone sees us?' said Mal. This was Lee talking, after all – Mr Botch-it-and-scarper. 'I don't fancy a run-in with the Five-O, know what I mean?'

'Nah, man, it can't go wrong,' Lee insisted, adding with a confident grin, 'I'll let you peel me nuts and dip 'em in acid if it does!'

'And I'll do it with pleasure, mate,' Mal half-joked. 'Right, then.' He turned to the others, rubbing his hands together. 'If we're all finished, I say we have a line to seal the deal.'

Reaching for the last of Lee's stash, he tipped it onto the mirror, telling Lee: 'Get a flick on, mate. A good stiffy should get us in the right mood to kick arse!'

Suzie woke with a start, unsure whether the pounding was coming from inside her head or from someone hammering on the door. It was definitely the door. Peering at her watch through sleep-blurred eyes, she struggled to focus on the wavy hands. Nine o'clock. Who the hell could it be?

Struggling upright, she dragged herself from the couch and limped to the front door. The bath had relaxed her, but falling asleep on the couch straight after hadn't done her any favours. She was aching all over, and didn't fancy talking to anyone. Peeping through the spyhole, her heart sank when she saw Wendy stamping her feet in the passageway, her fur coat pulled tight around her swollen belly. She slowly backed away from the door, hoping to creep back to the couch, but it was too late – Wendy's eagle eyes had detected the change in light behind the spyhole. She banged on the door again, shouting: 'Suzie, it's me. Hurry up, it's bloody freezing out here.'

Suzie knew there was no escape – and no excuse for not letting her in. A visit from Wendy was deemed an honour – like a royal visit. If she didn't let her in now, she'd really take the huff. Opening the door reluctantly, she forced a smile – instantly regretting it as the swollen lip tore itself apart and started to bleed again.

Wendy was shocked by the sight of her. 'Good God, girl!' she gasped, barrelling into the hall and pushing Suzie backwards into the light. She looked at her battered face with concern. 'What the hell happened to you?' she demanded. 'You been in a car crash, or what?'

'It's nothing,' Suzie insisted, twisting away from Wendy's hands and sloping back to the couch with Wendy hot on her heels.

'Doesn't look like nothing to me,' Wendy said, sitting down beside her. 'Here, let me have a proper look.' Gently tilting Suzie's face up to the light, she frowned, asking quietly, 'What happened, Suzie? And no bullshit, all right?'

Suzie hadn't meant to tell her, but Wendy was her usual persistent self, and she didn't let up until the whole story tumbled out.

'Well! I don't know what to say,' Wendy said when she'd finished. 'Oh, love . . . Come here.' Pulling Suzie to her like a child, she rocked her gently. 'How long has this been going on, then?'

'He's not normally this bad.' Suzie gulped back her tears, soothed by the rocking. 'And it's my own fault. I wind him up. I don't know why I do it, but I can't seem to stop myself.'

Wendy nodded wisely, listening to Suzie in sympathetic silence as she sifted through the information. She prided herself on seeing both sides to a story – unless it was hers and Sam's story, in which case there was only one side: hers. Still, despite how she felt about men hitting women, she knew it couldn't all be Mal's fault. He was always so nice to her. Anyway, Lee had been here – it was probably his fault!

'I know it must be hard,' she said, choosing her words carefully, 'but only you can know if you're pushing him too far. Can't you just learn to shut up before it gets to this? I'm sure he doesn't mean to do it. He's a pretty good guy, really.'

'I know . . . I know,' Suzie wiped her nose on her sleeve. 'You're right. He deserves better than me.'

Much as Wendy liked Suzie, she had to agree. The kid was way out of her league. What Mal needed was a strong woman – a real woman, like herself. Someone who'd give as good as she got. That'd sort him out. It had certainly sorted Sam out. He wouldn't dare pull a stunt like this.

'You know what,' she said with a wicked smile. 'If Sam ever tried any of this malarkey on me, I'd rip his balls off and force-feed them to him. I would – and, what's more, he knows it! That's how you've got to keep them, you know? On their knees – under your stiletto!' She laughed suddenly. 'I think I should be one of them wotsit women . . . Dominatrix! That's it!'

Suzie giggled at this, and bled some more. 'You wouldn't!'

Pulling a tissue from her pocket, Wendy gently dabbed at Suzie's lip. 'Too right I bloody would! And I'd be good at it an' all. Ooh, yeah! I could just fancy getting rigged up in rubber. That'd be a kick. A rubber basque, with cut-out titty bits. And a whip! God, that'd be fun. I'd skelp every one of the sad gits that walked through the door, whip the skin straight off of his sorry arse and get *paid* for doing it! And I'd laugh. My God, I'd laugh! Serve 'em right, the sorry bunch of bastards!'

Pausing, Wendy patted her stomach and narrowed her eyes thoughtfully. 'I might just give it a go when I drop this little load. Get myself down to the gym to tone up first, then a quick trip to one of those naughty-knickers parties to sort out some horny gear, and Bob's-yer-dominated-uncle! Tell you what, Sooze.' She nudged her. 'You can come and work with me if you want. I reckon we'd make a good team.'

Suzie blushed. 'Oh, I don't know about that. I'd be useless.'

Wendy drew her head back and snorted. 'Don't underestimate yourself, girl!'

Struggling to her feet, she rubbed at her back, then headed for the kitchen, saying over her shoulder, 'Why don't I make us a brew, eh? Coffee all right?'

'Yeah, thanks.' Suzie grinned as she wrapped the dressing gown tighter around herself. Wendy could be really funny sometimes. She could also be a terrifying bitch, but like this she was great.

Popping her head around the door a second later, Wendy grinned mischievously. 'Tell you what. How's about we sack the coffee and nip out for a bottle of wine.

We can watch a vid, get pissed . . . and have a little smoke!' She pulled the piece of draw she'd 'confiscated' from Sam out of her pocket and waved it triumphantly. 'Got any skins?'

'On the shelf.' Suzie pointed. 'Here, you *were* joking, weren't you? About doing the . . . you know?'

'No, I bloody wasn't!' Wendy exclaimed loudly as she waddled across to get the Rizla papers. 'And you don't need to look so shocked, Suzie. Women *are* allowed to like sex, you know. I might as well get paid for it, is all I'm saying. Here, start this off while I go to the loo.' She threw the papers to Suzie and made her way out, moaning, 'God, I can't wait to drop this. It makes me leak like a bleeding tap!'

Mal and Lee were high as kites by the time they set off. It was only eleven-thirty, but Lee insisted they needed the extra time to suss everything out. Reaching Hulme ten minutes later, Lee slowed down and turned onto City Road.

Turf of the posse that was out for Sam's blood, City Road was the only main road running through the estate. There were many minor roads leading off it, but they just provided access to the various mazes that made up the different parts of the estate, and they all led back to City Road. The one they wanted was the last on the right. Cornbrook Road – a short, narrow road with just a single dim street light at its corner.

On their right as they turned onto Cornbrook Road were the rear yards of the shops – each separated from its neighbour by a low wall, with just enough room for a couple of vehicles. On the left, stretching the entire length of the shops, was St Ignatius's Residential Home for the

Elderly. And straight ahead, at the end, sat a hulking twenty-storey high-rise, the car park of which overlooked both the Home and the shops, as well as providing a clear view of the City Road entrance. It was here that Lee had spent the past four Sunday nights – just out of sight of the flats' security camera as it slowly scanned the area.

Slowly making his way into the car park, he reversed into the familiar shadows and cut the engine. Killing the lights, he peered out through the windows for any signs of movement in the surrounding darkness. As he'd expected, there were none. The area was deserted – anyone going out was already long gone, and would probably not be back until much later. The Home was also in complete darkness, each of its residents soundly asleep by now, and probably too deaf or short-sighted to notice any irregularity even if they had been awake.

Now Lee and his mates just had to get on with the wait as best they could.

It was exactly twelve-fifteen when the three figures emerged from the shadows at the side of the supermarket. Pasha's nephews – or 'The Goons', as Lee called them. They were illuminated for a split second by the street lamp before disappearing around the gate into the rear yard.

'And they're off,' hissed Lee excitedly. Slouching down in his seat, he pulled his mask over his head.

A jolt of electricity charged the air in the car. The windows fogged over as the men's body heat surged, and adrenalin flooded their veins.

Mal rubbed a small hole in the condensation to watch the van drive away. 'Let's go!' he yelled as soon as it disappeared around the corner. Grinning, he pulled his mask on and reached for the door handle.

Lee grabbed his arm and held him back. 'Hang about, speedy bollocks! We've got to wait while he bags up.'

Mal slumped back, a petulant pout pushing up through his mouth-hole. 'So what do we do now? Sit here with our masks on like a load of bleeding terrorists?'

'We've just gotta time it right,' Lee explained. 'If we go too soon he'll see us on the cameras. Too late, and he'll be off in a flash.'

'Don't you think we'd better leave the masks off till we get over there?' Ged suggested quietly. 'We don't want to look too suss, do we?'

'Good thinking, Batman,' Mal agreed. Ripping his mask off, he angled the mirror to smooth his hair.

'You vain shite!' Lee laughed. 'All right, leave 'em off, but keep your heads down, yeah?'

Sam felt a trickle of sweat run down his back as he pulled his mask off. He felt safer covered up, especially knowing that one of the posse's girlfriends lived in the flats behind them. Even behind the car's blacked-out windows he'd felt exposed, visible from every angle. Stepping out unmasked, he really would be. But he had to agree that it wouldn't be too smart to walk the fifty or so exposed yards in a mask.

Another ten minutes passed before Lee turned and gave them the nod. Climbing out of the car as quietly as possible, they darted across the road, keeping tight to the shadows until they reached the supermarket wall. Crouching low in the bushes beside it, they had a further agonizing five-minute wait before they heard the back door creak open and footsteps shuffle out onto the concrete step.

Lee let out a nervous giggle, earning himself a fierce jab in the ribs from Mal who was hyped beyond belief – eaten up with the thrill of the hunt. A commando waiting to strike the enemy.

Squatting beside Mal, Ged could smell the urge to wreak havoc pouring from the man's glands. It didn't bode well, and again he silently cursed himself. If he had any sense at all he'd be a thousand miles away from this raving coke-head right now.

But it was too late to back out now.

Like a prison door slamming home, the shutters came down to the concrete with a loud metallic clang. Clicking the padlock firmly into place, Pasha Singh straightened up slowly. Wincing at the sharp protesting pops of his kneecaps, he arched his stiff back and rubbed a hand around his aching neck. He was getting too old for these late nights. It was time to start delegating responsibilities to his nephews. He'd have to do it sooner or later, or he'd never get back home. And that had been his intention all along. The sole reason he'd spent every waking hour in this stinking country working his fingers to the bone, building his empire. Because when he eventually did go back home, it would be as a success – or not at all.

Picking up the heavy money bag, he yawned long and hard. A quick trip to Moss Side to drop The Man's money off, then home to his own plump, accommodating wife and his nice warm bed. He couldn't wait.

He'd just stepped out into the pitch-dark yard, heading for his beautiful new jeep, when a noise stopped him in his tracks. Narrowing his eyes, he held his breath and tried to make out what it was and where it was coming from. Whispering, shuffling sounds. Close by.

A cat?

No way – cats didn't whisper.

His nephews, then? Maybe they'd forgotten something and come back?

Peering around the dark yard for the van, he saw that it was gone and knew it couldn't be them.

It had to be trouble, then – which was surprising, given his backer. But, luckily, he was prepared.

Holding his breath, he eased himself down in the dark and crouched beside the huge wheelie bin to the side of the shuttered door. Sliding his hand between its wheels, he tapped his fingers silently along the ground until he reached the gun – tucked at the back, tight against the wall behind a brick. Pulling it out slowly, he pushed the money bag under the bin. If he was being done over, they weren't getting their hands on that. Most of it wasn't even on the books. He'd have a hell of a time explaining it to the police – and an even harder one explaining it to The Man.

He couldn't afford to lose The Man's money. That was more than his life was worth.

'What's he doing?' Mal hissed impatiently, straining to see into the pitch-dark yard.

'Probably having a piss!' Lee sniggered.

Sam was growing more nervous by the second. 'Let's just get it over with,' he said. 'Take him by surprise.'

'Don't do anything stupid,' Ged urged cautiously.

'Fuck that!' Mal scoffed, his manic grin hidden by the mask. He was going in – alone if he had to. He was invincible. Untouchable. 'Give us the gun, Lee!' he demanded, holding his hand out.

Lee shook his head, pulling the gun tighter to his chest. 'No way, José! This baby's stayin' with Papa!' Ignoring

Mal's protestations, he snaked over the wall and rolled himself into the yard.

Mal was close behind, cursing through gritted teeth. So it was Lee's gun? So fucking what? Lee wouldn't know what to do with it, but he would.

'Hang about,' Ged hissed, gripping Sam's arm as he made to follow. 'No one mentioned guns to me!'

Sam hesitated. He trusted Ged, but they'd come this far – and he needed that money. Shaking off the restraining hand, he cocked his leg over the wall. 'Come on, Ged. It'll only be for show. You know what Lee's li—'

He was cut short as a thunderous roar shattered the silence, followed almost instantly by a second. As the reports echoed through the darkness, he was knocked totally off balance. Falling back, he landed heavily on Ged, his eyes bulging wildly through the mask.

'What the . . .? What was that?'

'Shooting, man!' gasped Ged, scrambling to his feet and hauling Sam up roughly by his collar. 'They're bloody shooting! We've got to get out of here!'

Just then, Mal dived over the wall, dragging a heavy cloth bag behind him. Leaping frantically to his feet, he tore his mask off and hurled it aside, yelling, 'MOVE! MOVE!' as he kicked his way through the bushes.

Colliding in their panic, Sam and Ged half-pushed, half-pulled each other out of the undergrowth and followed Mal, who was already some way ahead, running hell-for-leather across the road.

Slamming into him at the car, Sam tore his mask away and gripped his arm, shaking it frantically. 'Where's Lee? Where's Lee?'

'Get in the car!' Mal hissed, twisting his arm away and wrenching the door open. 'And shut the fuck up!'

Sick with terror, Sam jumped into the back. A glance at Ged's face as he jumped in the other side said it all. He was white as a ghost, wide-eyed and shaking.

'Where is he?' Sam asked again, acutely aware of how high his voice sounded.

'Back there, next to fucking Pasha!' snapped Mal. Searching for the keys, he became almost hysterical when he realized Lee still had them. 'Shit! Shit! How am I supposed to start the fucking car without keys?' He slammed his fist down on the wheel and the horn blared like a siren.

Come and get us! . . . Come and get us!

'God *damn* it!' Ged roared down his ear. 'Pull the fucking wires, man!'

A full agonizing minute later, the engine sparked to life. Throwing it into gear, Mal rammed his foot to the floor and hurtled forward over the pavement, heedless of the high kerb scraping the underside of the car as he rocketed towards City Road. Turning the corner with an ear-splitting screech of tyres, he gunned towards the safety of the Crescents.

3

Wendy had left at eleven-thirty, by which time Suzie was so exhausted she'd climbed into bed and fallen asleep almost as soon as her head hit the pillow. Now, like Mal earlier, she was startled awake by the phone.

Half expecting it to be Mal saying he was staying over at Lee's, she was surprised to hear Wendy asking for Sam. After checking to see if they'd come back and finding that they hadn't, she promised to send him straight home, then hung up and tried to go back to sleep.

A couple of restless minutes later, she knew it was impossible. Her head was banging from the wine, her body aching all over. Reaching into the drawer for a painkiller, she got up and wandered through to the kitchen to make herself a hot drink. She'd just put a pan of milk on the stove when she heard the frantic scuffling outside the front door.

Someone was trying to break in!

With her heart in her throat she reached for the baseball bat Mal kept behind the kitchen door and, gripping it tight with both hands, leaned hard against the wall, raising it high above her head as he'd shown her. As she stood there, shaking like a leaf and praying she'd have the strength to use it, the front door flew open – so hard it rocked the wall behind her. Then she heard Mal shouting: 'Lock the door . . . Lock the fucking door!'

Replacing the bat, she stood stock-still, listening as the hushed voices filtered through the wall. She was so shaken, she didn't notice the sizzling behind her as the milk began to boil, bubbling up and over the side of the pan onto the flame, filling the room with its sickly-sweet aroma.

'That you in there?' Mal called through the door. 'You burning something?'

Snapping to, Suzie turned and saw the milk spewing out onto the cooker. 'It's just milk,' she called back, grabbing the cloth off the sink to wipe it up before he saw it.

'Put the kettle on, doll,' he said. 'And Ged and Sam are here,' he went on, opening the door, 'so put enough for . . . Oi! Watch it!'

Looking down, she realized the cloth was dangerously close to the flame and jerked it away. Mal shook his head, smiling indulgently.

'Can't leave you alone for two minutes, can I?' he said, and, opening his arms, he cocked his head to the side and called her to him. 'Come 'ere, you silly cow.'

Tripping across the sticky floor, she fell into his arms with a sob, pathetically grateful for another tiny crumb of affection.

Cupping her chin gently in his hand, he tipped her battered face up and peered at her tear-streaked face. 'Here, what's all this, then? What you crying for, doll?'

'N-nothing,' she sniffed as he wiped the tears away. 'I . . . I just got w-worried, that's all.'

He smiled softly. 'There's nothing to worry about, doll. I'm home now. Everything's all right. Mal's here.'

He allowed her only a few seconds before easing her from him. He was beginning to get that itchy, clutching feeling deep inside his gut, and he didn't want to feel the horrible sensation of skin on skin when it sprang to the surface. Turning her towards the sink, he said, 'Clean yourself up, doll. And make those brews, yeah?'

Leaving her splashing cold water on her face, he went through to the living room. Sam had turned on the lamps and the TV, but the warm glow they cast hadn't managed to soften the stark whiteness of their faces. Shivering, Mal lit the fire and knelt in front of it. He was still there, hogging all the heat, when Suzie came in with the cups.

'Isn't she a babe, guys?' he crooned, oblivious to Ged and Sam's expressions of disgust and horror as they got their first look at her face. Badly bruised and swollen, the cut lip had crusted black around the edge. She looked hideous.

'Yeah,' Sam mumbled, dropping his eyes as he took his cup with trembling fingers. 'Thanks, Suzie.'

'Thanks,' Ged muttered, also unable to look at Suzie as he began to seethe inside. *The psychopathic little shit*! He would gladly strangle him when all this was over.

Having forgotten her battered face in the heat of the moment, Suzie didn't connect their shocked expressions to herself. Knowing nothing of the job – Mal seldom saw fit to explain his movements to her – she tried to think what could have happened to shake them up so. Had they had a fight? Had they been arrested? She had no idea, but whatever it was, it must have been bad. And she wondered if Wendy knew what they'd been up to. She hadn't said anything, but now that Suzie thought about it, it was a coincidence, Wendy's turning up out of the blue and now this.

Taking her own cup over to the couch she sat down,

drawing her legs up beneath herself as she waited to hear what was going on.

Sitting cross-legged on the rug, Mal rolled himself a strong spliff and took a lung-deep pull. Exhaling a huge plume of blue-grey smoke, he closed his eyes and leaned back, sighing. 'Man, did I need that!'

A few moments of heavy silence later, Sam said, 'So what happens now? Do we just—'

'Just a minute,' Ged cut in solemnly. 'Mal – you've still not told us what happened back there?'

'Yeah – what about Lee?' said Sam. 'Is he dead, or what?'

Suzie's heart lurched into her throat. She hadn't even noticed that Lee was missing until they mentioned him. And now they were saying he could be *dead*? What the hell was going on?

Mal shrugged. 'I don't know, man, I didn't really see anything.' Leaning back on his elbows, he squinted up at them through the smoke as he explained what had happened in the yard. 'I followed him over the wall, as you know, and the next thing I knew they were shooting. I rolled off to the side when I heard the first one, and I think it was Lee who got hit 'cos he made this weird sound – sort of a grunt, like. Anyhow, I rolled out of the way and banged into this bin thing, Then the other one went off, and the next thing I knew, Pasha landed at my bleeding feet!' Laughing nervously, he brushed a cone of ash off his chest. 'Shit! I didn't know if he was gonna turn round and shoot me or what, so I pushed myself back against the wall, just in case, like. And that's when I felt this . . .'

Leaning sideways, he pulled the bag towards him.

Sam sat forward. 'What is it?'

Mal shrugged. 'I reckon it's the dosh, but I ain't exactly had a chance to look yet, have I?'

Ged gulped a mouthful of tea. 'Well, don't you think you'd better?'

'Yeah,' said Sam. 'At least then we'll know it wasn't a waste of time.'

Mal held his hands up. 'All right, all right!'

Releasing the drawstring, he reached into the sack and pulled out a handful of notes.

Sam's eyes widened. 'Shit, man!' he gasped, reaching out to touch the money. 'How much is that?'

Mal pushed Sam's hand away and spread the notes fanlike across the coffee table. Looking up, he grinned. 'They're all twenties.'

Plunging his hand back into the bag, he pulled out another bundle.

'Wow!' Sam squeaked. 'How much more is there?'

'Hang on!' Mal laughed, putting his hand in and pawing the rest of the money out.

Suzie's jaw dropped as she saw the huge pile of notes. Mal and Sam looked at each other in amazement. Then, whooping joyfully, each grabbed a handful and waved it in the air ecstatically. Only Ged seemed troubled. He sat forward, his hands clenched so tightly between his knees his knuckles turned white.

'Man, oh man!' Sam laughed. 'There's got to be nine, ten grand here. Let's count it.'

Mal picked up the bag and gave it a shake. 'Hang about. There's something else in here.'

A large package fell to the floor with a dull thud. It was wrapped in plain brown paper, bound tightly with string, and there was something written on the top right corner.

Sam craned forward, his eyes on stalks. 'What is it? What's it say?'

'Will you just wait!' Mal laughed at Sam's impatience. He picked the package up for a closer look. 'It's just initials. An S and an M. That's all it says.' He turned it over in his hands with a shrug.

'Open it, then!' Sam was itching to get his hands on it. 'It's probably more.'

Unravelling the string, Mal carefully unfolded the package. 'Holy shit,' he whispered when he saw what lay inside.

'What? What is it?' Sam was becoming frantic. 'Is it more?'

'It's more, all right,' Mal told him, his voice husky as he fondled the three bulky wads. 'A *whole lot* more.'

Sam whistled quietly. 'We're rich, man. We're bloody rich.'

'Aren't we forgetting something?' Ged spoke so softly it took a moment for his words to penetrate their bubble of euphoria.

'What's that, Ged?' Mal looked up dazedly. 'What did you say?'

'I said, aren't we forgetting something?'

'What d'y' mean?'

'Lee?' Ged didn't much care for the bloke, but this was outrageous. 'He's lying back there, dead or dying, and you two are drooling over the bloody money like a pair of vultures. If you had a brain between you you'd be thinking about the police. Don't you think someone would have heard the shots and called them by now?'

Mal clutched at the money possessively. 'Oh, come on. No one saw us. You're just being paranoid.'

'Jeezus!' Ged snorted. 'I don't believe you. They might

not have seen us, you idiot, but Lee's still lying back there with a bullet in him. How long do you think it'll take for the police to identify him and start looking for his associates – and that's us, in case you've forgotten? And just think for a minute, man. How did we get back here?'

Mal shrugged. 'In the car. What's the big deal?'

Ged nodded slowly. 'That's right. In the car – Lee's car. If the police start sniffing about it won't take them long to trace it, and it's sitting right outside your bloody flat covered in our prints. How incriminating is that?'

Mal and Sam exchanged a worried glance. They hadn't thought of that.

'Do you think I should go and move it?' Mal asked.

Ged looked at him coldly. Not so cocky now, was he? 'Did you have gloves on?' he asked.

'No,' Mal admitted, feeling stupid. 'Should I go and wipe the wheel down, or what?'

'What about your masks?' Ged reached into his pocket, breathing a sigh of relief when he felt his.

'Mine's in the car,' bleated Sam, his face losing its colour again.

'Where's yours, Mal?'

'It's cool . . . I got rid of it,' Mal said, proud that at least he'd got that right.

'Where?'

'In the bushes, at the . . . shops . . .' His voice trailed off as the implication hit him.

'Oh, Mal! You didn't!' Suzie groaned. Even she knew that was stupid.

Ignoring her, Mal turned to Ged. 'What if they find it? What'll happen?'

Ged felt the heavy burden of responsibility passing

onto his head. Sighing, he rubbed a weary hand across his eyes before answering. 'They'll send it to forensics, and with your record they'll trace it straight back to you. Shit, man!' he hissed in exasperation. 'What did you leave it there for?'

'I don't know,' Mal moaned, slapping his forehead. 'All I could think was not to get caught with it on me. What am I gonna do?'

'Someone will have to go back for it,' suggested Sam. 'We can't afford to just leave it there. They're bound to find it.'

Ged sat back and folded his arms. 'Well, you can count me out.'

'Thanks for nothing!' said Mal, his face falling even further. 'At least if you got pulled with it there wouldn't be any of your hair or nothing on it. You could easy say you'd just picked it up. But me? I'd be fucked, wouldn't I? Well, thanks, mate!'

'You shouldn't have been so bloody careless!' Ged retorted angrily. 'Why the hell should I put my neck on the line for you?'

'I'd do it for you!'

'Yeah, right!'

'Do you want me to go?' Suzie offered, her voice little more than a whisper.

Mal's eyes sparked with sudden hope. 'Yeah, doll! Yeah! You go. It's in the bushes near the road, you'll find it dead easy!' Raising himself onto his knees, he gave her a tender look. 'God, you're a knockout. What would I do without you?'

Suzie smiled faintly. Standing up, she reached for a cigarette with shaking hands.

'You're not seriously going to let her go, are you?'

demanded Ged. 'The place is probably crawling with filth by now.'

Mal waved a dismissive hand. 'It'll be cool, man. I chucked it close to the road. They'll be in the yard if they are there. They wouldn't even see her going past the front way.'

Ged shook his head in disbelief. 'You selfish bastard! They'll be watching everything – the road, the shops, the flats. They'd see her and you know it. But you don't give a damn, do you? As long as you're all right.'

'Don't give me that shit,' Mal scowled. 'You just want me to go and get myself busted, don't you?'

Sensing a fight brewing and knowing she'd somehow get the blame, Suzie said, 'It's all right, I'll go. I don't mind. I'll just walk past and see what's going on, and if it's all clear, I'll go and find the mask. Just give me a minute to get dressed.'

Mal caught her hand as she passed, squeezing it tightly. 'You'll be fine, doll.'

'Yeah.' With another faint smile, she walked towards the door. Then, remembering Wendy's call, she turned to Sam. 'Oh, by the way, Sam. Wendy rang just before you got back and said to tell you to go straight home.'

Sam's face fell. 'Shit! I can't go home while all this is going on.' He turned to Ged and Mal helplessly. 'What should I do?'

'Better ring her.' Mal gestured to the phone with a wave, then turned his attention back to the money. Now he was in the clear he could afford to luxuriate in the moment. Picking up a thick bundle he sniffed it, closing his eyes in ecstasy.

Sam stared blankly at the floor. He didn't want to talk to Wendy. They'd only argue and he didn't think he could cope with any more aggro. But it'd be worse if he didn't call her. Reluctantly, he reached for the phone and dialled his number, resting his burning forehead against the cool wall as he waited for Wendy to answer.

Behind him, Ged was still trying to change Mal's mind about sending Suzie out. 'It's wrong, man. What if she gets pulled?'

Mal looked up from the money slowly, his eyes narrowed with suspicion. 'Why are you so bothered about her all of a sudden? What's it to you, eh? You gone sweet on my woman now, have you?'

'Give me strength!' Ged snorted, shaking his head as he stared off into space.

'Well?' Mal persisted, sure he'd stumbled across the real reason for Ged's concern. 'Want a piece, do you? Not got none of your own now, so you just thought you'd help yourself to a little piece of mine, eh?'

'Behave yourself,' snapped Ged. 'You know me better than that!' Snatching his cigarettes off the table, he lit one and blew a fierce stream of smoke at the carpet. Mal was pissing him off – big-time! But no good would come of ripping the little shit's head off his shoulders – no matter how much he'd like to do just that. Tapping ash onto his knee, he rubbed it in slowly and struggled to regain his calm.

'Look,' he said eventually. 'Just think about it, will you? It's not just your head on the line if she gets pulled, is it? She's only a kid. She won't stand a chance if the police get hold of her.'

Mal shrugged. 'She might be young, but she's not stupid. She knows how to keep her mouth shut.'

Ged gritted his teeth. 'But she shouldn't have to. It's nothing to do with her.'

Mal frowned. He just wanted to count the money, but he couldn't concentrate with Ged moaning like a little old woman. 'Look, just chill out, will you?' he snapped. 'Everything's gonna be fine. For God's sake, look!' He swept a hand across the money. 'We've got a shed-load of dosh, and you're still not happy. What's up your arse tonight? A fucking wasp?'

Ged looked away in disgust as Mal laughed at his own joke.

'Wendy, I've told you . . . I can't!' Sam whined into the phone behind them. 'No, don't, Wendy! Oh, shit!'

Slamming the receiver down, he flopped heavily down on the floor next to Mal and plucked at a loose thread in the carpet. 'She's coming over.'

'You what?' Mal stared at him. 'She can't!'

Sam blushed and lowered his eyes. 'I tried to tell her that, but she wasn't having it.' Grabbing one of the bundles off the table, he ran his thumb through it, mumbling into his chest: 'You know what she's like.'

'Great. That's all we need,' Ged muttered darkly.

'Ah, well . . .' Mal shrugged and turned back to the money. 'Too late to worry now. We'd better just get this little lot sorted before she gets here.' Picking the largest wad up, he threw it to Ged with a grin. 'Here, you miserable bastard . . . Count that!'

Catching it, Ged fingered the money with a heavy sigh, then reluctantly started counting.

They fell silent as they immersed themselves in the task, the only sound in the room the noisy licking of fingers as they carefully flipped back the layers of notes.

In the background, the front door clicked shut as Suzie let herself out. None of them noticed.

After a while, Sam looked up, his eyes glittering

brightly as thoughts of Wendy's impending arrival were overtaken by greed. 'There's three thousand, two hundred here,' he whispered.

'And I've got two thou six,' Mal whooped joyfully, pushing another bundle across the table to Sam. 'What's that come to, Ged?'

'Five eight,' said Ged, without looking up from the wad he was halfway through. 'And I've counted twelve up to now.'

Mal laughed. 'Better get a move on, man! We're well ahead of you here!'

'Twelve grand,' Ged said quietly, smiling in spite of himself.

'You're joking!' Mal looked up wide-eyed. 'Twelve thou? And you're only halfway through?'

Ged nodded, leafing rapidly through the notes. 'Fifteen now.'

'And there's another nine hundred here.' Sam gave a childlike grin. 'Bloody hell! We should open our own supermarket if this is the kind of dosh they make in a week!'

'Sack that!' Mal laughed. 'We'd make more in a tits-'n'-tush shop! Bluies and vibrators, an' that!'

When the money was all counted and heaped in neat piles on the table, they sat and stared from it to each other in wordless wonder. It was Sam who finally broke the awed silence. Whistling long and low, he shook his head slowly, wiping a glistening sheen of sweat off his forehead onto the back of his hand.

'Man, that's beautiful. How much altogether, Ged?'

'Sixty-eight thousand, six hundred – give or take a few quid,' said Ged slowly.

Mal and Sam couldn't keep the grins from creeping

across their faces. Sixty-eight thousand pounds! More money than they'd ever seen in their lives. Jumping to their feet, they threw their arms around each other and danced around the room, yelling: 'Yes! Yes!'

Breaking the dance, Sam squatted down beside Ged. 'How much is that each?'

Ged cast him a sideways glance, a small smile lifting his lip. 'Twenty-two and a half, and some small change.'

'Oh . . . my . . . God!' gasped Mal, dropping to his knees and staring at the pile in wonder. 'Lee only expected about ten gees altogether!'

The mention of Lee brought them back down to earth with a bang. How could they have left him lying back there, not even knowing if he was dead or alive?

Ged's conscience pricked him sharply. Clearing his throat, he said, 'Um – better split it four ways. Just in case, yeah?'

'Yeah,' Sam shamefacedly agreed. 'How much is that, then?'

Ged did a quick calculation. 'Seventeen thousand.' He smiled, shrugging lightly. 'Still not bad, eh?'

'This calls for a celebration!' Mal rubbed his hands together greedily. He was rich! Rich! 'Sam, go and get some cans out of the fridge while me and Ged share this out.'

Splitting the pile roughly, Mal pushed half across the table to Ged, while Sam, feeling more than a little left out, sloped off to the kitchen to get the cans.

It took Suzie almost fifteen minutes to half walk, half run to the shops. When she got there, she was more relieved than she'd ever been in her life to find nothing amiss. No police vans, no crowd of onlookers – nothing. Only too aware that this could soon change, she hopped over the low fence and ducked into the dark undergrowth.

Already petrified, her nerves jarred at every sound as she began her frantic search for the discarded mask. Every twig she stepped on seemed to echo loud and clear through the still night air, and every leaf rustling in the slight breeze became a forest in a raging storm.

When she'd been at it for ten minutes, paranoia began to take hold. It suddenly occurred to her that the police might have already been. They could have been, taken the bodies away – and the mask – and be lying in wait at this very moment, praying for an idiot like her to come along and wrap the whole case up for them. She was a sitting duck!

Her heart was already firmly lodged in her throat when she heard the car turning onto the road behind her. A shock wave coursed down her spine as it came closer and closer. Crouching lower as the approaching headlights illuminated the bushes, she winced as a prickly branch dug its spikes into her tender face. Holding her breath, she bit down on her hand to stop herself crying out as the car came alongside, then sailed past.

When the road was quiet again, she exhaled with a sob and rested her forehead on her knees to stem the rising nausea. Wobbling unsteadily as her head began to spin, she felt herself falling forwards. Clutching at the bushes to stop herself, her hand brushed against something cold and damp—

Wool!

The mask!

Oh, thank God!

Snatching at it, she yanked it to herself, snagging it on a bramble in her haste. Wrenching it free, she hugged it to her breast, then rolled it into a tight ball and stuck it deep into her pocket. Forcing herself to stand on legs that felt like liquefied jelly, she pushed her way out of the bushes, then, with a quick prayer of eternal gratitude for the deserted road, hopped over the fence and headed for home. Willing herself invisible, she rammed her hands deep into her pockets, keeping a tight grip on the mask, afraid that it might somehow escape her if she let it go for even a second.

Every quaking step was torture. She felt exposed. Vulnerable. Afraid that if anyone saw her they'd be sure to remember when the police started asking questions.

Her heart thundered in her ears as another car turned onto the road. Quickening her step, she only just managed not to break into a guilty run as it came closer, but when it was just yards away, a bubble of panic rose into her throat. She was going to scream.

Suddenly, the car began to slow, then it was pulling in to the kerb alongside her, and she could hear the squeak of a window going down.

'Suzie?'

Her heart stopped, her brain refusing to recognize the voice.

'Suzie,' it said again. 'What on earth are you doing, girl? Get in. You can't be walking around out here at this time of night – you'll get attacked!'

It was Wendy.

Gasping for breath, Suzie turned, wide-eyed as a rabbit caught in headlights. When Wendy leaned across and pushed open the passenger door, she fell onto the seat with a whimper.

'What's going on?' demanded Wendy, crunching the gears as she eased away from the kerb.

Suzie panicked. Mal would go ballistic if she told Wendy, but she was waiting for an answer, and she wasn't an easy woman to ignore.

'I . . . I just needed a w-walk,' she said at last, stuttering out her lie. 'Anyway, what are you doing back up here? I thought you said you were going to bed?'

'I was,' Wendy snorted, a cynical smile twisting her lips. 'Until Sam rang with some bullshit about the job going wrong, so I decided to come and get him.' She flicked Suzie a sidelong glance. 'You must know what happened? So come on – out with it.'

'I don't really know,' Suzie croaked. 'I didn't know anything about it till they came back. Then Mal said something had gone wrong and he needed me to come back here and get his mask.'

'You what!' Wendy barked, gripping the wheel tight as she threw the car round the corner. 'He sent you?'

Suzie pulled the seat belt on as Wendy put her foot down hard. 'No. It wasn't like that. I offered.'

'Sure you did.' Wendy sighed, shaking her head. 'I suppose you asked for the beating too?'

Suzie blushed but said nothing. The sympathetic Wendy of earlier was obviously long gone.

'Don't worry,' Wendy muttered, more to herself than Suzie. 'I'll get to the bottom of it.'

Turning in to the Crescents a minute later, Wendy pulled into the space alongside Lee's car and killed the engine. Leaning over to the back seat for her handbag, she nodded towards the Escort.

'I see shithead's here. Hasn't he got a home of his own?'

'He's not here,' said Suzie. 'Mal drove it back.'

Wendy opened the door and stepped out, shaking her

dress down. 'You mean to tell me that lazy little shite walked somewhere for once in his life?'

Suzie shook her head, keeping her gaze pinned to the concrete as she stepped out the other side. There was no way she was telling Wendy what had happened. She'd leave that unpleasant task to the others – let them weather the storm of her rage.

Wendy's eyes narrowed with suspicion. There was definitely something funny going on here, and Suzie wasn't telling. Well, she'd soon get it out of Sam.

Hustling Suzie up the stairs as fast as her belly would allow, Wendy waited impatiently for the door to be opened. The instant Suzie turned the key, she barged past her and marched up the short hallway, charging through the living-room door like a rhino and shocking the hell out of the men sitting around the money-laden table rolling spliffs.

'Holy fucking shit, Wendy!' squawked Mal, knocking tobacco every which way as he dived to cover the drugs. 'I thought it was a raid! How did you get in?'

'Suzie,' Wendy snapped. Then, standing over them like a fearsome headmistress, hands on hips, she looked at each of them in turn. 'Now, who wants to tell me what's going on? Sam?' She raised her eyebrows expectantly.

Mal glared at Suzie as she hovered nervously in the doorway. Shrugging helplessly, she mouthed: 'Sorry.'

'Well, Sam?' Wendy tapped her foot impatiently. 'I'm waiting!'

Mal motioned Suzie to the kitchen with his eyes, and, with a painfully thudding heart she went, sure that he would kill her for this latest gaffe. Seconds later, he joined her.

'Why did you let her in?' he hissed, flicking the door shut with his heel.

'I'm sorry,' she whimpered, leaning tight against the fridge. 'I couldn't stop her. She p-pushed past me.'

Mal glared at her for several moments. Then, remembering his share of the loot, he felt the anger seep away.

'Ah, sack it,' he said. 'It's not your fault. She said she was coming round. I just thought we'd be able to ignore her. Still, she's Sam's problem, not ours, eh?'

Suzie nodded quickly, relieved not to be in trouble again. She decided not to mention the fact that she'd spent the evening with Wendy drinking wine and smoking spliffs. If he thought they'd been discussing him he'd go really ape. She just hoped Wendy wouldn't say anything.

Nudging her aside, Mal pulled open the fridge and rooted inside, pushing yoghurts and soggy lettuce aside. 'I thought I had more beers in here,' he called over his shoulder. 'Where've they all gone?'

Suzie wiped her sweaty palms on her skirt. 'There was a six-pack in this morning. You lot must have drunk them all.'

'Must have done.' Shrugging, he closed the fridge door, then thought for a moment. 'Could be a blessing,' he said at last. 'Did Wendy bring her car?'

Suzie nodded. 'Yeah, she picked me up on the way back from the shops.'

Mal suddenly remembered the reason she'd been out. 'Oh, yeah. How was it? Did you find it?'

Suzie nodded, pulling the damp mask from her pocket.

'Oh, you beauty!' Mal snatched it from her and kissed it with sheer relief before throwing it into the bin. As an afterthought, he pulled the bag out and tied the neck in a tight knot.

'Better take that to the rubbish chute,' he said, handing it to her and shooing her out of the way as he made for the door. 'I'll get Wendy to drive over to the all-night Spar for a few bottles. I think we'll have some real nice stuff to celebrate my little windfall, eh?'

Leaving Suzie to deal with the bag, he went back to the living room where he found Wendy still grilling Sam – and Sam, the wuss, giving it all up like Mr Loose-gob. Mal sighed. It was time for a bit of the old diversionaries.

Coming up behind Wendy, he put his hands on her hips and squeezed, cooing seductively: 'Wendy, darlin', if I didn't know you were a married woman, I'd be very tempted to—' nuzzling his mouth to her ear, he whispered the rest '—*fuck the arse off you*!'

'Maaaal!' Wendy jumped, squirming as his hot breath tickled her neck.

Sam's face reddened. He might not have heard the words, but he could imagine what they were. Sometimes he really hated Mal. He was a disrespectful bastard. And as for Wendy – she wouldn't be acting like that if she knew what a git Mal could be. Look at what he'd done to Suzie.

'Couldn't do me a favour, could you?' Mal was saying now, his voice pure silk.

'Oh yeah?' Wendy smiled coyly. 'And what would that be, then?'

'Go down the Spar and get us some bottles?'

Wendy looked at his puppy-dog eyes for a moment, then sighed and held her hand out for the money. Taking two of the twenties from the pile on the table, Mal, folded them into her hand with a suggestive wink.

'Anyone ever tell you that you are an angel of mercy?' he crooned, herding her out of the door.

Seconds later he came back, rubbing his hands together as he told Sam, 'I reckon you owe me one, mate. I've just bought you a bit of time to have a line without your jailer breathing down your neck!' Nudging the still-glum Sam with his elbow, he laughed. 'Come on, you sad git! Put a smile on it – it might never happen!'

Sam tried to return the smile but only managed a grimace as Mal disappeared into the bedroom to get the last of his stash – which he didn't mind sharing now he had money to get a whole load more.

Suzie came back from the rubbish chute while he was gone and perched on the arm of his chair. Lighting a cigarette, she gazed at the carpet, exhausted by the events of the night.

Ged watched her with a frown of concern. 'You all right, sweetheart?' he asked quietly.

'Yeah, thanks, I'm fine.' She smiled without meeting his eye.

'Did you have any problem finding the mask?'

She shook her head. 'It took a while, but I got it. I've just dumped it down the chute.'

'Oh no.' Sam slapped his forehead. 'I forgot! You could have got mine out of the car while you were down there.'

'I'll get it now if you want?' she offered, standing again. 'I'll take yours too, Ged.'

'No!' Jumping up, Ged put his hands on her thin shoulders and gently eased her back down. 'I'll sort it out. You've done enough already. Just sit down and relax for a bit, okay?'

She nodded gratefully. 'Okay, thanks.'

'Was the place crawling with cops?' Sam asked.

'No,' she said, mid-yawn. 'It was deserted.'

Ged was almost at the door when he heard this. He turned back. 'What? There was no one about at all?'

'No one,' she confirmed. 'I was thinking maybe they'd already been and gone, but there was no sign of anything.'

Ged considered this, one eyebrow raised, then smiled. 'Well, I suppose that's good.'

'What is?' Mal asked, coming through the door with his stash in his hand.

'Suzie says there was no one down by the shops,' Ged told him. 'No coppers, nothing.'

Mal smiled. 'See, I told you it'd be cool. It'll give us more time to move the car.'

'Well, don't leave it too late,' Ged warned grimly. 'It won't be long before someone finds them. On the subject of which, I was thinking – maybe we should go back to see to Lee?'

'You can if you want,' said Mal. 'But I'm not going anywhere near the place. It's way too risky.'

'And what if he's alive?' argued Ged. ' 'Cos if he is and someone finds him, you can bet your life the police will squeeze everything out of him in two seconds flat.'

'Come off it. Lee wouldn't grass.'

'Don't be so bloody stupid!' Ged barked, his voice booming loud in the quiet room. 'He's not gonna take the rap for us.'

Mal shrugged casually. 'Think what you like, but I still reckon it's too risky going back.'

'And *I* reckon it's too risky leaving him there,' countered Ged. 'I'm going back.'

'See you later, then.' Mal gave a dismissive wave and turned back to his drugs.

Ged glared at him, fighting down the overwhelming urge to grip his scrawny neck and throttle the life out of him. Turning his anger onto himself instead, he cursed himself yet again for getting involved with this stupid scheme in the first place. Easy money, Lee had said. Hah! He should have known better. Nothing ever came that easy.

Which reminded of something that had been nagging him all night. The money. Sixty-eight grand was too much for a skanky little estate supermarket to take in one week. Even if it was the only shop in the area – which it wasn't – it couldn't be taking that much. There was definitely something not right about all this. He was on the verge of mentioning these suspicions when a car pulled noisily into the parking lot down below.

With the tube hanging from his nostril, Mal motioned Suzie to the window.

Sam licked his lips nervously. 'Hurry up, man. It's probably Wendy. Let me do mine before she comes in.'

'It's all right,' Suzie told them. 'It's only that bloke from upstairs. The weird one with the dogs.'

Mal laughed and passed the tube to Sam. 'Chill, baby, chill! You're gonna land yourself in an early grave, the way you're going on.'

Sam snorted his line quickly, then held the tube over his shoulder for Ged who was still in the doorway.

'No, thanks,' Ged snapped tensely. 'I've had enough of that shit, and so have you, Sam. As for you—' he jabbed a finger at Mal '—you're just losing the bleeding plot, you are!'

'What you talking about?' Mal snapped back. '*You*'re the one who's losing it. Look at you, standing there like the self-appointed voice of fucking morality!'

Ged's nostrils flared dangerously. 'Rationality, I'd say.'

'Yeah, well, whatever,' said Mal. 'You're doing me head in, going on all the time. Anyhow,' he went on, 'I've figured a way to sort this.' Turning to Suzie, he said, 'Get your coat on, doll. You can go back and check on Lee.'

'You're not serious?' Storming back into the room, Ged pointed at Suzie. 'Look at her, man. She's dropping on her bloody feet. She needs to go to bed, never mind back there!'

Mal didn't appreciate Ged's interference. What him and Suzie did was nothing to do with anyone else. Snapping his fingers at Suzie, all the time staring at Ged, he growled: 'I said get your coat on!'

Suzie desperately didn't want Mal and Ged to fight over her. Getting up quickly, she crept past Ged into the hall, wishing with every fibre of her body that she could just crawl back into bed and sleep for ever.

'See, Ged?' smirked Mal. 'She's my girl, and she wants to help me. Your obvious concern, touching as it is,' he placed a hand on his heart and bared his teeth in a malicious grin, 'is beginning to perturb me somewhat!'

Ged laughed mirthlessly. 'Have you heard the crap you start spouting when you fill your head with that shit?'

'Sticks and stones, me boy!' Mal pulled a childish face. 'Sticks and fucking stones!'

As Suzie opened the front door, Ged shouted for her to wait, then turned back to Mal. 'Mal, I'm telling you, man—'

'What?' Mal growled nastily. 'What you telling me?'

Ged just about managed to hold his temper down. 'Tell her she doesn't have to go,' he said quietly.

'She's going,' said Mal. 'And she'll be fine!'

'What about you?' Ged turned to Sam for support. 'Do you think she'll be fine?'

'I'm not getting involved,' said Sam, picking up a newspaper from the floor beside his chair and using it to cover his face. 'Just sort it out between you. Leave me out of it.'

'So you're not bothered if she leads the police back here?' demanded Ged.

'I wouldn't do that,' Suzie piped up nervously from the open door.

'Course she wouldn't,' said Mal. ''Cos, like I've told you, she's not that stupid.'

Ged turned on him furiously. 'Oh? And why is that? 'Cos she knows what she'll get if she messes up? Is that it? Yeah . . . you're such a big man, aren't you, Mal? Beating the shit out of the kid, then sending her out to do your dirty work. You're nothing but a spineless little bastard!' Balling his hands into fists, he loomed over Mal. 'Man – one of these days . . .!'

'One of these days what?' Mal retorted, knowing full well he was pushing his luck but unable to stop himself.

As the tension crackled like static in the air, Sam's headache resurfaced with a vengeance. He felt nauseous and his nerves were screaming. Finally, he could stand it no longer.

'For God's sake!' he yelled, the uncharacteristic force in his voice stunning the others into silence. Slamming the paper down he jumped up from his seat. 'I'll go – and don't you dare laugh at me, Mal, 'cos Ged's right. You shouldn't be sending Suzie!'

'Don't be stupid!' Ged snapped at him. 'You're already in hiding. Fat lot of good it'll do us if you get spotted. We'll be even deeper in the shit than we are already.'

Just then, Wendy appeared in the doorway and demanded to know what all the noise was about.

'Sam just volunteered to put his life on the line,' Ged blurted out – glad to his heart that she'd come in just then, because if anyone could talk sense into Sam she could.

'Well?' Wendy turned on her husband. 'What stupid scheme is it now?'

Wilting beneath her withering glare, Sam muttered, 'Someone's got to go and see to Lee. And I'm sick of these two arguing about it, so I'm going.'

'Oh, no, you're not!' Wendy slammed the three bottles of brandy she was carrying down onto the coffee table and pushed him back down on the chair. 'Listen here, matey!' she spat, thrusting her livid face into his. 'I got that house to get you off these streets and keep you alive – and now you think I'm gonna let you walk about out there, you bloody clown? If that crew sees you they'll waste you, you know that!'

'But, Wendy . . .' Sam protested weakly.

'Don't "but, Wendy" me, you bloody moron!' she screamed.

As the argument escalated, Suzie took the opportunity to escape and, for the second time that night, found herself heading along City Road – hoping against hope that she'd find it still dark, still undisturbed by the flashing lights and pandemonium of police vehicles she dreaded would be there by now.

It was still deserted.

Breathing a sigh of relief, she slipped into the

shadows of the fence encircling the Home and peered across to the dark yard. She had to go over there to find Lee. He was either dead or dying, and she had to find out which.

And to do that, she'd have to touch him!

The very thought filled her with dread. She'd never even *seen* a dead person before, never mind touched one. What if she fainted? Oh God!

But no – she couldn't let Mal down. She had to be strong, pull herself together and get on with it.

Taking a deep breath, she pushed herself away from the fence and hurried across to the open gates. But once there, her resolve began to disintegrate. It was so dark and eerie. She couldn't see a thing except the outline of Pasha's jeep, and the sight of it still sitting there long after he should have been gone made her heart sink. Steeling herself, she stepped through the gate.

It took a few moments for her eyes to adjust enough to make out the shape of the wheelie bin to the right of the door. Mal had said he'd been lying next to it when Pasha fell, so at least she knew where to start looking. Dreading the moment of discovery, she took a hesitant step forward, then another – sliding her feet one in front of the other in an attempt to feel her way without falling. She'd gone almost halfway when her foot connected with something soft. She froze, her toe still touching whatever it was. And then she heard a groan, so soft that she half thought she'd imagined it.

Her mouth filled with saliva as her heartbeat gathered momentum, going faster and faster, pounding, rushing, deafening, until she thought she was going to faint.

Then the thing spoke.

'Help me . . .'

It was Lee.

Dropping to her knees before she fell, Suzie fumbled for his hand. 'Lee,' she whimpered. 'It's me – Suzie. Are you all right?'

'It hurts,' he croaked. 'Head hurts . . .'

'Oh God, Lee, God! What should I do? I don't know what to do!'

But Mal would.

As the thought occurred to her, she pushed herself back onto her heels and shook Lee gently, sounding much more confident than she felt as she said, 'I'm gonna phone Mal. I won't be long. Will you be okay?'

Groaning, he flapped a hand feebly.

'I won't be long,' she said again, then gave his hand a reassuring squeeze and stumbled out of the yard.

Running around to the phone box, she almost cried in relief to find it was working for once. Tapping out the number, she hopped from foot to foot as the ringing tone trilled down her ear.

Come on, Mal! Come on!

'Yeah?' Mal's wary voice came to her at last, flooding her with relief.

'M-Mal – it's me,' she gabbled frantically. 'He's alive! Lee . . . He's still alive! And, oh God . . . You've got to come! Come now! He's alive!'

'Calm down, Suzie.' Mal's tone was sharp.

'Mal, please . . .' Suzie swiped at a tear as it trickled down her cheek. 'I don't know what to do!'

'Suzie?' It was Wendy.

'Yeah, Wendy, it's m-me. Please do something. Lee's hurt.'

'Where are you?' Wendy's calm voice helped.

'In the ph-phone box at the f-front of the shops.'

'Right,' said Wendy. 'Go back to Lee. We'll be there in a minute.'

Back in the yard, Lee had propped himself up on his elbows. Suzie could hear his heavy breathing from the gates.

'Oh, Lee . . . please keep still,' she urged and, squatting behind him, she tried to make him relax and lie back on her knees. Her fingers became sticky with grease and sweat as she stroked his hair, but she didn't notice. 'Everything's gonna be okay now,' she crooned. 'Wendy's coming.'

Lee groaned.

'What is it?' she asked. 'Am I hurting you?'

'Wendy to the rescue,' he croaked in reply. 'What a woman!'

4

In his heavily fortified flat on the thirteenth floor of a high-rise overlooking Moss Side's fire station, The Man waited for Pasha Singh with growing irritation. Lovers' rock pumped out from four powerful speakers tilting down from each corner of the sumptuous leather-and-chrome-furnished room, flooding the air with meaty, pounding bass and swirling, crystal-clear strings.

Rocking his head in time to the music. The Man was outwardly calm – inwardly, though, he was seething. Only the dangerous glint in his slanted catlike eyes gave any hint of the fire blazing within.

Linda, his latest pick-up, lay beside him in a blissful haze of drug-induced euphoria, her white-blonde hair splayed out across her pale shoulders, her long legs curled beneath her, sending her short skirt high on her slim white thighs. With one glossy red talon, she idly scratched at his knee as her hot breath gently penetrated the crotch of his Armani trousers.

The Man shifted irritably. It was two-thirty in the morning and he was not in the mood for any of her sex shit. A week down the line, and already she was beginning to irritate him. She had no sense of when to leave him be.

Drumming his wide, gold-heavy fingers on his meaty thigh, he frowned, his glittering eyes narrowed to slits. He was angry. A deep, smouldering energy was building inside him as the minutes ticked by. Pasha should have been here two hours ago. What the fuck was he playing at?

He inhaled deeply through his nose, then released the breath slowly, telling himself there was bound to be a good explanation. Pasha was no fly-by-night kid. He was a businessman. He wouldn't be foolish enough to think of ripping The Man off.

Jake wasn't so willing to wait and see. Pacing the floor, his short dreads bouncing around his handsome face as he repeatedly slapped a fist into his palm, he said, 'Let me go and look for him, boss.'

The Man shook his head slowly. Jake, his right-hand man, was too rash. Half Jamaican, half Irish, Jake had a racist streak bordering on the psychotic. He particularly hated Asians, and viewed Pasha Singh as all of them rolled into one. He'd have liked nothing better than to take a pop at him, but reason told The Man to wait a little longer. Pasha had been reliable up to now.

And there was time enough for revenge if it were warranted.

'Not yet.' The Man's voice was husky and low. 'I'll give him a little more time. But, see, if him mek me wait too long . . .' He let the sentence hang and kissed his teeth.

Jake grinned and settled a little, satisfied that his services would be required at some point tonight. Pasha Singh had messed up good this time.

A car horn sounded down below. Muted by the distance, it floated up like a remote banshee wail, barely audible beneath the music. The Man nudged Linda, clicking his fingers at her.

Sitting up lazily, she stretched and yawned, then uncoiled herself and wiggled across to the window. She knew what was required of her. Draping herself prettily around the place was only part of it. She was also the looker-outer, the spliff-roller, the general whatever-he-wanted-getter, and the whatever-he-desired-giver.

Sticking her face through the curtains she peered down towards the road. 'It's just that big guy,' she slurred. Letting the curtain fall back, she drifted back to his side.

Jake shot her a filthy look. 'Who the fuck's she talking about?' he muttered sarcastically. 'The big guy? Ten–fifteen big guys come by this yard every claat day! Cha!'

Stomping across to the window, he leaned flat against the wall and eased the edge of the curtain back to look for himself. He couldn't risk revealing himself fully, not with all the drive-bys going on at the moment – however unlikely it was that someone would score an accurate hit on a target this far up. Spotting the gleaming silver BMW he relaxed.

'It's just Max,' he said – more than a little pleased that it wasn't Pasha. The longer he took to arrive, the less likely it was that he would – and the more likely that Jake would get to inflict some serious damage on him.

Shoving Linda aside, The Man reached for the remote to turn the heart-thudding bass down to a low throbbing pulse. 'Tell him to come up,' he said.

Jake motioned to Max through the window, then took the keys from the shelf and went to let him in. It took a few minutes to open the heavily protected front door, but it was a necessary precaution. The Man was still on top for now, but things were getting heavy. Exception was being taken to the hold he had on the market. Still . . . no one was going to get through all these locks unless they blasted the wall away first. Picking up the intercom as it buzzed, he pressed the button to release the lock of the main door on the high-rise's ground floor.

'Yo, Jake,' Max said, coming up the communal stairs a few minute later.

'Max.' Jake nodded, stepping around him to scan the stairway for unwelcome followers before rebarricading the door.

In the living room, Max pressed his fist to The Man's in greeting but said nothing, waiting for the girl to be dismissed before delivering his news.

Waving him into a chair, The Man nudged Linda and motioned her from the room with his head. Leaning forward, he took a pre-rolled spliff from an ornate black-lacquered box on the coffee table and lit it, drawing on it deeply as he waited for her to go.

Reaching for her purse, she staggered to her feet and did as she'd been told without argument. Jake side-stepped her as she tottered past him on spiky stilettos, gripping the purse tightly to her breast as though it were a precious jewel.

'She off to powder her nose again?' he sniped, closing the door behind her.

'Leave her be,' The Man reprimanded him sharply. Turning to Max, he raised a questioning brow. 'So?'

Max grinned widely, revealing a row of large square teeth with a valley-wide gap in the centre. 'It dealt wid!' he purred, running a finger like a knife across his throat. 'The man 'im gahn!'

'Nice, nice!' The Man said. 'An' no one checked you?'

'No one 'cept the fishes,' Max said. 'An' they be too busy chewin' junkie to chat!'

The Man pulled an envelope from his waistcoat pocket

and threw it across to Max. 'There's a lickle extra this time,' he said. ''F' bein' quick.'

Opening it, Max flipped his thumb through the notes inside and smiled. 'That's sound, star!' Standing, he slipped it into his pocket and said, 'Well, better make tracks. Got me a hot little gal waiting. Thanks again for this.' He patted his pocket. 'It'll come in han—' His voice trailed off as he saw the deep scowl on The Man's face. An icy prickle raised the hairs on the back of his neck. ''S up?' he asked, backing up a step as he wondered if his luck had just run out – had The Man found out he'd been skimming from the collections?

'You'd better tell me you didn't bring no pussy round my yard!' The Man growled, his easy patois replaced by a broad Mancunian accent. 'You know I don't want no fucker knowing my business!'

'What d'y' take me for?' Max asked, his face a picture of wounded integrity as he breathed an internal sigh of relief. 'I ain't never done nutt'n stupid like that, an' I ain't gonna start now. She's hanging at the blues, man!'

'You sure?'

Max nodded quickly. 'Course, man. I wouldn't do that to you.'

The Man held his hand up in a sign of acceptance and settled back into his seat. 'I had to ask, Max. You know how it is these days. Can't be too sure of no one. See you later, yeah?'

Max nodded. He knew the score. Everyone was stabbing each other in the back since smack became such hot business, and no one was taking any chances.

Turning to leave, he stopped when The Man called out to him again. The icy prickle returned.

'Where you headed?' The Man asked.

'Down The Nile,' Max told him. 'Why, what's up, bro'?'

'Just want you to do one more thing,' The Man said, holding the spliff out towards him.

'Sure,' Max agreed, leaning across to take it. 'So long as it ain't popping no one else, 'cos I ain't equipped no more.'

The Man shook his head. 'I just want you to drive past the estate and see if Pasha's still there. You got your mobile?'

Max nodded and patted his pocket, smoke swirling up from his nostrils. Taking another pull, he handed the spliff back. 'Is that all, just drive past? You don't want me to go and see him?'

The Man shook his head. 'Nah. If the lights are still on, it's cool. I just want to know if he's there or not.'

'I'll bell you as soon as I see anything,' Max said and, waving, he hotfooted it out of there before they thought of anything else to detain him.

Jake let him out, waiting until the heavy security door on the ground floor swung firmly into place before closing The Man's door. While he was relocking it, Linda emerged from the bathroom and staggered past him into the living room.

Kicking off her stilettos, she floated down to the floor at The Man's feet and sifted lazily through her purse for the lump of soft black draw he'd given her. Finding it, she attempted to roll a spliff. Her head lolled forward in deep concentration, her mouth hanging slack and wet.

Coming back, Jake looked at her with disgust. 'She'll be a junkie in a week,' he declared venomously. 'She like it too much.'

'She'll be paying for it if she wants to carry on,' The Man said. 'I ain't keeping her supplied.'

'She working?' Jake asked.

'Not yet,' The Man said. Leaning forward, he coiled Linda's long hair around his hand and pulled her head back. She looked up at him, her eyes rolling heavily. Laughing softly, he let go and sat back. 'Not yet,' he repeated.

'So what you gonna do with her?' Jake asked. 'You ain't planning on keeping her round, are you?'

The Man shook his head. 'Nah. I've done everything I want with her already. Anyhow, Patrice is coming home soon, so she best be gahn, else she'll be losing all them Goldilocks – and she won't be earning much without them, eh?'

Jake laughed. Patrice was The Man's baby-mother. A gorgeous, crazy black queen. She wouldn't take too kindly to this bimbo, that was for sure. A white woman getting it on with her man was a soon-to-be-dead white woman.

'She got her own place?' he asked.

'Dunno.' The Man shrugged. 'But I'm thinking to move her into a nice place of her own anyway. Get her away from her lickle friends, mek her more high-class.' He nodded thoughtfully, voicing the idea that had been growing all week. 'I'm thinking she'd be good for business types with them baby blues.'

'So long as she can keep them open!' spat Jake, throwing Linda another filthy look.

Standing up, he stretched, rolling his tongue around his dry teeth. 'You want a drink?'

The Man nodded and glanced at his watch with a frown. His patience was beginning to wear paper-thin now. Pasha Singh was pushing his luck big-time. This was pure disrespect, and he couldn't afford to let it go unpunished. If the cunt was playing games, he'd have to pay the price. Even if he wasn't planning a rip-off, he was pure taking the piss with his timekeeping, and he'd have to be dealt with. He'd decide how when Max reported back.

Back at the shops, Suzie was just beginning to think Wendy wasn't coming when she heard a car turn onto the road behind her. It came to a stop outside the gate, its lights already dead as the door opened and soft footsteps headed towards her.

'Suzie?' Ged hissed into the dark. 'Where are you?'

'Over here,' she croaked.

Ged hurried across to her and gave her a quick, reassuring hug. 'Are you all right, sweetheart?'

'Yeah, I'm okay,' she said, leaning gratefully into his solid warmth. 'But we've got to get Lee out of here.'

Giving her icy hand a squeeze, Ged reached out to Lee and shook his shoulder gently. 'Lee, mate. We're going to get you in the car. Do you think you can walk if we get you on your feet?'

'Dunno,' Lee mumbled. 'It hurts . . .'

'You'll just have to try, mate,' Ged said, putting an arm under Lee's back and pulling him upright. 'Come on. Let's get you out of here. Give me a hand, Suzie.'

With one of Lee's arms around each of their shoulders, they walked him to the car. Suzie leaped in the back to pull him in as Ged pushed, and as soon as they were all in, Wendy reversed back out onto City Road and raced away, tyres squealing.

'He'd better not be bleeding on my seat!' she snapped

over her shoulder. Then, more gently: 'You all right, Sooze?'

'Yeah,' said Suzie quietly and, flopping her head back, she closed her eyes.

Halfway down City Road, a silver BMW streaked smoothly past them heading towards the shops. Instinctively checking the rear-view, Wendy saw the red glow of the other car's brake lights shining back at her like a pair of demon's eyes. She put her foot down hard as a sharp pain gripped her stomach.

In the kitchen, Jake was adding ice to two tall glasses when he heard the phone ring. Carrying the drinks through as The Man answered, he waited to see if his moment had come.

The Man was frowning, making 'Hmmm . . . mmmm' noises as he listened. After a minute, he said, 'Yeah, tek a look. I'll wait.' Covering the mouthpiece, he explained the conversation to Jake. 'Max says the lights is all off, but the jeep's still there.'

'Want me to go round?' Jake asked hopefully.

The Man shook his head, then held his hand up for quiet as Max came back on the line.

Walking over to the table, Jake put the glasses down heavily, splashing juice onto his hand. He licked it off, waiting for the nod he felt sure was coming.

'What's his fucking game?' The Man shouted. 'No one at all? Nah, man, just tek a look in the yard! Yeah, I'm holdin'! Shit!'

With a furious scowl, he held his hand out for a glass.

''S up?' Jake asked, passing one over.

The Man took a long drink and slammed the glass back down on the table. Leaning down, he peeled the draw from the sleeping girl's hand and tossed it to Jake. 'Mek a smoke, man – a strong one. Something ain't right.'

Jake could feel a kicking coming on. Rolling the spliff, he psyched himself.

'What? Where?' The Man barked. Then, suddenly, his tone changed, becoming edgy and cautious. 'Nah – don't, man! Leave him be. Don't touch him! Shit! What about the bag?' he asked then. 'Is the raas bag there? Fuck! Nah, man. Just clear out of there fast! In fact, come back here. No! I'm deadly fucking serious!'

Slamming the receiver down, he turned to Jake with blazing eyes. 'Fucking guy's lost his face, star!'

'Who?' Jake frowned. 'Pasha?'

'Shit, yeah!' thundered The Man, slamming his fist into the arm of the couch. 'Some raas pussy's smoked my man and took off with my fucking money!' Jumping to his feet in a furious rage, he kicked the girl out of the way and began to pace the room.

'Ooowww . . .' she whined, picking herself up and pushing her hair away from her face as she tried to locate him through the haze. 'Whassamatter?'

Without looking at her, The Man thumbed towards her. 'Get rid!' he demanded, his voice pure ice. 'I don't want her listening when Max comes back!'

Although he'd have liked to have heard what Max had to say himself, Jake was more than happy to oblige. Gripping Linda's arm, he hauled her to her feet none too gently, saying, 'Get ready, darlin'. You're going home!'

Sobering fast, she struggled against him. 'But I don't wanna go . . . I wanna stay here. Simeon, tell him—'

Jake grabbed her face and squeezed her cheeks together, puckering her lips. 'I said, *get . . . ready*! You are leaving!'

'Owww!' she screeched, sticking her nails into his hand and kicking out at his shin.

Smiling maliciously, he opened his mouth wide.

'JAKE!' The Man shouted. 'Don't! Things are hot enough without that shit! Here—' Picking his keys up from the table, he threw them across to Jake. 'Tek her home – and be nice, seen?'

'Seen!' Jake grinned. He turned back to the girl. 'Come, darlin'. We're tekkin' a ride!'

'I want my bag!' she yelped as he dragged her towards the door. 'I can't go home without my keys. I won't be able to get in.'

Still gripping her arm, Jake dragged Linda the few feet back to where her bag lay open on the floor. Picking it up, he snapped it shut and slammed it into her hands. 'There! Now let's go.'

Protesting all the way, she just about managed to grab her shoes and, hopping along the hallway behind him, got her feet into them, half sobbing as Jake pushed her roughly up against the wall. She made a half-hearted attempt to duck past him as he undid the locks, but he was too quick for her.

Slamming her into the wall with his elbow, he grabbed her hair, twisting her head to the side. 'Listen up,' he spat into her terrified face. 'The more you fight, the more I like! You got that?' He ground his pelvis into hers to emphasize his meaning.

She nodded quickly, her eyes wide and wet.

Jake lowered his face to within an inch of hers and opened his teeth over her mouth. He was gratified to see the horror in her eyes. Sniffing loudly, he said, 'You pissed yourself, darlin'?'

Linda shook her head, yelping as he tugged her hair again.

'Good. Now stop fucking about or I won't be nice to you no more!'

Ged carried Lee up the stairs to Mal's flat and laid him down on the couch. Suzie kneeled beside him, holding his hand to comfort him as Wendy looked him over.

He seemed to have perked up a bit now that the icy chill had left him, but they were all dreading the worst. It was obvious from the damage to his sleeve that he'd been shot – the leather was scorched and shredded. How badly his arm was hurt was what they were dreading finding out.

Cutting the sleeve away from the cuff to the shoulder – about which Lee complained bitterly – Wendy was soon able to put their minds at rest. The bullet hadn't penetrated his skin, it had just skimmed it, leaving an inch-wide groove of rawness in its wake.

The real damage he'd sustained was a gaping wound to the back of his head where he'd hit the floor when he fell. This was two inches long and half an inch deep, and a lot of blood had drained from it already. It was this that had laid him flat.

As she tended to this, Wendy kneeled directly in front of Lee, with her aching stomach resting on her thighs and her breasts at such an angle that he was afforded a fantastic view of her cleavage each time she bent forward. Unaware of the enormous pleasure she was granting him, she dabbed at the wound with a sponge, regularly squeezing the blood into the bowl of water

Ged had placed on the floor beside her. When this needed changing for the second time, she sat back with a frown.

'This needs stitching. It's too deep and it won't stop bleeding.'

Lee shook his head – as best he could lying face down with Wendy holding his crown in her vicelike grip. 'No!' he squealed, his voice muffled by the cushion. 'I'm not going to the sick house. Stick some plasters on it, it'll be all right.'

'Don't be stupid,' Ged scolded him gently. 'If it needs stitching, it'll have to be stitched. I'll take you to the Infirmary.'

As Ged reached for his jacket he noticed Wendy wincing for the fourth time since they'd picked Lee up. It suddenly occurred to him that she might be in labour, and he asked if she was okay.

'Yes!' she hissed through gritted teeth, releasing a series of short, sharp breaths. 'I'm . . . absolutely . . . fine!'

'Ooowww!' squawked Lee, twisting his head as her fingers dug in hard. 'Wendy! I know you love me, but can't you control your passion?'

'Fuck off!' Wendy snarled, then bent double as another pain tore through her stomach. 'Oh . . . God!' she groaned, gritting her teeth again and pressing down on the rock-hard bump as she waited for the pain to subside. Her face turned purple.

Lee's face, just inches from hers, was a picture of puzzlement. 'What's up, Wend'?' he asked. 'You constipated, or what?'

'You stupid prick!' Wendy laughed despite the pain. Lee came out with the most absurd things. 'I'm having the bloody baby, you moron!'

Sam sat bolt upright in his chair. 'You what?' he squawked. 'Now?'

'Yes, now!' Wendy hissed, shooting him a filthy look. 'Not that you'd notice, dickhead!'

Sam's hands fluttered ineffectually at his sides. He didn't know what to do. He wanted to help, but what could he do?

'Should I get some towels?' he asked eventually. 'Boil some water, or something?'

Wendy gripped her stomach, thrusting her chin hard onto her chest. 'Why? Planning to wash the car, are you?'

Mal, who'd been lying on the mat in front of the fire, clutching a bottle of brandy to his chest throughout, now rolled lazily onto his side and propped his head on his hand to watch the floor show. Seeing the expression of amazement on Lee's blood-drained face, he sniggered and waved the bottle tantalizingly.

'Yo, Lee! Y' look like you're in shock, mate. Wanna little drinky-poo?'

'Too right!' Lee's wide eyes shifted from Wendy's pain-racked face to Mal's drunken grin. Reaching for the bottle, he made to roll off the couch, but Wendy, temporarily recovered from her latest contraction, shoved him back with her fist.

'Owwww!' he yelped, rubbing at his shoulder where he could feel the imprint of her knuckles. 'What a woman!'

Wendy launched herself at him then, teeth bared, eyes blazing as she grabbed the front of his T-shirt and shook him viciously, bouncing his head off the cushion. 'You . . . stupid . . . little . . . BASTAAARD! It's your fault I'm having it now. If you hadn't started this, none of us would be here now! I hate you!'

'Ooohhh, baby . . .' Lee leered, blood trickling down

his hair onto the cushion. 'You're sooo sexy when you're mad!'

As another pain ripped through her, Wendy had to let go of him. Doubling over, she screamed, 'Get me to hospital! It's coming!'

Suzie staggered to her feet, her own body a mass of aches and pains. 'I'll call an ambulance,' she said, tottering over to the phone.

'Nine, nine, friggin' nine,' Mal drawled. 'Nee nah, nee nah! Yeah, that's a fucking great idea, that, innit? Some cunt gets shot an' the next thing you know, there's a fucking ambulance shooting round to my fucking gaff! Yeah, great! Let's call the dibble while we're at it, eh? And how about the National fucking Guard? That'd be a fucking big laugh, that would!'

Pulling the bottle round, he tipped it up for a drink and smacked himself in the teeth. Laughing crazily, he rolled around on the mat, splashing brandy everywhere.

Ged watched him in undisguised disgust for a moment, then turned back to the others. Seeing Sam's pasty face, and Suzie helplessly wringing her hands by the phone, he sighed heavily, once again feeling the burden of responsibility falling on him.

'Sam?' He spoke calmly, waiting until Sam's helpless eyes swung from Wendy to him before going on. 'You've got to get ready to go to hospital. Go and get some water on your face and sober up, yeah?'

Nodding mutely, Sam stumbled into the kitchen. When he'd gone, Ged turned to Suzie and told her not to phone for an ambulance because it would be quicker in the car. Suzie said she'd get her coat and go with them, but Ged shook his head.

'Thanks, sweetheart, but I don't think you should. It'll

look funny enough taking Lee in like this without anyone seeing the state of you. Stay here and get some sleep. Okay?'

'Okay,' she agreed reluctantly.

Ged smiled. She was a good kid. All she needed was a bit of affection.

Turning to Lee and Wendy, he waved them to the door. Lee opened his mouth to protest, but Ged held up a firm hand, telling him: 'In the car. No arguments. Can you make it down?' he asked Wendy then. 'I can carry you, if you want.'

'I can walk!' she snapped indignantly and, pressing her fingers in hard below the bump as if she could hold the baby in by will-power alone, she staggered to the door.

Max passed The Man's Jag as he drove into the car park. He caught a brief glimpse of the girl in the passenger seat and wondered if she knew about Jake. He shook his head. That shit was nothing to do with him.

Parking, he jogged across to the doorway and pressed the intercom button, peering around all the while to see if he was being watched. After a short wait the buzzer sounded, releasing the lock. Max went in quickly, pulling the door firmly into place behind him and rattling it to make absolutely sure it was locked tight before walking up the stairs to where The Man was waiting in the doorway – his face clearly displaying his anger and disquiet.

In the living room, Max flopped into the same chair as before and lit a cigarette, nervously watching as The Man stalked into the room.

'So what the fuck's going down?' The Man shot at him, his eyes glittering slits in his sweating face.

Max shifted in the chair, pulling his leather coat-tails free. He shrugged. 'Just what I said. It was all dark at the front, so I cruised round the back to look in the yard, and I see the jeep sitting there. So then I bell you, and you say tek a look.' Pausing, he reached out for Jake's untouched juice. 'Can I?'

The Man nodded and Max took a long drink, wiping his mouth on the back of his hand.

'Anyhow,' he went on at last. 'I get out, leaving my lights on so's I can see into the yard, yeah? And at first I don't see nutt'n, so I think to check the jeep – see if he's kipping in the back or something. But he's not. And then I see him lying by the door, and when I go over I see all this blood.' He paused again, taking another long drink.

'And?' snapped The Man impatiently.

'And so I feel 'is neck, but I can't feel no pulse, yeah? And that's when I tell you he's dead and you say come back here.'

'Shit, man!' The Man sat heavily, punching the chair arm with a dull thwack. 'I said don't touch him! Wha'pp'n to your raas brain?' He jabbed a finger at his own forehead. 'Y' lost all your sense now, is it? Shit, man!' With a heavy sigh, he put his elbows on his knees and stroked the corners of his mouth with his thumbs, deep in thought.

'I didn't really touch him,' Max said quietly. 'I only rest my finger just so . . .' He lightly touched a finger to his throat to demonstrate.

Watching this from beneath his brows, The Man shook his head slowly. 'You know the Babylon got them dee-en-ay tests,' he said, his voice low and grave. 'All it tek is one strand offa them pretty dreads—' he jabbed a finger at Max's hair '—and they'll swarm all over you!' He kissed his teeth. 'Raas!'

Max slouched in his chair, resting his head on his clenched fist as the enormity of the situation began to sink in. If he'd gone straight to The Nile earlier as planned, he'd be rocking his gal's ass by now. Instead, he was sitting here, getting depressed.

He knew full well the implications of his actions tonight. The junkie he'd dispatched to a watery grave was one thing. That would be eaten by the fishes along with any trace of himself by the time the Babylon found it. But a respected businessman lying dead in a yard, just feet from a main road and only a matter of hours from discovery, with traces of himself on the corpse, was another thing altogether. And he hadn't even done it!

'So the bag wasn't there?' The Man was asking now.

Max shook his head unhappily. 'I could see clear by the time you axed me to look for it, and there wasn't no bag in the yard. How much you lost?'

The Man's face darkened. 'A lot!'

Max rolled his eyes. 'Shit!'

'Listen,' The Man said after a minute. 'You'd better go meet your gal.'

'Nah,' Max shook his head dejectedly. 'It's too late. Anyway, I don't feel like it now.'

'Go,' The Man insisted. Standing up he headed for the door. 'Don't keep her waiting, man. Go get seen so you got an alibi, yeah? Forget all this for tonight, but keep your ears open, yeah? Anyone mentions Pasha or the shop, or someone having money to burn, come and tell me about it, yeah?'

Max nodded, following The Man to the door in a cloud of despondency.

'Look, don't worry,' said The Man as he waved Max down the stairs. 'If you only touched his neck a little bit, I don't think it'll show. Peace, man.'

Max gave him a sick smile, then continued down the stairs. It was all right for The Man to say 'Don't worry' when he himself hadn't been within a mile of the crime scene tonight.

5

Jake still hadn't uttered a word, but Linda was oblivious to the heavy silence in the car. She was too busy stroking her seat, enjoying the sensual feel of the smooth leather beneath her fingers. She'd become very attached to this car in the short week she'd been Simeon's girl. She loved the luxury of it. The touch and smell of hot leather. The musky scent of Simeon's aftershave. The sexy music throbbing from the expensive system. Money and danger – a heady combination. Sophisticated. A world she'd craved to be a part of for the longest time. And now that she was, she had no intention of letting it go.

Linda smiled as she thought of Simeon. The Man . . . her man! So big and strong – and wrapped around her little finger! Anything she wanted, she only had to ask and he'd be sure to give it to her.

Simeon was special, there was no denying that. Like a lion – powerful, demanding respect. Everything she'd always dreamed of, in fact. Yet, somehow, tonight, some of his appeal had faded. For tonight, she had seen Jake as something other than his right-hand man, and it had excited her beyond her wildest dreams. If Simeon was a lion, then Jake was a caged tiger. Gorgeous, unpredictable – and definitely dangerous.

Glancing across at the still-silent man, Linda drank in the details she had previously overlooked. The mocking curve of his lips. The surprisingly slender nose speckled with light freckles. The muscles in his arms, rippling like waves as he turned the wheel. As the heat of desire spread across her thighs, she wondered how it would feel to be with him. To have those arms around her, his husky voice whispering words of love as he moved deep inside her.

Running her fingers through her silky hair, she stretched languidly and raised her arms snakelike to stroke her fingertips along the roof. She wished he wasn't taking her straight home. Wished he'd take her somewhere nice and secluded.

Jake's lips fluttered in the tiniest smile as he watched Linda from the corner of his eye. Far from rousing his interest, her little snake-charming display merely confirmed what he'd felt all along – that she was a cheap little slut. And a stupid one at that, if she thought her little show would make him want to be nice to her.

Easing the Jag off the Princess Parkway, he considered taking her out into the countryside for a bit of fun. The Man wouldn't have a problem with that. She might, but The Man wouldn't.

'Jake . . .?' Linda interrupted his thoughts in her best seductive voice. When he still didn't look at her, she played a talon slowly down her cleavage. 'Why don't you like me, Jake?'

He glanced at her then, the infrequent street lights casting a demonic glint on the strange green of his eyes as a teasing smile curved his lips. 'Whassamatter?' he drawled, his voice low and deceptively soft. 'You wanna play?'

Excitement and fear flooded her eyes, sending a thrill of anticipation through his groin. Shifting in his seat, he eased down harder on the accelerator and smoothly changed course, heading the sleek car towards Styal. If the slut wanted action, he was more than happy to oblige.

Linda's heart fluttered wildly in her chest. Excited? Scared? She couldn't decide. Maybe both. But it didn't matter. He'd opened the door – shown that he liked her. Something was going to happen. Stretching her legs deeper into the footwell, she slowly crossed them, sending her skirt even higher as she twirled a lock of hair slowly around her finger.

Her eyes strayed to the clock face glowing red in the dash, and she got a momentary shock when she saw it was three-thirty. Her mum would go berserk! As soon as she thought it, she shrugged it off. So what? Let the old bag have a shit-fit. She couldn't spoil her fun for ever. In a few weeks she'd be old enough to do whatever she wanted – even leave home. Simeon had already hinted at getting her a flat of her own. If she played her cards right she'd be set for life. Simeon could set her up, and Jake could be her secret lover.

Smiling, she closed her eyes to concentrate on her fantasy. Jake would fall madly in love with her. And he'd be so gentle. The animosity he'd displayed so far, the aggression – that was just a cover. He was just wary of stepping on Simeon's toes, which was understandable, but she'd soon put his mind at rest. She'd assure him that she'd be discreet, then she'd cook for him, clean his clothes, and satisfy his every need. And in return, he'd worship her.

Jake noticed Linda's head nodding forward as she fell asleep. Only then did he look at her fully. He refused to give them the satisfaction of seeing him looking. Give them the impression he liked them or something? No way! He liked them frightened – like she'd been in the hall back there. That was good.

Nosing the car onto a short stretch of unlit motorway, he lit a spliff and changed the tape. Brimstone and Fire. Heavy dub to make the blood pulse through his veins. Then minutes later, he pulled onto a dirt track and rolled quietly to a stop.

Linda opened her eyes slowly. 'Whazzup?' she slurred, her mouth dry from sleep.

'Sshh,' Jake crooned.

'Where are we?' Hardly able to see in the pitch darkness, she tried to sit up to look out, but found she couldn't move her head.

Jake grinned and twisted her hair another turn around his hand as he stared into her soul with his unblinking green eyes. 'Wakey, wakey, darlin',' he purred. 'Time for some fun.'

'Oh, Jake,' she murmured, parting her lips in anticipation of his kiss as she reached out to touch his beautiful face.

Jake tightened his grip, amused by her obvious confusion. 'What should we play, then?' he asked in a voice like melted syrup.

'W-whatever you want,' she whispered, her voice tiny as she struggled not to cry out against the pain.

His eyes sparkled mockingly as he watched her pupils dilate – jet spreading out to overtake the blue. An absolute turn-on. Still holding her hair in a vicelike grip, he unzipped his jeans and pressed her head firmly down. She gagged as he forced himself into her mouth, but he held her fast, furiously bucking his hips against her until she thought she would faint.

Pulling her head back minutes later, he viewed his handiwork dispassionately. Her lips were puffy and red, her eyes dark and watery – and huge with fear. He felt satisfied, despite not having released one drop of seed. He'd never waste that on a white girl. That wasn't the point at all. The point was the mute terror he could see, feel, smell. That was what did it for him.

Pushing her back on the seat, he laughed as she raised her hands to her throat. 'What's up, darlin'? Too much man for you? Don't you like me no more?'

Linda nodded quickly, still uncertain, but still willing to believe he liked her. He must do to have had such a hard-on.

'I do l-like you,' she stuttered. 'Please don't be mean. Just let me . . .' She trailed off with a gasp as the moon suddenly emerged to illuminate his mocking eyes – liquid gold streaking through the green. A hell-cat.

Jake smiled and moved in for the kill. Running a finger gently along the exposed skin of her stomach, he slowly eased it under the Lycra hem of her skimpy top and traced it along the soft underside of her breasts. He listened to her ragged breathing as his eyes bored into hers – daring her to stop him . . . willing her to try.

She didn't.

Easing his hand in, he cupped her breast. Then, as she quivered with desire, he began to dig his nails in, raking them down in long, even stripes. Softly at first, then harder and harder, watching intently as her expression changed from pleasure to uncertainty to pain. Then, just as he knew she would cry, he pushed the top all the way up to her chin and gently traced his tongue along the rising welts. She began to moan softly.

'You like that?' he husked.

'Mmmmm . . .' she murmured.

And then she screamed as his teeth clamped down on her tender flesh.

6

Slouched in his seat in the hospital waiting room, Ged winced in sympathy as Wendy's screaming reached him all the way down the corridor. She'd been so far gone when they'd arrived, the midwife said he'd probably have had to deliver it himself if he'd hit a red light.

Rubbing a hand across his tired eyes, he had a sudden vision of Sam's ghostly white face in the back of the car. The poor sod would have been as much use as a chocolate fireguard if she'd had it in the car. As for Lee . . . well, he was no use, full stop. All he'd done was twist himself around so he could peer over into the back, no doubt praying she'd have to take her knickers off. Perverted little bastard. Giving birth was sacred in Ged's book, but Lee had tried to turn it into a peep-show.

As he thought about Lee, the man himself let forth a bellow from the other end of the corridor. Hearing a nurse yelling back, Ged tutted loudly. What was the little prat up to now? Was he determined to make them call the police? Sighing heavily, he pushed himself to his feet.

The receptionist glared at him reproachfully as he passed by her desk. *You brought him in, you sort him out*! her eyes seemed to be saying. Embarrassed and ashamed, Ged averted his eyes and hurried towards Lee's cubicle.

Pulling the curtain aside, he almost laughed out loud at the sight that greeted him: Lee, flat on his back on the blood-smeared examination couch, being artfully man-handled by a chunky nurse, whose round, flat face was a picture of determination – and she was definitely win-ning. Outweighing Lee by a good few stones, she was using every ounce to squash him flat as they argued furiously.

'You are staying until the doctor has seen you, Mr Naylor! Do I make myself clear?'

'Fuck off, Godzilla! You can't make me stay, so fuck . . . you!'

'It's for your own good. And if I have to get the security guards in here, believe me, you'll be sorry!'

'Get the fuckin' ARMY if it makes you feel good, it won't make no difference. I'm NOT . . . STAYING!'

'YES . . . YOU . . . ARE!'

Ged leaned against the wall and folded his arms. 'You might as well give up, Lee,' he laughed. 'She's well and truly got you.'

Glancing around in surprise, the nurse gave Ged a tense smile. 'At least someone's got sense. Now stop struggling, Mr Naylor. Doctor Laycock will be here any minute, and if he sees you like this he'll give you a tranquillizer!'

'Watch what you're saying,' Ged chuckled. 'He'll get worse if he thinks he'll get a reward.'

As the nurse turned again to look at Ged questio-ningly, Lee saw his opportunity and went for it. Sticking his hand up her skirt with lightning speed, he grabbed a handful of soft fat flesh, squeezing for all he was worth.

Shocked, she reflexively slapped his face, yelping, 'Get your filthy hands off me!'

Lee clung on tight as she struggled to get away, almost falling off the bed in his attempt to reach Nirvana. And he almost made it. Reaching the soft flesh at the top of her thighs, he pushed forward, only to find his progress blocked by the resistance of her panties.

Ged had been laughing so hard, he hadn't seen what Lee was actually doing, but when the frantic nurse began to scream in earnest, he suddenly realized and pushed himself away from the wall to go to her aid. Before he'd taken two steps, however, the curtain flew back and a white-coated, red-faced doctor stood glaring at them.

'What the HELL is going on in here?' he demanded. Then, quickly sizing up the situation, he barked at Lee, 'YOU! Unhand that nurse!'

Lee immediately withdrew his hand and stopped struggling, cowed by the total authority in the doctor's voice.

Turning to the furious nurse, the doctor said, 'Send security in. And bring me the shots.'

'Yes, Doctor. My pleasure!' Throwing a look of pure hatred at Lee, she turned on her heel and flounced out through the curtain.

Almost instantly, two uniformed thugs appeared. Swatting back the curtain they strode in and flanked the doctor, arms folded, no-nonsense faces hard as flint.

Shrinking into himself with fear, Lee scrabbled backward on the couch, but his heels quickly lost their grip on a slippery pool of blood and he slipped down prone.

The doctor picked up the chart and studied it. 'Naylor, is it?'

Lee nodded up at him. 'Yes, sir.'

'Well, Mr Naylor, we're going to administer a tranquillizer, so if you wouldn't mind rolling your trousers down . . .?'

The nurse reappeared with an evil-looking syringe and

a couple of sealed phials of clear fluid. Ged grimaced as she prepared the injection, then passed it to the doctor, who proceeded to savagely stab it into one of Lee's buttocks. It was like watching a horror film.

Within seconds, the tranquillizer took effect, stealing all the fight from Lee, replacing his hostile scowl with a stupid grin. Satisfied that he'd be no more trouble, the doctor and security guards left, leaving the nurse to repair the wounds.

With great delight, she shaved off a wide strip of Lee's dirty hair, then set about stitching the gash with fierce, even strokes. That finished, she started on his arm – pouring an undiluted solution of noxious-smelling anti-septic straight into the torn flesh before scouring at it like a demon for a good deal longer than was absolutely necessary.

Lee couldn't have cared less.

Fuck me! he thought as a blissful rush vibrated through his body. *I gotta get hold of some of them tranqs*!

Meanwhile, down the corridor in the delivery suite, the midwife was busy shouting encouragement. Drifting up from between Wendy's splayed thighs, her voice was distant and muffled.

'Don't push until the contraction stops. Good girl . . . You're doing very well!'

Wendy bore down and screamed – a low, animal grunt that rose in intensity until she was bellowing: 'GET . . . IT . . . OOOUUT!'

The midwife calmly carried on with her manipulations as if she were deaf. After a while, she turned to Sam and gestured him over. 'Want to feel baby's head, daddy?'

Sam's hand fluttered around his mouth. He felt sick.

'I don't want him touching any-fucking-thing!' Wendy roared. 'Get him out of here! AAAAGGGHHH!'

Sam's eyes swam as the bloody head slid out. He could still hear Wendy screaming, and the midwife talking, but they sounded odd. Buzzing. In the distance. Not here and now.

Back at the flat, Suzie's eyes were burning. It was almost quarter to five in the morning, and she was so tired she was having a hard time keeping them open and focused. But she couldn't go to sleep. Mal wouldn't let her.

She watched nervously as he paced the floor, puffing on his millionth cigarette. She was dying for one herself, but he wouldn't let her have one so she had to make do with breathing in his smoke as he blasted furious streams of it her way.

He was really angry again, and she didn't know why. He'd started soon after the others had left to go to the hospital, but he'd ranted on about so many different things in the meantime she couldn't pinpoint the cause. And he was drunk, which didn't help, his breath venomous with brandy fumes – having finished almost two of the bottles by himself.

'Well?' He abruptly stopped pacing and stood directly in front of her, his hands balled into fists. 'WELL?'

'I d-don't know what you m-mean,' she stuttered. And it was true, she didn't. She hadn't even heard the question.

Leaning over her with a fist on each arm of the chair, he snarled into her face, 'I said: Are . . . you . . . shagging . . . Ged . . . sweetheart?'

Shrinking away from him, her voice little more than a whisper, she said, 'No, of course I'm not.'

He grinned, his face an evil mask. 'I don't believe you!'

'It's true,' she said. 'Mal, please believe me. I wouldn't do that to you. Honest to God!'

He stared at her for a moment, weighing up whether to believe her or not, then with a grunt, he pushed himself away and began to pace the floor again. Taking yet another cigarette out of the packet, he lit it and sucked deeply on it before turning to torment her again.

'Want one, doll?' His voice was teasing. 'Want one? Want me to give you one?' He came towards her slowly, a malevolent smile curling his lips as he cocked his head to the side, saying again, 'Want one, doll? Want this one?' He waved the cigarette under her nose, almost touching, but not quite. 'I said . . . do you want this one?'

She called on every ounce of will-power not to make a sound as he touched the glowing red tip to her bare arm – tentatively at first, then gradually increasing the pressure, until she could smell her own flesh cooking, and hear the fine hairs crackle. Biting down hard on the inside of her cheek, she tasted the copper tones of blood on her tongue.

Suddenly – mercifully – the phone rang. As its shrill insistence broke the tension, Mal pulled the cigarette off her skin and put it to his lips. Sucking on it hard, he blew a thin stream of smoke into her eyes, patting her cheek as they began to water. 'There, there. Don't cry!'

Dropping a kiss onto the top of her head, he strolled calmly to the phone and snatched up the receiver, saying, 'Yeah?' in a shockingly normal voice. Taking a last drag on the cigarette, he dropped it and ground it out on the carpet. 'Oh, hi, Ged. How's it going down there?'

Suzie didn't move an inch, sure that he'd be back to finish the job as soon as Ged put the phone down. And he'd be twice as bad if she tried to escape.

'No kidding, man!' Mal laughed suddenly. 'A girl? That's great! Hey, Suzie.' He kicked the back of her chair. 'Wendy's had a girl!'

Suzie smiled and nodded.

Mal leaned against the wall, grinning broadly. 'Yeah, man, sound . . . sound! So what about Lee? How's he doing?' He listened for a moment, then laughed out loud. 'Hey, Suzie, listen to this. Lee felt up some nurse so they give him a knockout shot! Kinky bastard! Pass us one, doll.' He gestured to the cigarettes on the table.

Suzie reached for the pack and went to hand one to him. When he motioned for her to light it for him, she breathed an internal sigh of relief. He'd calmed down.

'You not having one?' he asked when she passed it to him. Scared that he might change his mind, she quickly lit one and inhaled deeply.

When he finally put the receiver down, Mal rushed across the room and pulled her up out of her seat. Holding her around the waist, he twirled her around and around, yelling ecstatically: 'A baby girl! A baby girl!'

Suzie laughed along with him, and wondered – not for the first time – how he'd feel if she got pregnant? Would it make him as happy with her as he was for Sam and Wendy?

Back at the hospital, Sam slumped further down in his seat, watching Ged make the calls Sam should have been making. He'd just told Mal, and was now trying to get through to Sam's babysitter, Louise. She wasn't answering, which was hardly surprising, given the time. Sam was just glad she'd decided to stay over last night, or they'd have been well and truly stuck. He'd have to remember to pay her extra.

He was also truly glad he'd had Ged to help him through this terrible night. Ged had been fantastic. Taking control when Sam had fallen apart. Getting Wendy here in the nick of time. Sorting Lee out. And now, making the calls. If he hadn't been here, Sam didn't know what he would have done. As it was, he was still recovering from a very humiliating faint. He dreaded to think what Mal and Lee would say when they heard about it. He'd never live it down.

The birth had been horrible. Blood and gore running down Wendy's legs. Green snotty gunk covering the baby's head. Revolting! And Wendy screaming and yelling, telling him she hated him. The midwife had told him to take no notice, but she didn't know Wendy like he did. She'd meant it, all right.

Again, he thanked God for Louise. There was no way he could face going home to his kids right now. Much as he loved them, he couldn't bring out their good sides like Wendy did. All he got were the petulant sulks – the fighting and screaming.

And now there was another to add to the fray. Another to walk all over him.

Sighing deeply, he closed his eyes and let his head fall back. Aggro. That was all he ever got these days.

Putting the phone down, Ged looked at his watch, frowning. Surely Lee was finished by now? Pushing past a stinking wino who was approaching him with a begging look on his face, he strolled towards the snotty receptionist to ask her to check. Just as he reached the desk, Nurse Frosty-knickers herself came around the corner, pushing Lee in a wheelchair. She half-smiled at Ged as she unceremoniously shoved the chair out through the doors.

Ged called Sam and they followed them outside, wincing in the blinding early-morning light.

'Bleedin' 'ell!' Lee moaned, throwing his good arm across his eyes with a grimace as a burst of birdsong shattered the silence. 'Where's me gun? Let me shoot the twittering bastards!'

'Shut up!' Sam hissed.

'Here, nursey,' Lee said. 'You gonna give me a kiss before I go, then?'

Ignoring him, the nurse asked Ged to please bring the chair back when his friend was in the car, then marched back inside with her head held high.

'She fancies you, mate,' Lee slurred, an inane grin on his face.

'Shut up!' Ged hissed, shoving the chair towards the car.

When they were all in the car, Ged suggested they go back to Mal's and, to his relief, they agreed. He didn't want Lee at his place – he'd never get rid of him. As for Sam, he'd have gone anywhere rather than home to his kids right now. And Lee's place wasn't high on anyone's list – including Lee's – as somewhere nice to relax after the night they'd had.

Anyway, their money was still at Mal's. They had to go back for that if for nothing else.

Fifteen minutes later, Suzie opened the door to let them in, then quickly scuttled into the kitchen. Filling the kettle, she busied herself with the cups as she listened to them through the open door. She'd intended to stay out of the way so Mal couldn't accuse her of anything later, but when he shouted to her to come and join them, she went through reluctantly. Perching on the arm of Mal's chair, she pulled her cardigan sleeve down to cover the burn on her arm and looked at the floor.

Lee had a bulky white bandage wrapped around his head like a turban, and another around his arm beneath his T-shirt that gave him the appearance of bodybuilder's biceps. Lying on the couch, he gazed at his arm in wonder, angling it this way and that – on a total high as he saw himself with muscles for the first time ever.

'Shee-it, man!' he laughed. 'Wish I knew what they put in the tea in that place! It sure makes you feel good, whatever it is!'

'Go on, you cunt!' Mal teased. 'From what I hear it wasn't the tea that got you going, it was you getting your hand up that nurse's knickers!'

Lee grinned, relishing the memory of almost forgotten female flesh. 'She had a right arse on her, though, didn't she, Ged?' he leered. 'What was she like, eh? A right slap-arse face on it too!'

'Yeah,' Ged agreed, smiling indulgently. 'She was a bit of a monster. Didn't put *you* off though, did it? Still, at least she was an adult.'

'Phwoaar, yeah!' said Lee, totally missing the sarcasm. 'All woman!'

'Oh, come on!' Sam yawned. 'She was one of the ugliest birds I've ever seen in my life.'

'You would say that,' Lee said. 'You've got Wendy.'

'How is Wendy?' Mal asked.

'Fine.' Sam yawned again and stretched out on the

chair. 'Sleeping it off when we left, lucky cow! I'll tell you what, I'm going for the snip after this. No way am I going through that again!' Closing his eyes, he was snoring within seconds – wiped out, physically and mentally.

'He's got the right idea,' Ged said, yawning. 'I think I'll head home and get my head down for a bit.'

'Nah, man!' Mal said, throwing Ged his stash tin. 'Don't break up the party. Make a smoke. Anyhow, Suzie's making a brew, ain't you, Sooze?'

Suzie nodded and went to the kitchen, glad of an excuse to escape.

Ged yawned again. He was dog-tired. 'All right.' He relented. 'One smoke, one brew, then I'm off!'

'Good man!' Mal smiled – his earlier suspicions forgotten for now. 'This is good, innit?' He grinned, looking from Ged to Lee. 'The gang's all here. And what a night, eh?'

'Y' can say that again,' Lee laughed, gingerly patting his head. 'Anyhow, talking about what a night . . . How was it?'

'How was what, mate?' Mal asked.

'You know,' Lee said. 'The night?' He looked from Mal to Ged, but their faces were blank. 'The job,' he said finally. 'How did it go?'

'Oh, yeah!' Mal slapped his forehead. 'I forgot all about that. Well . . .' He flashed a grin at Ged. 'You'll be pleased to know it went very well indeed!'

'How well?' Lee squawked. 'How much? Come on, don't keep me in suspenders!'

Mal waved a hand towards Ged. 'I'll let the brains of the operation tell you.'

Ged licked the edge of the Rizla papers and carefully stuck his roach in, taking his time to light the spliff before answering, by which time Lee was crackling with excitement.

'Sixty-eight thousand, six hundred.'

Lee's mouth fell open. 'You're joking? Tell me you're joking!'

Ged grinned, shaking his head.

'He's not,' Mal said. 'We've counted it, and it's right.'

'I don't believe it!' Lee said, and raising a hand, fingered the dressing on his head. 'Shit! That's the best compensation I ever got for taking a whack! How much each?'

'Seventeen grand!' Mal's face was glowing. 'Seventeen grand, matey! What d'y' reckon to that then?'

'I reckon we should be celebratin'!' Lee whooped, throwing himself back on the couch and kicking his legs up in the air. 'Ow! Seventeen grand! Oh yes! Oh yes! Ow!'

Ged nodded towards the empty brandy bottles on the floor. 'Mal's been celebrating already.'

'Is that what it was for?' Lee said, vaguely remembering Mal offering him a swig. 'Looks like I've got some catching up to do.'

'Wait till the drugs wear off first,' warned Ged, 'or we'll be taking you back in with an overdose.'

Lee shrugged. 'Who cares? I can buy me own stomach pump with me seventeen grand! Jeezus! I can't believe it! Wa-hay!'

Mal laughed, leaning over to take the spliff from Ged. 'Never expected that much, did you?'

'No way.' Lee grinned. 'Shit, that Pasha's got some business going down there! We'll have to do him again!'

Mal and Ged looked at each other. Lee obviously didn't remember what had happened.

'Er . . . I think you did him for the first and last time already, mate,' Mal said, pulling hard on the smoke.

'What d'y' mean?' Lee asked, totally bewildered by their grim expressions. 'I didn't do nothing . . . Did I?'

'You shot him,' Ged said quietly.

'Yeah,' Mal added, a little too gleefully. 'He went down like a ton of bricks. Sure looked done in to me.'

Lee shook his head dazedly. They were winding him up – they had to be? He'd only taken the gun to wave about and frighten Pasha – not shoot him. Nah! He couldn't have!

He grinned at them hopefully. 'You're having me on, aren't you?'

Ged shook his head. The smile slid off Lee's face. Now he was really confused. He couldn't remember anything between hiding in the bushes and Wendy sponging his head – and even that wasn't too clear after the elephant shot.

'Is he dead?' he asked at last.

'I reckon,' Mal said.

'So what exactly happened?' Lee asked.

Between them, Ged and Mal outlined the events of the night. Lee listened in stunned silence.

'Still,' Mal concluded. 'At least it wasn't you. That's something, isn't it? He tried to kill you first. You just happened to be a better shot – and a good job too!'

'Yeah!' Lee agreed indignantly. 'The bastard could have killed me, innit?'

Mal nodded. 'That's right, mate. So he deserved it, didn't he? It's his own fault.'

Ged didn't say anything. This was Mal's twisted logic for you. It wouldn't occur to him that the bloke was only trying to defend himself and his property. Oh, no! He shouldn't have done that. He should have just let them come and take it – or maybe he was supposed to just hand it over with a smile?

'So what happened to me gun?' Lee was asking now. 'Who's got it?'

'Ahhh . . .' Mal grinned sheepishly. 'We didn't think about that. Sorry, mate.'

Lee slumped down on the couch, his face as sad as could be. 'You mean I've lost it, and I haven't even finished paying for it?'

Mal shrugged. 'Looks like it.'

Ged steepled his fingers beneath his chin, deep in thought. He'd totally forgotten about the gun. Things could get very bad if the police got their hands on that. But there was nothing they could do about it now. The best they could hope for was that Lee's prints would be too smudged to be identifiable if it was found.

'Do you want me to go and have a look for it?' Suzie offered, coming back with the brews.

'Don't even think about it!' Ged warned as Mal's eyes lit up. 'None of us is going down there again. Someone's bound to have found him by now.'

Even Mal had to agree that Ged was right this time. It was gone six in the morning and completely light outside.

'Yeah, all right,' he said. 'We'll just have to wait and see what happens, eh?' Turning to Lee, he said, 'You could get life if they find it. How d'y' reckon you'd cope with that then?'

'Probably better than you,' snapped Lee, totally sober now. 'Don't forget your prints are all over it an' all!'

7

'Who found him?' Detective Chief Inspector Ted Jackson asked without looking up from his notepad. 'One of ours or a civvy?'

Tilting his head to the side, he put the finishing touch to his rough sketch of the body before closing the flap of his pad over with a snap and turning his full attention on the young constable who immediately blushed. 'Come on, lad. It's not that difficult a question!'

'Er . . . the milkman, I believe, sir.' PC Paul Dalton wilted beneath the DCI's gaze. 'We took the call at five-thirty. I believe it came from that box round there.' He pointed out of the gates towards the front of the shops.

Jackson nodded and abruptly turned away. Dalton retreated with relief. The man had the aura of an alligator circling his prey. And they were on the same side! God only knew what he did to his suspects.

Jackson squatted down beside the body for a better look. The Asian victim, Pashratar Singh, had been shot through the head. But since he was lying on his side in a macabre travesty of the recovery position this wasn't immediately apparent. He was approximately five foot five, Jackson assessed. Well padded, and – he glanced at the hand-made leather moccasins – well-heeled. Obviously making a fair profit if the brand new jeep was anything to go by. A bit surprising, given the location of his business, but Jackson knew from experience that

Asian shopkeepers had a knack of turning pennies into pounds wherever they were. Something to do with working their arses off morning, noon and night. A lesson their British counterparts could usefully learn, in his opinion.

Taking a pencil from his breast pocket, Jackson leaned closer and moved the blood-stiffened collar of the expensive suede jacket aside with the pointed end. There was no tie. Not a business meet gone wrong, then. Moving a cuff back revealed a very nice Rolex watch strapped to the wrist. Not a simple mugging, either. And a prod with the pencil told him the wallet was in the inside breast pocket – probably full, given the bulky feel of it.

Easing the pencil beneath the victim's chin, he carefully raised the heavy head a couple of centimetres. Congealed blood, tissue and hair remained on the concrete below – an imperfect circle marking the place of death. Jackson dipped his head to look at the underside of the face. Dead a good few hours, he guessed, judging by the squashed, sunken quality of the skin. Already, a pencil-thick groove was forming in the waxy flesh.

Laying the head back in its grisly cast, Jackson recorded his findings. Glancing at his watch, he marked the time at six forty-five a.m.

Less than an hour into his shift. Beggar of a way to start the day.

Standing, he brushed the dirt from his knees and scanned the assembled crew for a familiar face. Not finding one among the crush of young, eager-faced uniforms, he ambled across to the yard's entrance for a quiet look around. Leaning against the wall beside the open gates, he crossed his feet at the ankle and folded his arms. A passer-by would have taken him for a nosy onlooker.

He certainly didn't look official. At fifty-two, his salt-and-pepper hair was a little long to be considered respectable, his craggy face too villain-like, and his mismatched clothes too cheap.

A couple of minutes into his solo surveillance, his eagle eyes had detected a number of things that he felt warranted investigation – starting with the bushes edging the small wall. Flatter in the centre than at any other point, the trampled grass looked recently disturbed. He'd check them out after he'd done the yard.

Pushing himself away from the wall, he walked slowly forward, flicking his eyes from side to side as he scanned the concrete for signs. He'd only gone a few steps when he found something. Pushing a couple of PCs aside, he bent double and peered at a sizeable bloodstain that was partially concealed by a leaflet advertising an upcoming Simply Red concert.

'I bloody knew it!' he muttered to no one in particular.

'What's that?' Detective Sergeant Macintosh asked, appearing at his side. 'Thinking of going, were you?'

Jackson glanced up at his fat friend, saying without rancour, 'You're late.' Then, kicking the leaflet aside, he pointed at the bloodstain. 'That there, Mac, confirms what I was just thinking.'

Mac raised his thick eyebrows and waited.

'See where the body is?' Jackson continued. 'This is too far away, and there's no trail across the yard. If it's our man's, and he fell here and dragged himself – or was dragged – over there, there'd be a trail, wouldn't there? And given the size of the exit wound and the amount of blood lost, there'd be a damn' sight more in this spot than over there, wouldn't there?' Without waiting for an answer, he walked towards the bushes.

'Forensics here yet?' he asked as Mac followed him over the low wall.

'Graves is on his way,' Mac said, smirking as Jackson tutted.

'That prick!' Jackson was scathing. 'Get a sample of that stain before the bollock destroys all the evidence, will you? And while you're at it, get one off the stiff, and have it secured – just in case.'

Turning back to the business at hand, he motioned with a nod to the flattened undergrowth. 'Recently trampled, you reckon?'

'Herd of bloody elephants,' Mac said, kicking the undergrowth aside with his toe.

'Mmm,' Jackson murmured. 'And not kids.'

'Not if those prints are anything to go by,' Mac pointed to a mess of adult-sized footprints in the mud.

Jackson bent low with his hands on his knees. 'Think we'd get a clear cast?'

'Doubt it. Too mushy.'

Jackson nodded. 'Looks like a scuffle. Do you reckon it started in here?'

Mac mulled it over for a minute, then shook his head. 'The stiff came out of the back door, and he'd only gone a few feet before falling. I don't reckon he'd have had any reason to come in here, then go back out there. More likely whoever did him was hiding here and had a bit of a panic. We found the weapon yet?'

'Not yet. But there'll be a search of the immediate area as soon as.'

'What d'y' reckon for motive?'

Jackson shrugged. 'There's no sign of robbery. He's still got his wallet and watch on him, and they didn't have the jeep away. I'd bet the shop keys are still here, too. You can check that.' He paused, shrugging again. 'Grudge, maybe?'

Hearing a car pull up outside the gates of the yard, Mac turned to look. 'Heads up,' he warned. 'Graves.'

Jackson stood up and peered across the yard, frowning at the sight of Greg Graves climbing out of his official car. A gangling wimp of a man, with side-parted carroty hair and abnormally long wrists, everything about him set Jackson's teeth on edge. Quite apart from the fact that he was notoriously blind to the most obvious evidence.

'Shit!' he hissed. 'Get in there, Mac, and sort those samples before he puts his size thirteens right in the middle of 'em!'

As Mac leaped over the wall to do his bidding, Jackson squatted down to study the footprints in the hopes of finding a good one. But Mac had been right. The ground was so churned up, it was impossible to tell one from another.

He was about to give up when he spotted a tiny scrap of material stuck to a bramble. Pulling a pair of latex gloves out of his pocket, he slipped them on and reached for the scrap. It was black wool, probably from a hat or a balaclava. It was so small it would probably prove nothing, but there was always a chance.

Dropping the wool into an evidence bag, Jackson sealed it and slipped it into his pocket, then stood and made to go back into the yard. Just then, a convoy of TV-equipment trucks rolled up to the gates. 'Oh, great!' he muttered. 'Just what I need.'

A car pulled in behind the trucks. Jackson's eyes narrowed as Liz Jardine, the glamorous Granada news-reader, stepped out, trailing a make-up woman. He wished someone else had come to cover the killing.

She would nose around until she knew everything, then give it all out on air at the first opportunity.

'How did they get wind?' Mac said, rushing over.

'God knows!' Jackson frowned. 'But I suppose I'd better do some damage limitation. Do you think you can keep the nappy brigade out of the way while I stop the silly tart giving away vital info?'

'My pleasure,' Mac grinned. Then, rubbing his hands together, he turned to the crowd of PCs and bellowed: 'Right then, lads and lasses . . . Let's have you all over here, out of harm's way, eh? Come on, come on – move yourselves!'

Sighing heavily, Jackson made his way towards Liz Jardine.

8

Mal woke, groaning. He was still on the rug in front of the fire, but the fire was out now and he was freezing. Shivering, he peered blearily around the room. Everyone was flaked out. Sam, still sprawled half-on, half-off his chair, his mouth hanging wide open, snoring softly. Lee, his face drained of blood, curled up on the couch with his ruined jacket over his shoulders. And Ged, over-flowing the chair near the window, his long legs stretched out before him, his meaty hands clasped together on his stomach.

'What time is it?' Mal croaked, pushing himself up on his elbows, yawning hard. 'God, what a night. I'm shagged.'

'Ten to seven,' Ged said, rising from his dream with surprising ease and squinting at his watch. 'Must have dropped off.'

'Is that all?' Mal moaned. 'I've only had half an hour. No wonder I feel like shit!'

'You don't look too hot, either,' Ged commented.

'Says the bloke who looks like he's been slapped round the mush with a kipper!' Mal retorted grumpily.

Struggling to his knees, he dug his cigarettes out from the mess, sparked the fire and dipped his face towards it to light up. Then, grumbling loudly, he kicked aside the heap of empty bottles and cans and huddled up to the heat.

'Whassamatta?' Lee croaked. Lifting his heavy head from the cushion, he quickly dropped it back when a starburst of pain shot through it. 'Shit!' he groaned. 'I feel like I've been run over by a sixteen-tonner!'

'Serves you right!' Mal snorted.

'Get back up yer arse where you come from!' Lee said. 'But give us a fag before y' go!'

Mal threw him one, then offered one to Ged. Ged reached for it, then lumbered to his feet and headed for the kitchen to put the kettle on. Seconds later, he popped his head round the door to tell Mal he had no milk.

Mal tutted, then yelled: 'SUZIE! WHERE'S THE MILK?'

In the bedroom, Suzie struggled awake as Mal's voice disturbed her sleep. The quilt had dropped to the floor, and the cold bit into her when she moved. With a shiver, she rolled onto her side and forced herself to sit up, tapping her feet around until she found her slippers.

'SUZIE!' Mal yelled again. 'Get your arse in here!'

With a sigh, she went to see what he wanted.

'About bleedin' time!' he snarled when she came in.

'Sorry. I didn't hear you.'

'Clean your ears out, then,' he snapped. Then, nodding towards the kitchen, he said, 'Ged needs milk. Go and get some, and don't take all day about it.'

'Here,' Lee piped up, raising his head gingerly from the cushion. 'She can check for my gun while she's there, innit?'

'Good idea,' Mal said. He turned back to Suzie. 'If you hurry up, you might still make it before the pigs.'

'Don't be stupid,' Ged said, coming to stand in the doorway. 'It's gone seven. They'll have well sussed it out by now.'

Mal shrugged. 'So? She can still have a mooch.'

Ged stared at him in disbelief. 'You really are an arsehole, aren't you? First you send her to get your mask, then back to check on Lee because you didn't want to risk it . . . and now a gun! A gun you weren't even supposed to have! Well, I've had it! I'm off.' He stomped across the room to grab his jacket, a scowl of pure disgust on his face.

Mal watched him with a smirk. 'See that little old woman what's fighting to get out of you?' he said. 'Well, I'd watch it if I was you, 'cos she's winning! When d'y' start the knitting classes?'

Ged shot him a bad look, but Mal shrugged it off. Now he was properly awake, he was beginning to remember his good fortune, and that made him too happy to argue.

'Chill out, dickhead!' he laughed, rolling his eyes. 'All right, you win. She don't have to look for the gun. But she can still go for milk – if that's all right with you? Aw, come on, man,' he went on when Ged didn't answer. 'Don't take off now. We ain't even started celebratin' yet!'

'Okay,' Ged grunted, sitting back down. 'But I'm telling you, man. You've got to stop treating that girl like shit, 'cos it's pissing me off.'

Sam was woken by their voices. 'God, my head's splitting,' he groaned. 'You got any tablets, Mal?'

'Think yours is bad?' Lee said, tapping two fingers gently along the neat line of stitches throbbing painfully beneath the bandage. 'You wanna feel mine. It's mashed. I'll need a whole bottle of pills to sort this out!'

Mal shook his head in despair. 'Listen to youse, y' pair of demics! You don't want pills, you want some Charlie!'

Standing up, he stretched. 'Right. I'm getting changed, then I'm off to the coke shop.'

'Can I use the phone?' Ged asked. He had planned to wait till evening before he called his daughter, but he couldn't wait. If he called now he'd catch her before she went to school.

'Use it . . .' Mal spread his arms wide. 'Shit, keep it if you want! I'm so fucking rich, I'll buy another while I'm out!'

With that, he grabbed his jacket from behind the door and trotted out of the room, high on life.

Ged tapped out his old number like second nature – which just about said it all, he thought. Old habits die hard – even the crappy ones. Like hanging about with these tossers just because they'd been to school together.

Lee clutched at his head when the front door banged shut behind Mal. 'Me head's busting!' he moaned. 'I think I'm dying.'

'I've got two aspirins left,' Suzie said, coming through from the bedroom. 'You can have them if you want.'

'I need more than that,' Lee moaned.

'I'll get some more at the shops,' she said, pulling her coat on and going to get her purse from the kitchen drawer. 'Does anyone else want anything?'

'You can get me twenty cigs,' Ged said, sticking the still-ringing phone under his chin so he could root through his pocket for change.

'Will you be long, Ged?' Sam asked. 'I'd better try Louise again. Let her know about Wendy before she thinks we've abandoned her.'

Suzie smiled as she remembered the good news – the only good news – of the night before. 'Oh, yeah, Sam,' she said. 'I meant to say congratulations, but it was a bit hectic this morning. Will you be going to see her later?'

'Yeah,' Sam said. 'You'll be coming, won't you?'

'Course,' she smiled. 'I wouldn't miss it. Won't be long.' Waving, she left.

'Hello?' Ged said when the phone was finally answered. Hearing his daughter's voice, he smiled – relieved that it wasn't her mother. 'Hiya, sweetheart. You all right? Yeah, look, I'm glad I caught you. I want to see you. No, not now. Later . . .'

Mal had taken Lee's car, cutting his journey down from fifteen minutes to five. Now he was in Stevo's living room, the corners of his mouth twitching in amusement as he pulled his wad out and saw Stevo's jaw drop to his knees.

He leafed through the notes, slowly, deliciously, all the time watching Stevo from the corner of his eye. Like all the other Scots Mal had ever met, Stevo was usually an arrogant shite. But not today. The guy was practically drooling. Mal chuckled softly as he imagined the pound signs dinging round and round in Stevo's eyes like a cartoon.

'How much ye after?' Stevo asked, his voice husky with money lust.

'How much you got?' Mal asked nonchalantly. 'I might want a fair bit this time. Depending what it is, like.'

'I've got some top gear,' Stevo said. 'It's the best! Just let me know how much, and I'll see what I've got left. Been going like hot cakes, this stuff . . .'

'Yeah, yeah,' Mal drawled, looking at Stevo with contempt. 'It's always the best, innit? Don't be taking me for a mug, Stevo. You're not the only dealer around, you know. And I might be in the market for a big score, so you'd better treat me good.'

Stevo held his hands out. 'Mal – I'm offended, mate. Have I ever treated ye any way but good, eh?'

Mal smirked. It felt good being in control. Sauntering across to Stevo's grotty old couch, he plonked himself down, casually crossing his legs. This was the life. Stevo had never been so willing to please. He usually couldn't wait to get him out the door. But not today. Now he'd realized Mal was a serious buying prospect he was falling all over himself.

'I don't want to rush ye, pal,' Stevo said suddenly, interrupting Mal's little daydream of power. 'But I've got someone coming round, and it's a wee bit delicate, like.'

'So what you sayin'?' Mal's voice was flat. 'You want me gone, is that it?' Half rising, he began to repocket the money. ''Cos if me money's not good enough to get you to treat me with respect, I'll—'

'No!' Stevo held his hands up quickly, his eyes swivelling furtively as he considered how best to get rid of Mal and at the same time get him to leave the wad of dosh behind. He badly needed it to pay his own dealer off. He was due any minute and he'd kick off good-style if Mal was still here.

'Look, Mal,' he said after a minute. 'I can get ye any amount ye want. Just let me know what ye need and it's yours. But just now, I'm no being funny, but y' cannae hang about. Y'understand, don't ye?'

'So what have you got on you right now?' Mal asked coolly.

Stevo jumped up and pulled his last bag out of his pocket. Inside this there were four tenner bags. His dealer would be bringing more, but he wouldn't leave it unless Stevo had the money he owed for the last lot – which he didn't. But Mal did.

'Look, this is all I've got,' he said. 'I know ye want more, so I'll do ye a favour . . .' He dangled the bags from his fingers so Mal could see the white powder through the plastic. As he expected, Mal's eyes lit up. *A proper coke-fiend!* Stevo grinned inwardly. This should be easy.

'As y' know,' he went on, as sincerely as possible, 'I don't normally deliver. But for ye, mate, I'll make an exception. What y' after altogether? A quarter? Half?'

Mal eyed the bags greedily. 'Depends how much you're asking for it.'

Stevo did a quick calculation and said, 'I'll let you have a quarter for five.'

Mal nodded slowly, ticking it over. 'Sounds okay. How much off for a half?'

'Aw, come on,' Stevo moaned. 'I cannae go any lower than that. I've already knocked thirty offa the quarter, an' that's ma absolute rock bottom – I won't make a single penny at that price!' He paused, considering his next words carefully. 'Only thing is, I haven't got it all here anyhow, see. So what I'll have to do is take the money off y' now, and bring the whole lot round to ye later.'

'You what?' Mal stared at him incredulously. 'You reckon I'm gonna leave a grand with you and trust you to bring me the stuff? You must think I'm off my bleedin' head, mate!'

'Aw, come on,' Stevo whined. 'I've never ripped y' off, have I? I always give ye good deals. And, look.' He shook the bags temptingly. 'You can take these now, and I'll only charge ye half for them. Can't say fairer than that, can I?'

Stevo fidgeted nervously as Mal took his time thinking it over. Glancing nervously at the clock, he saw it was nearly time. He had to get Mal out – quick.

'Look, ye can have these for nothing if y' leave the money!' He thrust the four bags at Mal. 'But y' gonna have to go. Take it or leave it. What d'y' say?'

Mal snatched the bags with a grin. 'All right, you're on. But I want a good half. None of your bicarb specials, know what I mean? I want the real deal, man, or I won't be pleased.'

'Y've got it,' Stevo agreed with relief. 'Only top notch for ye, mate. Just the matter of the upfront, like . . .?'

Mal counted off a grand and handed it across reluctantly. 'I'm telling you, Stevo,' he warned. 'Any funny shit and I'll have your balls!'

'Aye, nay worries,' Stevo said. And, grabbing the money before Mal could change his mind, he hustled him out the door.

Mal shook his head as the door slammed to behind him. What an arsehole. Still, he had four nice little bags for nothing. He couldn't complain. That'd do till Stevo brought the rest round.

A grand's worth of pure! He could cut it to fuck and triple the buying price easy!

Turning from the door he almost ran headlong into a tall black guy.

'Sorry, mate,' he muttered, sidestepping to let him pass.

The man sucked his teeth, glaring down on Mal as he shouldered past. Mal didn't retaliate – the guy was way too big. Instead, he walked on, looking back with a sneer before turning the corner. Who did he think he was in his long leather coat? Shaft?

Humming happily, Ged's daughter ran up to her bedroom to get dressed. She'd been feeling quite low before her father had phoned but she'd cheered up immediately when he'd said he had something for her. She hoped it was money. It had *better* be money. There was a lovely little dress she had her eye on in town. A silver strapless, clingy number. Great for going out in – really sexy and sophisticated. Alison would be dead jealous.

Oh, what a nice daddy. And such a pushover.

No, daddy, I'm not in school today. It's teacher-training day. I can meet you any time. An hour? That'd be great!

Taking a rarely worn polo-neck jumper from her drawer, she pulled it on – wincing as she struggled to get it over her tender breasts. When it was on, she turned to look in the mirror, and was pleased by what she saw. They were getting big, and they were lovely and firm. No wonder her mum was always telling her to cover them up, she thought, smiling slyly. Jealous old bat! Just because *her* body had turned to lard.

Throwing her waist-length hair back, she secured it with a couple of sparkly clips – the girlie effect, to please Daddy. And the same with her make-up – just a hint of pink gloss on her lips and a fresh swipe of mascara on her lashes. It wouldn't do to upset him with her usual full-on look. He might just change his mind about the present, and that would be a total pisser!

Finished at last, she wriggled into her Levis and posed for the mirror. Pouting her lips, she looked up through spider-leg lashes. Gorgeous! Blowing herself a Monroe kiss, she dragged herself away from her reflection and checked the time.

Seven forty-five. Good. She had just enough time for a spliff before setting off.

9

Suzie saw the army of vehicles blocking the road as soon as she rounded the bend. Even from this distance, some two hundred yards away, the noise was deafening. She'd expected the police, but the TV crew took her completely by surprise. They were milling about like ants, shifting tall lights into different positions, putting up screens on stands to deflect the glare, and swinging fluffy microphones in great arcs above the crowd.

There was so much activity, she had to force herself to keep going. It would be stupid to run. Anyway, under normal circumstances, she'd be one of the first to gawp at something like this. As it was, there was a fair-sized crowd already gathered on the pavement, and more spilling over onto the road – local people, craning their necks to see beyond the line of police guarding the strips of blue-and-white tape separating them from the crime scene. There was a buzz in the air – everyone thrilled that yet another awful thing had happened, but disappointed not to have witnessed it.

Suzie casually made her way into the crowd, sure she'd be able to pick up what was happening by hanging back and asking a few discreet questions.

'Suzie?' A hand grabbed at her sleeve. 'Jeezus! Long time no see!'

Suzie looked around in surprise and saw that it was Elaine Dixon, a girl she hadn't seen since leaving school the previous year – and didn't particularly want to now. But once Elaine latched onto you, there was no getting away.

'What about this, then?' Elaine twittered. 'Eh, I'm bloody glad I ran out of cigs and had to come to the shops. I would have missed all the fun otherwise!'

'What's going on?' Suzie asked, trying not to look too guilty. 'Has one of the shops been done over?'

'Haven't you heard?' Elaine's eyes were wide with excitement. Suzie shook her head. 'That Pasha got done in last night,' Elaine told her gleefully. 'He's still in there, but you can't see him 'cos they've got this big tent thing round him.

'That copper,' she went on, pointing out PC Dalton who was valiantly holding back an army of tattooed local women, 'told Val Medlock – remember her? – that Pasha got battered to fuck! So bad they couldn't even make out who it was at first. God . . .' she sighed. 'I wish I'd seen it!'

Suzie shook her head, folding her arms tightly around herself. 'Who did it then?'

'Dunno,' Elaine shrugged. 'Probably to do with drugs, though,' she said, pursing her mouth and raising a knowing eyebrow.

'Mmmm,' Suzie murmured. 'Probably.'

'Oh, bound to be,' Elaine asserted, getting into her stride. 'They wouldn't have the telly down if it wasn't a biggie. Have you seen who it is, by the way? Only Liz Jardine!' she went on with a grin. 'That blonde piece from the six o'clock news. I hope she asks me what I think, 'cos I'll tell her a thing or two!'

'Like what?' Suzie asked.

'Like that shop's just a front!' said Elaine knowingly. 'I know for a fact they're selling more than just beans!'

'What you talking about?' Suzie asked, genuinely puzzled.

'Oh, come on,' Elaine huffed incredulously. 'Everyone knows that! Where've you been, girl? He was making a packet! More junkies go in that shop than proper customers, and they never come out with shopping.'

'I didn't know,' muttered Suzie, frowning as a glimmer of realization began to creep in. It was all starting to make sense now. The amount of money they'd got. How they'd thought it was too much for a shop.

'Is the newsagent's open?' Suzie asked, eager to get away from Elaine. 'I've got a few things to get, and I'm in a real hurry.'

'Yeah, it's open,' Elaine said. 'Tell you what, I'll come with you. We can't see nothing anyhow.' Linking her arm through Suzie's, she pulled her away from the crowd. 'So what you been up to? I've not seen you for ages. Heard you got off with some old bloke. Is that right, then, or what?'

Suzie felt a little swell of pride at this. 'Yeah, Mal,' she said. 'But he's not exactly old. He's only thirty-two.'

Elaine grinned. 'Well, I never! He got a bit of dosh, then, eh? Sugar Daddy, is he?'

'No, it's not like that,' Suzie said. 'He's not like an *older* older man. He's more like my age. We get on really well . . . like friends, you know?'

As they rounded the corner they nearly bumped into a PC guarding the still-shuttered front of the supermarket.

Oblivious to his presence, Elaine nudged Suzie in the ribs, asking in a loud whisper, 'So what's he like at you-know-what? Is it true what they say?'

Suzie blushed, sure the copper had heard. 'I don't know what you mean.'

'Come off it!' Elaine persisted. 'They reckon older blokes know more about it, you know – how to get you going and that?'

Suzie began to feel decidedly uncomfortable. Mal would go berserk if he thought she was discussing their sex life. Apart from which, she didn't feel right about it herself. She hadn't seen Elaine for ages, and they hadn't exactly been best mates even then. Elaine had been – and it was obvious she hadn't changed – the biggest gossip in school, always spreading rumours and stirring things up.

She was trying to think of a way to change the subject when Elaine did it for her. Pointing at Suzie's bruised face, she said, 'So, did he do that to you, then?'

When Suzie sighed, Elaine's eyes lit up. 'I knew it!' she yelped, sounding too gleeful by far. 'You lucky bitch! God! I wish my fella cared enough to lay a good one on me! Come to think of it,' she snorted. 'I wish he was capable!'

Suzie was puzzled by Elaine's reaction. 'What do you mean?'

'Well, it proves he really loves you, don't it?' Elaine said. 'If he didn't, he wouldn't bother doing that. My bloke – oh, hang on, you know him. Tommy? Tommy Randall? Used to be in our English class? Anyhow, him. I've been with him for ages, and he's dead soft. I thought he was well hard when we was at school, and I suppose he was, with other lads, like, but not with me!' She grinned. 'I can wrap him round me little finger – only I don't feel like it most of the time 'cos he bores the tits off me!'

She stopped to light a cigarette, offering one to Suzie.

'Thanks,' Suzie took it and bent down for a light. 'Why don't you just finish with him, then?'

'I probably will,' Elaine said. 'When I find a bloke like yours. Someone with balls! He got any mates, your fella?'

'Yeah, loads.' A vision of Lee floated into Suzie's head. Lee would love Elaine.

'You're dead lucky,' Elaine went on enviously. 'I mean, look at you!'

'What?' Suzie looked down at herself. She was mortified to see she'd forgotten to put her tights on – hairy legs on full display.

Elaine didn't seem to have noticed. 'You look dead grown up,' she was saying. 'Older, like. Don't you feel good? I would.' She looked down at herself with disgust. 'Better than looking bleedin' seventeen, innit?'

Suzie was shocked. Elaine looked how she should look. Young and carefree – not old and knackered, like Suzie felt most of the time. Yet here was Elaine envying her. Maybe it wasn't so bad after all, this maturity lark. Elaine certainly seemed impressed, and what she'd said about Mal made sense. He must love her.

Going into the crowded newsagent's, they had to push their way through to the fridge. All around them, women were gossiping about the incident, and as they waited to get to the counter to pay, Suzie strained to pick up whatever information she could.

'. . . *said it was his nephews what done it.*'

'. . . *making snuff movies in the back of the shop!*'

'. . . *seen him passing a wrap to that wotsisface the other day.*'

'. . . *cut his heart out an' stuffed it in his belly!*'

'*He-llo-o!* Anyone in there?' Elaine waved a hand in front of Suzie's face.

'Oh, sorry,' Suzie said. 'I was miles away.'

'No kidding!' Elaine laughed. 'I was saying, that woman back there reckons she saw a load of guys in there with baseball bats last night. She was walking past when they come piling out, and when she looked through the door, Pasha was on the floor, covered in blood!'

'You reckon?'

'Yeah! She saw the whole thing.'

'What?' Suzie pulled a disbelieving face. 'She just stood there watching and they didn't do anything to her? They would have caved her head in!'

Elaine shrugged. 'I'm only telling you what she said.'

Suzie paid for her things and they pushed their way out of the shop.

'So, when can I come?' Elaine asked when they were outside.

'Eh?'

'To your place. Can I come now?'

'No!' Suzie shook her head quickly. 'Honest – I'd have to sort it with Mal first. Look, I've got to go. Call round in a couple of days, all right?'

'Give us the address, then.'

After reluctantly telling Elaine her address, Suzie ran home. She dreaded Mal's reaction when she told him Elaine would be calling round. But at least he'd be happy when she told him what people were saying about Pasha.

Mal was laughing when Suzie let herself into the flat, and she was relieved, having expected him to be in a mood about how long she'd been out. Hanging her coat in the hall, she wondered how to broach the subject of Elaine coming round. He was likely to get really pissed off about that.

Mal glanced up when she walked into the living room, an ecstatic gleam in his eye. His mirror was on the coffee table with a sizeable mound of coke in the middle.

'What did you get, doll?' he asked. 'Hope you got something for breakfast, I'm starving!'

'We've got some bacon in the fridge,' she said, heading into the kitchen. 'I'll make butties.'

Lee sat up at the mention of food. 'Great!' he said. 'And a gallon of tea while you're at it. I'm dry as a desert shithouse!'

'All right,' she smiled. 'I'll put the kettle on. Do you still need those aspirins?'

'Probably not,' he said, 'but I'll have 'em anyway. It's all drugs, innit?'

'You don't know what drugs is till you see what I've got lined up for later, mate.' Mal looked up, grinning, from his chopping. 'It's party time at Mal's mansion tonight!'

'Yeah?' Lee asked, catching the bottle of aspirins as Suzie threw them. 'How's that, then?'

'Wait and see!' Mal tapped his nose smugly. 'Bit of patience, eh?'

'Where's Ged?' Suzie asked, taking the cigarettes out of the bag.

'Gone to see his daughter,' Sam told her. 'He'll be back later.'

'Oh, right. I'll put these in the drawer for him, then.'

'Sack that,' Mal said. 'Giz 'em here. He'll get more while he's out.'

Suzie asked Sam if he'd spoken to Wendy yet as she handed the cigarettes to Mal.

'Not to Wendy,' Sam said. 'But I spoke to the ward sister, and they're both doing fine.'

'Which is more than can be said for his babysitter,' Lee laughed. 'His little 'uns are running rings round the poor cow! I said I'd go and give her a hand, but Sam's not having any of it, are you, mate?'

Sam rolled his eyes. 'Too right I'm not! Look what happened last time I let one of my mates loose on my babysitter.' He nodded towards Suzie, saying to Mal: 'Robbed us of a great sitter, you did. Best we ever had.'

Mal snorted. 'You must have been desperate! She certainly ain't the best I've ever had!'

'Mal!' squawked Suzie.

'Only joking, doll,' he laughed. 'You're one of the best little shaggers in Hulme, you are. Now, where's me bacon butties?'

'Subject of babysitters, I'd best be making a move,' Sam said, getting up and pulling his jacket on. 'I can't leave Louise with my two all day.'

'Behave yourself!' Mal said. 'You've not even had a line yet. 'Ere, cop this.' He threw the tube to Sam. 'Get some of that down your neck!'

Sam hesitated for a second, then dropped his jacket and kneeled beside the table. 'Oh, all right then. But just one, then I'm out of here.'

'Eh! Save some for me, you greedy cunts!' Lee squawked, struggling to get off the couch as he watched the line disappear up Sam's nose.

'Plenty more where this came from,' Mal assured him. 'Anyhow, get your dosh out, you two. I've just paid through the nose for this little lot!'

'That a pun?' Sam's grin was creeping up to his hairline. 'You can be a right funny bastard sometimes!' He laughed, slapping Mal's shoulder.

'Yeah, but you make the best spliffs!' said Mal.

'Not as good as your Manchester landmarks!' Sam countered. 'I've heard people as far away as London talking about yours!'

'His what?' Lee sniggered. 'His big fat juicy cones – or his big fat dick?'

'Not as big as yours, though, eh? Lee?' Sam laughed, nudging Mal.

'Piss off!' Mal snorted. 'Mine's bigger than his any day!'

'But not as big as Sam's legendary donkey dick, eh? Eh?' Lee leered. 'Famous in fucking America, that!'

'Well! If I do say so myself,' Sam chortled, 'it *is* a bit of a monster!'

'Lying bastard!' Mal threw a mock punch at him.

'Straight up!' Sam laughed, ducking quickly. 'Ask Wendy!'

'Oh, don't mention her,' Lee groaned. 'I'm getting a hard-on!'

In the kitchen, Suzie laughed at their efforts to out-compliment each other. She'd never seen them on such a buzz. She only hoped it would last.

When she brought in the plate of fragrant bacon butties, they'd finished their lines of coke and had pushed the mirror over to the side to give them more room to play with their money. Remembering the lesson of the previous day, she waited until Mal cleared a space before putting the plate down. They immediately pounced on it, taking huge continuous bites out of the butties. She shook her head in amazement. They couldn't even be tasting it, they were eating so fast.

Taking a cigarette from the open pack on the table, she went over to the couch for a lie-down. Turning the bloodied cushion over, she put her head down and sighed happily. The vibes in the flat were good this morning.

Then she remembered her news and pushed herself up onto her elbow to tell them. 'Oh, by the way, guess what I heard when I was down the shops?'

'What's that, doll?' Mal asked, tomato ketchup leaking down his chin.

'Oh, it's good, Mal,' she smiled. 'The police were there, loads of them. And guess what? The telly people were there, too!'

'No way!' Lee gasped. 'Shit, man, we're famous!'

'Is that right?' Sam asked, wide-eyed. 'Who was doing it?'

'That Liz Whatserface from the six o'clock news,' Suzie told him. 'She was right there in front of me, talking to a copper. I couldn't hear what they were saying, but there were loads of people there. Anyhow, that's not the best bit,' she said, bursting to tell them. 'You'll never guess what people are saying!'

'What? What?' the men chorused.

'They're only saying Pasha was battered to death by a load of guys with baseball bats!' she told them, relishing her moment in the spotlight. 'A woman in the shop told my mate Elaine – oh, she'll be coming round sometime, by the way – anyhow, this woman said she'd seen them doing it! Can you believe it? Says she was in the phone box and watched the whole thing!'

'Fuck me!' Mal laughed, nudging Lee. 'Couldn't ask for better than that, could you, mate?'

'What else?' said Lee. 'Did anyone mention me?'

'No,' Suzie smiled. 'Not a single word. But they were saying plenty of stuff about Pasha that I thought might interest you.'

'Like what?' Sam asked.

'Well . . . like he was dealing smack from under the counter, for a start. And that it was probably junkies who'd done him over, or his nephews.'

The men looked at each other and laughed.

'What a beautiful world this is!' Mal held his hand up for the others to slap palms.

'Like a fucking rainbow,' Lee said. 'And we've got the pot of gold!'

Mal put an arm around Lee and Sam's shoulders and smiled into their faces. 'My brothers. I do believe we are home and dry. Let's celebrate!'

Gathering the money together he put it to the side, then pulled the mirror back into the centre of the table and tipped another bag onto it.

Finishing her cigarette, Suzie settled back and closed her eyes. At last everything was going right – it must be if Sam was laughing. Always worrying about everything, he'd be the first to say if he had any doubts that they were in the clear.

Minutes later she was woken from her light doze by Lee tugging on her sleeve.

'About this mate of yours who's coming round. What's she like, then?'

10

The Man had fallen asleep on the couch, and, rather than waking him when he got back, Jake had covered him with a quilt.

Waking up hot and sticky, The Man saw that it was light outside.

'What time is it?' he asked, rubbing the sleep from his eyes.

'Going on nine,' Jake said. 'You feeling okay?' he asked then, taking in the deep lines etched in The Man's face.

'Yeah, I'm cool,' The Man said. Pushing the quilt aside, he sat up and stretched his legs out. His trousers were badly creased, and he could smell his own sweat from the restless few hours tossing and turning on the hot leather couch. 'I need a shower!' he muttered, wrinkling his nose.

Jake handed him a freshly made cup of coffee. 'I'll go get some eggs and stuff while you're in there,' he said. 'I'm starving.'

The Man groaned. 'That all you ever think about?'

Jake grinned. 'Among other things!'

'Oh, yeah . . .' The Man stretched his arms, grimacing at the stench from his underarm. 'Did you drop her all right?' He peered at Jake from beneath his brows. 'Didn't get too heavy?'

'Nah, man,' Jake assured him. 'We had a bit of fun, that's all.'

The Man nodded. 'So long as that was all. We can do without any more shit right now.' Standing, he put his cup on the table and headed for the bathroom. 'I'll be ten minutes.'

Knowing full well it would be more like half an hour before The Man had scrubbed and scoured every inch of his body, Jake relaxed back onto his chair to finish his smoke. When the phone rang, he leaned across and pressed the hands-free button, growling, 'Yeah?'

'Yo,' said Max. 'Where's The Man?'

Jake took a long drag before answering. 'Tekkin' a shower. 'S up?'

'Got something I think he should know,' said Max. 'I'll come round.'

'Leave it half an hour,' Jake told him. 'I'll be back then to let you in.'

'Half an hour, then,' Max said, then hung up.

Stubbing out the part-smoked spliff and leaving it in the ashtray for The Man, Jake grabbed his coat and the car keys and went out.

Max put the phone down and finished polishing the sleek matt barrel of his latest find. Folding the duster, he put it and the tube of polish back in the cupboard under the sink. Then, with a last loving stroke, he wrapped the gun in a square of black cloth and carried it down to the cellar to stash in the strongbox with the others.

Guns were his passion. Ever since he could remember he'd longed for one of his own. And now he had six. Six little beauties, picked up from various sources. The two he'd been lucky enough to find last night were very nice. Both were special, but the matt black .35 Magnum Colt was a real beauty. And very unusual. There weren't many like that knocking about.

All in all, it had been a profitable night. Now all he had to do was give The Man the information he had, and – with luck – get paid for it, which would cap it off nicely.

Half an hour, Jake had said. He'd better get a move on. Pushing the steel bar firmly across the cellar door into its reinforced socket, he clicked the heavy-duty padlock into place and gave the door's handle a couple of good hard testing pulls. He couldn't take any chances with security, not with the little arsenal he had down there. Satisfied that it was secure, he dusted his hands down and headed out.

The sunlight hit him straight between the eyes, but it didn't bother him. Despite just a couple of hours' sleep, and the early-morning debt-collecting run, he wasn't tired. Forty minutes snatched here and there was enough to reinvigorate Max. He was lucky like that. Always active, always alert – and always out for what he could get.

He took great pride in being clear-headed, never touching anything stronger than weed drugs-wise and just the occasional bottle of Budweiser. There were too many gouchers out there already. Too many druggies who thought they had it taped but couldn't see what was staring them in the face. People like that always ended up losing everything they had. Junkies were the worst. They were stupid. Ignorant, blind scum. Stupefied by the drug they held so dear. Max would never be that dumb.

Closing his front door with a heavy slam, he locked it with the mortise, then bounced the hundred yards to the single row of garages. His was on the end, fortified with huge steel bars and padlocks. No thief was ever gonna get their filthy hands on his things – least of all his gorgeous silver BMW 325i. His pride and joy. His face lit up when he saw her. Nestling snugly inside the confined space, she looked to Max like an untamed silver panther, waiting for the love of her life to arrive.

'Here I am, darlin',' he crooned, stroking her smooth, still-warm body.

Sliding onto his seat, he felt the heat spread through his loins as it always did when he entered her. Better than any woman! Firing up the engine, he flicked the concealed cassette player on, then backed her carefully out. Pausing only to jump out and relock the garage, he headed for The Man's flat, singing along soulfully to Sade.

'Mummy . . . mummy?' The voice was insistent, creeping into Wendy's brain like an invisible plague. Reluctantly, she opened her eyes.

'All right, all right – I heard you!' she snapped, shrugging off the nurse's hand.

'Baby's awake and looking for food.' The nurse – a simpering idiot, in Wendy's immediate opinion – smiled down into her face.

'Well, give it a bottle then!' Wendy snarled. She winced as a stitch snagged on the sanitary towel. 'Jeezus!' she howled, turning her back on the nurse. 'Have I died and gone to Hell, or what?'

The ever-helpful nurse, fresh from lessons about coping with post-natal mothers, wheeled the baby around to the other side of the bed. 'Look. That's your mummy.' She simpered into the perspex cot. 'If you're a good girl, she might pick you up and give you breakfast and a lovely little cuddle. Mmmm?' She looked at Wendy for confirmation.

Wendy gave her a filthy look and rolled onto her other side. 'Look, Little Miss Muppet,' she spat. 'Take *baby* away and give me a break, will you? I'm knackered.'

'Oh dear, Mummy seems a bit upset,' the nurse cooed at the squalling baby. 'Never mind. We'll go and have some breakfast, and when we come back, Mummy will be in a much better mood, won't she?'

'Oh, will you piss off!' Wendy moaned, pulling the pillow up around her ears.

The nurse wheeled the baby away down the ward. Wendy waited until the awful din had faded before rolling onto her back. God! What had she done? She didn't want the child anywhere near her. Maybe it was something to do with the way it had been forced upon her last night. There had been none of the joy she'd felt with the others – just pain and anger. Anger at shit-head Lee for bringing it on. And anger at her wimp of a husband for— For what?

For just being!

Grabbing at the bedside cabinet, Wendy hauled it around and threw the little top door open. Fuming silently, she pushed roughly through her neatly folded clothes for her cigarettes. All she wanted to do was go back to sleep and forget she was alive – forget the baby. But that was impossible now.

She decided to call Louise while she was having a smoke – make sure she was coping okay on her own, because no doubt Sam would have gone straight back to Mal's. Pulling her purse out, she pushed the covers back and swung her legs over the side of the bed, grimacing as the stitches stretched tight. It hurt like hell. She hoped they'd done it properly, not left her scarred for life. She'd sue the bloody arse off the hospital if they had.

Stepping down gingerly, she hobbled slowly to the plug-in pay phone and dragged it into the day room. Making for the chair with the most padding, she dialled her home number and lit herself a much-needed cigarette.

Louise answered quickly, sounding as if she were on the verge of tears. Josh and Annette were fighting in the background.

'Is Sam there?' Wendy asked the distressed girl. 'Huh! No, I didn't think so. Well, has he rung you? Okay, that's something, I suppose. Yes, I did. A girl. No, I've no idea. I was kind of banking on a boy, so I hadn't thought of any girls' ones. Still, plenty of time, eh? Right, love, I'm off. Can you cope for a while on your own? Oh, good. Well, I'll make it up to you when I see you. Now, just make sure those little buggers don't walk all over you. Tell them I said I'll see to the pair of them when I get home if they don't behave, all right? Yeah. Okay. Speak to you later, love. Bye.'

Pulling another couple of twenty-pence pieces out of her purse, she lit another cigarette from the butt of her last and dialled Mal's number. Suzie answered.

'Hello, Suzie,' Wendy said. 'Yeah, yeah . . . I'm fine, thanks. Yes. She's fine too. Is Sam there, love?'

She pulled deeply on the cigarette as she waited for Sam to come on. When he finally did, she blasted him.

'What the hell do you think you're doing? Why is Louise still looking after your kids? Get your arse back home and let the poor girl go home. Never mind me! What do I want to see you for? It's the kids that need to see your stupid face, not me! Yeah? Well, make sure you do as well, 'cos if I'm the only one in this ward tonight without flowers I'll bloody kill you when I get my hands on you. And bring me some more cigs. Right, yeah . . . Well, I'm going. Yes. She's fine – as far as I know. What do you mean, what do I mean? I mean as far as I know! No, I haven't. A nurse is feeding her. I'm going. See you later.'

She slammed the phone down angrily. Why wasn't she feeding the baby herself, indeed! Why the hell should she? That was what the nurses were for, wasn't it?

Getting up, she was about to walk out of the room when a picture of Pasha's supermarket flashed up on the TV. Turning the sound up quickly, she sat back down to watch.

'. . . *sometime in the early hours, according to our sources. No details have been released as yet, other than the name of the victim: Mr Pashratar Singh, the forty-six-year-old owner of the supermarket.*

'*It is believed that Mr Singh was attacked shortly after leaving the premises but, as yet, the police are uncertain of the motive. More details will be given on tonight's six o'clock news, when we will show Liz Jardine's interview with Detective Chief Inspector Jackson of Greater Manchester Police.*'

Wendy watched avidly as the camera panned around the crowd. Off to the rear, she could clearly see Liz Jardine in conversation with a man. She scanned the locals, hoping to catch a glimpse of someone she recognized. Then she saw Suzie. What the hell was she doing there? Picking the phone up quickly, she dialled the flat again.

'You're on telly, girl!' she laughed when Suzie answered. 'No, I'm not joking. Channel three. Can you see it? Way to go, kiddo!'

*   *   *

Max sat on his usual chair, grinning broadly.

'Well, what have you got for me?' The Man asked.

Reaching into his inside pocket, Max pulled out a thick wad of notes and passed them across the table.

'What's this?' The Man asked with a frown.

'Have a look,' Max said, leaning forward.

The Man turned the wad over in his hand. It looked perfectly normal. He looked at Max questioningly.

'The eyes,' Max told him, excited by his discovery. He hadn't noticed at first, not until he'd counted it for the third time. Then, turning the notes so they all faced the same way when he stacked them, he'd suddenly noticed the smudges in the Queen's eyes. At first he'd thought it was the trade-mark defect of a batch of forgeries, but when he'd looked real close he'd seen it clearly.

The Man scrutinized the notes carefully, and suddenly it was crystal clear. 'What the fuck?' he growled, sitting further forward and peering hard at the note in his hand. 'Is that what I think it is? Jake, pass me my glasses.'

Max leaned back with a grin. 'I wasn't sure at first, but it sure looks suss to me.'

Jake passed The Man's glasses to him and leaned over the back of the couch for a look. 'What is it?'

The Man handed him a note. And there it was. One in either eye. The tiny identification marks that Pasha had used to mark out The Man's money, separating it from whatever other money might make its way under his counter – for the back-of-the-lorry stereos, videos and suchlike that were Pasha's business alone. 'S' in the right eye, 'M' in the left. A routine Pasha had adopted after his first and only mix-up. Barely visible, and something The

Man had forgotten about because it had been so long since he'd felt the need to check on Pasha's handling of their business.

'Where did you get this?' The Man shot at Max, agitatedly flapping the note he was holding.

He knew without a doubt it was part of his missing money. And it had to be part of the latest batch, because none of the money ever stayed in Manchester for more than a few hours once he had it. It went directly to his contact in London, and from there straight over the waves to Ireland, from where his dealer's dealer operated his empire.

'One of my dealers had it,' Max explained, beginning to feel a little wary of the turn in The Man's tone. 'I went round there this morning to pick up a little debt he owed me, and this is what he had.'

'Who?' The Man snapped. 'And how much did he give you?' He folded the note back into the wad and stuck the lot in his shirt pocket.

Max opened his mouth to protest, but thought better of it as The Man's face darkened. He was just glad he'd only brought part of the money with him, or it would all be going the same way.

'It's just some little shit-head who teks an ounce or so of coke off me every week,' he said at last. 'No one big. He owed me some money and, truth to tell, when I went there this morning I expected to be kicking his arse for any of it. But as you can see—' he waved towards The Man's pocket '—he paid up.'

The Man jumped up to pace the floor, slapping a huge fist into his palm as he contemplated the fate of the man who'd been foolish enough to rip off his money.

'Tek me to 'im!' he demanded after a minute, turning

to Max and glaring furiously. 'The dude's got some explaining to do! I'm gonna fucking kill 'im!'

Max saw his weekly turnover diminishing before his eyes. The Man would wipe Stevo out in one fell swoop, leaving Max to find another mug to offload his cut coke onto, and that wouldn't do at all. He had a nice regular income from his dealings with Stevo, helping him to live a fairly legal life. That income would soon disappear if The Man whacked Stevo.

Apart from which, that money was Max's. Stevo had owed him that. Now it looked like his big mouth was about to lose him the whole lot.

'Hold up . . . hold up,' Max said, squirming under The Man's brutal glare. 'Let's not be too hasty. There's probably a good explanation—'

'Yeah!' The Man thundered. 'Like your boy stuck his nose in my bizzness! Claat!' He leaned over Max, prodding himself viciously in the chest to punctuate his words. 'And like he ripped off one of my best men and smoked 'im, tekkin' my money, star! He can't have no explanation to justify fucking with me!'

Cursing loudly, he turned and sat heavily on the couch, drumming his fingers and breathing fire. He needed to calm down and clear his head. Work out what to do with this information.

'Why don't you let me speak to him?' suggested Max. 'Find out what he knows? You said yourself there could have been thousands. If you go round, he'll know you're onto him and disappear. Let me check him, yeah? At least then you might be able to get most of it back. What do you think?'

Jake laughed nastily. 'He'll disappear anyway. Soon as he knows who he's dealing with!'

Max shook his head, desperate to buy time. He'd as good as lost the two hundred The Man had just pocketed, but if he could get to Stevo before they did, he might stand a chance of recovering the ounce he'd laid on him that morning. He shouldn't have got rid of too much of it yet.

'Look, just think about it,' he almost pleaded. 'The police were all over the shops this morning. Stevo would know that. Let me sound him out like I don't know nothing. If I get his confidence he might let it slip where he's stashed the rest.'

'And then again, he might just up and do a runner!' said Jake.

The Man mulled it over quietly. They both had a point, but on balance, Jake's made more sense. Turning to Jake, he said, 'Call Rico and the boys and tell them to come over straight away.'

Stevo tipped the last of the coke from the ounce into the biggest bag, and carefully sealed it so none of the powder could escape. Mal should be well satisfied with it – even bulked out as it was with just a bit less than the usual cut of glucose, and a dash of unscented baby powder and bicarb. It wouldn't do him any harm and, as long as he wasn't shooting it, he'd never even know.

Sitting back, Stevo rolled his head on his shoulders and looked at the pile of bags on the table with satisfaction. It had taken a couple of hours to get it all done, but it had been time well spent. He'd bumped up the weight so that the ounce had become an ounce and a half – not including the generous amount he'd skimmed off for himself before cutting it. Obviously Max would have cut it before bringing it – and probably his dealer before him

– but it was still good-grade stuff. Probably better – and certainly no worse – than the other shit doing the rounds at the moment.

Gathering the bags together, he stashed them in his jacket pocket and set about clearing his stuff up. Wetting his finger, he carefully wiped it around the dishes of his Chinese weighing scales, picking up whatever powder was still there and licking it from his finger. He got a good buzz just from that. It was good stuff, all right. When the dishes were clean, he gently laid the set in its box, put it back under the hinged floorboard and smoothed the dog-eared flap of carpet back into place. Then he placed the equally dog-eared yucca back in its spot on top of that.

Getting busted with coke already bagged was bad enough – Stevo might just manage to convince a judge that it was for his own personal use. But getting caught with the elaborate weighing machine . . . No chance! Intent to supply was worse than anything.

Standing, he patted his back pocket, smiling at the bulky wad of money he still had over from the grand Mal had given him.

'Good one, Mal, y' scummy shite!' he said aloud. 'Saved me a right good kicking, so ye did!'

Pulling his jacket on, he headed for the door. He wasn't expecting anyone to call round until later in the evening, so he'd decided to get round to Mal's place pronto and drop the stuff off. He didn't know why, but he had the feeling he should get it and himself out of there ASAP. *Must be getting paranoid*, he thought. A bit of the old fresh air would soon clear that up.

Locking the door behind him, Stevo set off down the stairs at a trot. Halfway down, he stopped, wondering if he'd left the cooker on when he did the freebase earlier. He contemplated going to check, then decided against it. It was just the paranoia talking.

He had his head down as he rounded the corner and ducked under the garages. He heard a car pull up sharply in the car park, but thought nothing of it.

Suzie was up to her elbows in suds at the kitchen sink when she heard the doorbell. She was about to go and answer it but stayed put when she heard Mal grumbling his way down the hall. He was still in a mood with her for getting her face on TV, but at least he hadn't got nasty about it. He just hadn't spoken to her for a couple of hours. She'd been busying herself with the cleaning ever since, staying out of his way. Hopefully, he'd be back to normal after they'd been to the hospital to see Wendy and the baby.

'Oi, Suzie,' he shouted suddenly. 'You've got a visitor.'

She frowned. A visitor? No one visited her. It was only ever Mal's mates who came round. Drying her hands, she went to see who it was. Her heart sank when she saw Elaine standing in the doorway with a big stupid grin on her face. What was she doing here? She'd said a few days – not a few hours!

'And who's this lovely lady, then?' said Lee, pulling himself up on the couch to get a better look at the girl. She wasn't exactly a babe, but she wasn't barking either. She had a fair old pair of tits on her, and the black roots showing through the dyed blonde hair would look dead sexy in the right light! Definitely worth a legover. 'So you're Suzie's friend, are you?' he asked.

'Yeah, that's right,' Elaine said, looking around her with a mixture of surprise and envy. Suzie had really landed on her feet. It was a great flat, with a carpet, and curtains – not blankets tacked up at the window like at her dump – and a proper three-piece suite. There was even a wall unit with neatly stacked books and nice ornaments on its shelves. She smiled broadly when she saw Suzie – her new best friend.

'Hiya, Sooze,' she said. 'Hope you don't mind me coming early, like, but I had to find out if you saw us on telly earlier?'

'Mmmm . . .' Suzie murmured, casting a worried glance at Mal. But Mal was too busy playing lord and master to remember he was in a bad mood.

'Sit down, luv,' he said, waving Elaine onto his chair by the fire and offering her a cigarette. 'Smoke?'

'Ooh – ta!' Elaine chirped, taking one and leaning forward to get a light.

Her eyes sparkled as she got a good close look at Suzie's older man. Quite a looker, she decided, real smooth and sexy. Not very big, but with his black hair slicked back and his dark blue, black-lashed eyes, he looked a bit Tony Hadley-ish.

'So, it's Elaine, is it?' Mal said as he kneeled on the rug beside her, rolling a spliff, his chest puffed out like a mating bird's. 'How come I haven't seen you before?'

'I haven't seen Suzie since school,' Elaine said. Turning to Suzie, she raised her eyebrows in mock admonition. 'Eh, you! You never said he was this gorgeous!'

'So what exactly did she say?' asked Mal, smiling slyly at Suzie who was still hovering nervously in the doorway. 'Give me a good report, did she?'

'Nah! Said you were a right ugly old tosser!' Elaine said. Then she laughed, leaning forward to squeeze Mal's arm. 'Only joking! She said you were great. And I said she was a lucky cow – didn't I, Sooze?'

'Mmmm . . .' said Suzie, folding her arms around herself defensively. This was going to be bad, she could feel it. Elaine thought she was being funny, but Mal would remember every word she said and use it as evidence later, judging and convicting Suzie on the strength of it – however many times she said she was only joking!

Determined not to be outdone by Mal, Lee was waving his arms to get Elaine's attention. 'Yo, Elaine, me darlin'! Come and park your arse over here and tell me all about yourself.' Moving over, he patted the cushion beside him.

Giggling, Elaine obligingly trotted over to the couch. And when Mal had finished his rolling, he went and sat on the other side of her. Seeing her scrunched between the two of them like that, with a catlike smile on her fat face, Suzie's heart sank. God! She'd never leave now. What had she been thinking of, giving her the address?

'Want a brew, 'Lane?' Mal asked, passing the spliff to her and blowing his smoke into her face suggestively.

'Ooh, yeah,' gushed Elaine, blushing at the way he'd said her name. 'Tea, please. Three sugars.'

'Shove it on, doll,' Mal told Suzie as if everything was hunky-dory.

Sam felt awful for Suzie as she traipsed into the kitchen. He'd noticed her expression drop when she'd seen who her visitor was. Now, after just a couple of minutes, he understood why. This girl was a common little tart.

Getting up, he stretched, then casually strolled into the kitchen. Suzie was filling the kettle, looking very down-hearted.

'You all right?' he asked. She nodded, but he could see she was shaking. 'Don't let it get to you,' he whispered, squeezing her arm. 'She's not a patch on you, and despite everything, Mal does love you, you know?'

'Thanks,' she murmured with a tight little smile.

'Any time.'

Suzie sighed when Sam went back into the living room. She wished she did know that Mal loved her, but it was hard sometimes – especially when he was flirting with other women. She could hear Elaine giggling as Mal and Lee tried to outdo each other, and it cut her to the heart. At least Lee was single, she consoled herself. If Elaine was going to get off with one of them, it would have to be him. Anyway, Mal wouldn't stand her filthy mouth for long, whereas Lee would find it a turn-on. Mal hated hearing women swear, and Elaine was one of the worst.

When the doorbell rang again, Mal didn't move. 'Oi!' he shouted. 'Get the door!'

Suzie went, knowing full well he was talking to her. It pissed her off when she heard Elaine giggle again as Mal said: 'She knows her name, don't she?'

The man at the door looked weird, and Suzie immediately wanted to slam the door in his face. It wasn't his scruffiness, or the dank smell of sweat and rotten socks she found disturbing, it was his shifty eyes. The way he furtively looked every which way, as though he was psyching himself up to whip his coat open and flash his dick at her.

'Mal in?' he asked.

'Yeah,' she said. 'Who should I say wants him?'

'Just tell him it's Stevo,' he said, slightly irritated to be kept on the step by this stuck-up little madam. 'And don't take all day, eh?' he added, flashing her an insincere grin. 'Nay offence, pet, but I'm not too fond of hanging about in strange places.'

Mal jumped up when she told him who was at the door. 'And you left him outside, you daft cow?' Shoving past her, he rushed to the door. 'Stevo! My main man! Come in . . .'

Suzie heard them going into the bedroom. She sat down and lit herself a cigarette, wondering why she couldn't go even one full day without screwing up. Never mind a day – even an hour would do.

'Eh – you'll never guess what, Sooze!' Elaine beamed at her from the couch. 'Leo's asked me out, haven't you, Leo? Great, eh?'

'Lee!' he corrected her. 'Leeeee . . . Leeeee!'

'Oh, yeah, right,' she laughed. 'Lee-Lee! Don't worry, I won't forget.'

'It's all right, I forgive you,' Lee said. 'E'yar – d'y' wanna look at me stitches?'

'Cor, yeah!'

Sam raised an eyebrow at Suzie as Elaine jumped up onto the back of the couch and pulled Lee's head back between her legs. She carefully unwound the bandage, then set about examining the war wound with morbid fascination.

Mal bounced back into the room minutes later, rubbing his hands together gleefully. Stevo had done him proud. He stopped short just inside the door when he saw what Elaine was doing. 'What's this?' he said. 'A chimps' nit-picking party?'

'I'm looking at his stitches,' Elaine said. 'It's 'orrible! Come and have a look!'

'You must be fucking joking!' Mal shuddered and pulled a face, then turned to the others, yelling, 'Is this a bleeding morgue, or what? Let's get some music on. It's party time!

'Get a spliff going, Sam,' he said, throwing his stash tin at Sam. 'And where's those brews, Sooze?' He laughed. 'Hey, that rhymed! Brews – Sooze! I'm a bleeding poet and no way did I know it! Your mam had the right idea calling you that, didn't she, Sooze?

'Which reminds me.' He turned back to Sam. 'Subject of names, what are you calling the sprog?'

Sam shrugged. 'No idea, mate. Hadn't thought beyond Benjy. Wendy was sure it was going to be a boy.'

'Ah, that's nice,' Suzie said. 'And it could still work for a girl.'

'Have you heard her!' Mal howled. 'Benjy for a girl! It's not a girl's name, that!'

'I like it,' Suzie said quietly.

But Mal wasn't listening any more. Flipping through his tapes he pulled one out and stuck it in the machine, turning the volume up full blast.

'Ooh! Bob Marley!' Elaine squealed. 'I love him!'

'Me too!' said Lee. 'Well, not "love", 'cos I ain't a batty boy, but you know what I mean! Looks like we're gonna hit it off, me and you!'

The doorbell rang again – barely audible above 'Buffalo Soldier'.

'Bleedin' 'ell, it's like Piccadilly round here today,' Mal shouted. 'Suzie, go and get it, will you?'

It was Ged. Much more relaxed than when he'd left, having had a couple of hours' sleep, a shower, a change of clothes, and a visit with his daughter. He screwed up his eyes at the volume of the music.

'Bloody hell, mate!' he yelled to Mal. 'Bit overboard, isn't it?'

Elaine's eyes widened as she spotted Ged. He was gorgeous – a real hunk. Well over six foot and built like a bouncer, with his hair shaved down really close. Really manly. For a second she forgot all about the bandage she was rewrapping – until Lee nudged her. Winding it on quickly, she slid back down onto the couch and waited to be introduced to Ged, who was busy talking to Suzie.

'Well, you're a sly one, aren't you?' he said. 'I saw you on TV earlier. Budding film star, eh?'

'Don't be daft,' Suzie said, blushing furiously.

'Did you see me, too?' Elaine chirped up. 'I was there and all, wasn't I, Sooze? We looked brill, didn't we? Proper glamour pusses and no mistake!'

Ged noticed her for the first time – and immediately didn't like what he saw. *Slut on the make*, he decided.

'Sorry, can't say I noticed you,' he said politely. Then, turning back to Suzie, he smiled. 'You looked good, Suzie. You should think about taking it up profession-ally. Right make-up, right hair-do, you'd run rings round the likes of Liz Jardine. Which reminds me – we've got to watch the six o'clock news, 'cos they're doing the full story.'

'We already know, mate,' said Mal. 'So what did you make of it, then?'

Ged shot a warning glance towards Elaine. They shouldn't discuss any of this in front of her. She definitely wouldn't be trustworthy. 'Tragic, really,' he said guard-edly. 'He was a nice bloke, from what I remember.'

'No way!' Elaine jumped in, eager to dazzle them all with her inside knowledge. 'He wasn't all kosher, him, you know. I was telling Suzie earlier, wasn't I, Sooze? He was dealing all sorts of stuff, him, under the counter, like. Smack, and that. And I know this woman, right, who saw him getting attacked. I was talking to her about it just this morning, wasn't I, Sooze? She said it was a big gang of blokes what did it. About nine or ten of them at least, she reckoned – with baseball bats. They laid right into him, and she was watching the whole thing from the phone box. Anyhow, she's told the police all about it, so you might see her on the news and all, 'cos she got interviewed—'

'You what?' interrupted Suzie. 'I never saw that.'

'Oh, yeah,' Elaine said. 'It was after you left, like. When I went back round, the news people was walking round asking everyone if they knew anything, and my friend went trotting over to tell them.'

'Did they believe her?' Ged asked.

'Course!' said Elaine. 'Well, she saw it, didn't she? Anyhow, they must have, 'cos she had to give a statement to the pigs after.'

Ged and the others exchanged a quick look. It certainly looked hopeful – as long as the police believed the bullshitting cow who claimed to have witnessed the whole thing. And if she was anything like the mouthy one on the couch, Ged thought, she'd probably convinced herself she was telling God's honest truth, and the police would take it reasonably seriously.

'Well, this calls for a celebration,' Mal said. 'We've still got a bottle of bevvy to get through, and I've got me lovely Charlie in the bedroom.'

'Ooooh – kinky!' Elaine giggled.

Mal gave her a look. What the fuck was she on, the silly cow? Still – never mind her. They had celebrating to do.

'Lee, off yer arse and set the mirror up,' he said. 'And haven't you made those brews yet, Sooze?' Laughing again, he went to the bedroom to get his coke, chanting, 'Brews – Sooze . . . Brews – Sooze.'

*   *   *

Stevo turned the corner from the stairwell and stopped dead in his tracks, looking at the splinters of wood scattered around the landing outside his front door. His stomach flipped over. Someone had been in – someone with very big feet. Even from here, he could see the huge imprint of a boot where the lock should have been.

Maybe they were still in there, waiting for him?

He instinctively backed up into the shadows of the recess beneath the stairs, and peered at his door through the narrow gaps. His breath came in ragged little bursts as he waited for signs of movement from within his flat. After a few minutes, having heard nothing, he began to think it would be safe to go in. Maybe whoever it was had been in to rip him off but, finding nothing, had left quickly?

Just as he began to step out, he heard footsteps coming from inside his flat. Edging back as far as possible, he peered out fearfully. It was either the police or a rip-off crew. Either way he'd get his head kicked in if they spotted him.

'I'll come back later,' The Man said, slamming the door back on its hinges as he stepped outside. 'And when I get him, I'll rip his fucking head off and shove it up his raas fucking arse!'

Stevo's knees turned to water. What the hell was The Man doing in his flat? And why was he talking like that? What had he done to upset The Man, for God's sake?

Jake came out next, rubbing his fingers down his leg as if he'd touched something nasty. Then three enormous men Stevo had never seen before, followed by Max.

Stevo's mouth dropped open when he saw Max. What the hell was he doing here? He'd paid him what he owed this morning. If he'd had a problem, he wouldn't have laid that ounce on him – would he? His mind raced. Was it the coke? Had it come from The Man? Had word got around that he'd cut it too much, or bumped his price too high? Or was Max setting him up – saying he hadn't paid what he owed?

'I've a good mind to leave Jake here till he shows his face,' The Man said now.

Stevo was filled with dread. There was no way he wanted to get into it with Jake. He was a raving psycho. The Man was a definite heavyweight, there was no denying that, but at least he had a reputation for being fair. But Jake! He'd just as soon torture and mutilate someone as listen to reason.

'Cha!' Jake exclaimed loudly. 'I ain't hanging about in this filthy dump!'

Stevo just about managed to hold in his juddering sigh of relief.

'Look, why don't you let me do it?' Max suggested. 'I'll speak to him, suss out what he knows.'

The Man looked at his watch. 'All right,' he said at last. 'I'll give you two hours to find him and get his story. But after that, Rico and the boys are on it – and believe me, Max, I ain't fooling! Seen?'

'Seen,' Max agreed glumly.

Stevo shrank back into the brickwork as The Man, Jake, and the heavies marched past just inches away. He held his breath, knowing full well he'd be thrown head first over the balcony if one of them saw him. And he didn't even know what he was supposed to have done.

He waited until he had heard the car doors slamming and the tyres squealing out of the car park down below before exhaling and opening his tightly shut eyes. Max was bad enough, but even he'd sounded scared just now. There was something heavy going down.

As Max went back into the flat, Stevo made a decision. Whatever he was supposed to have done, Max was his only hope. Hadn't he just pleaded for time to talk to Stevo? Taking a deep breath, he edged out of the shadows, checking carefully that The Man hadn't blagged him and left someone on the stairs to catch him out.

'What do you make of it?' Jake asked when they'd dropped Rico and the boys off at their own car.

'Stinks like rotten pussy,' The Man said.

'Tell me about it!' Jake sniffed. 'That's the filthiest yard I ever stepped in!'

The Man checked his watch again. Two hours he'd given Max. He had plenty of time to shower again – get the stench of that scum out of his skin. And he needed to eat. He rolled his head, clicking the little bones in his neck. He felt like crap, and this business was beginning to wear him down.

'Pull in at the gym,' he said on a whim. 'I need a sauna to sweat the stench of that gaff out of my system.'

Jake eased the car to the left, heading for the Princess Parkway. He'd drop The Man, then go and sort some of their other business. Marie had rung the mobile when they'd been on the way over to Stevo's to tell them that one of the other girls was getting out of line. It was Jake's job to slap her back in – his job and his pleasure.

Glancing sideways at The Man as he idled at a red light, Jake frowned. His eyes were shut, his head back on the rest. Where was his energy these days? Jake hoped it wasn't a signal of bad things coming. If The Man was getting lazy, the other posses would soon catch on and it wouldn't be long before one of them stepped up in his face.

Pulling up outside the gym, Jake nudged The Man awake. After arranging to come back in an hour to collect him, he pulled away, watching in the rear-view as The Man strolled inside. It was time to start seriously contemplating his own future.

11

Wendy was in the day room, having a cigarette, when the nurse popped her head round the door to tell her she had visitors.

'Can't you send them in here?' she asked.

'Sorry.' The nurse smiled apologetically. 'It's against the rules, I'm afraid.'

'Well, I'm afraid rules are made to be broken!' Wendy snapped. Then she relented when the nurse looked about to cry. Heaving herself out of the chair, she said, 'Oh, all right! Where are they?'

'By your bed,' the nurse said, adding, 'Would you like a cup of tea, Mrs Donaldson? I think the trolley's coming round soon. Shall I bring you one?'

'Yeah, thanks.' Wendy sighed. She knew she was being a bitch, but she was wound up. 'What time's dinner?' she asked. 'I'm starving.'

The nurse checked her watch. 'Should be about an hour, but if you're hungry I could make you a sandwich.'

She looked so eager to be liked, Wendy allowed her a smile. 'Yes, that would be nice. And . . . thanks, love.'

Watching her disappear into the kitchen, Wendy sighed again. It was really getting her down, being stuck in here. She just wanted to get home – and get to grips with what Sam and his idiot friends were doing. Sort it all out before things got any worse than they were now.

They were all crowded around her bed when she

pulled the curtain aside: Sam slumped in the only chair, Mal fiddling with the radio headphones, Ged talking quietly to Suzie. But what immediately pissed her off was Lee and some tart she'd never seen before cosy-cosying on her bed.

'Oi! You two!' she snarled. 'Shift!'

Mal dropped the headphones when he heard her voice. Coming around the bed with his arms spread wide, he hugged her. 'Look at you, then,' he said, pushing her back to look her over. 'Beautiful as ever! How was it, then? Shelling peas, or what?'

'Bloody painful!' she snorted.

'Well, you'd never know!' he said with a wink. 'Eh . . .' he dropped his voice. 'Where's the khazi in this place? I'll go and make you a spliff for tonight.'

'Out that door, and turn left.' Wendy pointed the way. 'But don't be putting bush in it. I don't want to stink the place out.'

As Mal headed off to the toilets, Wendy turned her attention back to Lee who was still on her bed. Shoving him hard in the back, she said, 'I won't tell you again. Shift!'

'Wendy, babe . . . love of my life.' Lee jumped up, pulling Elaine with him. 'How's it hangin'?'

Ignoring him, she climbed painfully onto the bed. 'Hope you brought my cigs?' she said to Sam. 'And where are those flowers I told you to bring?'

Sam stood up, pulling a beautiful bunch of roses and freesias from beneath the chair. He handed them to her, bending to kiss her cheek. 'Where is she, then?' he asked, looking around for his missing baby.

'Where's who?' Wendy asked, laying the flowers on the cupboard with hardly a glance.

'Where's who?' cackled Lee. 'What did I tell you, 'Lane? She's a right one, ain't she? Where's who? Ha ha ha!'

'Give me strength!' Wendy hissed, glaring at Lee. 'What did you bring him for, Sam? And what's that hanging off its arm?'

'This is Elaine,' Lee said, pushing Elaine forward into the freezing zone of Wendy's glare.

'Hiya!' Elaine chirped. 'I'm Leo's new girlfriend.'

'Lee!' hissed Lee.

' 'S what I said!' said Elaine. 'So you're Wendy, are you?' she said to Wendy then. 'I've been dying to meet you.'

Suzie shook her head, covering a grin with her hand. If Elaine only knew it, she had well and truly put the mockers on any hope of Wendy ever giving her the time of day. But Elaine didn't notice Wendy's sneer. She was actually a very good match for Lee – as thick-skinned and as oblivious to people's distaste as he was. If she'd decided that she and Wendy were going to be mates, she couldn't have been more wrong.

Halfway through Elaine's bubbling pot of questions about the baby, Wendy turned to Suzie. Her smile was deliberately warm as she said, 'Suzie, I'm glad you made it, darlin'. I've been waiting all day to see you.'

Suzie glowed with the special attention. 'I wouldn't have missed it for the world!'

'Neither would I,' said Ged. 'So where's the baby I almost delivered?'

Wendy rolled her eyes. 'Probably in the nursery.'

'Aaah!' Elaine cooed ecstatically. 'I love babies. Can I go and see her?'

'No,' said Wendy without even looking at her. 'Suzie,

you can go and check on her for me if you want. Just go and ask that nurse over there where she is.'

'I'll go with you,' Elaine said.

'No, you won't,' Wendy snapped. 'You can stay put and stop your boyfriend bothering me.'

'Oh, all right.' Elaine grinned, happy to stay in the presence of Queen Wendy.

'I'll come,' Ged said, following Suzie through the curtain.

'What time is it?' Wendy asked Sam when they'd gone.

'Just gone ten to six.'

'Better get into the TV room.' Wendy dropped her feet down. 'Don't want to miss the news. Oi!' she snapped as Lee and Elaine went to follow her through the curtain. 'You're not coming!'

'Aw, Wend,' Lee moaned. 'It was my idea!'

'What was?' Elaine asked.

Wendy gave Lee a contemptuous glare. 'Idiot!' she hissed. 'Right, come on, then – but stay quiet, or else!'

Suzie and Ged crept into the day room a few minutes later. Then Mal swanned in and slipped Wendy's spliff to her.

'Hey, this is the life,' he said, pulling a pile of chairs forward and positioning them in front of the TV. 'So what are we watching?'

'The news,' Ged told him, motioning with a finger under his nose for Mal to wipe some stray powder away.

'Me and Sooze are on it,' Elaine told Wendy proudly.

'She'd better not start yapping!' Wendy snapped at Lee.

'Here you go,' Mal said, dropping into a chair. 'It's on.'

The nurse poked her head through the door. She was about to remind Wendy that it was against the rules for visitors to sit in here but, finding them so quiet, she decided to leave them to it. They weren't doing any harm, and as the ward sister had nipped out, it was up to her. Pulling the door shut, she headed back to the nursery to have another cuddle of Wendy's baby.

The theme tune and titles came to an end, then Declan Maine, the studio newsreader, came on.

'*Good evening. Tonight's main story is the murder of prominent local businessman, Pashratar Singh.*

'*The body of Mr Singh, owner of PS Supermarket in Hulme, was discovered in the early hours of this morning. He was killed in what police are describing as suspicious circumstances. For the full story, we'll go over to Liz Jardine at the scene.*'

A picture of the supermarket flashed up on the screen.

'Ooh, look!' Elaine yelped. Lee quickly nudged her quiet.

Liz Jardine smiled gravely into the camera.

'*This morning, the body of a well-respected local businessman, Pashratar Singh, was discovered in the yard behind me . . .*' She gestured towards the gates with a sweep of her arm.

'*Mr Singh was murdered in what police are describing as an attempted robbery. It is unclear as yet who is responsible for this unprovoked, savage attack . . .*'

'Eh, up!' Mal laughed, throwing a mock punch at Lee. 'You savage git, you!'

'*. . . But the police are following up a number of leads. We will bring you up to date as and when we have information as to their findings.*

'*Earlier, I spoke to Detective Inspector Ted Jackson of*

Greater Manchester Police; the officer in charge of the investigation.'

The picture flipped to the morning scene and everyone surged forward on their seats, hoping to see Suzie again. The camera closed in on Jackson, looking extremely uncomfortable. His sharp eyes narrowed to slits as he waited through Liz Jardine's introductory waffle.

'Look!' Lee pointed at the screen. 'It's Wacko-Jacko!' He turned to Elaine, saying proudly, 'He busted me last year – right old bastard, he is. Nearly stitched me up good 'n'proper. Tried to plant a shitload of drugs on me!'

'Bollocks!' Mal sneered. 'You're lucky he didn't do you for possession!'

'He couldn't do me after nicking all me shit off me, could he?' Lee said indignantly.

'Thought you said he planted it on you?' Mal said. 'Anyhow, he probably needed it for the police Chrimbo party! You've contributed to the Dibble's benevolent fund, you cunt!'

'Ssshhh!' Wendy hissed. 'I can't hear what they're saying.'

'*Detective Chief Inspector,*' Liz Jardine smiled at Jackson. '*What can you tell us about this horrific crime?*'

Jackson cleared his throat and ran a hand through his hair.

'*Not a lot at this point, other than to confirm that the body is that of Mr Pashratar Singh, and that he was fatally wounded in what we are preliminarily treating as an armed robbery.*'

'*As we know, Detective Chief Inspector, Mr Singh was well known and respected by the people in this area,*' Liz Jardine went on, her face a studied mask of caring. '*And such a vicious crime must surely cause concern to such a* close-knit community. What can you tell these people to explain this terribly shocking event?'

'We've not, as yet, reached a definite conclusion as to the motive behind the attack,' said Jackson guardedly. 'But obviously we will be following every lead, and every care will be taken to ensure that no information is overlooked.'

'I believe there was an eyewitness? What can you tell us about that?'

Jackson rolled his eyes. 'Again, I can only confirm that we will be interviewing a person who has come forward with information relevant to this incident. But I'm afraid we won't be able to disclose any details at this time.'

'That'll be my friend!' Elaine giggled, looking around proudly. 'The woman I was telling you about!'

'Ssshhh!' Wendy hissed again.

'. . . When we have followed up this and other leads that we have, we will issue a more comprehensive statement.'

'Thank you, Detective Chief Inspector.'

The screen flicked back to the evening shot of Liz Jardine outside the supermarket.

'That was the situation this morning, just hours after Mr Singh was murdered. I can tell you that the police have now completed their interview with the eyewitness – who cannot be named for security purposes—'

'Which means they're taking her seriously,' said Ged.

'Mmmm.' Mal nodded sagely. 'Pigs love wallowing in shit!'

'. . . And details of the statement are being thoroughly investigated.'

Mal leaned forward in his seat suddenly, pointing at the screen. 'The fucking shop's open!'

Ged craned forward. 'It bloody is, as well!'

'Money-grabbing bastards!' Lee shouted, jumping up excitedly.

'Will you bloody well shut up!' Wendy glared at him.

He sat back down, muttering, 'But they are. Look. You can see the lights are on.'

'That could just be the police clearing up,' Suzie suggested.

'It's not, though, is it?' Mal snapped indignantly. 'You can see the cunts going in and out.'

'. . . *Keep you updated as we receive information*,' Liz Jardine said, concluding her report. '*Back to you in the studio, Declan.*'

Mal jumped up and turned the TV off.

'Top banana!' Lee cackled. 'We're well and truly off the hook!'

'What do you mean?' Elaine looked puzzled.

'Shut your gob, Lee.' Ged shot him a look. He pushed his chair back, looking at his watch. 'It's nearly half-six. Time we made a move.'

'Yeah.' Mal rubbed his hands together. 'Back to mine for a party, then?'

'Not you, Sam,' Wendy said, getting to her feet. 'You can stay here with me for a bit, then you can go home and see to your kids!'

They followed her back to her bed, delighted to find the baby fast asleep in her plastic cot. They all rushed over to her – except Wendy, who tutted loudly and climbed into bed.

Sam looked down at his little girl for the first time since the awful birth. 'Oh, she's beautiful,' he whispered, smiling, with tears glistening in his eyes.

'If you're just going to go all soppy, you might as well go now!' Wendy snapped.

'Aaahhh!' Elaine cooed, sticking a podgy finger into the baby's curled fist. 'She's gorgeous. Can I have a hold?'

'Right, that does it!' Wendy's face was livid. 'Piss off, the lot of you!'

'Ah . . . Wend,' Lee moaned. 'I want to have a look at the baby. Can't I wake her up and have a hold?'

'Piss . . . Off!' Wendy growled, closing her eyes to show she meant it.

They left quickly after that, knowing it would do no good to hang around, the mood Wendy was in. Only Elaine tried to hang back, and found herself being hauled away by Lee before she had her head bitten off.

Outside the main doors they huddled around Mal, blocking the wind so he could light the huge five-skinner spliff he'd made for them in the toilets. Sam was on a downer about Wendy's attitude towards the new baby, but he cheered up when Mal handed the spliff to him, and they headed back to Mal's flat, deep in excited discussion about the news report – ignoring Elaine's constant questions: 'What do you mean? Why are you celebrating? Why is it good news? I don't understand . . .!'

At the same time, Stevo was making his escape. Hiding in the shadows of the garages beneath his flat, he nervously scanned the car park and the small adjoining play area. The last thing he needed was to be spotted as he made his dash across the open grass to the line of pirate taxis parked alongside the pub at the end of the road. If he could just make it that far without being seen, he might stand a chance.

When he was sure there was no one about, he pulled the brim of his baseball cap down low over his shades and lunged out into the night. Switching the hastily packed bag from hand to hand, he fled across the grass, praying to God he wasn't being watched. Every window in the flats behind him felt like a pair of eyes whose stare was burning into his back. But he couldn't stop now. This was a matter of life or death.

It seemed to take for ever before he reached the taxis, but at last he made it. Wrenching the door of the first one open, he fell onto the back seat and gasped, 'Piccadilly Station!'

'Five,' the driver, a wrinkled, yellow-eyed Jamaican, grunted over his shoulder.

'Cool,' said Stevo. 'But put your foot down, yeah? I'm in a real hurry!'

Kissing his teeth, the driver crunched into first gear and edged away from the kerb as if he had all the time in the world. Stevo fought down a mad urge to batter him around the back of his head to make him get a move on. Instead, he slid further down in his seat and peered out into the darkness – hoping with all his heart that he wasn't being followed.

Max had given him until seven to find out where the rest of the money was, but he didn't know anything about it. He hadn't even heard about Pasha getting shot until Max had told him. And it had really freaked him out when Max said The Man was blaming him for it! How the hell was he supposed to prove it wasn't him when he'd been on his own watching videos when it happened? He knew what would happen if The Man got his hands on him now. He'd be very, very dead! And it wouldn't matter what he said, The Man would never believe him, because, as Max had pointed out, he'd had that marked money.

Fucking Mal! This was all his doing. He'd given him the bloody money. Stevo had told Max this, but Max hadn't wanted to bother tracking Mal down. He wanted Stevo to sort it out. But sack that! Stevo knew better than to hang around to get his head blown off for something that was nothing to do with him. He was off. Max had Mal's address. Let him sort his own shit out.

'Goin' to Jamaica?' the old driver chuckled, looking at Stevo's shades in his rear-view. 'Somewhere warm?'

'Uh? What? Oh, aye . . . aye.' Stevo nodded, pulling the cap down further.

'Best time of year.' The old guy wanted to chat. 'Plenty a gal a-wigglin' theirselves up dem beaches. Sheesh, y' should see 'em!' Slapping his hand down on the wheel, he launched into an account of his youthful exploits back home, growing more unintelligible with each word.

Stevo switched off, hearing nothing but his own heavy breathing and the unsteady pounding of his heart. He began to relax a little as they crossed over the Mancunian Way. Halfway there. He sighed heavily. Once he was on that train back to Glasgow, he was never coming back to Manchester. Never!

Half an hour later, Max rounded the corner to Stevo's flat. Finding the door ajar, he knew immediately that Stevo had done a runner. Cursing angrily, he kicked the door open and stormed inside to confirm his suspicions.

For a second he was confused. He'd expected the place to be cleaned out, but everything still seemed to be there. Furniture, TV, hi-fi – even the lamp was on. He wondered if he was wrong and Stevo was still out trying to track down the money, but on closer inspection he knew this wasn't the case. All the tell-tale signs were there. The yucca, which always stood in the corner beneath the window, was on its side halfway across the floor, its leaves twisted and mangled, its soil spilled out in an untidy heap. And the carpet was pulled back from the corner, revealing the gap where the floorboard should have been.

Max raced through to the bedroom, and found it in the same state. The bed was still there, as was the wardrobe, and the bedside cabinet with Stevo's things still littering its top: ashtray, skins, lighter, dirty mags, pile of half-full cups and glasses. The only sign of disturbance was the chest of drawers, which had the few clothes Stevo had left behind spilling from its dragged-out drawers. The shit-head had definitely done one!

'NO!' Max shouted in despair. 'No . . . No!'

He kicked the chest savagely, grabbing at the few remaining rags and tearing them to shreds in a frenzy. Then, in a blind rage, he made his way through the flat, wreaking destruction, only stopping when it was a chaos of broken glass, splintered wood and torn material.

Taking a breather, he considered his position. He had a real problem now. Not only had he lost the ounce of coke he'd laid on Stevo that morning, he now had to tell The Man that he'd let Stevo get away with all his money. This was not going to be easy.

12

At seven-fifteen, Jackson and Mac trailed wearily into Jackson's messy office. They looked and felt like a couple of whipped dogs, having spent a good part of the day at the murder scene and the rest trooping around the immediate area, taking statements. Things were pretty much back to normal now for the residents of Hulme, although Jackson suspected that the calm wouldn't last too long. Areas like that tended to have little time between major incidents.

Dropping the huge bundle of statements and notes onto his desk, Jackson flopped into his chair and took out the bottle of Scotch he kept in his drawer. Pouring two healthy slugs into a couple of already used plastic cups, he handed one across to Mac.

'You beaut!' Mac said, taking a drink and leaning back heavily in his chair. 'So what have we got?' he asked with a yawn. 'Apart from a bad case of being absolutely shagged out!'

Jackson rolled his head on his shoulders. 'Tell me about it! I've been on since six.' Grimacing at his warm drink, he slammed his cup down and rubbed his eyes with the balls of his hands. 'I could do with a freezing cold beer – and a bloody shower,' he added, sniffing himself with disgust.

Mac yawned again. 'Fancy popping down to The George? Nothing like a noisy watering hole to wake you up and get the grey stuff grinding.'

'Sounds good,' said Jackson. 'But I'd better give this a once-over first.'

Reluctantly, he pulled the paperwork towards him and read through the first sheet, snorting cynically every couple of seconds. When he'd finished he flipped it across to Mac. 'Biggest load of tosh I ever saw in my life! Eyewitness, my arse! She made every word of it up.'

Mac nodded. 'She didn't even know he'd been shot, silly bint. Baseball bats, I ask you! There was no evidence of a beating, was there?'

'None whatsoever. Only bruise on that body came from falling heavily on the concrete.'

'And that was definitely out back, where he was found?'

'Definitely. Not even the remotest sign of any sort of anything inside. Nah! She's talking bollocks, me old son. File it under miscellaneous!' Jackson nodded towards the bin.

Mac grinned, slapping the paper back on the pile. 'Best place for it, but I don't think the Super would be too pleased. So what have we got?' he asked then. 'Real stuff, that is?'

Jackson pulled another sheet from the pile. 'According to the lab prelim on those blood samples you got – thanks for that, by the way – there were definitely two different sources. The stiff was O-neg. And the other wasn't!'

Mac grinned. 'Human or animal?'

'Oh, definitely human,' Jackson said, adding with a scowl: 'If that's what you call the type of scum who pull off shit like this. Yep. Human – with a pretty bad wound, I'd say.'

'So where did they get to?'

Jackson shrugged. 'Lot of blood lost. You'd have thought they'd have been in a pretty bad way. But if they crawled off, they didn't leave any trace. No drag trail.'

'Maybe someone helped them?'

'Probably,' Jackson agreed. 'Remember all those prints in the bushes.'

'Mmm. So we've got at least one injured, and a helper. Have we checked the hospitals?'

'Someone should have done by now,' Jackson said. 'Remind me to check in the morning.'

'You know Graves gave heart failure as cause of death?' said Mac, smirking.

'Dickhead!' Jackson shook his head.

'Mind you . . .' Mac went on. 'I think *my* ticker would fail if I got blasted in the mug!'

'What heart?' Jackson jeered. Pushing his chair back, he stood up. 'Come on. Let's get out of here before I fall asleep.'

Just down the corridor, PC Paul Dalton was hanging up his uniform. He was dog-tired. All that standing around had wiped him out – and he'd had a bellyful of listening to the local women gossiping. Load of know-it-all bitches – and all of them claiming to know something scandalous about the shopkeeper. Poor sod! Dead less than twenty-four hours and villainized for ever. And as for the so-called grieving family – he'd never known the like. Opening the bloody shop just hours after the head of their family got murdered!

Closing his locker with a weary sigh, Paul wondered what he'd let himself in for by taking a placement in this murderers' paradise. Just thirty-odd miles away from his native Warrington, it felt like the other side of the Earth. Everywhere you turned someone was getting mugged, attacked, stabbed, raped or shot. He'd taken Moss Side because he'd liked the idea of working in a challenging environment. And the ghetto of the north was certainly proving to be that. In just three months he'd been to nine murders – five shootings, two machete attacks, a stabbing and a petrol-dousing.

The first was the one he'd never forget. A fifteen-year-old girl caught in a hail of bullets meant for her boyfriend – who had immediately denied all knowledge of her, claiming to be an innocent passer-by. If she'd died instantly, he'd have got away with it, too. But she hadn't. She'd lain on the floor in a widening pool of her own lifeblood, her pretty face ripped to shreds and bits of her stomach leaking out, crying out for 'Peppy' – which just happened to be this innocent bystander's rather distinctive name. Surprise, surprise!

Paul shook his head to clear his mind of the image of the girl. The first was always the worst, they'd been told in training. And it was true. But now he knew what a scummy world it really could be, he was hardening.

Going across to the sink, he splashed cold water onto his face to wake himself up. He really needed a shower, but that would have to wait until he got home.

The door opened as he reached for the towel, and Eddie Walker popped his head in. 'You all set for tonight?' he said.

'Why, what's tonight?' Paul asked.

'The party,' Eddie reminded him. 'At the nurses' home?'

'Shit!' Paul muttered. He'd forgotten all about the

party, and he really didn't feel like going. 'Oh, look, I don't know,' he said. 'I'm knackered. It's been a rough day.'

'Tell me about it.' Eddie laughed. 'I've been down at Maine Road all day, kicking arse at the City match. Sad lot, the City fans. Don't know why they bother – they never win. They only end up getting pissed off and laying into each other outside. Still, can't complain, eh? Keeps me fit, all that aggro.'

Paul shook his head. 'I thought we were supposed to stop the aggro, not join in with it!'

'Perks of the job!' Eddie winked. 'You'll learn. Anyhow, what are you doing? You'll be sorry if you miss it. Those nurses are a rum bunch!'

'What time?' Paul asked. 'I need a shower.'

'It doesn't start till nine,' Eddie said. 'We're meeting up at The George for a quick one before we go.'

'All right.' Paul nodded. 'I'll meet you there at half-eight.'

'Good man!'

As Eddie left to get ready, Paul tried to make himself feel enthusiastic. It was difficult when all he wanted to do was slope off home and get his head down. He hoped Eddie wouldn't mind too much if he left early. Pulling on his jacket, he flipped the light off and headed out.

Turning his car onto the Princess Parkway a few minutes later, his spirits lifted when he saw that, for once, he had a clear road ahead. He'd have plenty of time to get home, take a shower and change before coming back.

As Paul Dalton drove by below, The Man was furiously pacing his living-room floor. He looked ready to explode, the veins in his face engorged, his neck cords standing out like rigid bars.

Max had never seen him so livid, and he'd certainly never been the cause – either directly or indirectly. He was terrified. And Jake standing behind the couch watching his discomfort with a gleeful smirk wasn't helping matters.

'What do you mean, "gone"?' The Man thundered. 'How'd he manage that when I told you to stay with 'im?'

'I did!' Max spluttered. 'Well . . . for a bit, like. But he said he had nothing to do with it, and—'

'And you just believed him, like a raas sap!' Jake snorted incredulously. Turning to The Man, he thumbed towards Max, sneering. 'For all we know it was him all along! Did you think to ask him where he got all the sponds to be laying an ounce of coke on this scally dealer, eh?'

'Man, I swear to Jah, this ain't nutt'n to do with me!' Max protested his innocence to The Man. Then, jumping to his feet, he turned on Jake, spitting vehemently: 'No way are you setting me up for this! You can think what you like, but I ain't taking the rap for this!'

'Oh yeah?' Jake hissed, his eyes glittering dangerously. 'So how come you—'

'Shut it!' The Man bellowed. Standing between them, he glared at each of them until they snapped their mouths shut, staring at each other in sullen silence.

Turning to Jake, he said, 'It wasn't Max. He wouldn't have risked his neck going back to check on Pasha last night if it was. Now just cool it, 'cos we gotta sort this. Some little cunt is having a game at my expense, and I aim to find out who.'

Jake sniffed. He knew The Man was right, but it bugged him that Max had let Stevo get away so easily.

The Man sat down heavily. 'I need a minute to think this through.'

Max sat down on the edge of the seat and waited while The Man brooded. He shot a look at Jake who was leaning against the door casually twiddling his dreads, and thought if he wasn't so close to The Man he'd be getting a good kicking right now. He was well out of order with his snide remarks.

Not that Jake worried him. What did was knowing that this would escalate before it got sorted. And knowing that he was only tangled up in it because of his own big mouth really pissed him off. He'd lost his ounce, and now he'd lost his two hundred quid – all because he'd tried to do The Man a favour. Well, he wouldn't be that stupid again. The Man he could do nothing about, but if he ever got his hands on Stevo he was going to cut him up into a million pieces!

'Where did this Stevo say he got my money?' The Man asked, his voice calmer, if still sharp.

Max let out a breath. 'Some guy called Millie, or Melly? I think it was Melly. Stevo said he lived over in the Crescents. Robert Adam, I think. I forget what number.'

Jake snorted. 'No kidding!'

The Man turned on him. 'If you got nothing better to do, Jake, go make a drink.'

He waited until Jake had gone into the kitchen, then sat forward and took a spliff from his box. 'Don't pay no mind to Jake,' he told Max. 'He's just looking out for me. He'll come round in time.'

'Yeah, I guess,' Max conceded. 'But you do know it

wasn't me, don't you? And you understand what kind of position Jake is putting me in, saying shit like that.'

'Yeah.' The Man glanced up from beneath his brows. 'Like you must understand the predicament I'm in? You're the only one who knows how to trace where my money came from, and where the rest of it is. That's why I want you to stay on this, Max. I want you to keep digging until you find the thieving muthafucker who wasted my man and took what's mine. And when you find him, you let me know. I'll take it from there, yeah?'

Max nodded reluctantly and sat back, pondering his position. It wasn't good. Finally, he cleared his throat and asked the question that had been burning away inside him.

'Look, man – no offence, but what about my money? When I brought that two hundred round, it was only to show you.'

The Man looked up, his brow creased, his eyes narrowed. 'So what you saying, Max? You want me to give you my money?'

Max shifted uncomfortably. 'Well, no, not exactly. It's just that . . . well, it was your money, but at the same time it wasn't. I mean, it was mine too, wasn't it? Part of what Stevo owed me. It wasn't like he just gave it me for nothing. He owed it, man. I'm sorry it turned out to be part of the shit you lost, but I don't think it's right that I should lose out.'

The Man didn't answer. He carried on smoking his spliff, only looking up to take his glass from Jake when he came in.

Jake had also made a drink for Max – despite a burning desire to cut him up bad. He handed it to him without looking at him and took his own over to the window. Leaning against the wall, he stared out through the crack in the curtain.

Max sipped at the drink and waited. A few minutes passed before The Man finally looked up.

'Right. I've thought about what you said, and I'll tell you what I'm prepared to do. I'll split the difference. I'll give you a ton back now, and the rest when you find out where Stevo is – and who this Melly guy is. Lead me to my money, and I'll make it worth your while. What do you say?'

Jake shook his head in disgust. The Man was definitely going soft. He should be *forcing* Max to take him to these people, not offering a reward and asking him. If he had his way, Max wouldn't see a penny out of this – and he'd be out there now, sorting it out – or he'd be getting some concrete boots for breakfast.

Max wasn't altogether happy with the deal either, but he knew it was better than he could have reasonably expected, given the circumstances. He wasn't happy that The Man expected him to go searching, either. He wished he'd never got involved, and made a mental note to do for both Stevo and Melly when this was sorted – guilty or not.

The Man counted out a hundred and handed it across to Max, secreting the other hundred in his waistcoat pocket.

'Just keep hold of it for now,' he said. 'I want to be sure none of this marked money gets on the street, so I can keep track of it. Is it a deal?'

'Yeah, I suppose so,' Max said, stashing the money quickly before The Man changed his mind.

Just then, the intercom buzzer sounded. The Man motioned Jake to answer it, and watched, frowning, as he took his sweet time sauntering out. The vibes weren't right. Something was shifting between them, and it didn't bode well. If Jake started playing up, he'd have to be taught a serious lesson. Rebellion in his team was the one thing The Man couldn't afford right now. If word got about that his right-hander was hanging loose, the other posses would take it as a sign of weakness and start fucking him up. If that happened he'd end up killing someone, and that was the last thing he needed. He'd worked hard to rise above all that shit.

Still . . . If needs must.

When Jake finally picked up the intercom phone there was no one on the other end. Hanging up, he went to tell The Man. Less than a minute later, there was a knock at the door.

'What the fuck?' The Man hissed. 'Go tek a look, Jake – and be careful.'

Jake went to peep through the spyhole. He hadn't pressed the buzzer to release the door, so no one could have got in that way. And it certainly wouldn't be a neighbour. So who the hell was it?

It was the girl, Linda. Standing in the hallway, pulling at her little skirt and flicking her hair into place.

'It's that slut!' Jake snarled. 'What do you want me to do?'

'Shit!' The Man frowned. 'What's she doing here?'

'Preening herself for all the world to see,' Jake spat.

'Bring her in!' The Man snapped tersely, annoyed that she'd got past the security door without waiting for an invitation. She was starting to do his head in. She'd been amusing for the first week, but now she was becoming a pure irritation. She seemed to think she was something special. It was time to disillusion her.

'Shall I give her a slap?' Jake asked eagerly.

'No! I'll sort this one,' The Man said. Standing, he held his hand out to Max. 'I appreciate your help. And don't forget, I'll make it worth your while if—*when* you find this Melly.'

Max shook The Man's hand. 'Yeah, okay. I'll check you later.'

He followed Jake to the door, leaving without a backward glance as Jake dragged the girl inside, slamming the door behind him.

Wriggling away from Jake, Linda quickly ducked past him and ran into the living room. Rushing over to The Man, who was sitting again, she bent forward to kiss him.

'What's this shit?' he snapped, sticking a hand up to keep her at bay. 'Who said you could come round here?' he went on frostily. 'And how did you get in?'

She faltered. This wasn't the greeting she'd expected. 'A – a man came out while I was waiting, so I just came up . . . Thought I'd save him—' she shot a wary glance at Jake '—having to buzz me in.'

'You don't ever come here without being told to!' The Man shouted, waving his hand angrily. 'You think I want people seeing you come here in broad daylight? Cha! If I want you, I'll tell you!'

'What's wrong?' she whined. 'I thought you'd be glad to see me? Anyway,' she added sulkily. 'I'm your girl-friend. I should be able to come and see you without making an appointment!'

The Man jumped up furiously, pushing her to the floor. 'Don't you ever get sarcastic with me, bitch! And who said you're my girl? Eh? Did I say that? You're giving yourself airs, bitch!'

Linda covered her head with her arms when he raised his hand menacingly. 'Simeon . . . please! I didn't mean to make you angry. What did I do wrong?'

'You got ideas above your station, fool.' Jake grinned nastily. 'No one comes here without an invitation – no one!'

'But . . . but *you*'re always here,' she cried. 'Why can't I come when I want to?'

'What?' Jake snarled. 'You questioning my right to be here?'

The Man reached down and yanked Linda up from the floor. Throwing her down onto a chair, he towered over her, pointing a finger towards Jake as he yelled into her face: 'He is my spar! Whereas you are just a fucking tart! See the difference?'

He leaned closer then, forcing her to cringe back as he pinned her with an icy stare. 'You don't mean *that* to me!' He snapped his fingers in her face. 'Got that?'

Tears spilled from Linda's huge, terrified eyes. Rolling over her spidery lashes, they ran down her cheeks and splashed onto her breasts. As The Man watched their progress, his eyes narrowed suspiciously. Reaching out, he yanked the material of her top down, frowning darkly at the welted stripes and teeth marks adorning her breasts.

'Jake?' he demanded, turning to look at Jake over his shoulder. 'You do this?'

Jake shrugged. 'Yeah . . . so?'

The Man tutted, releasing the material. 'What the hell you playing at, man? I told you not to hurt her.'

'She didn't bleed,' Jake said. 'Anyhow, she enjoyed it!'

The Man shook his head and turned back to the girl. She cowered away from him. The last thing she'd expected was for Jake to tell him what they'd done. What would he do to her now?

'This true?' he asked, a slight smile lifting his lip. 'You enjoy that shit?'

'N-no,' she spluttered. 'I – I . . .'

'Could be useful,' he said, ignoring her as he looked back at Jake, a glimmer of an idea forming in his mind. 'Some a them big-money men like it like that, don't they?' he mused. 'It's usually hard getting these bitches to oblige. I reckon we could make a mint with this one if she likes it rough.'

'W-what do you mean?' Linda whimpered fearfully.

The Man leaned over her again, smiling now, his voice low and velvety. 'I mean, it's time we sorted out that nice little place I've been promising you, eh? You'd like that, wouldn't you, darlin'?'

She nodded, relieved that he wasn't going to kick her out, but confused by this sudden change in his mood.

Standing, he pulled a wad of money from his pocket and handed it to her. 'Tomorrow, I want you to go and buy yourself some nice, sexy things. Don't be getting none of this cheap shit you been wearing, though . . .' He plucked at her skimpy silver halter neck. 'Get some real sophisticated stuff, then go to a girlie place and get some nice innocent stuff: pretty little dresses, and ribbons for your hair, yeah?'

She nodded, taking the money.

'And here, darlin',' he went on, holding out a little folded wrap. 'Go and sort yourself out, there's a good girl. You look a fucking mess.'

Linda smiled happily, licking her lips as she took the wrap from him and tottered off to the bathroom. She'd sort out all that stuff about the big-money men and what-have-you later. For now, she was just glad she wasn't in The Man's bad books. And glad to have this little wrap of happy powder to kiss all those silly little fears away.

'Get on to Marie,' The Man told Jake when she'd gone. 'Get her to sort a place out. In fact, tell her to come over tonight. I want her to see this one – suss her out.'

'What time?' Jake asked. 'You got Max coming over later too, don't forget.'

'Marie's cool. It don't matter what she hears.'

'Yeah, maybe Marie's cool – but *she*'s not,' Jake countered, nodding towards the bathroom.

'Not yet,' The Man agreed. 'Anyhow, Max will ring before he comes.'

'I'll tell her to come at one,' Jake said, heading for the phone.

13

When Paul entered the main bar of The George, the first people he saw were DCI Jackson and his fat friend. They were sitting at a wonky table facing the door and he felt himself blushing as they simultaneously looked his way. Thankfully, they didn't seem to recognize him. He breathed a sigh of relief. One meeting with Jackson had been enough of an unnerving experience. The last thing he needed was to feel self-conscious in his social time.

He went to the bar to get himself a pint and looked around for Eddie. Spotting him in a crowded booth overlooking the pool table – out of Jackson and Mac's view – he made his way over and slid onto the bench seat beside him, nodding hello to the others already seated.

'We're not staying long, are we?' he asked quietly. 'Jackson's round there. I feel funny having him watching me.'

Eddie laughed. 'I've just invited them to come with us. I didn't think you'd mind.'

Paul nearly choked on his beer. 'Tell me you're joking!'

Eddie slapped him on the back and said, 'Do me a favour! Do I look like a brown-noser? They always come in here for a couple when they've finished for the day. What you so nervous of him for, anyway?' he asked teasingly. 'What you been doing, you naughty lad?'

'Nothing,' Paul said. 'It's just that I spoke to him this

morning and – I don't know.' He shrugged. 'He just made me feel a bit weird.'

'Scared you shitless, you mean?' Eddie grinned. 'Ah, don't worry about the old Dragon Master. He's all right – if you avoid him like the plague!'

'I intend to,' muttered Paul.

'Anyway, never mind them,' Eddie went on, pushing himself to his feet. 'We've time for another pint before we set off. What you having?'

'Lager, thanks.' Paul drained his glass quickly and handed it over.

'How are we getting there?' he asked when Eddie came back a few minutes later.

'Cab,' Eddie said. 'I don't know about you, but I'm planning to get well and truly plastered before the night's through, and there's no way I'm driving with that pair of dykes, Nesbitt and Wotserface, on drunk-driver watch!'

'Fake-Man Blake?' Paul volunteered, having heard the unflattering term being bandied around the station.

'That's the one!' Eddie laughed. 'Shit! Wouldn't they just love to pull us in for driving under the influence? They'd have us in cuffs and down at the station faster than they could turn that vibrating truncheon of theirs on!'

Laughing along with the others at the table, Paul began to relax. Maybe tonight wasn't going to be so bad after all.

An hour – and two drinks – later, the group made their noisy exit.

'Haven't I seen that lad somewhere before?' Mac gestured with a nod towards Paul Dalton as the group straggled out.

Jackson looked over. 'Yeah. A bit ago when he came in!'

'No.' Mac shook his head. 'Somewhere else. He's one of ours, isn't he?'

'Oh, that's right.' Jackson nodded. 'He was there this morning. I talked to him and he kept blushing.'

Mac laughed. 'The effect you have on people! They call you the Dragon Master, you know?'

Jackson chuckled. 'Yeah, I know. But they don't know I know. They forget we're shit-hot detectives and it takes us two minutes to learn their every little secret!'

'Talking of secrets,' Mac said, suddenly serious as he remembered something that had been bugging him all day. 'Did you notice how shifty the Singh family were this morning?'

'I noticed how bloody quick they were to get the shop open!' Jackson said, tutting disapprovingly. 'Times change, eh, Mac? Bloody hell, it was unheard of in my day. If someone in your family died – never mind got murdered – the whole place would shut down for a month at least!' He shook his head. 'Maybe I'm getting old, but I don't understand this whole the-show-must-go-on business.' He sighed, picking up his empty glass. 'Another?'

'Thanks.' Mac handed over his empty glass.

Jackson headed off to the bar, leaving Mac to mull over his suspicion that the Singh family weren't altogether kosher. It wasn't just the indecent haste with which they'd opened up the shop – although he had to agree with Jackson on that. Times had changed – for the worse. There was something else. He'd been a bit too busy today to put his finger on it, but something about the nephews niggled him.

'They need looking at,' he said when Jackson came back.

'Who do?' Jackson asked.

'The nephews – the family altogether.'

'Why? What've you got?'

'Just a hunch.' Mac shrugged, taking a swig and licking the foam off his moustache. 'Something about them doesn't sit right. Remember when they got there this morning?' he went on, eyes narrowed with concentration. 'The big one, Guppy – Guptar Wotsisface? Well, I thought it was a bit suss how he kept bugging us to let them in. Like all he was bothered about from the time they got there was getting access to the shop, even though his uncle was lying in a pool of blood in the back yard. Just doesn't feel right, that.'

'Maybe he couldn't face seeing his uncle in that state,' Jackson said. 'Does funny things to people when they lose a loved one in those circumstances.'

Mac shook his head slowly. 'No, it wasn't that. He was the one who did the ID, if you remember, and he went straight in without a flicker of emotion.'

Jackson considered what Mac was saying. He hadn't paid too much attention at the time but, on reflection, he supposed Mac was right. The eldest nephew had been very matter-of-fact in his viewing of his uncle's body. No tears, no shock – nothing. If anything, Jackson reflected, he'd looked pissed off. And he'd certainly sounded it when he'd been barking at his brothers in their own language – not a word of which Jackson had understood, which was probably why he'd switched off and not noticed the untoward behaviour.

'If you ask me,' Mac continued, 'he was more concerned about getting in the shop than anything. Like he was worried about something inside. Something he didn't want anyone else to get to first.'

Jackson frowned. 'I know what you're saying, Mac. Trouble is, it's only a gut feeling – not that I don't trust them, especially yours – but that's all it is at the end of the day. We'd never get the go-ahead to go over the shop. Not while it happened outside and the nephews aren't suspects. Their alibis are watertight.'

'Nothing's watertight,' said Mac. 'And if we're looking for motive, what goes on inside the shop might have some bearing.'

'We'll have a hard time proving they're involved,' said Jackson. 'They're on the video leaving the shop through the front door at twelve-fifteen, and Singh triple-locked the door behind them. They went straight to The Pink Casino down Canal Street, and the casino's video shows all three arriving at twelve twenty-five, while the shop video shows Singh leaving by the back door at twelve thirty-seven. There's no way they could have done it. It's just not possible.'

'All right, so maybe they didn't do the dirty work themselves,' said Mac. 'Maybe they paid someone to do it for them? It'd be easy enough, and they've definitely got the funds.'

'It'd be easy enough to arrange,' Jackson agreed. 'The place is crawling with scum capable of it. Good thing is, most of them are so stupid they'd slash their own throats for a few quid.'

'Good thing?'

'They're all so bloody thick,' Jackson explained, 'that it wouldn't take us long to weasel it out of one of them if someone had been paid by the family.'

Mac nodded, taking another drink and letting out a

loud burp. 'We'll take a look through the files tomorrow and line up some likelies, eh? Drag 'em in and give 'em a shake-up.'

'We'll need something pretty solid before we start ruffling any big bastards' feathers,' Jackson said. 'It's my bet the Singh family would sue the bollocks off us if we started casting aspersions without a bloody good reason. So we'll follow your hunch – but quietly.'

'Agreed,' said Mac, draining his glass. 'Another?'

The party was in full flow when they arrived. They didn't have tickets, but Eddie managed to get them in with a flash of his badge – and a promising wink at the two giggling young nurses manning the ticket table. 'All professionals together, eh, girls?'

As Eddie lingered to take the nurses' phone numbers, the others wandered inside to find a table. Paul stayed with Eddie, determined not to end up sticking out like a sore thumb.

Inside, the place was packed to the rafters. 'Who the hell's looking after the patients?' Paul hissed.

'Bugger the patients,' Eddie said. 'I need a bit of tender loving care myself!' Spotting three nurses chatting at the end of the bar, he nudged Paul, motioning towards them with his head. 'Mine's the blonde. Come on!'

Paul followed as Eddie pushed a path through the heaving bodies to the nurses. The blonde Eddie had earmarked was gorgeous, the other two plainer – one particularly so. As tall as both Paul and Eddie – and wider than either – she had a large, flat face and dull, dark blonde hair. Her warm, sparkly-eyed smile took Paul totally by surprise.

'Hi,' she said, holding out her hand. 'I'm Jane.'

'Er – Paul,' he said, shaking her hand. 'And that's Eddie.' He gestured towards his colleague who was busy chatting up the blonde.

Eddie turned and nodded hello, pulling an almost imperceptible face when he spotted Jane. Paul squirmed, embarrassed by his bad manners, but Jane didn't seem to notice – or, if she did, she didn't let it show.

'This is Vanda,' she said, introducing Paul to the other nurse. 'And the one whose bottom seems to fit your friend's hand so perfectly—' she nodded towards Eddie, who was indeed fondling the blonde's backside '—is Asia.'

Paul raised a brow. 'Asia? That's unusual.'

'Unusual girl,' Jane whispered with a giggle. Leaning closer she added: 'As your friend is sure to find out if he carries on.'

Paul looked at her quizzically. She laughed, then cupped her hand around his ear to whisper something. Almost choking, he shot a look at Eddie and wondered if he should warn him. Then he decided not to. *Let the lecherous sod find out the hard way*, he thought.

When Eddie went off to dance with his conquest, Paul didn't mind because he was having a good time with Jane and Vanda. It was almost an hour before they spotted an empty table. Paul sent them to grab it while he bought a round.

'So,' Jane said when they were seated. 'You're a copper, are you?'

'Yeah, that's right. This is my second year.'

'Ah, a baby,' Vanda said. 'Thought you were too polite to have been at it long.'

'Where are you stationed?' Jane asked.

'Moss Side,' he told her.

'Oh, we get a lot of your lads in,' she said. 'They're regulars down at Cas, aren't they, Van?'

'Yeah.' Vanda nodded. 'Never a night goes by without one of your lot bringing someone in in handcuffs. It makes it very difficult to treat them, you know.'

'Mmmm,' Jane added thoughtfully. 'And they're always so beat up. Makes you wonder what goes on in the back of the police vans!'

'It's not us!' Paul protested. 'Honest!'

Jane laughed. 'Don't worry, we're just teasing.'

'If you want my opinion,' Vanda said, 'I reckon some of them could do with a good kicking. Like that one you had in last night, cheeky sod!'

'I know!' Jane squealed. 'I couldn't believe it!'

'I'd have chopped his bloody hands off,' Vanda said.

'What's this?' Paul asked, intrigued.

'Oh, just this bloke who came into Casualty last night,' Vanda said. 'I'll let Jane tell you.'

Jane's eyes sparkled as she told the story, and Paul couldn't help but smile.

'. . . And the next thing I knew,' she said, coming to the end, 'he had his hand up my bloody skirt! Well, I just couldn't believe it!'

Paul was grinning now. 'What did you do?'

'I bloody well lamped him one!' she said, bristling with self-righteous indignation. 'And if it hadn't been for the doctor walking in, I'd have ripped his fucking head off! Oops!' She threw a hand across her mouth. 'Pardon my French!'

'Don't worry about it,' Paul laughed. 'Good to know you're human.'

'Gee, thanks!' she said, mock-offended. 'And just what did you think I was? Robot? Animal?'

'Oh, God! I'm sorry!' he spluttered. 'I didn't mean that!'

Jane laughed good-naturedly. 'Don't worry about it.'

'So was he with one of ours, then?' Paul asked, covering his embarrassment behind his glass.

Jane took a drink and slammed her glass down. 'No, but he bloody should have been! Handcuffs were invented for creeps like him – people who can't keep their hands to themselves. I'm so glad I'm on earlies now. The creeps don't like the daylight.'

'What was he in for again?' Vanda asked. 'Didn't you say he'd been shot?'

Paul's ears pricked up, a tingle of anticipation bristling the hairs on his neck. 'Pardon? Did you say shot?'

'Well, no,' Jane said. 'Not exactly. He'd smashed his head open, which needed quite a lot of stitching, and he'd cut his arm.' She motioned with her hand across her bicep. 'It wasn't too bad, as it turned out, but when I first looked at it, I don't know why, I just thought it looked like a bullet wound.'

'What made you think that?' Paul pressed.

She shrugged. 'Because it was a perfect line, I suppose. Like something had gone across it really fast and burned it.'

'So what was it?' Paul asked.

'He slipped climbing the fence at Alex Park,' she told him, rolling her eyes. 'You know the railings there? The big metal spiked ones? Well, he slipped on them and caught his arm on one of the spikes, and when he fell, he smashed his head.'

'Oh, I see,' Paul felt deflated. 'Still . . . while we're on the subject of shooting injuries, you didn't happen to get any in last night, did you?'

Jane shook her head. 'Not that I know of. Sorry.'

Eddie came over to the table then, his beaming face red and sweaty. He picked up the pint Paul had bought him and took a long swallow before slamming it back down.

'Having a good time with Asia?' Jane asked innocently.

'Wonderful!' he announced. He patted Paul on the shoulder then, winking as he said, 'Don't mind if I abandon you, do you?'

'Not in the slightest,' Paul smirked, wincing as Jane and Vanda kicked him under the table. 'I'll see myself home. Have fun!'

'Oh, I aim to!' said Eddie.

14

It was ten-thirty. Only a few hours since they'd left the hospital for their celebration party, but the events of the night before, added to the mixture of drugs they'd indulged in since arriving back at the flat, were beginning to take their toll.

Mal had got them all so coked up in the first hour back that Sam had eventually begged for something to bring him down. Now they were all zonked on the temazepam Lee and Elaine had managed to score from the junkie with the dogs on the floor above.

Ged was sleeping – naturally, having neither wanted the coke nor needed the temazepam.

Elaine – quiet, at last – was huddled on the couch with Lee, who had a possessive arm around her as they watched yet another of the videos he'd persuaded Sam to drive over to his flat for.

Mal and Sam were playing cards on the coffee table, with the entire contents of Suzie's copper jar spread before them as betting money.

Suzie herself was curled up on Mal's chair – fed up to the back teeth that Elaine was still here and seemed to have no intention of ever going home again. Suzie was also more than a little pissed off that she hadn't been offered any of the coke. Not that she would have taken it if she had been – it was the principle of the thing. Elaine was not only offered the stuff but actively encouraged to have some. It wasn't fair.

She was just wondering if anyone would notice if she slipped off to bed when Sam threw his cards down with a loud slap.

'Well, that's me!' he declared. 'I'm whacked. I'm off home.'

'Aw, not yet!' Mal said. Gathering the cards together, he shuffled them and started to redeal.

'I've got to,' Sam insisted, struggling to his feet. 'Have you seen the time? Louise has been on her own with the kids since last night. She must be going spare.'

'She'll be all right,' Mal said. 'Just give her another ring.'

'No, I can't.' Sam was adamant. 'Wendy's gonna flip as it is.'

'Fuck Wendy!' Mal snapped, annoyed that he wasn't getting his own way.

'Oh, yes, please!' Lee piped up, wincing as Elaine dug him in the ribs with her elbow.

Sam patted his pockets for his keys, then tapped Ged on the shoulder. 'I'm off, Ged. Do you want a lift?'

Ged stretched and bounced to his feet. 'Yeah. Thanks, mate.'

'Not got your car?' Lee asked.

'Nah.' Ged shook his head. 'It's not taxed or MOT'd so I don't drive it unless I have to.'

'It's a heap of shit anyway,' Lee went on with a smirk. 'My Mark II creams it!'

'The Mark I's got a better engine,' Ged retorted smoothly.

'Can we go?' Sam asked impatiently. 'I'm knackered.'

'Yeah, sorry,' Ged said, frowning at himself for getting into Lee's game of one-up.

'Think I'll go to bed as well,' Suzie said, getting up stiffly.

'Night, sweetheart,' Ged said, smiling as he followed Sam to the door.

'Yeah, night, Suzie,' Sam called, waving back at her. 'Night everyone.'

'Night-night, John-Boy and Jim-Bob!' Elaine yelled after them. 'Night, Grandma!' she added, looking pointedly at Suzie.

Ignoring her, Suzie went to bed.

Ged and Sam began to come alive in the cold night air as they lumbered down the stairwell a minute later. As they rounded the corner and stepped into the tunnel, a man turned in from the road end. They carried on walking, paying him no heed as he came towards them. He was big, but Ged was bigger, and Sam was glad to his heart to have him there. He was still paranoid about bumping into the City Road Posse, but with Ged to back him up he knew he'd stand a chance of escaping unhurt – unless they pulled a gun.

Max passed the two men, then turned back and called out to them. 'Yo!'

Turning, Ged jerked his chin up suspiciously. 'Yeah?'

'You live here?' Max asked.

'No, just visiting,' Ged said. 'Why? What's up?'

'I'm looking for someone called Melly,' Max told him. 'Millie, or Melly. Something like that. Know him?'

Ged and Sam looked at each other and shrugged. 'Nah, sorry, mate.'

'Right, thanks.'

Max turned and headed for the stretch of grass as Ged and Sam carried on walking down the tunnel.

'Hang about,' Sam said as they came to the road end. 'There is a bloke called Millie. Smack dealer – lives on William Kent.'

'Oh, yeah,' Ged said. 'Milton something-or-other. Little fella?'

'That's the one. Should we tell him?' Sam nodded towards Max who was standing on the grass, looking up at the flats.

Ged considered it, then shook his head. 'Nah. I want to get home. Come on.'

They got into the car and Sam reversed out. Driving past the tunnel they both looked to see if the man had gone. He was still there. Sam stopped the car and wound his window down.

'What are you doing?' Ged asked.

Sam wrinkled his nose sheepishly. 'Let's put him out of his misery, eh?'

Ged laughed. 'You're a right soft git, sometimes. Go on, then.'

'Yo, mate!' Sam called.

Max turned and peered at them down the tunnel. Sam waved him over.

'This bloke you're looking for,' he said when Max reached them.

'Yeah?' Max leaned down with his hands on his knees. 'You know him?'

'I know someone called Millie,' Sam said. 'Lives on the third floor of that block over there.' He pointed back through the tunnel.

'What number?'

'Sorry, I don't know that,' Sam said. 'But someone over there will. It's on the third floor, anyway. Just ask when you get there.'

'Respect!' Max put his fist into the car, touching it to both of theirs. 'I owe you one!'

'No problem.' Sam grinned and, waving, pulled away. 'Nice guy,' he commented.

Ged shook his head with a smile. 'Mr Bleeding Heart!'

Fuelled by a sudden rush of adrenalin, Max hurried across the grass towards William Kent Crescent. At least Stevo had given him the right name – just the wrong block. All he had to do was find out which flat it was, and this whole mess would be sorted.

Except for the ounce he'd laid out that morning.

He ground his teeth angrily. He was going to cut Stevo up so bad for taking off like that. And he wasn't in the mood for poncing about these flats either, but he had no choice. Stevo had a lot to answer for!

As luck would have it, just as he crossed the road heading for the stairwell, three young student types came out. So busy looking at whatever the one in the centre was holding, they didn't see Max until he stepped in front of them. They stopped dead then, their eyes wide with fright.

They were only too willing to point him in the direction of Millie's flat when they realized he wasn't going to mug them. They'd just come from there themselves, they told him, and yes – Millie was alone. Max thanked them, advising them to stash their gear away before the Babylon gripped them.

He shook his head with amusement as the boys legged it to an ancient Volkswagen Beetle to make their noisy escape.

Now to find number 327.

*   *   *

Elaine giggled as Lee and Mal coaxed her to take another line. She was being treated like a queen, and loving every minute of it. She was so glad she'd met up with Suzie again. But, God! What was up with the girl? She'd turned into a right miserable cow. She'd done nothing but whinge all day. Still. That was *her* problem. Elaine was having fun.

Taking the rolled-up fiver from Mal, she leaned over the mirror and snorted – wondering why she'd never got into this before.

'Go on, girl!' Lee encouraged her. 'Get the whole lot down yer neck!'

The rush knocked her for six. She clenched her fists, clamping her teeth together as a million starlight prickles coursed up through her body, from her feet right up to her head, lifting the hair right off her scalp.

'Oh, yeah, baby!' Lee leered, eyeing her nipples as they stiffened beneath her T-shirt. 'Let it ride!'

'Charlie loves a virgin!' Mal laughed.

'Eh! I ain't no virgin!' Elaine giggled, opening her eyes at last.

'Well, I never would have guessed!' Mal teased her.

Taking the tube, he bent his head over the mirror. 'Put another film on, Lee,' he said, snorting the fattest of the lines.

15

Dead on one o'clock, Jake pressed the buzzer to release the security door down below. Then he unlocked the flat door and waited. Finally, Marie appeared, hauling herself up the last flight with a hand on the rail.

'Wotcha, darlin'!' she puffed, stopping to take a breath. 'Bugger me, them stairs are a killer! He inside, is he?'

Jake nodded and waved her in with a smile. Marie was the only one of The Man's girls he could stomach. Well into her forties, she was sassy and smart. She might look a bit done in, with her dyed black hair backcombed like a poodle's tail, and the face of a seasoned battler, but she was sharp as a knife. She'd been on the game for twenty-odd years because she wanted to be, not because she'd been forced into it by a pimp, or lured by drugs. She never touched drugs – just alcohol. But she was in control of that and, in a funny way, Jake respected her.

The Man definitely did. Probably because he'd never had any sort of relationship with her, other than business. And she was good at that side of things. He trusted her judgement implicitly. And she was a real asset when it came to keeping the other girls in line – not averse to slapping them down if necessary, or tipping Jake the wink when they were on the fiddle.

Marie had her hands on her hips when Jake joined them, looking down at Linda who was sleeping in a heap on the floor by the couch. 'Bit young, Sim,' she was saying. 'You sure she's kosher?'

'She reckons she's nineteen,' The Man said. 'You think she's lying?'

Marie gave him a look, then shrugged. 'Far be it from me to call the kid a liar when I ain't even spoken her. You got anything to drink in this place?'

'Yeah, sure. What's it to be? Coffee? Tea?'

Marie gave a raucous belly laugh and flopped down into a chair, kicking her shoes off and rubbing her toes. 'Do me a favour! I'm bollocksed! Give us a Scotch.'

The Man nodded to Jake to pour the drink. Then he sat down, facing Marie. Leaning forward with his elbows on his knees, he nodded towards Linda. 'What do you reckon, then?'

Marie groaned and put her feet down. Reaching across, she moved the girl's hair away from her face and took a good look. Leaning back, she put her feet up on the coffee table and reached into her bag for a cigarette.

'Pretty,' she said at last. 'I can see why you picked up on her. But, if you want my honest opinion, she's never nineteen. More like sixteen, I'd say. Still, that's legal, so you haven't got a problem. Oh, thanks, luv.' Taking the Scotch and ice from Jake, she swallowed a mouthful and wiped her hand across her mouth. 'God! I needed that! Now then. You didn't get me over her just to tell you if I think she's pretty or not, did you? What's the plan?'

'She needs a place,' The Man said. 'Somewhere a bit decent.'

Marie raised an eyebrow. 'Think she's a bit special, then, do you?'

The Man gave her a lopsided smile and tapped the side

of his nose. 'Me hear tell she likes playing rough, so me figure she'd go down a bomb with the city-slicker men. Them we had to turf out last year, seen? The ones with all the money!'

'You mean them clowns what messed Samantha up?' Marie cast a worried look at the girl. 'Bit much for her, ain't they? Thought you said she'd never done this before?'

'Jake auditioned her.' The Man laughed. 'Seems she can tek it, no problem!'

Marie shot a glance at Jake. 'You been naughty?' she asked, mock-stern. 'Tut, tut!'

Jake grinned. 'She keen for it, Marie. Believe me – she keen!'

'Well, you got nothing to lose by trying her out,' Marie said. 'Needs a bit of work, though.'

'Yeah, I know.' The Man nodded. 'It's sorted. I gave her some money to get herself some gear. You tek her downtown tomorrow and help her choose some tasty stuff, yeah? You know better than me what them pervy guys like.'

'Sure,' Marie agreed. 'No probs. Now, about this place you want. How's about she comes in with me for a bit? That way I can coach her, and keep an eye on her – make sure she don't get too roughed up, like.'

'Hey, that'd be great!' The Man smiled. He pulled some money from his pocket and handed it to Marie. 'Take this, then – to keep her while she's learning. I'll give you more in a week, depending how it goes, yeah?'

'Sound as a pound!' Marie said, sticking the money in her shoe. 'How about family?' she asked then, the flicker of a frown crossing her face. 'I don't need no irate mother calling the pigs on me.'

The Man shrugged. 'Dunno, I ain't asked her. But she seems to come and go as she pleases.'

Marie nodded. 'Good. I can't be doin' with any of that shit. When do I get her, then?'

'Now, if you want,' The Man said – pleased to be killing two birds with one stone, since Max would be coming over soon.

'You wanna wake her up, then?' Marie said. 'Only you know I hate touching smack-heads. That *is* what she's on, innit?'

'She's only had a little bit.' The Man shrugged. 'Jake can carry her down and give you a ride home, yeah?'

'That'd be fantastic,' Marie said, smiling gratefully. 'Me feet are throbbing like a donkey's dick already, without having to traipse about looking for a taxi!' Gulping the remnants of her drink down in one, she swung her feet to the floor and, groaning, forced her feet back into her shoes.

Jake shook Linda's shoulder until she stirred.

'Whazzup?' she mumbled.

'It's time to go,' he said, pulling her to her feet.

She was confused, stumbling and clutching at Jake to keep her footing as he walked her to the door. 'Where we going?' she asked. 'What's happening?'

'You're going to stay with this nice lady,' he told her, leading her out of the flat and down the stairs.

In the doorway, Marie turned to The Man with a serious expression. 'There's just one thing, Sim. If I'm taking the kid on, I don't want her touching the gear again. It's different with them slags out there. They got on it all by themselves and don't need no help staying on it. But she's just a kid. It'll fuck her up.'

The Man shrugged. 'Do what you want with her. Just make sure she starts earning big – and quick.'

'Depends how long she's been on the shit,' Marie said.

'Only been doing it this past week,' The Man said. 'It shouldn't be a problem getting her off.'

'Well, I'll tell you what,' Marie said. 'I'll give her a week to sort her head out before I start training her. That all right?'

'Whatever you think best,' he said. 'I'll bell you to-morrow, yeah?'

'Yeah, okay.' Marie waved and headed down the stairs.

Max was downhearted as he pressed the buzzer ten minutes later. He'd found Millie, all right – had spent the last few hours kicking the shit out of him and trashing his gaff – but the little ponce had had nothing. He rehearsed what he was going to tell The Man as he trooped up the stairs.

'Well?' The Man demanded, waving him to his usual chair. 'You find him?'

'Yeah, I found him.' Max sat back nervously.

'And?'

'And . . . nutt'n,' Max admitted.

'What you mean, nutt'n?' The Man bellowed. 'You find the claat, then come tell me nutt'n?'

'He didn't have it,' Max said. 'I just spent hours going over him, trashing his gaff, and there was nothing there. I swear it!'

'He must have stashed it somewhere, then!' The Man bellowed. 'Did you even bother asking him?'

'Course I did!' Max wiped a hand across his sweaty

brow. 'But he said he's never heard of no Pasha, and didn't know nothing about this Stevo!'

'And what do you think?' The Man asked, looking hard at Max. 'Did you believe him?'

'I don't know,' Max said. 'But I don't think he'd have carried on lying so long, the kicking I gave him. I got the feeling he was on the level.'

The Man began to pace backwards and forwards the length of the room, kicking at anything in his way. 'I want my fucking money, Max! And I want the fucking cunt who did it. I don't care what it tek, I'm gonna find 'im. An' when I do – I'll kill 'im!'

'I don't know what else to do,' Max said glumly. 'I've been back to Stevo's place and he's not there. And this Millie ain't got nutt'n. What am I supposed to do?'

'All right,' The Man snapped. 'Tell me where this Millie is. I'll go round there myself, and if he don't give me what I want, I'll blow his fucking brains out. I'm through with playing games!'

Max groaned. This was ridiculous. Millie had been petrified. There was no way he knew where the money was. He'd have given it up if he did. The tasty cut Max had given him across the cheek would have guaranteed that if nothing else. He didn't see what good it was going to do if The Man went over there. More likely than not, The Man would end up killing the little scab, and where would that leave Max? In the shit – that was where! He'd been seen asking for the guy, and his prints were all over his gaff. If The Man did for him, it would be Max who'd end up in the frame. He tried to explain this to The Man.

'What you don't seem to understand,' The Man snarled back at him, 'is that apart from being lumbered with a shitload of gear Pasha should have been taking off my hands – that I've now got to unload on someone else – I lost a fuck of a lot of money last night! And so far this cunt of yours is the only lead I've got to get it back. And it ain't just the money at stake here,' he went on furiously. 'What d'y' think'll happen if I let this ride and word gets out? Every raas fucker out there will think I've lost it, that's what! I'm telling you, Max, I ain't gonna sit back and let every little ponce in the area think they can walk on my fucking head! I've got to make an example of this little rip-off smack-head! Now tell me where he is!'

Max moaned, flopping his head back and rubbing at his throbbing temples. 'Think what you're doing to me, man! You'll hand me to the Babylon on a plate if you go round there! Can't you see that?'

The Man punched the back of the couch. 'Shit, man! You want me to creep down like a raas pussy and bury my head in the sand? How can I, eh? There's too much at fucking stake here!'

'Look, man . . .' Max sat forward. 'Be reasonable. There's got to be another way. There's got to be something we can do without you dropping me in it. For fuck's sake, man, this wasn't nutt'n to do with me in the first place!'

'Oh, but it was,' The Man countered, his voice low and mean. 'If you hadn't been mixed up with these skanky smack-head rip-off merchants you wouldn't be in this mess now!'

'That's a pile of shit!' Max slapped a hand down on his leg. He was getting riled now. He'd always respected The Man, but now he was pure taking liberties. 'Nah, man!' He shook his head angrily. 'You ain't got no right involving me like this!' He jumped to his feet, his eyes blazing. 'I was doing you a favour, man – I didn't expect you to diss me for it like this! I've had it with this shit, man. I ain't sitting by while you drop me right in it. Nah!'

'Sit down,' The Man growled, glowering at Max over the back of the couch.

'Nah, man . . . It ain't right!'

'Sit . . . down!'

Max dropped back into his chair, huffing. The Man came around the couch and sat down, facing him. His nostrils flaring, he breathed deeply, consciously calming himself to regain a clear perspective on the situation.

'All right,' he said at last. 'I admit you've got a point, Max. I won't do nutt'n right now. I'll wait a couple of days . . . let some people see your boy Millie alive and well, so no one can finger you when I get round to him. Okay?'

'Okay,' Max grumbled. 'Only, let me know when you're planning to go so I can get myself an alibi, yeah?'

'Sure. I'll tell you when. Don't worry.'

Suzie's eyes were open before she even realized she was awake. She stared at the clock on the bedside table, unable to focus for a moment. Then the fog cleared and she saw that it was only one forty-five. She'd been asleep for just over three hours. So why had she woken up again?

Then she heard the sounds again – the ones that had penetrated her dream, alerting her subconscious that something wasn't right. They were coming from the living room. Hushed whispering, and muffled giggles. Surely it wasn't Elaine? She should have gone ages ago. Then again, if Lee was setting up camp on the couch she'd probably decided to stay with him.

Turning over, she was surprised to find that Mal

wasn't beside her. Why hadn't he left them alone and come to bed, she wondered. They were probably dying to get it on, and Mal was more likely than not cramping their style. He could be so thick-skinned sometimes. On the other hand, he was likely to have fallen asleep on the floor.

Rubbing the sleep from her eyes, she sat up and reached for the dressing gown lying across the foot of the bed. She'd go and check, she decided. Wake him if he was sleeping, or, if they were still partying, join them – try to make amends for being such a moody bitch all day.

All right, so Elaine had turned up a few days early – did it really make a difference? Anyway, Elaine was going out with Lee now, so she'd probably be around a lot from now on. And maybe it wouldn't be so bad to have a friend of her own again.

Pushing her feet into her slippers, she pulled the dressing gown tight and padded into the hall. The noises were louder here. She paused outside the living-room door, frowning. It sounded like Elaine and Lee were at it. But surely not? Not in front of Mal.

She hesitated with her hand on the door handle. Maybe Mal had nipped out? He could have gone over to Sam's, or down to the all-night garage?

When she heard Mal telling Lee to get the mirror out, she smiled. He was still here after all. The sex sounds must be coming from one of the videos.

Pulling on the handle, she pushed the door open. Nothing could have prepared her for the sight that greeted her. Elaine was at it, all right – but not with Lee. With Mal!

All three of them were naked, but Lee had obviously had his turn as he was now lining a heap of coke up on the mirror, watching Mal as he bent Elaine beneath him over the couch to take her from behind. And Elaine was squealing like a stuck pig, obviously enjoying every second!

Suzie stood there for an eternity of seconds, transfixed by the sight of the sordid scene. Unable to speak, she began to hyperventilate as her racing heart seemed to leap into her throat, blocking her breathing.

As a wave of dizziness overtook her, she felt herself falling and just about managed to clutch at the door to stop herself crashing to the floor in a dead faint.

Hearing the sound of her palm slapping against the wood, all three of them turned to look over to the door at the same time. Suzie saw their faces change like a slow-motion cartoon. Lee's was a picture of shocked horror. Elaine's crumpled, not sure whether to laugh or cry. But Mal . . . Mal looked neither shocked nor horrified. If anything, he looked perversely pleased.

His mouth lifted at the corner and, without missing a stroke, he said, 'Come to join the fun, doll?'

'Mal?' she wheezed. 'What are you doing?'

'Thought you'd be able to work that out!' he sneered, mid-thrust. 'Obvious enough, innit?'

Unable to bear it, she turned and fled from the room. Lee shouted after her, but she ignored him and ran into the bedroom, slamming the door behind her.

Leaning her back against the door, she stared around the room in wild disbelief. No . . . No! It couldn't have been real! She was still in bed – still dreaming! She had to be. Mal wouldn't do this to her – he wouldn't betray her like this. He loved her.

The door handle rattled against her back, and Elaine's voice came through the wood.

'Suzie – it's me. Open the door, Sooze. Come on. Let me in. I just want to talk to you. Suzie?'

'Piss off!' Suzie screamed, pressing back harder against the door. 'Just piss off, and leave me alone!'

'Aw, don't be like that,' Elaine wheedled. 'It's not how it looked. Just let me in so I can explain.'

Suzie gulped back a great sob as it bubbled up in her throat. Not how it looked? How could it be anything *but* how it looked?

'Suzie – please let me in,' Elaine persisted.

'All right!' Suzie yelled, wrenching the door open so suddenly that Elaine fell into the bedroom. 'Go on, then,' she demanded. 'Explain to me how it wasn't how it looked!'

'Aw, Sooze,' Elaine simpered, reaching out to touch Suzie's arm. Suzie snatched it away.

'Don't touch me!' she hissed, glaring at Elaine's moon face. 'How could you do this to me, Elaine? You're supposed to be my friend!'

Elaine closed the door and sat on the bed. Patting the space beside her, she looked up at Suzie sheepishly. 'Come and sit down, Sooze, please. I didn't mean to hurt you, and I am your friend. Honest.'

Suzie sank down on the bed, afraid that if she didn't she would fall. She felt as though she'd been knifed through the heart. And here was Elaine talking to her like it was no big deal.

Ahh . . . Sorry I ate your last Rolo, Suzie. I'll get you another packet tomorrow. Honest I will.

Elaine reached for her hand. 'I swear I never meant none of this to happen. It just sort of did. You know what it's like.'

'No, I don't!' Suzie sobbed, snatching her hand away,

amazed that Elaine was being so blasé. 'I would never have gone with *your* bloke like that!'

Elaine giggled. 'No, I don't suppose you would. Not with Lee, anyhow. But you're dead lucky, ain't you?' she added enviously. 'Your Mal's so gorgeous, I just couldn't resist. You understand, don't you? Bleedin' hell, girl, it's not like he *fancies* me or nothing.'

'He fancied you enough to get it up for you,' Suzie snapped, swiping at the tears with the back of her hand.

'Come off it!' Elaine scoffed. 'It was them bleedin' films of Lee's what done it! Gawd, girl – have you seen 'em? They're proper horny. Got us all at it, they did.'

Suzie gave her a withering look. 'I noticed!'

Elaine dipped her head and peered up into Suzie's face. 'Oh, come on. It wasn't personal. You got to see the funny side, ain't you?'

'Funny side? What's funny about walking in on my fella screwing my mate?'

'So we *are* still mates, then?' said Elaine. 'You don't hate me? You know I wouldn't have done it if I thought it'd hurt you.'

'So how did you think I'd feel, Elaine?' Suzie asked quietly. 'You couldn't have thought I'd be all right about it?'

Elaine shrugged. 'God. I don't know. I thought you might have seen it as a bit of a giggle. I suppose I even thought we might have done a bit of swapping, like.'

'Swapping?' Suzie spat the word out. 'You haven't even been with Lee two minutes, and you're talking about swapping?'

'How did you know Lee only took two minutes?' Elaine sniggered. Leaning forward, she whispered conspiratorially: 'Have you seen his thingy?' She stuck her little finger out and wiggled it. 'Talk about fish bait!'

Suzie couldn't help but smile. 'You're terrible!' she said.

Elaine smiled, obviously relieved. 'So, we're still friends then? Forgive me?'

'Mmmm, I suppose so,' Suzie murmured, then added sternly: 'Only don't let it happen again.'

'Top one!' Elaine exclaimed, throwing her arms around Suzie. 'You know what? You're sound, you are!'

'Yeah, well, don't think I'll be so forgiving if I ever catch you at it with Mal again,' Suzie warned, disentangling herself.

'Aw, I am sorry,' Elaine said. 'Honest, Sooze. I promise I'll behave from now on!' She pushed herself up from the bed. 'Are you coming in?'

Suzie shook her head. 'No. I need a bit of time to myself.'

'Okey-doke.' Elaine smiled and opened the door. 'See you in a bit, then.'

Lee was really concerned about Suzie. He'd nearly died when she'd walked in and caught them at it, and he didn't understand how Mal could be so cool about it. You had to admire him, though – the way he'd just carried on as if nothing was wrong while his woman looked on. Still, she hadn't half looked upset.

'Do you think she'll be all right?' he asked for the third time.

Mal snorted contemptuously. 'She'd bleedin' better be! She'll cop for a kicking if she starts any crap with me. I ain't taking jealous shite from her or no bird.'

'Must have been a shock, though, eh?'

'I don't give a flying fuck!' Mal barked. 'She can think

what she wants, but she ain't telling me who I can or can't shag!'

'Does that mean I can give your Suzie one, then?' Lee's eyes lit up. 'You give my Elaine one and I'll give your Suzie one?'

Mal's face darkened. 'I'll tell you what, mate,' he snarled. 'You ever lay a fucking finger on my Suzie, I'll slice your fucking dick off!'

'Eh?' Lee looked up to see if he was being serious. Seeing that he was, he went back to his task of chopping lines on the mirror.

'Tell you what,' he said a minute later, 'you want to let your Suzie have a bit of this. Did you see what it did to my 'Lane, eh? Turned her nympho, this stuff did.'

'Suzie ain't touching it!' Mal snapped. 'Anyhow – while we're on the subject, you still owe me some dosh for what you and her have had tonight. Cost me, that did. So come on – cough up.'

Elaine walked back into the room just as Lee pulled a huge wad of notes from his pocket. Her eyes widened at the sight of so much money – in her new boyfriend's hand!

'Cor! Where'd you get that?' she asked, dropping to her knees beside him. 'Here, let's have a look. Can I hold it?'

'She all right?' Mal asked, nodding towards the door.

'Thought you didn't care!' Lee piped up.

'Shut your trap,' Mal snapped. 'I just want to know where her head's at. You know what birds are like for sulking.'

'She's fine,' Elaine said. 'I told her it were them films sending us all nuts. She'll be out in a bit. Just wants to get her head sorted. Come on, Lee.' She turned her attention back to the money. 'Giz a hold!'

'There's plenty more where that came from,' Mal told her, relieved to hear that Suzie was all right – not that he was about to admit it. 'Play your cards right,' he went on, 'and Lee might treat you to something nice.'

'Will you, Lee?' She grinned.

'I might,' said Lee. 'If you behave y'self!'

'You're ace, you!' she said, snatching the wad and flipping her fingers slowly through it. 'Cor! There's hundreds here!'

'Thousands,' Lee corrected her smugly. 'Thousands and thousands!'

'Where did you get it?' she asked breathlessly.

'Ah, that'd be telling!' Mal teased.

'Aw, please!' Elaine begged. 'Go on – you can trust me!'

Lee didn't see why he shouldn't tell her – she was his girlfriend, after all. He shouldn't be keeping secrets from her. But rather than incur Mal's wrath, he waited for his permission.

'Go on, then,' Mal laughed. 'I know you're dying to tell someone. Might as well be her.'

'Okay . . .' Lee started. 'I'll tell you, but first you've got to promise not to breathe a word to no one!'

'Promise!' Elaine said. 'Cross me heart and hope to die!'

'All right. Well, you know Pasha . . .?'

'Suzie? You awake, doll?' Mal whispered, creeping into the bedroom a little while later.

Suzie didn't answer. She felt the bed dip as he sat down to take his clothes off, and wondered bitterly why he'd bothered putting them back on in the first place.

'You didn't half give me a heart attack when you

walked in back there,' Mal went on, still whispering. 'Here, she's a right dirty whore, that friend of yours, ain't she?'

Suzie ground her teeth silently.

'I didn't wanna do it, you know,' he went on, his voice taking on the whining edge he always used to elicit her sympathy. 'I don't even know how it happened. I mean, one minute we're just sitting there watching them films, and the next she's all over me. I couldn't stop her. She was like – I don't know – it was like the coke gave her super-strength, or something. And with me being so out of it, I didn't know what was happening till it was too late, like. Suzie . . .? You listening?'

Suzie had clamped her eyes tight shut. She didn't want to hear his excuses. She'd seen who'd been on top. He'd have a lot of creeping to do before she forgave him for this – if she ever did. Right now, she didn't know if that was possible.

16

Suzie pretended to be sleeping when Mal woke up the next morning, and it worked. He looked at her, then crept out, closing the door softly behind him. She heard him waking Lee and Elaine up. Then, ten minutes later, they all left. She stayed in bed for a few more minutes in case he came back. When he didn't, she pushed the quilt aside and got up.

Going through to the living room, she groaned when she saw the state of the place, and wrinkled her nose in disgust at the sour, sweaty smell hanging over the room like a cloud. The evidence of their betrayal still littered the room. From the mess of videos strewn across the floor, to the heaps of sweet-wrappers, empty cigarette boxes and ripped-up Rizla packets spilling off the table – right down to the disturbed cushions on the couch and chairs. And Elaine had forgotten her tights – they were draped sluttishly across the back of the couch.

With a tight-lipped scowl, Suzie snatched them up and marched into the kitchen, holding them at arm's length away from her. Hurling them into the bin, she went to the sink and scrubbed her hands with disinfectant. She didn't want a single flake of Elaine's skin contaminating her – or any other part of her disgusting anatomy, for that matter!

Going back into the living room, she threw all the windows open to clear the smell, then whirlwinded her way through the room, scouring and disinfecting every visible surface, brushing and hoovering both the carpet and the furniture. And she didn't stop until she felt she'd completely eradicated Elaine's presence. When she had finished, she made herself a cup of tea, sat down, lit herself a cigarette and tried to put her thoughts into some kind of order.

They must have thought they were so smart, sending Elaine in to calm the waters last night. But they were very wrong if they thought it had worked. She'd put up with everything Mal had done to her so far, but no more! She'd even blamed herself for winding him up. And why? Because despite it all, she'd really believed he loved her – that one day things would change. How stupid was that?

But everyone had their limit, and she'd reached hers. Let them walk around thinking stupid Suzie would forgive and forget. She'd show them. It might take time, but she would make them pay!

Mal and Lee arrived back at one that afternoon. By then, Suzie had calmed down enough to act as though nothing had happened.

'All right, Sooze?' Lee shuffled his feet, unable to meet her gaze.

'I'm fine, thanks,' she said, laughing inside at his obvious embarrassment. 'Why? Don't I look it?'

'No, you look great,' he said. 'I was just asking, like – you know . . .' His voice trailed off.

'You look a bit pale yourself,' she said, peering at him closely, making him squirm. 'You're not coming down with something, are you?'

'No, I don't think so,' he said, sitting down. 'I feel okay.'

'Do you?' she said. 'That's good. Sleep well, did you?'

He blushed. 'Um, yeah, thanks. The couch is dead comfy.'

'How about you, Mal?' she asked, smiling sweetly at him. 'You sleep all right? I didn't hear you come to bed.'

'Er, yeah, fine,' Mal said, looking everywhere but at her. 'Do you want a brew? I'm just making one.'

'That'd be nice,' she said, sitting down and lighting herself a cigarette. Her hands were shaking, but she was glad she was making the others uncomfortable.

'I think I'll have a bath,' she said when Mal came back with her coffee. 'I'm feeling a bit grimy. Don't know why – I haven't really done anything.'

'You want me to run it for you?' Mal asked.

'No, it's okay,' she said, getting up. 'I'll do it.'

'Want me to wash your back?' he said, a small, hopeful grin on his face.

'No, thanks,' she said. 'I can manage.'

Lee breathed a loud sigh of relief when she left the room. 'She's acting weird, mate.'

'You reckon?' Mal said, thinking the same thing himself.

'Too right,' Lee said. 'Can't say I blame her, but it's freaking me out. She was being dead cold when you was in the kitchen – like she hates me, or something. You don't think she blames me, do you?'

'I hope so,' Mal said.

Lee was upset by this. He liked Suzie and didn't want her to think he was a cunt just because Mal couldn't keep his dick in his pants. 'It wasn't all my fault,' he muttered.

'Yeah, it was,' Mal hissed. 'If you hadn't got Sam to go for them stupid films, none of this would have happened.'

'I never told you to shag Elaine!' Lee hissed back. 'Fucking hell, man! She ain't even your bird.'

'Didn't hear you objecting last night!' Mal snapped.

Lee looked down sulkily. In truth, he'd been so wasted last night, he wouldn't have cared who shagged her. Still, it wouldn't happen again if it caused this much trouble.

'You reckon she'll be all right?' he asked a few minutes later.

Mal nodded. 'Yeah, she'll be fine. I'll just buy her a few nice things to soften her up. She'll be sorted.'

'I hope so,' Lee said. 'I don't like it when she's like this. Anyhow, your brews are shit. Hers are dead nice.'

'Tell me about it,' Mal laughed.

'I thought you wasn't bothered,' Lee sniped. 'So how come you're creeping round her?'

Mal's pride stepped up a notch. 'It's not that I'm bothered so much,' he said. 'It's just, well, you know what birds are like. They take the huff about something and you can't get a fuck out of 'em for days. You have to play the game to get 'em back on side, innit?'

Lee thought about it and nodded. 'I'd forgotten all that shit. Pauline used to hold out for weeks at a time. Makes you feel like your bollocks are busting.'

'Exactly,' said Mal. 'So that's why we do it, innit? To stop ourselves getting fucked up. So I ain't creeping, I'm looking after me health.'

'You're a right clever cunt, you,' Lee said admiringly.

'I know.' Mal grinned. 'You watch, mate. She'll be right as rain in a couple of days. Now get a spliff built, I'm gasping!'

*   *   *

Suzie had just got out of the bath when Elaine turned up – carrying several bin bags packed full of her clothes and personal effects.

'All right, Sooze,' she said when Suzie opened the door. 'Jeezus! I thought I'd never get here without dropping the bleedin' lot!' She manoeuvred her load into the hall with difficulty. 'I had to stop twice to tie 'em back up again!'

'What is it?' Suzie asked, stepping back as Elaine dropped the bags unceremoniously at her feet.

'Me stuff,' Elaine said, shaking her hands to relieve the cramps. 'Left Tommy, haven't I? 'Bout time I dumped the pleb, wasn't it? He's a loser. Never gonna get nowhere, him.'

'So where will you go?' asked Suzie, leading her into the living room.

'I'm moving in with Lee!' Elaine declared.

Lee was sitting on the couch, putting a roach into another spliff. He looked up at this, shocked. 'You what?' he squawked. 'Moving in with me?'

'Yeah!' she laughed, rushing across and dropping herself down onto his knees, nearly squashing the spliff. 'You are me fella! Where else would I go? Don't you want me to, or something?'

'No, it's not that,' he said, pulling the bent smoke clear. 'I just wasn't expecting it, like.'

'That's sorted, then,' she said, planting a noisy kiss on his cheek and snatching the spliff from his fingers. 'Giz a light.'

Mal laughed and threw her a lighter. 'I hope you like cleaning up, 'cos his flat's a right manky hole!'

'We'll chuck it all out and buy new,' Elaine said. 'Spend a bit of that money we've got lying around doing nothing!'

'You what?' Lee spluttered. 'That's mine, that!'

'And what's yours is mine, now we're living together!' said Elaine sternly. 'So . . .' She slipped off his knee and looked around at them. 'We gonna celebrate, or what?'

Lee frowned, more than a bit pissed off about the 'what's yours is mine' business. But then he thought about the advantages of living with a bird again. Hot cooked food on the table every night . . . clean socks and scrods whenever he needed them . . . pussy on tap – no more solitary wanking! Maybe it wasn't such a bad idea, after all.

Grinning, he turned to Mal. 'Better give us a bag of Charlie . . . Get the show on the road!'

'Fuck off!' Mal said. 'I ain't giving you nowt. You'll pay for it!'

'That's what I meant,' Lee said. 'Mind you, though, you *could* give it me if you want – sort of a moving-in-together present!'

'Sort your menk out!' Mal snorted. 'You ain't getting nothing free off me! What d'y' think I am? A bleedin' charity? Flash the cash, matey!' He held his hand out.

Grumbling, Lee took a hundred from his wad and handed it across. Mal snatched it and went to the bedroom to get the gear.

'So tell me again about what happened with you and Pasha?' Elaine said to Lee when he'd gone. 'Did you really blow his face off?'

Suzie almost choked when she heard this. If Lee had spilled the beans, Mal would kill him!

Just then, Mal came back. 'What you talking about?' he asked.

'Lee's just gonna tell me about him and Pasha again,' Elaine said admiringly. 'Gawd, I can hardly believe it was my fella what done it! Wait till Tommy gets wind of this!'

Suzie looked at Mal, wide-eyed. Surely he wasn't going to let Elaine run around opening her big mouth? They'd all be done for if she did.

'Oh, no, you don't!' Mal said, giving Elaine a dark look. 'You don't tell *no one*! I thought I made that clear last night?'

'I know,' said Elaine. 'But I don't mean just anyone. I'd only tell Tommy. He wouldn't say nowt!'

'I thought you said he was a pleb?' Suzie asked quietly. 'A loser, you said.'

'Fuck Tommy!' Mal said vehemently. 'You ain't with him no more, so you don't tell him nothing, right?'

'Yeah,' Lee said, snatching his spliff back. 'You're with me now, so you'd better not go nowhere near fucking Tommy again!'

Elaine giggled. 'Are you jealous?'

'Nah,' he said sulkily. 'It just ain't right, my bird hanging about with her ex, that's all.'

'Ah, you don't have to worry about him,' Elaine said.

'And you'd better make sure it stays that way,' Mal warned her quietly. ''Cos I'm telling you now, if I find out you're fucking around behind Lee's back, I'll sort you out myself. Got that?'

Elaine looked at him adoringly. She could certainly see why Suzie liked him so much. He was a proper man! If she had her way, Suzie would be out on her arse and she'd be moving in! Fuck skanky Lee and his little excuse for a dick! As soon as his dosh was spent, she was dumping him and making a move on Mal.

'All right, Mal,' she simpered. 'Whatever you say.'

Suzie watched this with amusement. She knew exactly what Elaine was thinking, but she wasn't worried. Mal obviously didn't like her very much, and it looked like he didn't trust her either. Well, good! But that didn't mean he was forgiven.

Ged and Sam arrived a couple of hours later. Suzie let them in, then sat back to watch what would happen when they found out Elaine knew everything.

Mal and Lee were nervous, and tried their damnedest to control Elaine. But it wasn't long before she blew the gaff. She just couldn't help herself. Desperate to prove that she was part of the 'gang' now, she plonked herself next to Ged and nudged him.

'Here, what you gonna do with all your dosh, then?'

'What you talking about?' he asked, casting a dark glance at Mal.

'Elaine, button it!' said Lee, going white in the face.

Turning her back on Lee, Elaine went on coyly, 'You know – the dosh from Pasha's? I bet you were dead brave when them bullets went off. I would've been shitting myself, but I bet you didn't, 'cos you're well hard, aren't you?' She reached up and stroked Ged's arm. 'Dead muscly and all.'

Ged went ballistic. 'What the fuck did you tell her for?' he demanded, shoving Elaine out of the way to glare at Mal and Lee. 'You might as well have sent a signed fucking confession to the pigs as tell this cheap little slag! I don't fucking believe you!'

'Oh, God . . . oh, shit!' Sam muttered over and over, gripped by an awful, absolute certainty that it was now only a matter of time before they were hauled in and charged with murder.

'What's wrong?' Elaine spluttered. 'What have I done?'

'You get the fuck away from me!' Ged bellowed into

her face. He jumped up and began to pace the floor. 'Oh, shit! I can't fucking believe this is happening! How could you, Mal? I knew that fucking ponce had no sense, but *you*? How could you tell this – this little slag our business?'

Elaine burst into tears and ran to Suzie like a hurt child seeking the comforting arms of its mother. Suzie sat impassively, allowing Elaine to think she was comforting her as she patted her shoulder. Elaine would have been chilled to the core by the cold look in Suzie's eyes.

'Right,' Ged said at last. 'Kitchen – now!'

Silently, the men trooped into the kitchen. Ged slammed the door shut behind them.

'What's he going to do?' Elaine asked fearfully as their hushed, angry voices rose and fell behind the door.

'They'll be talking it through,' Suzie said. 'Ged's sensible. He won't do anything.'

'I wouldn't tell anyone, you know?' Elaine said.

Suzie looked at her and said quietly, 'I hope not.'

A few minutes later, Mal came out and motioned Suzie into the bedroom.

'Look, take Elaine to town for a bit, will you?' he said, taking a wad of money from his pocket with shaking hands.

'What's going on?' she asked.

'The shit's hitting the fan,' he told her. 'Ged and Sam are really pissed!'

'Can't say I blame them,' she said quietly. 'It wasn't one of your brightest ideas, was it?'

Mal frowned. 'You're not helping.'

When the girls had left, the men came back into the living room to thrash it out. Ged was still furious.

'You've totally blown it, you know that, don't you?' he said to Mal and Lee, who sat before him like a couple of schoolboys waiting to be caned. 'You couldn't be trusted for one lousy night! You don't know this slag from Eve, but you had to go and open your fucking stupid gobs!'

'It was him,' Mal said, pointing at Lee. 'He was flashing his money at her, and she wanted to know where he got it!'

'It wasn't my fault!' Lee protested. 'You made me get me dosh out to pay you for the fucking coke!'

'I never told you to fucking tell her!' Mal yelled.

'You fucking did, you cunt!' Lee yelled back. 'You said, "Go on, then!"'

'Shut the fuck up!' Ged shouted. 'As far as I'm concerned, you're both to fucking blame! Now, what we gonna do to sort it out?'

Mal and Lee looked down guiltily.

'We've got to minimize the risk of her telling anyone else,' Sam said quietly.

'Yeah, right!' Mal sneered. 'Minimize the fucking risk? What's that supposed to mean when it's at home?'

'Don't start with me,' Sam told him icily. ''Cos the mood I'm in right now, Mal, you'll be lucky if I don't break every bone in your fucking body!'

Again, Mal looked down. He wasn't brave enough to take Sam and Ged on when they were this mad. Apart from which, he knew they were right. He and Lee should never have told anyone what they'd done – least of all a tart like Elaine.

'What we supposed to do?' Lee asked.

'We have to make sure she can't tell anyone,' Sam said. 'That's your job, Lee.'

'How am I supposed to do that?'

'By never letting her out of your sight,' said Ged.

'What if she wants to go somewhere without me?'

'You don't let her,' Ged said, adding bitterly: 'I'm sure Mal will give you lessons in keeping her in line!'

Mal folded his arms and averted his eyes.

'Not only do you not let her out of your sight,' Sam went on, 'you also make sure she doesn't get to speak to anyone on her own.'

Lee groaned. 'How? I can't exactly stop her using the phone, can I?'

'No,' said Ged. 'But you can monitor what she says.'

'I don't think you understand what a threat she is,' Sam went on grimly. 'And not just to you – to me and Ged as well. Not to mention Wendy and the kids. Fuck knows what she's gonna say when she finds out what you've done.'

'Aw, shit,' Lee muttered, sinking further down. Wendy would have his balls for this. He'd blown any chance he might have had of getting into her knickers now.

'What about you two?' Mal asked. 'It ain't just us who'll have to keep an eye on her.'

'I don't see why the fuck we should do anything!' Ged yelled. 'It wasn't us who couldn't keep quiet. If I had my way, I'd never have to look at the bitch again!'

'She already knows you can't stand her,' Lee said grumpily. 'What if she gets funny with you? She might take it into her head to drop youse in it.'

Ged glared at him. 'I'll hold you personally responsible if she does.'

Sam frowned. 'What if she does, Ged?'

Ged considered the possibilities and came up with the only solution he could find. 'Much as I hate the idea, I suppose we'll just have to keep her sweet, won't we?'

'We'll be all right if we stick together on this,' Mal said, looking at Ged contritely.

Ged shook his head, saying darkly, 'I don't even want to talk to you right now, Mal. I'm going home to chill out. And you'd better sort her out before I get back, or there'll be trouble.

'Come on, Sam,' he said then. 'Drop me at mine before you go for Wendy.'

Without another word, they left.

'Fucking hell!' Lee spluttered when the front door slammed shut behind them. 'They went a bit overboard, didn't they?'

Mal looked at him hard. 'They were right. You should never have told her.'

'Get out of it, you cunt!' Lee laughed. 'They've gone now, you can stop blaming me.'

Mal raised an eyebrow. 'I *am* blaming you, mate. If she drops us in it, it won't just be them holding you responsible.'

'So what are we going to do?' Sam asked as he pulled away from the car park.

Ged shrugged. 'Keep a close eye on them, and hope to God they can keep that little bitch under control.'

Sam shook his head. 'I can't believe they did it. It's like giving a child a machine gun and lining yourself up to be shot! She's dangerous.'

'I know,' Ged muttered darkly. 'And all it'll take is one argument with Lee, and that'll be it. She'll blow our lives apart.'

'Well, they can't be trusted,' Sam said. 'So one of us is going to have to go round every day to keep tabs on them. And we'll have to keep each other up to date.'

'Yeah,' Ged agreed glumly. 'Not that I fancy setting eyes on either of them ever again!'

'You reckon we should do them in?' Sam asked, half jokingly.

Ged snorted softly. 'Don't think the thought hasn't crossed my mind!'

Pulling up outside Ged's flat, Sam smiled weakly. 'I don't think I'd better tell Wendy just yet.'

'I wouldn't if I was you,' Ged said. 'Anyway, it isn't fair to land something like this on her right now. Give her time to get home and settled first, eh?'

'I was thinking of days rather than hours,' Sam said.

'Don't leave it too long,' Ged warned. 'Best she's prepared if worse comes to worst.'

They exchanged a gloomy look, then Ged got out. Sam waved and pulled away. He was dreading Wendy's reaction to this latest cock-up. What a day this had turned out to be!

A few miles away in Marie's flat in Wythenshawe, Linda went to bed thinking much the same thing.

She'd been totally confused when she opened her eyes that morning to find herself in a strange bed in an unfamiliar room. She'd had no idea where she was, and couldn't remember how she'd got there. In fact, she couldn't remember anything between going to see Simeon and waking up.

She'd been on the verge of crying with the fear and frustration of it all when, suddenly, a light had begun to shimmer in the midst of the void. Jake! He must have brought her here. He'd taken her down the stairs from Simeon's flat to the car, then . . . then what? Nothing.

As if that wasn't frightening enough, she'd been

further petrified when the door opened and a strange woman came in with a cup of tea. Having no idea who Marie was, she'd assumed she must be connected to Jake in some way and had asked if she was his mum.

Marie had laughed. 'Good God, girl! Do I look that bleedin' old? Jake's mum, indeed! No, love – I'm definitely not his mum! I'm Marie – a friend of Simeon's. Now drink your tea and get up so we can have a chat, eh?'

Marie had done her level best to make Linda feel comfortable, and it had worked. She'd soon loosened up, and by the time they went to town for the clothes The Man wanted her to get, she was chattering away as if she and Marie were old friends.

They'd arrived back at Marie's flat at seven, and soon after she'd begun to get her first inkling of what Marie was to mean to her.

'You're gonna knock them blokes for six,' Marie had said as Linda paraded around the living room, modelling the clothes with girlish delight. 'With them dresses and your hair up like that, they won't be able to resist you.'

'Blokes?' Linda had asked, puzzled.

Marie had nodded. 'Yeah, they'll be queuing up for you. And I reckon you'll get a fair few wanting to take you regular. Sim won't half be pleased if you make good for him.'

'What are you talking about?' Linda had demanded, afraid now.

Looking at her hard, Marie had said, 'You don't know, do you?' Linda had shaken her head, and Marie had muttered, 'Oh, well, I guess it's only fair to tell you . . .'

Although she hadn't fully understood at first, it had

gradually dawned on Linda that she'd been sent to Marie to be trained as a whore. She'd cried then, hurt to the bone that Simeon would do such an awful thing to her. But Marie had explained his ways, and somehow managed to convince her that he wasn't such a bad guy.

But it wasn't Marie's praise of The Man that finally piqued Linda's interest. It was the idea of men paying her that much money to do what she'd already been doing with Simeon, Jake – and quite a few before them. And as Marie said – she herself had been doing it for years, and she'd never come to any harm. She had her own flat, and never had to scrape to pay the bills. A healthy bank account to see her right in her old age. And she was free to choose whether or not she wanted to work – which was more than most people could say!

Marie had missed her forte – she could have been a first-rate recruitment officer. By bedtime, Linda had not only agreed to give it a go but was actually excited about it, and was even pressing Marie to show her the ropes as soon as possible.

Tucking Linda into bed – in a motherly fashion that surprised even herself – Marie left her to her dreams of wealth and went to call The Man.

He was pleased to hear that things were going so well, especially when Marie told him how enthusiastic Linda was to get started.

'I knew you'd sort it out,' he said, his voice thick with admiration. 'You're a star! We'll be raking it in soon. I'll have to find you some more to train up!'

'No, thanks,' she said. 'This one's enough for the time being. And while we're on the subject of this one,' she went on, 'I've a few concerns about her.'

'Oh yeah?' he asked guardedly.

'Yeah. More to do with your choice of clients, actually.'

This was something she'd been considering all day, and it needed saying before it was too late.

'I'm not too happy about dropping her in at the deep end. She's just a kid, and I think we'd do better to let her start off easy. No point scaring her off before we make anything out of her, is there? And I'm not sure Jake was right about her liking it rough. I think it's a front, if you want my honest opinion. Anyway, there'll be plenty of time for that later on, if that's what she wants. And she'll be a lot more cooperative if she's allowed to find her own way, won't she?'

The Man listened to Marie's speech in silence and decided she was probably right. When she asked him what he thought a moment later, he gave her the go-ahead to deal with it in whichever way she felt fit.

'I'm sure you'll get the best out of her, but keep me up to date, yeah? Oh, and by the way,' he said before hanging up, 'I've decided to give you a lickle cut of whatever she makes. So don't take too long, eh?'

Marie was a lot happier when she hung up. She'd guessed right away that Linda was no angel – she could tell that just by looking at the clothes and make-up she'd arrived in. But she was certainly not the slut Simeon and Jake had made her out to be, either. Just as she was no natural junkie. If she were, she'd have been in a terrible state by now. Given this, Marie had had her doubts about Simeon's plan to train her up. But, in the end, the kid had been so enthusiastic that she'd decided to keep her for the time being. She'd certainly be safer here than abandoned to Jake's mercies.

And there was still time for the kid to change her mind – which she probably would. If Marie was right, and she usually was, Linda was just a screwed-up little girl desperately looking for love.

17

Paul Dalton was in the incident room when the call came in on Wednesday morning. He wasn't too amused when the Duty Sergeant handed him the memo to take along to DCI Jackson.

'Thanks a bundle!' he moaned.

'Think nothing of it, kid,' Sergeant Booth replied sarcastically, folding his arms over his belly and leaning back on his chair, grinning. 'It's a caring, sharing team we've got here.'

Paul rolled his eyes. 'Well, I would have preferred if you'd shared this with someone else!'

'Perks of my rank, delegation,' Sergeant Booth winked. 'Now bugger off before I do you for insubordination!'

Pushing his way out of the door, grimacing, Paul made his way to Jackson's office. He wasn't looking forward to seeing the DCI again. Every time he laid eyes on him he blushed, and it was beginning to get him down.

'Yes?' Jackson's gruff voice barked from the other side of the door when Paul knocked.

Paul swallowed hard and went in.

Jackson was at his desk, surrounded by a mess of paperwork. Three untouched plastic cups of tea sat precariously close to the edge – one of which was very likely to go over should Jackson move a single sheet of paper an inch to the right.

'What is it?' Jackson asked, without looking up.

Paul stepped forward hesitantly. 'Em, there's been a call, sir. Sergeant Booth said I should bring you this.' He held the memo out.

Jackson sat back wearily. Taking the glasses from the end of his nose he rubbed a hand slowly over his eyes before pushing them back on. 'Let's have a gander, then.' He held his hand out.

Paul passed him the memo and waited while he read it, taking the chance to have a look around the office – the think-tank of the formidable DCI. It was a mess. Dead plants lined the window-sill, their forlorn tendrils snaking out of the pots in stringy fibres; a multitude of overflowing ashtrays covered every surface, vying for space with the thousand or so full, half-full or spilled-over plastic cups – some of which sported plant life much healthier than the potted variety. And everywhere, there was paper. Official paper covered in jottings, plain paper complete with diagrams and scribbles, and rolled-up balls of the stuff all over the floor. Paul wondered how it had got into such a state. The cleaners were usually very thorough – had they missed this room?

'What is this?' Jackson asked, interrupting his thoughts.

'It's got the basic details right there, sir.' Paul leaned across the desk to point it out.

'I can read!' Jackson snapped. 'But as you said, they're basic. I want you to fill in the missing bits!'

'Er, the call came from Iggy's, sir,' Paul explained. 'St Ignatius's, that is. The old folks' home opposite the supermarket. One of the residents reckons she's got information about the murder, sir. The sarge said you'd want to be told.'

'Name?'

'Dalton, Sir. PC Paul Dalton. 926.'

'Not *yours*.' Jackson's voice was pained. 'The resident – what's *her* name?'

'Oh! Sorry, sir. It's a Mrs Ivy Lilley, I believe.'

Jackson jotted the name down in his notepad and pushed his chair away from the desk. 'So what's she saying?'

'Just that she might know something about the murder, sir. The sarge reckoned you'd want to have a chat with her – see if there's anything to it, I suppose.'

'First rule, lad.' Jackson stood and came around the desk, grabbing his jacket from the back of the door. 'Don't suppose!'

'No, sir?' Paul was puzzled.

Jackson explained. 'Don't suppose this is a load of bollocks just because the informant happens to be old. That's what you were thinking, wasn't it?'

'No, sir! Of course not!'

'And don't suppose I don't know what you're thinking,' Jackson continued. 'Because I do. Lads your age assume anyone over the age of thirty is a bit iffy in the old mental stakes. Am I right?'

Paul blushed.

Opening the door, Jackson stepped aside and ushered Paul out. Then he followed, locking the door behind him.

'Can you drive?' he asked as he strode away down the corridor towards the main desk.

'Yes, sir. But—'

'No buts. You can take me over to St Iggy's. Never could stand driving, myself.'

Stopping briefly at the desk, Jackson got a set of keys

and flipped them to Paul, telling Sergeant Booth as he motioned Paul out: 'He's with me, if anyone asks.'

Ten minutes later, Paul turned onto Cornbrook Road and pulled up outside the front doors of the home – into the space Jackson pointed him towards. The space that specifically stated: 'No Parking. Ambulances only'. He didn't protest. By now he was realizing that Jackson was a law unto himself – the three red lights he'd ordered Paul through on the way being a perfect testament to that fact.

After gaining entry to the foyer, they had to wait a full five minutes before Jacqueline Fenton, the live-in warden, put in an appearance. She was a shocking sight: overly pancaked and blushered, with mascara-caked eyelashes and a fresh blast of Rive Gauche so strong that it preceded her down the stairs.

Jackson cast an amused glance Paul's way as she came towards them with her hand extended, gushing: 'I'm so sorry I kept you. If you'd like to come through to my office . . .'

'If you don't mind,' Jackson said, 'we'll get straight along to Mrs Lilley.'

'Of course,' said Ms Fenton, nose firmly out of joint. 'If you'd like to follow me . . .?'

As they followed the perfume cloud down the corridor, Jackson whispered to Paul out of the corner of his mouth, 'Sees herself on the news telling the world how she was the vital link in solving this case. Nothing else would explain that trowel job! Probably thought we'd have a camera crew in tow!'

Ivy Lilley was eighty-nine years old, and in no way, shape or form senile, dotty or incapacitated mentally. She was a straight-backed, immaculately dressed lady, with a neat halo of powder-white hair, and the keenest pale blue eyes Paul had ever seen. He was more than a little surprised.

Jackson shot him a look that plainly said 'Never suppose' as they followed Mrs Lilley into her neat apartment.

'Won't you sit down?' she offered in a smooth, cultured voice. 'Maybe you'd like a drink? Coffee? Tea?'

'No, thank you,' Jackson replied, smiling and sitting down. 'We don't want to trouble you, and we shan't keep you any longer than necessary.'

'It's no trouble at all,' she replied.

'Very kind of you. Now if I may, I'd like to ask you a few questions?'

Mrs Lilley nodded, then held up her hand in an unmistakable 'wait' motion. Standing, she turned to the hovering warden and gestured her towards the door.

'I'm sorry about that,' she said when she came back moments later minus the warden. 'But Ms Fenton is an unashamed gossip, and I don't much relish being her latest topic.'

Jackson and Paul both smiled at this.

Mrs Lilley smoothed her skirt over her knees, considering her words carefully before speaking.

'I'm aware that I'm in a very precarious position, having witnessed the shooting,' she began after a moment.

Jackson shot a glance at Paul to see if he'd picked up on what she'd said. Seeing the lad looking visibly more alert, he was pleased.

'As I'm sure you'll appreciate,' she continued, 'I have not taken the decision to inform you lightly. I sincerely hope you won't jeopardize my safety in any way?'

Jackson looked her straight in the eye. 'I give you my personal assurance that I won't.'

Mrs Lilley regarded him closely for a second, then nodded.

Jackson smiled, then took his notepad from his pocket and flipped it open. 'I'll just take a few details, if I may, and then you can tell us what you saw.'

Mrs Lilley related her account of the events of the night of the murder in a clear, precise manner, with no embellishment whatsoever. And Jackson wrote down every word – without, at any time, even thinking about 'filing it under miscellaneous' back at the station. This was a statement he intended to take very seriously indeed.

'That,' he told Paul when they left an hour later, 'is going to be a dynamite witness when we get this to court.'

'If she's still alive,' Paul murmured.

It was an obvious dig at the grinding, tedious legal processes that lay ahead, and Jackson nodded sadly, only too aware of the meaning. At Ivy Lilley's age every waking morning must be a bonus. He shuddered involuntarily, remembering that he was well on the way to a ripe old age himself. Letting out a sigh, he shook the thought away.

'See you've sorted your problem with those dodgy gears,' he said, referring to Paul's crunching, grinding efforts on the way to the home.

Paul grinned. He'd been nervous as hell earlier but, having seen Jackson in action, he'd settled down. The fear had been replaced by respect.

'Pull in at a shop, will you?' Jackson said then. 'I'm dying for a fag – don't suppose you smoke?'

Paul shook his head. 'Sorry.'

Jackson tutted. 'Didn't think so. You kids are all on health kicks nowadays. Still, each to his own vice, I say. Mine's fags and booze, and I'm not apologizing.'

As Paul waited for Jackson to get his cigarettes, he went over what they'd learned from Mrs Lilley. First and foremost, she'd obviously been telling the truth. She wouldn't have known it was a shooting otherwise. That detail hadn't been released to the press, and, as the 'eyewitness' had claimed to see men wielding baseball bats, this was the weapon people believed had been used. Only someone with intimate knowledge would know the truth.

'Well, that was a turn-up, wasn't it?' Jackson remarked when he slipped back into his seat moments later. Tearing the cellophane from his cigarettes, he rolled the window down and tossed it out. Lighting himself one, he sucked deeply on it, filling the car with noxious fumes.

'Yeah, stroke of luck, that,' he went on. 'Shame it was so dark she couldn't get the reg. on the cars, but we've got a lot to go on – particularly the big silver job.'

'Sounded like a Merc or a BM,' Paul volunteered.

'Mmmm.' Jackson nodded. 'We'll get some pictures over to her, see if she recognizes it. In the meantime, I'll get my head together with Mac – that's DS Macintosh to you – see if we can get a book of mugshots over to her. You never know, she might just recognize the scabs if she sees their mugs. Particularly the girl she mentioned. I'll have to see if I can get hold of a tape of that news broadcast, see if we can spot her.'

'Bit strange for a girl to get involved in something like this, isn't it?' Paul asked.

Jackson pulled a world-weary face. 'Shame to say, but no. In places like this the women can be as bad as the men. Never turn your back on them or underestimate them. They might not be the one holding the gun, but they're usually right there, screaming at the one who's got the shooter to pull the trigger!'

As they pulled into the car park at the rear of the Station, Jackson turned to Paul, his expression serious. 'Don't breathe a word of what we just heard to anyone in there. I want to keep Mrs Lilley's identity safe for the time being. It'd take just one of these idiots to blab to the wrong person, and her life would be in danger. You understand?'

Paul nodded.

'Good lad.' Jackson smiled and patted Paul's shoulder before climbing out of the car. Leaning back in, he said, 'By the way, I'll want you to run me and Mac about tomorrow, so keep yourself free.'

Jackson stopped by the desk on the way in and told Sergeant Booth to send DS Macintosh straight to his office when he came in. He also told him to make sure the lad and the car were available for the next day.

'Well, well – who's teacher's pet, then!' Booth teased Paul when he came to hand over the keys a minute later. 'Only wants you again tomorrow! Shall I put in a request for a chauffeur's uniform for you, then? By 'eck! You've got it cushy, haven't you?'

Paul grinned sheepishly and headed off towards the canteen.

Eddie Walker collared him as soon as he sat down. 'I've been looking for you,' he hissed, looking around furtively. 'You haven't told anyone about the other night, have you?'

Paul smiled slyly. 'Your little walk on the wild side, you mean?'

Eddie groaned. 'Don't! I feel bad enough already without you taking the piss! Why didn't you tell me?'

Paul sat back with a look of innocence. 'I thought you were being "right on"!'

'The only thing I was right on was the last bus home when I felt that *thing* between its legs!' Eddie snapped. 'Swear you haven't told anyone?'

Paul laughed. 'Stop panicking. I haven't breathed a word. And if it's any consolation, I'm sorry, mate! It was cruel. I should have told you. But honestly – would you have believed me?'

'No,' Eddie conceded. 'Probably not. Anyway, I don't want to talk about that any more. Is it true you've been out with the Dragon Master all morning?'

'Yeah,' Paul admitted. 'And he's not that bad.'

'Come again?' Eddie pulled his head back.

Paul laughed. 'Honest, mate, he is so on the button it's frightening! He's not bad when you get to know him, and he's even got a sense of humour.'

'I'll take your word for that,' Eddie said doubtfully. 'So what were you up to?'

Paul shrugged, remembering Jackson's warning. 'Just a bit of driving about. He wanted to take another look at the supermarket.'

'So what about that call from Iggy's?' Eddie persisted. 'Booth said you took the message in. Did you go over there with him?'

Paul shrugged again and opted for a lie. 'Yeah, I took him there, but I didn't go in. I waited in the car while he had a word with the warden. I don't think it came to anything, though. He didn't say anything when he came out, anyway.'

'Yeah, he's well cagey, that one,' Eddie said. Glancing at his watch, he pushed his chair back with a scrape. 'Shit! I should be at Barton Street. You want to come to The George again tonight?'

'I was going there anyway,' Paul said. 'I'm meeting Jane and Vanda.'

Eddie gave him an incredulous look. 'Since when?'

'Since you abandoned me with them and we had a good laugh,' Paul told him.

'At my expense, no doubt?' Eddie said, grimacing.

'Only for the first couple of hours.' Paul grinned. 'But, seriously, they're sound.'

'Each to his own, eh?' Eddie said, jumping up with another glance at his watch. 'See you tonight, then.' Waving, he dodged through the crowded tables and disappeared through the door.

Paul watched him go, grinning. It was a shame he couldn't tell him what was going on – it'd be good to get his head together about these cars. But if DCI Jackson didn't want anyone to know, he'd have to abide by that.

18

Ged had just stepped out of the shower when the phone rang. Grabbing a towel, he threw it around his waist and went to answer it. He was shocked to hear Caroline's voice. His ex-wife never rang him! He was even more shocked when she told him their daughter hadn't been home for two days and demanded to know if she was with him.

'No, she bloody isn't!' he snapped. 'D'y' really think I'd have kept her here without telling you? Jeezus, Caroline. You never change, do you?'

Caroline went quiet, and for a moment Ged thought she'd hung up. Then he heard her breathe deeply, and realized she was making an effort to calm down.

'She's not been home since Monday morning,' she said at last. 'I'm not accusing you of kidnapping her or anything, I just thought she might have come to you?'

Ged breathed out through his teeth, consciously relaxing his grip on the phone. She was making an effort so the least he could do was be civil.

'She didn't,' he said after a moment. 'So what happened?'

'Nothing *happened*,' she retorted angrily. 'She's just bloody well disappeared!'

'Look, there's no point getting into an argument over this, is there?' Ged said.

'No,' she agreed quietly. 'That wasn't my intention.'

'Yeah, well, I'm sorry. Look, why don't you come over and we can talk it through? See if we can work out where she's gone.'

Caroline hesitated for a moment, then said, 'No, I'd best not leave the house in case she turns up or tries to phone. Can you come here instead?'

Ged sighed and bit his lip. He hadn't set foot in the house for over a year – never thought he would again. But this was too important to play petty games.

'All right,' he agreed. 'I'll get there as soon as I can.'

He replaced the receiver with a frown. His fifteen-year-old daughter had gone missing, and Caroline was seriously worried. She must be. She'd never have phoned him otherwise. And she had every reason to be worried. It was Wednesday now – two full days since she'd seen or heard from her.

He only hoped it was nothing he'd said or done on Monday morning that had sparked this off. He didn't think he'd said anything bad about Caroline, but he might have made the odd snipping remark. Would that have been enough to make his daughter run away? He wouldn't have thought so, but it was hard to tell what ran through a teenage girl's mind when her parents were pulling in opposite directions.

Half an hour later, dressed and dried, Ged grabbed his jacket and headed out the door. He hesitated at the car, loath to drive it illegally – especially now. But this could be serious. Deciding to take a chance, he hopped in, amazed when the engine immediately fired into life. Maybe it'd be worth getting it MOT'd now that he had the money. It was a damn sight better than catching buses or cadging lifts.

* * *

The house looked exactly the same as it had when he'd left, and Ged felt his stomach lurch as he stepped through the door.

Closing it behind him, Caroline edged past him into the living room. He followed, flicking his eyes around at all the old familiar things. He realized with a shock that Caroline had kept his photo. It was on the fireplace with the school pictures.

'She wanted to keep it,' Caroline muttered, following his gaze. 'I would have put it away ages ago otherwise.' Sitting down, she pulled her cardigan tight around herself, shivering despite the gas fire raging beside her.

Ged sat awkwardly on the edge of the couch and watched her. She looked awful – drained, older. This business was obviously taking its toll on her.

'So, how are you?' she asked, lighting herself a cigarette with shaky hands.

'So-so,' he answered. 'You?'

She looked at him with haunted eyes, a quiver puckering her chin. She bit her lip to keep from crying and raised the cigarette to her mouth.

He knew she was struggling to keep her emotions in check and felt he should give her a moment to regain her composure.

'I'll make a coffee,' he said.

Caroline had pulled herself together by the time he came back.

'Thanks for coming,' she said, taking the cup from him. 'And I'm sorry about that just now. I'm just worried . . .' Trailing off, she looked away, pulling long and hard on another cigarette.

Ged felt sorry for her. 'So, she's been gone for two days?' he asked softly.

Caroline nodded, letting the smoke trail from her nose. 'I saw her Monday morning before I went to work, but I haven't seen her since. I thought she'd gone to her friend's – a girl she hangs about with, Alison. But I rang there yesterday and Alison said she hasn't seen her.'

'Had you had a row or something?' Ged asked.

'No!' she snapped. 'And I hope you're not implying this is my fault?'

'I'm not implying anything,' he said. 'I'm just trying to put together a picture of what might have happened.'

'Well, it was nothing I'd done!' Her chin wobbled again. 'I thought you'd come to help, Ged? You're not just going to sit there being sanctimonious, are you?'

He sighed. 'No, I'm sorry – I didn't mean to make it sound like that. Let's not get into a fight, Caroline. Let's just try and find out where our little girl's gone.'

She smiled sadly. 'That's half the problem. She's not so little any more. She's growing up fast. Too fast!' Lighting yet another cigarette, she looked him full in the face, saying almost accusingly: 'You probably couldn't see it because you haven't seen that much of her. I wish she *was* still little. It would be a damn sight easier keeping an eye on her.'

He frowned. 'You make it sound like you've got no control over her. She can't be that bad?'

'I'm not saying she's *bad*,' she told him quietly. 'But she's definitely out of control. She's stays out later and later all the time. Sometimes she doesn't come back till the early hours. I've tried everything to stop her, but nothing works.' She looked at him resentfully. 'It's all right for you. You come and go as you please. But I've got all the responsibility. And I've got to work to keep the house going, so I can't be here to make sure she stays in. Every time I come home, she's already been and gone.'

'Have you tried putting your foot down? Telling her to stay in after school?'

Caroline laughed bitterly. 'I've told her, and I've threatened her. I've even tried slapping her, but it doesn't make any difference. She just nips in while I'm at work, changes her clothes and takes off again. At least before, I knew she'd come back at some point. What am I supposed to do now?'

'Have you tried all her friends?'

'Yeah – the ones I know, anyway. Trouble is, most of them reckon they haven't seen that much of her lately. Seems she's got herself a new boyfriend. Some fella she met at a blues in Moss Side.'

'A blues?' Ged snapped. 'What the hell was she doing at a blues? Jeezus, Caroline! She's only fifteen!'

Caroline's face hardened. 'Maybe now you're getting an idea of what she's like! She's running wild, and there's nothing I can do to stop her.'

Ged shook his head. But angry as he was, he knew he couldn't blame Caroline. She was a working single parent, with precious little time to be enforcing time restrictions on a headstrong teenager. And if they were going to get into the blame arena – he had to admit to his fair share, didn't he? He'd walked out without a backward glance. Best thing for everyone, he'd said at the time. And maybe he'd been right, but there was no excuse for the sporadic nature of his contact with his daughter ever since. He'd blamed it on Caroline's bitchy attitude, but if he was honest, he couldn't blame her for that either. He'd behaved like a pig.

'Do you want another coffee?' Caroline asked, breaking into his thoughts.

He nodded. 'Yeah, please.'

Following her to the kitchen, he leaned against the door frame, watching as she filled the kettle. 'So, who is this boyfriend?' he asked.

She shrugged. 'Your guess is as good as mine. She doesn't tell me anything these days. And we were so close once,' she added wistfully.

'I know,' he murmured softly. 'I remember. I was a bit jealous, if I'm honest.'

Caroline turned and gave him a strange look. 'Jealous? What of? You never said.'

He shrugged and grinned at her sheepishly. 'I know. Sounds stupid now, but I was. I suppose it was the attention you gave her when I thought you had no time for me.'

'More like you had none for me!' she snorted softly. 'You were never here. I was always competing with your friends. I just got fed up in the end.'

'I don't blame you,' he said. 'I was selfish, wasn't I?'

'Yes,' she replied matter-of-factly. 'You were.'

They lapsed into silence as they waited for the kettle to boil. Ged looked around the familiar kitchen, surprised to see the habitually cluttered surfaces now free of mess, and sparkling clean.

'You got a cleaner, or something?' he teased. 'I don't think I ever saw it like this before.'

'Amazing how much you can get done when you're not bogged down and depressed,' she answered quietly. 'It took a few months, but I got there in the end. Anyway, it's done now, isn't it?' She handed him his coffee, her smile tight, and led the way back to the living room.

'So where do we go from here?' he asked.

'Well, I suppose we could get on to Alison again,' she

said. 'Find out what she knows about this boyfriend. She was at the blues with her, so she must have seen him.'

'What did she say when you spoke to her yesterday?'

Caroline shrugged. 'Not a lot. Only that she hasn't seen her or spoken to her since Sunday. She was supposed to meet her on Monday but she never turned up.'

'Okay. Give me her address. I'll go and have a word with her.'

Ged finished his coffee and pushed himself to his feet. As Caroline wrote down Alison's address, he took his wallet out and removed a bundle of notes. He handed these to her when she gave him the address.

She eyed the money guardedly. 'What's that for?'

'Take it,' Ged pushed it into her hand. 'I owe you much more than this. Take it.'

She looked at him uncertainly. 'Are you sure? It's an awful lot.'

'I'm sure,' he insisted, folding his huge hands around her small ones. 'Take it, please. And my apologies for everything I've put you through this past year.'

'Thanks,' she whispered, close to tears. 'But it's not all your fault. I did my fair share to muck things up.'

'Let's just forget all that now,' he said. 'Friends?'

'Friends!' she agreed, smiling properly for the first time since he'd arrived.

Ged felt the weight he'd been carrying for the past year lifting from his shoulders – and it felt good.

Alison was apprehensive when she answered the door to an enormous man with a very serious face and what her dad called a copper's knock.

'Can I help you?' she asked.

'Alison?' Ged queried.

She nodded, eyeing him nervously.

'I'm Linda's dad,' he told her. 'Can I come in for a minute and have a word?'

Alison peered nervously at the living room door, afraid her mum might come out and hear something she shouldn't.

'Em – yeah, okay,' she said at last. 'Come in the kitchen.'

Opening the door wider to allow him to come in, she led him into the kitchen – praying he wasn't going to blast her for whatever Linda had done.

'You know why I'm here, don't you?' he asked when they were sitting at the kitchen table.

'Yeah,' she admitted, looking down. 'Linda's mum rang yesterday. Hasn't she gone home yet?'

'No, she hasn't,' he said gravely. 'Now, I know you told her mum she never turned up on Monday, but I need to know if that was true. Was she here? Maybe there was something she didn't want you to tell her mum? Something bad she thought she'd get into trouble for?'

Alison shook her head. 'No. Honest, she never came.'

Ged looked at her from beneath lowered eyebrows, aware that he was making her squirm as he assessed whether or not to believe her. He decided he did.

'I've not come to have a go at you,' he said. 'But I need to know what's happened to her. Can you think of anywhere else she might have gone?'

'No, I'm sorry, I haven't got a clue,' she told him. 'None of our mates have seen her, either.'

'What about this boyfriend she got herself at the blues?'

Alison blushed. 'I don't kn-know him,' she stuttered,

flicking a worried glance at the door. 'Linda met him a couple of weeks ago, but I don't know him.'

'Where were you?'

'At the R-Reno,' Alison stammered in a tiny voice.

'Don't worry,' Ged said gently. 'I'm not here to get you into trouble. I just need to know about this boy so I can find Linda before something happens to her.'

Alison nodded. 'If I knew anything I'd tell you – honest I would. But I only ever saw the guy once. That night, when he took your Linda home.'

'Back to her house? Did you go with them?'

Alison blushed again and looked down at her nails. She didn't want to grass, but Linda's dad didn't look the sort to let things drop. He was staring at her now, waiting for her answer, and the longer she left it, the more obvious it would be that she was covering something up.

'No,' she whispered. 'She didn't want to me to. She said she was going back to his flat, and would I be all right getting a taxi back. She went off in his car.'

Ged didn't like what he was hearing. 'She went back to his flat?' he demanded 'And he had a car? How old was he?'

Alison shrugged nervously. 'I don't know? Thirty – thirty-five?'

Ged clenched his fists. 'What was his name?' he asked through gritted teeth. 'This bloke – what was his name?'

Alison edged back in her seat, shocked by the white-lipped livid expression on his face. 'I-I don't know. Simon, I think. No, *Simeon*! That's it.'

'And what does he look like?'

'I hardly saw him.' Alison was near to tears now. 'Only for a m-minute when she told me she was going. He was standing by the door, waiting for her.'

'So what did he look like?' Ged demanded. 'Big? Small? Fat? Thin? Black? White?'

'Well, he was big. Muscly, kind of. And he was black, and bald.'

Ged nodded, scowling. 'And where does he live?'

Alison was shaking in earnest now, her voice jerky and high with fright. 'I don't know, Mr Grant. Honest I don't! All I know is it's in that big block of flats in Moss Side behind the fire station.'

'Are you sure?'

Alison nodded. 'Positive. Linda pointed it out to me last week when we were on the bus going to school.'

'But you don't know the number? Come on, Alison – think! It's important. She might be in trouble.'

'No. She never said. It must be somewhere near the top, though, 'cos she pointed up.'

Ged pushed his chair back and stood up. Looking down on the frightened girl, he forced himself to smile. 'Thanks for your help, love. I'll see myself out.'

Ged sat in his car outside Alison's house, mulling over what he'd learned. It was a shock to find out that his little girl had willingly gone off with a bloke she'd only just met – at a blues, of all places! He'd never dreamed she was the kind of girl to get into that kind of scene. She wasn't even sixteen yet. What the hell was she doing going off with a man old enough to be her father? Jeezus!

And what the hell kind of man picked up a girl that young? What kind of sick, perverted bastard?

Throwing the car into gear, Ged pulled away from the kerb, seething with a white-hot rage. If Linda was staying with this child-molesting piece of scum, there was going to be murder! He'd castrate the filthy bastard when he got his hands on him!

Before he knew it, he'd arrived at the flats Alison had mentioned. For an hour he sat, just staring at the door, watching the comings and goings – hoping to see Linda. He even played with the idea of going across to the door and ringing every bell on the off chance that at least one would answer and that, once inside, he'd be able to knock on every door until he found her.

But, much as he'd have liked to do just that, a small voice of reason told him this would only alert whoever Linda was with that he was looking for them. It would be far better to wait until it was dark. Then he could get in, do what he had to do, and get out again without being seen. A lot more sensible than walking in in broad daylight and setting himself up to get busted.

Having decided this, he began to pull out of the car park. Then, just as he was about to turn onto the road, he looked in his rear-view and saw a man coming out of the flats. He slowed to a crawl, racking his brains to remember where he'd seen him before. Then it came to him. It was the bloke who'd stopped him and Sam the other night when they'd been coming out of Mal's. The one who'd been looking for Millie.

Winding his window down, he reversed back, coming alongside the man as he unlocked his own car door. 'Excuse me, mate,' he called.

Max looked up with a frown.

'I don't suppose you remember me,' Ged said, 'but I met you the other night, in Hulme. You were looking for a bloke called Millie, and me and my mate told you where to look.'

Max narrowed his eyes. He remembered the meeting,

although he wouldn't have recognized Ged because it had been dark that night. Now, in the fading afternoon light, he looked like a Babylon.

'Wha' you want?' he grunted suspiciously.

Ged nodded towards the flats. 'You came out of there just now. Maybe you can help me out? I'm looking for a bloke who lives here. His name's Simeon? Oh, and he might have a young blonde girl called Linda staying with him?'

'Why you want him?' Max demanded, his suspicion growing stronger by the minute. 'What's it to you?'

Ged frowned. 'I've got my reasons. Do you know him or don't you? It's a simple enough question, man!'

'Raas!' Max snarled. 'Who the fuck you talking to like that, eh? Axing all kind of t'ing that ain't none of your raas bizzness! Cha!'

'I'm only asking,' Ged snapped back at him. 'No need to have a shit fit! Fucking hell!' he went on incredulously. 'That's what you were doing the first time I saw you! What's the bleedin' difference?'

Max drew himself up to his full height and put his hand inside his jacket. His eyes swivelled every which way as he advanced on Ged, muttering: 'No one talks to me like that, muthafucka!' Pulling the gun out, he pointed it at Ged's face from the cover of his jacket.

'Shit!' Ged hissed, holding his hands up as he edged away from the window. 'Shit, man! Look, just forget it, yeah? There's no need for this! All right?'

He took his wallet out then and held it open so that Max could see the hefty wad of notes. 'Here, man—take it. Just put the gun away, yeah?'

'Raas!' Max growled. 'You think I'm a fucking mugger? I look like a fucking mugger to you?' He jabbed the gun through the window. 'All you white cunts are the same! Muthafuckin' bastards!'

'No . . . Look – I'm sorry, all right?' Ged gulped as Max became more agitated. 'Shit! I don't believe this!'

Max kissed his teeth. 'Pussy claat! Gimme that!' Snatching the wallet, he waved the gun under Ged's nose, growling, 'I see you round here axing questions again, I'll blow your fucking raas brains out. Now mooove . . .'

Max sneered as he watched Ged tear out of the car park, then looked down at the wallet in his hand with disgust. Mugger! He'd never mugged anyone in his fucking life!

Flipping it open, he looked again at the bulky wad of notes inside. It wasn't exactly how he'd planned it, but this would make up for some of the money he'd lost when Stevo did a runner.

As he stared at the notes, he spotted the tiny marks. His heart skipped a beat. *No way*! It couldn't be!

Ripping the top note out, he peered at it closely. It bloody was! The marks were there in each of the Queen's eyes.

Leaping into his car, he pulled the rest of the notes out and scrutinized them. Some were clean, but the rest were marked. He separated them into two piles on the seat beside him. There was forty-five quid in the clean pile; one hundred and seventy in the marked.

Reinserting just a few of the marked notes into the wallet, he pocketed the rest and got back out of the car. If he was going to take this to The Man, he sure as hell wasn't losing it all again!

*   *   *

Ged drove to Mal's flat in a fury. That thieving bastard's face would be indelibly marked on his memory, and when he saw him again, he'd make him regret the day he did what he'd just done.

No one had ever pulled a gun on him before. It had totally freaked him out. But now the shock was wearing off, he felt like turning his car around and hunting the cunt down. And when he found him, he'd rip his head off and stamp all over the hole!

Mal and Lee were up in arms when Ged stormed in and told them what had happened.

'Why didn't you pan his bleedin' face in?' Mal said. 'I'd have battered the fuck out of him!'

'Bit hard when you're stuck inside a car with a gun in your fucking face!' Ged snarled back at him. He slammed his fist down onto his knee. 'But I'll kill him when I get my hands on him, man! I swear I will!'

'Who was it?' Lee asked. 'Did you know him?'

'Yeah!' Ged spat. 'That's why I stopped him in the first place. He stopped me and Sam when we were leaving here the other night and asked where that smack dealer, Millie, lived. Then the cheeky bastard's got the nerve to pull a gun on me for asking him where this Simeon lives!'

'You say he was looking for Millie?' Mal asked, narrowing his eyes. 'Well, that'll be it, won't it? He'll be a bleedin' junkie! And you know what they're like, man. Head cases!'

Ged shook his head. 'No, he wasn't a junkie. He was too smart looking. And his car was a top-of-the-range BM.'

'Probably nicked it,' Mal snorted. 'Like he nicked your wallet. Cunt! So, what you gonna do about it?'

Ged shrugged, pursing his mouth furiously. 'I don't care about the wallet – there was only about two hundred in it anyway. It's him sticking that gun in my face I'm pissed off about!'

They discussed the mugging for a while. Then they got onto Ged's reasons for going to that block of flats in the first place, and why he was so eager to find Simeon. They were shocked when they heard about Linda. They'd known her since she was born, and had never imagined she'd go off the rails like this.

'You want to go and drag her out of there, give her a good hiding and lock her in her bedroom,' Mal suggested. 'And batter the fuck out of the guy for messing about with her while you're at it!'

' 'S right!' Lee added indignantly. 'The guy wants locking up! Bleedin' pervert!'

'What do you think I was there for?' Ged snapped, flicking a disbelieving glance at Lee for making that statement in the light of everything Ged had heard him say about schoolgirls. 'I was planning to find out which flat he lives in,' he went on. 'And if she was in there, I was gonna break his door down and get her out!'

'So what's stopping us?' Mal asked. 'Let's get down there!'

Ged shook his head. 'No. I'd already decided to leave it till it got dark. I think that'll be better – especially now.'

'Right, then,' Mal said. 'We'll go when it's dark.'

'Eh!' Lee jumped up, fired by a sudden revelation. 'You don't suppose it was him, do you? That Simeon you're looking for?'

'No.' Ged shook his head. 'Linda's friend told me he was bald, but this bloke's got dreads.'

'I bet he knows him, though.' Mal arched a knowing

eyebrow. 'Why else would he go psycho like that? He must have been covering for the guy.'

'Whatever . . .' Ged rolled his head on his neck. 'I can't do anything about it right now, so there's no use winding myself up, is there?'

'Just so long as we sort this Simeon creep out when we find him!' Mal said. 'Poncey cunt he must be and all, with a name like that!'

'Oh, believe me,' Ged said. 'I intend to. *And* the thieving bastard who took my wallet! Now, how's about one of you makes me a brew while I let Caroline know what's happened?'

'Yeah, I reckon we could all do with one,' Mal said, pushing himself to his feet. 'Here you go, mate.' He handed his stash tin to Ged. 'Make yourself a spliff, eh? And don't worry about Linda. We'll find her – together, mate!'

Ged looked up at him gratefully. Of them all, Mal was the last one he'd expected to show genuine concern. But here he was, doing exactly that – and, looking at his face, Ged knew without a doubt that he was genuine.

'Thanks, Mal,' he said. 'I really appreciate that.'

Mal shrugged modestly. 'What are mates for, eh?'

19

Max held the wallet out towards The Man. The Man snatched it and threw it open, pulling the notes out and riffling through them.

'How did he come to have this?' he growled angrily. 'That's sixty quid of my fucking money! How come?'

'I don't know,' Max said – glad he'd decided to replace just a bit of the money as he watched it disappear into The Man's pocket. 'I didn't exactly get to ask him.'

'And how come he gave it to you?'

'Like I said.' Max shrugged. 'He pissed me off axing questions about you, so I pulled my gun on him!' He laughed nastily. 'And the pussy turn yellow and give me his wallet!'

'It's not funny!' The Man bellowed. 'Who was he? And why was he asking about me? What exactly did he say?'

'Just that he was looking for you. That he knew you lived in these flats . . . And that you might have a young girl called Linda with you!'

'How did he know that?' The Man barked. 'Who's been chatting my business?'

'And how come he stopped you?' Jake interrupted, a suspicious gleam in his eye.

Max rounded on him furiously. 'How the fuck do I know?'

'So you're saying he just got lucky?' Jake snorted. 'Yeah, *right*!'

'Nah, hang about!' Max said. 'He stopped me 'cos I stopped him the other night! I axed him where to find that Millie!' He sat back, smiling smugly. 'So you can stop your insinuations, Jake. Trying to make out like I'm a fucking informer, or something!'

'Hang on, hang on!' The Man cut in. 'So you seen him the other night? You asked him where this Millie lived, and he told you, yeah?'

Max nodded. 'Yeah. Well, roughly. Didn't know the number, though, so I had to ax someone else when I got over there.'

The Man's face darkened. 'Bit of a coincidence, isn't it? You talk to him just before you give Millie a going-over, then the man comes looking for me? Knows my name – and even mentions that slag Linda. Something ain't right with this!' He shook his head, pursing his mouth. 'Nah! It's wrong!'

'You sure he wasn't Babylon?' said Jake.

Max shrugged, slumping down in the chair. 'That's what I thought when I first saw him, but I don't think so.'

'And what makes you so sure?' The Man asked.

Max grinned. 'Well, I never seen a Babylon give up 'im wallet before!'

Jake shook his head and wandered over to the window. Max could be such a dickhead. This man sure as hell sounded like a Babylon. And it was too much of a coincidence that he just happened to have been hanging about when Max went looking for the dealer who supposedly had the money, and now he was here asking about The Man. People walked in and out of these flats

272

all day long – how come he hadn't stopped anyone else? How come he'd chosen Max?

'What car was he in?' The Man asked.

'Ford,' Max told him with the true sneer of a BMW driver. 'Dark blue. Pretty old.'

'MNE plate?' Jake asked.

'I didn't notice,' Max admitted.

'All the undercovers in Moss Side use dark Escorts and Cortinas, and they all got MNE plates,' Jake said. He turned to The Man. 'If I was you, I'd start wondering if the Babylon haven't been watching you.'

'You think?' The Man asked quietly. Jake shrugged and went back to looking out of the window.

The Man looked down at his hands. This was definitely too much of a coincidence. In all the time he'd been dealing with Pasha, he'd never been fingered. Yes, the police had been getting a bit more active on the scene lately, but they'd never connected him to anything, had never tried to bust him. Even when they did that mass raid a month before Pasha copped it, they hadn't set foot near him or Pasha. But now, ever since that money had turned up with Max's boy, Stevo, things were starting to happen. It wasn't good.

In light of this more pressing matter, it slipped his mind that Max had also been asked about the girl.

'I don't like this,' he said to Max a minute later. 'It's too close. Seems to me this guy gave you my money knowing you'd bring it straight to me.'

'What good would that do?' Max asked.

'Could be a set-up,' The Man said grimly. 'If Stevo and his boy Millie had already been gripped by the Babylon and had the money taken off them, that would explain why they didn't have none of it when you went looking.

And if that Millie one was warned not to say anything, that's why he wouldn't give it up when you put the arm on him. They probably figured whoever it belonged to would go looking for it, and held onto it to use as a trap. What we've got to do is figure out what's really going down here, and make sure we don't get fucked up.'

'It's a bit late for that,' Jake muttered darkly. 'Seems like it's already started.'

'Well, they ain't got nutt'n on me,' The Man snapped. 'Even if they have got the money, there's nothing to say it's mine. No one knew about the marks except us in this room.' He looked at Max hard. 'You didn't tell no one, did you?'

'Course I didn't!' Max protested. 'I'm not that stupid!'

'Well, the only other one who knew was Pasha – and he's not telling no one nothing!'

'Not now,' Jake agreed. 'But what about before he was hit?'

'What you talking about?' The Man shot at him. 'You know he was safe!'

'You don't know, though,' Jake countered. 'That might be what this is all about. Think about it. He had his family working with him – they *must* have known what he was doing for you. He couldn't have hidden it from them, not when he was doing it from the shop. They might think you're behind him getting whacked. They could have gone to the Babylon and worked out this deal to set you up so they could get revenge.'

The Man didn't speak. He hadn't thought of this, but now realized it was altogether possible. *Damn*! If that was the case, he had his work cut out for him. He couldn't afford to sit back and let the nephews think their uncle's death was anything to do with him. Apart from anything else, his pride wouldn't allow him to let his reputation be sullied like that. He would have to go and see them, sort it out.

'Max, you'd better go now,' he said. 'Call me later and we'll arrange a meet. Where you gonna be?'

Max stood up. 'I'm going home for a shower and something to eat. I'll stay there. Just give me a ring when you're ready.'

The Man nodded and turned to Jake. 'Come on – we're going to see the nephews.'

Jake frowned at him from the window. 'Is that a good idea? Supposing the Babylon are still sniffing about down there?'

'So what?' The Man retorted. 'Man's gotta eat, ain't he?'

Ten minutes after Jake drove The Man out of the car park, Lee drove in. Scanning the cars already parked, he said to Ged, 'What did you say it was?'

Ged had already looked. 'It's a BM,' he said, 'but it's not here.'

'That's all right,' Lee said, reversing into a space and cutting the lights. 'We can wait.'

'All night if we have to,' added Mal. 'I've got the necessaries!' He held up a handful of five-skinners he'd rolled earlier. Lighting one, he put his feet up on the dash and filled the car with smoke.

'Let's play I-spy!' Lee said, ignoring the groans of the others. 'I'll go first. Er, right, I've got one! I-spy with my little eye, something beginning with L.'

'Lift?' said Sam.

'Nah.'

'Lorry?' said Mal.

'Nah.'

'Loser?' muttered Ged.

'Nah, come on, youse ain't even trying!'

'Lemon?'

'Lilac tree?'

'Nah! Youse are never gonna get it!'

'Just tell us!' said Mal, handing the spliff over the seat to Ged.

'Loada fuckin' sad gits sittin' in a car!' Lee cackled. 'Get it? Loada fuckin'—'

'Shut up, you bleeding pillock!' Mal laughed, smacking Lee around the head. 'Right, my turn. I-spy with my little eye, something beginning with G.'

The nephews were surprised when The Man and Jake walked in. In fact, the late Pasha Singh's relatives looked decidedly hostile, and it occurred to The Man that Jake could have been dead right about them. He looked around at the customers milling about in the aisles, and gave Jake the nod to remove them.

It took Jake just two minutes to persuade them all to leave. When the last one had gone, he shut the door and flipped the 'open' sign to 'closed'.

The Man removed his shades and pocketed them, all the time staring straight into Guptar Singh's reticent eyes. He knew quite a lot about this man already. Pasha had been very proud of his nephews.

Guptar Singh was twenty-six. A good-looking, well-educated, intelligent man, who, according to Pasha, was the natural successor to the Singh throne, possessing an astute business sense. He was also exceedingly arrogant, The Man deduced. Fancied himself as a law-abiding citizen and therefore, more likely than not, classed himself as a cut above these drug dealers standing in front of him. The Man, who was by no means unintelligent himself, knew that his initial approach was all-important.

'We've come to offer our condolences,' he began when the shop was finally cleared. 'For the untimely demise of your uncle.'

Guptar Singh's head jerked back indignantly. Although he'd never actually laid eyes on the large man standing before him, he knew who he was. Simeon Marchant. The so-called Man. Major smack dealer. His uncle's supplier. A situation he had never countenanced.

'What did you come here for?' he hissed, his voice betraying his suspicion and anger at this unexpected and unwanted intrusion.

The Man stepped slowly up to the counter and leaned forward until his face was just inches from Guptar's – his slightly flared nostrils the only indication that he was annoyed by the other man's tone. His voice was deliberately low and controlled.

'I came to offer my sympathy for your loss. So I'm a little disturbed to be treated in such a disrespectful manner by the nephew of the man I had much respect for. If you have a problem, then I suggest you air it right now.'

Guptar Singh snorted disbelievingly. Looking around at his brothers for support, he said, 'This man comes to offer insincere sympathy to us for the death of our uncle, then threatens me when I don't fall at his feet!'

The Man smiled icily. 'I think we'd better get something clear here. I had a lot of time for Pasha, but that won't affect how I deal with you. I don't like your attitude, and I won't think twice about putting a bullet through your raas head if you keep it up!'

'Like you did to my uncle?' Guptar retorted, equally icily.

'Now, that's what we need to clear up,' The Man said quietly. 'I'm going to tell you this just once, so you'd better listen up. I did *not* kill your uncle, and I didn't arrange to *have* him killed. His death was nothing to do with me. I don't expect you to understand,' he went on. 'But your uncle and me had a good thing going. We both gained from it and, needless to say, I'm grieved that it should have ended like this!'

'Of course you're going to say it wasn't you!' Guptar shot back at him. 'Stands to reason you would. This is *murder* we're talking about, not some little fight that went wrong. *Murder!*' he stressed the word. 'And if you ask me, you're the main suspect!'

'No one is axing you, claat!' Jake snarled. 'We're *telling* you how it is!'

'Well, tell it to the police!' Guptar shouted. 'You go tell them how much you liked and respected my uncle, and why, and let them decide if you're guilty or not!'

'You really are stupid!' The Man growled, slamming his fist down hard on the counter. 'Me and Pasha had a good thing going. I don't need to tell you how much money he was making.' He waved a hand around the shop. 'Look for yourself. You think he made enough to keep you and yours in the style you're accustomed to by running this shit-hole?'

'This isn't our only business,' Ranjit Singh said quietly. A slightly shorter version of his brother, he stepped behind the counter to stand beside him now. 'We know our uncle had business with you, Simeon,' he went on.

'We're not so stupid that we didn't see what was going on. Apart from which, our uncle discussed everything he did with us. He planned to retire soon and go home. We'd have been running the businesses when he left, so he had to make sure we knew everything – including his business with you.'

'I'm glad to hear Pasha trusted you that much,' The Man said, giving his full attention to the younger, more reasonable nephew. 'So you should know enough to realize I respected him and had no part in his murder. I came here today hoping we could reach an agreement regarding the set-up we had going. I'm sure you know your legitimate profits won't be enough to maintain you. That's why me and Pasha had our thing. He was a wise man, your uncle.'

At this, Guptar turned to Ranjit and began to argue noisily with his brother in their own language, punctuating his words with waving arms and looks of pure hatred directed towards The Man. Ranjit managed to keep an even tone as he answered, seemingly winning the argument when Guptar eventually threw his hands up and walked away.

Ranjit turned back to The Man and smiled tightly. 'I apologize for my brother, but this is hard for him. He's head of our family now, and it's his responsibility to avenge our uncle's death. I've told him I don't believe you were involved, as I don't think my uncle would have done anything to cause you to do something like that.'

The Man nodded. 'Your uncle was honest, and I had no problem with him. The only problem I've got now is with the scummy bastard who killed him. If it was planned, then someone has made a direct attack on me, and I promise you I'll find them and take my own revenge!'

'I understand,' said Ranjit. 'But there's no need to trouble yourself. The family will deal with this. God will lead us, and help us take revenge in whatever way He sees fit. Whatever happens, the piece of shit that did this will suffer!'

'All well and good,' The Man said. 'An eye for an eye, Jah says – and between us, we'll take an eye each! All I ask is that you tell me if you find out who it is before I do. And likewise – I'll let you know. Deal?'

Ranjit considered the request and then nodded. 'Deal.'

They shook hands to seal their understanding. Then The Man got back onto the subject of continuing the business he'd had going with Pasha.

'It wouldn't be wise, under the circumstances,' Ranjit told him. 'But I'm not ruling it out as a future possibility. You know the police are watching us?' He shook his head in disgust. 'I'm sure they've got us down as suspects. They confiscated the shop's security videos, and we've been told they got hold of the videos from the casino we were at when it happened.'

His face became suddenly angry, and he slammed a fist down on to the counter. 'If we'd waited just ten more minutes instead of racing off to gamble our uncle's money away, we would have been here to protect him! We could have saved him!'

'Don't blame yourself,' The Man said wisely. 'Jah takes His people home when He sees fit. All we can do is accept His decision, then settle the score when we can. Remember – anything I can do, just ask, yeah?'

'Thanks.' Ranjit nodded gratefully. 'My uncle respected you, and I'll make my brother understand. As for your offer, I'll consider it again when the time's right. But right now, I think it would be unwise for both of us.'

The Man nodded. 'We'll wait, then. Contact me when you want to talk again. Or if you hear anything.

'Come, Jake,' he said then, motioning Jake to the door. 'I need to go see Rico.'

The Man was quiet as they drove away from the supermarket, and Jake glanced at him every now and then – angry glances that, had The Man seen them, would have alerted him that something was afoot. In fact, Jake was rapidly losing respect for him – thought he was turning soft. Not so long ago, Guptar Singh would have been taught a hard lesson for the disrespect he'd just displayed. But The Man had done nothing, and Jake couldn't understand why he seemed so willing to sort things out with Pasha's nephews.

The more The Man moved towards diplomacy in his dealings, the more Jake could see him losing his control over things. He'd built up his various businesses on the strength of his reputation, but he was changing. Soon someone else would see it – and war would break out. And right now, Jake wasn't sure he was prepared to fight for him if he couldn't be bothered to fight for himself.

The seed of an idea began to grow in Jake's mind. If the Man was just going to give up on things, then it was only fitting that Jake should take over. It was still early days, so he'd have to tread carefully, but the way things were going, it wouldn't take too long to destroy The Man's credibility and step into his shoes. The other posses already wanted The Man off the top spot, and it wouldn't be hard to lure some of them over to his side.

The more he thought about it, the more he knew it was the right thing to do.

The Man watched Jake from the corner of his eye. It was clear that Jake was turning against him but, while it angered him beyond belief, it didn't worry him unduly. He was stronger than Jake could ever hope to be – and a great deal smarter. He had the ability to let not even the dimmest flicker of what he was feeling cross his eyes, and he never allowed foolish temper to betray his innermost thoughts when he was outside his home. Jake's face, however, was a moving-picture testament to the plotting and scheming taking place in his mind. His plans might as well have been written across his face in indelible ink for all the world to see.

Knowing that Jake was plotting against him, he began to plot his counteraction. He'd wait and watch. Then, when the time was right, he'd act. He'd let Jake set the tempo. If he were smart enough, he'd remember where his loyalties lay and that would be the end of it. But if he persisted, he'd be punished – leaving no one in any doubt of the consequences of crossing The Man.

Back at the supermarket, Guptar Singh was not at all pleased with his brother for having been so agreeable towards the man he was convinced was behind their uncle's murder.

They'd begun to argue furiously as soon as The Man and Jake had left the shop. Guptar accused Ranjit of committing a sin by fraternizing with the murderer when their uncle was still warm in his grave. Pulling rank, he then demanded that his brother pledge his loyalty to the family and drop all thoughts of any kind of future dealings with The Man.

Ranjit didn't believe The Man was connected to the murder, and tried in vain to make Guptar see that their late uncle's business partner only wanted to help them find the murderer and exact revenge. But this just made Guptar even angrier. This was family business, he said – and the revenge would be, too.

When Guptar left to go and check on their aunt a short while later, Ranjit had a quiet word with their younger brother, Raj, to sound him out about his views on the subject.

Raj agreed that it wasn't the right time. But, like Ranjit, he didn't discount the future possibilities. He, too, realized that the business couldn't survive without the added income, and agreed that once the police relaxed their surveillance the Singhs should consider contacting The Man.

The only thing they all agreed on was the missing money. If anyone turned up at the shop with money bearing their uncle's marks, they would definitely let The Man know. It was his money that had been taken, and to honour their uncle's name it would be returned to The Man if it turned up.

By eleven, Sam was getting twitchy. They'd finished the spliffs ages ago, and there'd been no sign of anyone going in or out of the flats for over an hour.

'Look, I'm sorry to break this up,' he said. 'But I promised Wendy I'd be home by now. I'm sorry, Ged.'

Ged shook his head. 'It's all right. I've been thinking I should get back to check on Caroline.'

'You what?' Mal said, twisting in his seat to look back at Ged. 'We're only doing this for you.'

'I know, and thanks,' said Ged. 'But I'm worried about

Caroline. I'm sure she wants to call the pigs, and if she does, we'll be bollocksed.'

'Yeah,' Mal agreed grimly. 'And you can kiss goodbye to seeing Linda again if they get in on it!'

'Or us getting our hands on this Simeon one,' added Lee.

'All right, youse go,' Mal said. 'We'll stay for a bit.'

'Bollocks to that!' yelped Lee. 'If they're pissing off to be with their birds, I'm going back to Elaine!'

'I need a lift back to yours to get my car, anyway,' Sam said.

'Okay,' Mal said grumpily. 'But you'd better stop at the Spar for a bevvy, Lee. I ain't sitting with you and your fat slag all night without getting bladdered – and you're paying!'

'Piss off,' Lee said, starting the car. 'You won't give me no free Charlie!'

Dropping Sam and Ged in the car park a little while later, they arranged to try again the next night.

'But one of youse can bring the spliffs next time,' Mal said.

20

On Thursday morning, Jackson received the videotape of Monday's news report. Liz Jardine had sent it by courier – along with a handwritten note wishing him a speedy and successful conclusion. It was all too obvious that she was hoping he'd alert her to any breakthrough the moment it occurred. She could swivel, as far as he was concerned.

Taking the tape to the video suite, he sent for Mac to come and watch it with him.

By eleven, they were almost brain-dead, having played it through numerous times – squinting at all the people in the crowd as they looked for a girl who matched Mrs Lilley's description. If they spotted any likelies, they would get some stills blown up and get them over to her.

It was a long shot, but anything would help right now. They had nothing. No weapons, and no reported shooting victims treated at any of the hospitals. It was an obvious possibility that their man could have gone out of Manchester, but it wasn't very likely, given the amount of blood they'd found at the scene. The only other explanation was that the person had died and their corpse was lying somewhere, rotting away and in the process of decomposition destroying the forensic evidence that would link them to the murder.

This was what Jackson was hoping wouldn't happen. In areas like this, bodies often went undiscovered for months. The various disgusting stenches that lingered around the hallways of these high-rises could override even the smell of rotting flesh. He couldn't recall the number of times that he'd been called to a suspect flat only to find a reeking jellified mess melting into the carpet.

It was now four days since the start of the case. The longer this went on, the less likely they were to get it sorted and closed.

'Do you think you could have looked any more bored than that?' Mac asked, pointing at Jackson rolling his eyes on screen.

'You're not supposed to be watching me,' Jackson grunted. 'But I do look a bit like a fucking St Bernard, don't I?' he griped, stroking his chin and fingering the saggy rolls of flesh below. 'Whoever said the camera never lies is an arsehole,' he muttered. 'Anyway, Mac – apart from me, have you spotted anyone worth checking out?'

'Three or four.' Mac leaned forward to point at the screen. 'Just freeze it for a sec and I'll show you.'

'I wonder what goes through their minds?' Jackson mused as he rooted for the remote under a mess of papers on the desk. 'When they go back to the scene and see us digging about?'

Finding the remote, he pointed it at the screen, freezing the crowd. 'You'd think their faces would give them away, wouldn't you?'

'They can be crafty bastards, though, can't they?' Mac muttered, staring hard at the crowd. 'Look how many we catch red-handed, and they come over so innocent you end up questioning your own judgement. If you want my opinion, it's the innocent ones who look guilty, and vice versa. There you go . . .' He pointed at the screen. 'That's one of them.'

Jackson leaned forward for a closer look. Mac was pointing to a blonde girl standing off to the rear of the crowd. She was on tiptoes, peering around with big eyes. Jackson noted the counter number to get a still shot of the frame.

'Looks very interested, doesn't she? But I suppose that's to be expected. Kind of reminds you of those French women knitting at the executions, doesn't it? Who else?'

'There's another two standing together a bit further on,' Mac said. 'Just over to the right a bit, and further forward . . . Stop. There they are.'

Jackson peered at the two – another blonde, with a ponytail and black roots, and a redhead. Something about the redhead struck him as odd.

'Funny look on her face,' he said. 'See how the blonde looks excited, like our French Revolution girl? Now take a look at the redhead. She looks freaked. And she's not looking in the direction of the body like all the others. She's watching us.'

'A lot of them do that,' Mac remarked. 'It doesn't really mean anything. I mean, come on, you were being filmed! Half of them are just there hoping to get their mugs on telly, aren't they?'

Jackson shook his head slowly. 'I hear what you're saying, Mac, but I don't think that's her game. Let's just run it for a sec and see what she's up to, eh?'

They ran the film and watched the girl intently. She was indeed watching the police, furtively glancing around at them, but not, as they'd supposed, at Jackson or the film crew.

'You know what's making me twitchy?' Jackson commented. 'The way she's watching the obvious coppers – the uniforms. It's like she's keeping an eye on them to see if she's been spotted, know what I mean?'

Mac frowned. 'What? Like she's expecting to be?'

Jackson nodded thoughtfully. He hadn't quite got it straight in his own head what it was exactly. Just a gut feeling. But whatever – she was definitely one to check.

'Maybe she's just got a thing about men in uniform?' Mac suggested, managing to leer and grin simultaneously.

'Or maybe she's guilty as hell about something?' Jackson countered.

'Could be anything.' Mac shrugged. 'Unpaid leccy bill, pending court case? She might even have a warrant out on her.'

'She wouldn't be stupid enough to turn up there if that was the case.'

Mac pulled his head back and gave Jackson an incredulous look. 'Oh, please!'

'All right.' Jackson waved a hand towards the screen. 'Where's your other suspect?'

'Further back,' Mac said. 'Just before you do your hound-dog bit!'

The fourth likely was another blonde – extremely thin and scruffy, and sporting a pair of dark shades.

'Junkie,' Jackson grunted.

'Bit early for a smack-head.'

'Not if she's a lifter,' Jackson said. 'The early worm gets all the bargains, and all that. Right, I've had enough of this.'

Pressing the rewind button, he waited for the tape to pop out of the machine. Then he put it back in its case and wrote across the front: JACKSON – DO NOT ERASE.

'Here's the counter numbers of the frames we want stills off,' he said, handing a note and the video across to Mac. 'Get down to the lab and tell them what we want. Oh, and Mac, tell 'em to be quick, eh?'

'Yes, sir!' Mac flipped a salute and jumped to his feet. 'Anything else, sir?'

'Yeah!' Jackson grinned. 'Don't be so disrespectful to your elders and betters!'

Even at a rush, it was a full hour before the lab technician carried out the folder and handed it to Mac.

'I've managed to get them pretty clear,' he said. 'But with the size he wanted, I'm afraid they're a bit on the grainy side. Now then – will that be cash, or credit?'

'Ha, ha, very funny!' Mac drawled. 'See you later, and thanks for this,' he said, waving the folder as he turned and rushed out the door.

'Here you go, boss,' he said when he reached Jackson's office. He flipped the folder across the desk.

Jackson caught it and tipped the prints out, lining them up side by side on his desk. He spent a good few minutes scrutinizing them before looking up.

'Do us a favour,' he said, picking up the phone and tapping out an internal number. 'Go and pick up the mug books – and make sure they give you the Rastas, too. I only mentioned that one at the last minute, they might forget if you don't remind them.

'Hello, yes.' He turned his attention to the phone, waving Mac out. 'That car I wanted, I need it in five minutes. And the lad – Dalton. Tell him to get his arse over here quick smart!'

Slamming the receiver down, he pushed his chair back and gathered the prints together, stuffing them back into the folder. He'd just locked his door when first Mac, then Paul Dalton appeared from opposite ends of the corridor.

'Took your bloody time, didn't you?' he snapped as he headed for the back door. 'Come on. We haven't got all day!'

Paul Dalton's nerves returned with a vengeance. DS Macintosh was an added pressure. It had been bad enough driving just DCI Jackson, but the two together – old mates, obviously – made him feel inadequate. He needn't have worried. Mac had already decided he must be all right, or Jackson would never have picked him out to come along.

'You know the way, don't you?' Jackson asked as they jumped into the car.

'Yes, sir.' Paul nodded. 'Oh, by the way, I got these out of some car mags.' Reaching into his uniform jacket, he pulled out the folded wad of magazine pages he'd assembled the night before. 'I thought we could show them to Mrs Lilley and see if she recognizes those cars.'

'Good lad!' Jackson took the pictures and winked at Mac over his shoulder. He'd forgotten all about the car pictures. The lad was proving to be an asset. 'Well, off you go, then,' he said. 'And don't forget – I'm colour-blind. Red means green, right?'

'Don't be telling him stuff like that!' Mac admonished from the back seat. He tapped Paul on the shoulder. 'Don't you be listening to him. I want to get there in one piece. You go through one red and I'll nick you myself!'

'Yes, sir,' Paul said with a grin.

* * *

Jacqueline Fenton was surprised to see them – and distinctly cooler, having been ousted from their meeting the day before. Opening the door to let them in, she said, 'I presume you're here to see Ivy again?'

Jackson smiled. 'If she's available?'

'I'm sure she is,' Ms Fenton answered, flicking a glance at the mug books he was carrying. So they were taking old Ivy seriously, then. 'I'll just let her know you're here,' she said, and swept off down the corridor.

'What's eating her?' Mac asked in a hushed voice as they followed.

'I don't think she was expecting us,' Jackson hissed back. 'She's only got half her face pack on!'

'Bit of all right, though,' Mac commented. 'Nice arse!'

'Only 'cos it matches yours for size,' said Jackson.

Ms Fenton didn't even try to enter when Ivy invited the officers into her apartment this time. Turning on her heel, she rushed off to have a gossip with the visiting hairdresser. She still hadn't forgiven Ivy for snubbing her yesterday, but maybe she'd relent later – after the officers had gone. Find out what was going on?

'Can I get you a coffee?' Mrs Lilley asked when they were all seated.

'No, thanks,' Jackson said. 'We don't want to put you out. And I don't mean to rush you, but I'd appreciate it if you could have a look at some pictures for us.' Opening the folder, he pulled out the stills and handed them to her.

'These were taken from a videotape of the news broadcast,' he told her. 'They're not brilliant, but they're not too bad. Now, I know you said you couldn't be absolutely sure if the girl you saw that night was the same girl you saw the next morning. But, based on your description, we picked out four likely girls. All I ask is that you take your time to look them over. You're under no pressure, so if you don't see the girl, don't worry. Just do your best.'

'Of course,' said Mrs Lilley.

The first print was the junkie in shades. Mrs Lilley looked closely at her, then shook her head. 'I've seen this girl around, but she's not the one.'

She took longer with the second print. This was the one with the two girls standing together. As she peered long and hard, her face creased into a thoughtful frown. Jackson and Mac exchanged a glance. This could be it.

'I wouldn't like to say I was one hundred per cent certain,' she said at last. 'But I'm almost sure this is the girl.'

Jackson felt his heart jump in his chest. He pushed himself to the edge of his seat. 'Which one?' he asked, knowing in his heart that she was going to say the redhead.

'That one.' She pointed at the redhead and Jackson almost cheered. 'I'm pretty confident she's the one I saw on the night, and again the next morning. But I'd hesitate to swear under oath that I was certain. It could just be her familiarity.'

Jackson's heart slowed to normal. 'Are you saying you already know her?'

'Not know her, exactly,' Mrs Lilley explained almost apologetically. 'But I've certainly seen her going to and from the shops. It's hard not to notice the regulars when my window overlooks the only route from the main road. I would venture to say I'm ninety-nine per cent certain, but I don't know if that's good enough?'

Jackson smiled reassuringly. 'It's good enough for us

to find out who she is and have her questioned. If she is our girl, we'll soon work it out. Please don't think you've let us down. You've been very helpful.'

'Oh dear,' Mrs Lilley sighed almost regretfully. 'I hope I'm wrong. She seems such a pleasant girl. Whereas I'm afraid the same can't be said for her friend!'

'Oh?' said Jackson. 'You mean the blonde?'

'Mmmm,' Mrs Lilley murmured, pursing her lips. 'Unpleasant girl. Spends a lot of time hanging about at the back of the shops with a very unruly mob. Until recently, that is. Probably all the police activity has chased them away for the time being.'

'And you're quite sure she's not the girl you saw there that night?' Jackson asked.

'Not at that time.' Mrs Lilley shook her head. 'Earlier, yes. She was sitting on the wall at the side with her friends. They were drinking and smoking and making a racket, as usual. In fact, there was an altercation between them and Mr Singh.'

'An altercation?'

'Oh yes, quite noisy too. Lots of shouting, some pushing and shoving. As I said, they're very unpleasant characters, and that was certainly not the first time they'd been aggressive towards Mr Singh.'

'What time would that have been?' Jackson asked.

'Ten o'clock,' she told him confidently. 'The news was just coming on and I missed the first ten minutes because of all the shouting. I'm sure if you ask Mr Singh's nephews they'll be able to give you more details.'

'They were there?'

'Oh yes. They came out and chased them away. They'd probably know who they are, because, as I said, it wasn't the first time.'

Jackson made a mental note to visit the supermarket on the way back to the station. It was a bit of a coincidence that these two girls were together the morning after the murder, when one had been involved in a scuffle with the dead man the night before and the other was supposedly spotted going into the yard very late on the same night. This was starting to take shape, and he wanted to be sure he'd covered every possibility.

'I wonder if you'd look at some cars now?' he asked Mrs Lilley when he'd finished jotting his notes. 'With luck, there should be one that's similar to the one you saw that night.'

Mrs Lilley pored over each of the pages Paul Dalton had ripped from his magazines, then pointed out two cars that she thought were very like the silver one.

Jackson tipped Paul a wink. They were both BMWs, as he'd suggested. One was a 325, the other a 318. So similar that it was understandable she couldn't pinpoint exactly which model she'd seen. As for the darker car, she wasn't certain, but thought it looked like a Ford Escort. The only problem she had was that the ones in the pictures looked much plainer than the one she'd seen. Jackson was delighted. Even without knowing the exact makes, it narrowed the range down considerably. It would make their work so much easier.

Next he showed her the mug books, but this didn't go quite so well. Page after page of photos of criminals, but none that Mrs Lilley felt sure enough about identifying to be significant. All she could say about the three men she had seen running away from the supermarket after the shots had been fired was that one was very broad and tall, another was shorter but still quite well built, and the third a fair deal shorter. And she was pretty sure they were white, whereas the man in the silver car was black.

'I'm so sorry I can't be more helpful,' she apologized. 'I'm much surer of the girl because she was alone, and she stood right outside my window. I wouldn't even like to hazard a guess if one of the men in your books was one of the men I saw. I'm sorry.'

'Don't be,' Jackson said quickly. 'You've been a tremendous help. I only wish all of our witnesses were as astute as you. You've given us a lot more than we expected.'

'Canny old bird,' Mac said as they left the home. 'Shame she has to spend the last days of her life stuck in that rathole. Must be hell when your mind's as sharp as a pin. Still, a few days in court will give her something to occupy her.'

'Mmmm.' Jackson nodded towards Paul. 'But as me laddo here was only too quick to point out – only if she lasts as long as it takes us to catch these scummy little shits and get them to court! I don't know,' he went on, sighing long and hard. 'Eighty-nine. And we're not that far behind, Mac. Will you visit me when I'm stuck in a place like that?'

'No way!' Mac retorted. 'I'll be long gone. But you're the Dragon Master. Don't you possess the secret of eternal life or something?'

Paul's foot pressed down harder on the accelerator with shock when he heard them joking about the nickname the lads had given Jackson. He felt the blush suffuse his face in a burning wave.

Jackson nudged him. 'Like I said . . . I know everything! Now, pull in round the front of the supermarket.'

* * *

Guptar Singh felt a stirring of panic in his gut when the three officers walked in. He was dreading the day they discovered the other business his uncle had been running. And even though he knew he had scoured every inch of the shop and found no leftover drugs, he could almost feel the handcuffs snapping into place as Jackson approached him.

'Good afternoon, Mr Singh. I wonder if we could have a quick word?'

Guptar glanced at a couple of customers who had stopped shopping to blatantly gawp at the scene. 'Just let me call my brother and we can go through to the stockroom,' he said, adding pointedly, 'It'll be more private back there.'

He went to the door off to the side of the counter and called through. Seconds later, Raj appeared and took over. Guptar led them through to the back of the store.

'Business good?' Jackson asked on the way, more out of politeness than any real interest.

'Been a bit slow, actually,' Guptar said. 'But it's the recession, isn't it? Businesses are closing up all over the place.'

Jackson raised an eyebrow. 'Can't be that bad,' he said, looking pointedly at the expensive colour monitor and recording machine showing a crystal-clear image of the shop floor.

And then there was the new jeep Guptar's uncle had recently acquired. Not to mention the brand new Mercedes van. Or the luxury detached house with all mod cons Jackson had visited after the murder.

Walking slowly around the stockroom, peering nonchalantly into cartons, he said, 'Is this your only business, Mr Singh?'

Guptar was visibly agitated by the questioning, which Jackson thought suspicious in itself.

'No. We've another shop in Moss Side.'

'Same as this?'

'Smaller,' said Guptar, glancing nervously at Mac and Paul Dalton standing in the doorway. 'Look, what is this, Inspector? Why are you asking these questions? I hoped you'd come to tell us you'd caught whoever murdered my uncle.'

'Unfortunately not,' Jackson replied, sitting on the edge of the desk beside the monitor. 'But I *do* have some questions regarding the night of the murder.'

'I'll be glad to tell you what I know,' Guptar said. 'But I'm afraid I don't have too long to spare. I've dragged my brother away from his work to cover for me as it is.'

'Oh, it won't take long,' Jackson drawled. 'Now then, on the night in question, at approximately ten p.m., I believe there was a confrontation between your uncle and a gang of local youths?'

Guptar nodded, folding his arms. 'That's right. But it wasn't anything, really. Just some kids getting lippy. We got rid of them easily enough.'

Jackson made a note on his pad. 'Could you be a bit more specific, sir? What exactly do you mean by "lippy" for example? Were they threatening your uncle?'

'No, nothing like that,' said Guptar. 'They're always doing it. They come in and buy their beer, then sit out back drinking it. And when they start getting drunk, they think it's funny to knock on the back door and shout things. You know what kids are like. It's not serious.'

'Shouting things?'

'You know, the usual. "Piss off back to Paki-land", "Paki bastards" – the usual rubbish.'

'So they've never threatened you or your family? Never said anything that worried or annoyed you?'

Guptar snorted. 'If I got wound up by every piece of white trash that called us names, I'd be in an early grave!'

'Like your uncle?' said Jackson quietly.

'Is this some kind of a joke?' Guptar demanded. 'You think my uncle was shot through the head by some kid, just because they called us names and we chased them away? They were always doing it! Don't you think they'd have shot him before now if they were capable of that?'

'Depends how angry they were about being chased away that particular time,' Jackson countered.

'They weren't angry,' another voice said. 'They were laughing, as they usually were at the climax of their night. They knew what would happen, just as it did every other time. It was a game to them. Cat and mouse.'

Jackson hadn't heard Ranjit come in. He acknowledged him with a nod, waiting until he'd put down the boxes he was carrying before asking, 'I believe you were also here when this gang was arguing with your uncle? Is there anything you can add? Your brother doesn't think it was in any way related to the murder a few hours later.'

'Neither do I,' said Ranjit, wiping his hands on a small towel. 'They're just kids who got a kick out of winding my uncle up, that's all.'

Jackson pulled the print of the two girls together from the folder and held it out towards Ranjit. 'Do you recognize either of these girls?'

'Yes, both of them.' Ranjit nodded. 'The blonde's part of the gang we were just talking about, and the other's a regular customer. Why? What have they got to do with anything?'

'Do you know their names, or where they live?'

'The blonde's called Elaine,' Ranjit told him. 'She lives with one of the lads in the gang. Tommy, I think his name is, but I'm not sure. They've got a flat in Trent Court, the flats across the way. You don't think she had anything to do with this, do you?'

'What about the other girl?' Jackson asked, ignoring the question.

'Em, Susan, or Suzanne, something like that,' Ranjit said. 'She lives somewhere over that side.' He pointed through the back wall in the direction of the Crescents. 'Nice girl, very polite.' He handed the print back. 'But I still don't understand why you're interested in them.'

'I'm not, not specifically,' said Jackson guardedly. 'I'm just trying to fit some pieces together.'

'Yeah! Adding one and one and coming up with five, instead of chasing the people responsible!' Guptar butted in angrily.

'I assure you we're doing everything we can to trace whoever murdered your uncle, Mr Singh,' Jackson snapped at him. 'And in doing so, we have to follow up every lead, however small.'

'And you're saying one of those leads has led you to investigate these girls?' Ranjit interjected, eager to clarify the matter in his own mind – and shut his excitable brother up at the same time.

Jackson pushed himself to his feet. 'No, Mr Singh. I'm not saying we're investigating them. I'm saying it's been drawn to my attention that one of them was involved in an argument with your uncle on the night he was murdered. To eliminate her, I need to question her. Nothing more sinister than that. I'm hoping she may be able to tell us if she saw anyone suspicious hanging about at the time.'

The explanation was plausible and both Guptar and Ranjit settled visibly as they accepted it. Jackson was relieved. The last thing he wanted was for the family to think they were accusing the girls. That could be very tricky. He knew they'd be out for revenge when they found out who it was, and it was his job to keep such information from them until they had their suspect – or suspects – safely locked up.

'Well, I won't take up any more of your time, gentlemen,' he said at last. 'I'll be in touch as soon as we have anything to tell you, and please don't hesitate to contact me if you hear anything. Good afternoon.'

He inclined his head to the men and walked towards the door. Reaching for the handle, he stopped and turned back.

'Oh, by the way – just out of interest, where did you say your other shop was?'

21

Even as Suzie was being discussed by the police, her own thoughts were on them – how she'd like nothing better than to walk into the station and tell them exactly what she knew. It would be the ultimate payback for what Mal had done to her. If he'd left it at just the one time with Elaine, she might, in time, have found it in her heart to forgive him. But it had taken all of two days for him to slip back into his old way of talking down to her. And she knew for a fact that the three of them were still at it. Only now, instead of doing it at Mal's place, they sloped off to Lee's flat. Did they really think she didn't know?

There were two major problems with grassing them up. The first was her own involvement. She wasn't so stupid that she didn't know that what she'd done in going to collect first the mask, then Lee made her an accessory. She'd be putting herself at a very real risk of going to prison for the part she'd played.

The second was what it would do to Ged and Sam – and then, of course, to Wendy and the kids. She knew she couldn't do something like that to them. Much as she'd like to go and inform on Mal and Lee, she knew for a fact that they wouldn't go down without making sure Ged and Sam went with them.

Sam and Ged were upsetting her too at the moment, but not enough to make her grass them up. It was the way they were treating Elaine. She'd thought they hated her as much as she did, but ever since they'd found out that Lee had told her about Pasha, they'd been really nice to her.

'Oi!' Mal interrupted her thoughts. 'I thought I told you to make a brew! Gawd! You're going fucking deaf, you are!'

Suzie gritted her teeth as Elaine squealed with laughter. She was a permanent fixture now, having 'moved in' with Lee – which was a laugh, seeing as he seemed to have moved in with Suzie and Mal! And now she squealed about everything. How much she loved this flat. How she simply couldn't imagine how she survived before she came here. And how much she loved being Suzie's 'bestest friend'!

Yeah! Such a good friend that she laughed every time Mal made a crack like that!

Pushing herself to her feet, Suzie went to put the kettle on – shooting a killer spark of hatred at Elaine on the way. Not that the thick-skinned cow even noticed!

As she prepared the cups, she slipped into a dark fantasy of revenge. She had got to the point of visualizing herself pouring petrol over them all while they slept and striking the match when Mal yelled at her from the living room.

'Oi! What you doing in there? Sewing the fucking tea bags up, or what?'

Suzie's nostrils flared. 'Won't be a minute,' she called back, hissing 'Bastard!' under her breath.

Pulling the cupboard door open, her hand hovered over the packet of laxative powders she kept at the back. A nasty grin crept across her face as she read the word 'Flavourless'.

* * *

Sam ran his hands through his hair and prepared to be blasted. He'd finally told Wendy about Elaine knowing everything, and she was absolutely furious.

'How could you be so bloody stupid?' she screamed at him. 'Of all the imbecilic, moronic . . . crazy things to do!'

'It wasn't me,' he muttered. 'It was Lee and Mal.'

'So why didn't you stop them?' she demanded. 'You must have known they were going to do it? Why didn't you make sure they kept shtum? Bloody hell! You're such a goddamned idiot, Sam! And I thought Ged had more sense!'

Upstairs, the baby began to wail.

'Jeezus!' she hissed. 'Great timing that brat's got!'

'That's enough, Wendy,' Sam said, his voice low.

She wheeled on him, her eyes narrowed with disbelief. 'What did you say?'

Sam looked up at her slowly, and for the first time ever, wanted with all his heart to slap her stupid! He'd had about all he could take. The way she talked down to him was so ingrained by now that it was like second nature to hear it. But it was the way she spoke to and about the baby he couldn't stomach.

'I said that's enough!' he repeated slowly. 'Enough of throwing your weight around all the goddamned time, and enough of slagging me off for things that have got nothing to do with me. But especially enough of blaming everyone else for every little thing that happens!'

'And just what is *that* supposed to mean?' she hissed. 'Do I have to remind you that I was the one who tried to stop you getting involved in this in the first place? Have you forgotten that it was me – *me* – who got this house sorted out? Not you! And now, because of you—'

Sam jumped to his feet and lunged towards her. Pushing her down on a chair, he towered over her, forcing her to crane her head back as she tried to face him down. Well, not this time.

'Isn't it about time you got off that fucking pedestal you've built for yourself?' he spat into her face, punctuating his words with a few vicious prods in the shoulder. 'Never a day goes by without you reminding me how much you've done for me, and how little I give in return! You think you got this house all by yourself, but you seem to forget the council gave it to us. *Us*, you hear? Because we were having a baby. A baby I helped create, in case you think you did that all by yourself as well? And while we're on the subject of the baby,' he went on furiously. 'Her name is Melissa! Remember? *Mel-is-sa*! Not "brat"! And if I ever hear you talk to her like that again, so help me, Wendy, I'll shut your nasty mouth once and for all!'

Wendy sat stock-still, her mouth gaping, as Sam stormed out of the house. How dare he speak to her like that! Of all the ungrateful . . .

Outside, Sam leaped into his car, shaking with rage. It had been a long time coming, but he'd finally got it said – and he'd meant every word. If he had to listen to one more of her diatribes he'd cheerfully strangle her. And if she carried on treating Melissa like a little sack of shit that had been flung on her to blight her life – he'd kill her! Sure, she fed her, bathed her and changed her nappies. But that was all she did. He'd never once since she came home seen Wendy cuddle her, or kiss her. And he'd never heard her call her by the name they'd eventually chosen. At best she said 'she' or 'her'. But today was by no means the first time she'd called her 'that brat'.

In fact, ever since she'd come home, Wendy had been treating all the kids badly, and if she didn't stop – and quick! – he'd take them all over to his mum's and apply for custody.

With this settled in his head, he started the car and roared away from the kerb. He hoped Ged was at Mal's when he got there. He'd help him put things into perspective. He was the only person in the world who understood how he felt about his kids.

The further Sam got away from the house, the more he felt the tension ease. He let his breath hiss out long and hard between his teeth. He'd never thought it possible to love someone as absolutely as he'd loved Wendy – to adore them, even when they treated you so badly you forgot what it meant to be a man. And he'd certainly never thought it possible for anything to kill that love. But that was starting to happen. Seeing her hold their beautiful, innocent baby at arm's length as she fed her, refusing to meet the child's searching eyes, had filled him with such rage, he doubted if he could ever feel the same way about his wife again.

But he knew he'd have to tread carefully now that he'd antagonized her. She had an awful lot of information about his activities on Sunday night. If she wanted to, she could blow him sky-high.

Ged arrived ten minutes before Sam. The second he stepped in, he was almost knocked off his feet by Mal hurtling around the corner, racing Lee to the toilet.

'What's going on?' he asked Suzie. She smiled but didn't answer.

Elaine greeted him weakly from the couch where she was rocking herself backwards and forwards, clutching at her stomach. Then, looking beyond him to Suzie, her face pained, her voice desperate, she said, 'Have they finished yet? I don't think I can hold it much longer.'

'Well, you'll just have to!' Suzie snapped – so sharply that Ged shot an enquiring look at her.

When Suzie turned then and gave him a sweet smile, he wondered if he'd walked onto the set of *The Stepford Wives*.

Elaine started groaning. '*Ooohh . . . Aaawwhhh*! It's terrible! Tell 'em to hurry up, Sooze. Please! I'm desperate!'

Suzie rolled her eyes and sat down.

'What's wrong with everyone?' Ged asked.

'Sumfink we ate!' Elaine moaned. 'Oh, gawd! It's 'orrible!'

Sam arrived just as Mal and Lee limped back into the living room. Elaine barged straight through them, heading for the foul-smelling bathroom at a run. Sam gave Ged a puzzled look.

'Don't ask!' Ged warned him.

Mal, looking very sorry for himself, slumped onto his chair. ''Ere, doll . . .' he called to Suzie. 'Go down the shops and get us something, will you? I feel like shit!'

'You mean you feel like *having* a shit!' Lee joked feebly from the couch. 'Oh, me poor arse. It feels like it's on fire!'

'Thanks, Lee!' Sam groaned. 'Just what I wanted to hear!'

'It does!' Lee protested. 'It's like when you've had a biryani and thirty lagers and end up with the raging trots.

Only I ain't had no biryani, just tea. Can you get the shits off tea?'

'Shut up, will you!' Mal snapped. 'I'm trying not to bleedin' think about it. How long's that silly cow gonna be in there?'

Lee pushed himself to his feet. 'I'll go and ask her.'

'Oh, God!' Sam said in disgust. 'Can't you just leave her alone for a minute!'

'She might let me in,' Lee said hopefully. 'We could have half the bog each!'

'You're such a disgusting little pig!' Suzie said nastily.

Lee was stunned. He just couldn't get used to Suzie being nasty to him – and she was still smiling, which unnerved him even more. He slumped back down onto the couch. 'I'll just wait, eh?'

Sam exchanged a curious glance with Ged as he sat down beside him. Ged shrugged lightly. Suzie *was* acting strangely, there was no denying that. These idiots must have pissed her off. Best if he and Sam stayed out of it.

'I've just had a row with Wendy,' Sam told him quietly. 'I wanted a bit of advice.'

'You've been upsetting Wendy when she's only just come home?' Suzie cut in sharply. 'Typical!'

Sam looked at her, puzzled by her reaction. 'I didn't mean to,' he protested weakly. 'But you know what she's like. I told her something she didn't want to hear and she completely lost it.'

'Huh!' Suzie muttered. 'I bet!'

'Oi!' Mal snapped at her. 'What the fuck's got into you lately? You're being a right sarky little bitch. Now belt up, or I'll give you what for!'

'I'm sure she didn't mean anything,' Sam said, jumping to her defence.

'Yeah?' Mal snarled. 'Well, I reckon she did! She's been making cracks for days now.' He turned to glare at Suzie, saying, 'And she'd better bleeding stop it, 'cos it's doing me head in! Oi!' he yelled at her. 'Are you bleeding listening?'

'Sorry? Were you talking to me?' Suzie looked over at him innocently.

'What the fuck kind of game are you playing?' Mal screeched, clutching his stomach. 'I'm telling you, girl! Push me too far, and I'll pan your bloody face in!'

Elaine came hobbling back from the bathroom. Immediately, Mal and Lee jumped up and raced for the door, jamming themselves shoulder to shoulder for a second, until Mal got himself free and forced Lee back.

'Sorry for snapping at you, Sam,' Suzie said, feeling guilty for making him look sad. None of this was his fault.

'It's okay,' he said. 'I'll make a brew, eh?' Jumping up, he headed for the kitchen to escape the madness, calling over his shoulder: 'Anyone else want one?'

'No!' Elaine moaned.

'Don't talk to me about tea!' Lee said, hobbling back to the couch. 'It's running out of me like water!'

When Sam was washing the cups out, he spotted the powder residue at the bottom of one. He peered at it, tipping the cup towards the light, and suddenly realized what was going on. Suzie heard his laugh and smiled to herself. She heard the cupboard door open as Sam looked to confirm his suspicion.

'Here, Ged!' he shouted moments later. 'Come and give us a hand, mate!'

Mal came back just then, his pale face glistening with sweat. 'Suzie,' he moaned. 'Go and get me something, can't you? We're supposed to be going to look for Linda, but I can't go like this. Tell them you need something to stop diarrhoea, and hurry up. I'm dying!'

'Don't be such a drama queen!' Suzie snapped, grabbing her coat and walking out as Mal stared openmouthed at her retreating back.

Suzie took her time strolling to the shop. When she got there, she walked slowly down the first aisle, picking up items here and there and studying their labels intently. She was determined not to hurry back. She wanted Mal, Lee and Elaine to suffer for a bit longer. She walked up and down each aisle several times, stopping to look at everything, picking up a few bits and pieces along the way. Shampoo, toothpaste, toilet rolls!

She smiled as she popped this into the basket, enjoying the small revenge. Just part payment for what they'd done to her. She only hoped Sam wouldn't let the cat out of the bag while she was out, or Mal would be doubly bad when he recovered.

After fifteen minutes she had circled the shop three times and was bored. She made her way to the counter, where all three of the Singh brothers were now standing watching her. She felt distinctly uneasy as she approached with her basket. Why were they staring at her so intently? Did they know she was involved in the robbery? Her palms were slippery with sweat as she put the basket down, and she realized her hands were shaking. She just hoped the brothers hadn't noticed.

Ranjit tilled the items up, while Raj put them into a bag. 'Anything else?' he asked when he'd finished.

Suzie was relieved to see that he was smiling, and

scolded herself for being paranoid. 'Er, yes,' she said. 'Do you have anything for diarrhoea?'

'Sure,' he said. 'Diocalm's very good.'

'I'll have a box, please,' she said, then: 'In fact, you'd better make that two.'

Ranjit raised an eyebrow. 'Someone got a gippy tummy?'

'Something like that.' Suzie grinned, casting a nervous glance at Guptar, who was still staring at her very oddly.

Ranjit put the boxes into the bag and said, 'That's eleven pounds seventy-six, please.'

Suzie pulled one of the twenties Mal had given her from her pocket and handed it to him, casting another nervous glance at Guptar.

She took her change and left the shop quickly. But before she had taken ten steps she heard Ranjit shouting at her.

'Suzanne! Suzanne!'

She turned back and saw him waving to her from the shop door. She glanced around nervously to see if there was anyone about who could help her if anything kicked off. But, for once, the area was deserted. Looking back at Ranjit, she saw that he was smiling and relaxed a little. Maybe he'd just forgotten to put something in the bag?

'What's up?' she asked, walking towards him. 'Did I leave something?'

As she reached the door a hand shot out and grabbed her, dragging her inside. She started to scream, but it was too late – they had locked the door behind her, and now they were advancing on her, their faces twisted with anger and suspicion.

22

Millie wasn't in when The Man and Jake called at his flat. But they decided to wait for a while, watching the entrance to his stairwell from the car.

They'd been there for almost an hour before the taxi pulled up. Instantly alert, they both sat forward to watch as the passenger got out. He was a small, thin, nervous-looking man, with a long straggly ponytail and scruffy clothes. They knew it was their man as soon as he turned around and they saw the line of bumpy black stitches adorning his left cheek – Max's handiwork. They gave him a minute to get to his flat before they followed him.

Milton Payne had barely closed the door and dropped his bags of shopping when he heard the knock. Without thinking, he leaned back and opened it again. As soon as he saw the two vicious-looking men he knew he'd made a mistake, but it was too late to do anything. He made a half-hearted attempt to throw his weight against the door, but Jake effortlessly knocked him flying, and they came in, pushing him across the hallway until his back was against the far wall. He cowered there, hunching his body over in preparation for the kicking he knew would come.

'I h-haven't g-got anything,' he whimpered.

'That's not what I heard!' The Man said, reaching a massive hand out to pin Millie's neck to the wall.

Jake grinned. *Action at last*! 'You want me to start searching?' he asked.

The Man nodded. 'Yeah, sure.' And, turning to Millie, he said, 'And you're gonna help by telling us where to start, aren't you? Or do we have to tear the whole place to pieces, and you into the bargain?'

'I don't know what you're looking for!' Millie squealed. 'I've got no drugs!'

The Man laughed, a cruel barking sound that filled Millie with dread. 'Drugs? I ain't interested in drugs, you skanky smack-head! It's my fucking *money* I want – and you'd better tell me where you stashed it, or I'll rip your fucking head off your neck – slowly!' To emphasize this, he threw his other hand across Millie's face, pressing down on the raw stitches and hooping his fingers into the jawbone, digging in and applying pressure – hard and slow.

Millie felt as though his skin were ripping, and he felt his jawbone bend beneath the huge fingers as his face began to distort.

'Pleeashhh . . .' he moaned as tears dribbled from his eyes. 'Don't hurt me, pleeashhh!'

As suddenly as he'd begun, The Man stopped squeezing and let go, slapping the swollen stitched cheek none too gently. 'Just tell me where you stashed it, batty bwoy?'

Millie began to sob as he felt the blood trickle down from his burst stitches. 'I – I honestly don't k-know what you m-mean! Someone came a few d-days ago asking the same thing, but I don't know anything. I s-swear on my life!'

Jake tutted. 'Let's waste him!' he said. 'Stop his whingeing!'

'Nah!' The Man shook his head. 'I want to talk to the guy.'

'Talk!' Jake spat furiously. 'What's with all dis talkin' shit? It's all you ever wanna do these days. I don't understand you, man! You should be whackin' these dickheads, not chattin'! What's wrong wi' choo, man!'

The backhander caught Jake totally by surprise. His hand flew to his cheek where The Man's ring had scored the flesh. He touched the thin, oozing stripe and looked at the blood on his fingers disbelievingly.

'You ever talk to me like that again,' The Man hissed, 'I'll do more than slap you back into line! You're heading for a big fall, star!'

Jake pulled his head back angrily. 'Wha' you do that fe?'

The Man's eyes glittered dangerously. 'Like I said, you're heading for a fall. Now you take one step too many and I'll push you right over! You're supposed to be my spar and I should be able to trust you, but something in you is going turncoat and that bothers me. If I can't trust you, dread, then I got no use for you! And I'll tell you, man: you make me reach that decision and you'll have to go – for real!'

Millie watched the exchange in petrified silence. These two were friends, but if they could threaten each other like this – what would they do to *him*? The air was so thick with malice, he felt his stomach churn. If he survived this day, he was moving out of this place for ever! He didn't care if he had to live in a box in the drains at the back of the abattoir! Anywhere would be better than this!

Satisfied that Jake didn't want to press him any further, The Man turned his attention back to Millie.

Seizing his lank ponytail, he pulled him away from the wall and hauled him through the doorway into the living room. Jake followed sulkily, folding his arms and leaning against the door frame as The Man threw Millie down onto a chair.

Everywhere around them were the signs of Max's recent visit. The smashed TV lay on its side, against the wall now where Millie had shoved it to clear up the shattered glass. The furniture had been slashed from corner to corner, the material hanging in thin strips – the beige inner foam scored like an uncooked pork roast. The worn carpet still glittered with embedded shards of broken glass and pottery, although Millie had brushed and hoovered many times. In fact, he'd gone over the place like a maniac after getting home from the hospital that night, determined to wipe out the awful memory of the man who'd violated his space.

And now it was happening again – and he still didn't know anything about this money they kept going on about.

The Man pulled a twenty-pound note from his pocket and snapped it open in front of Millie's face. 'What you know about this? he demanded.

Millie looked from the note to The Man in utter confusion. 'N-nothing. What d'y' mean?'

'You saying you never seen this before?'

'I don't understand!' Millie squeaked, flinching as The Man snapped the note again. 'It's just money.'

'What about them marks?' The Man jabbed a finger at the eyes.

Millie peered at the eyes, but without his glasses he couldn't see any details. He shrugged nervously. 'I don't know what you want me to say.'

'That's part of my money that was ripped off when Pasha got smoked!' The Man snapped. 'You telling me you don't know nothing about that?'

'No, honest I don't!'

Mercifully, The Man's mobile began to ring. He reached into his jacket and pulled it free, his face a mask of irritation at the interruption.

'What?' he barked. He listened for a moment, then slapped the phone shut. Marching towards the door, he motioned Jake to follow. 'C'mon. We've got something!'

Jake caught the undertone of excitement in his voice and followed without question, leaving Millie wondering what on earth was happening.

He couldn't believe it when he heard the front door slam behind them. He waited a minute, trying not to breathe as he strained to hear sounds that would tell him it was just another part of the game. Would he open the living-room door and find them waiting for him? Finally he decided to brave it. He opened the door an inch at a time until there was enough room to peep through. The flat was empty. With jelly legs he ran to the front door and threw both bolts into place, then the chain and, finally, the mortise.

Then he went to pack.

'Where we going?' Jake asked, sliding into the driver's seat.

'The shop,' The Man told him, jumping in the other side and slamming the door. 'And get a move on.'

'Why? What's going on?'

'Some girl just turned up with some of the money,' The Man explained, grinning. 'They've got her locked up in there, waiting for us!'

*   *   *

Suzie had been crying. Her nose was glowing red like a beacon, her eyes were puffy and sore-looking. She'd been strip-searched by Guptar, and had received a few hard slaps for struggling. She instinctively knew not to carry on fighting. These men were not like Mal. Mal hurt her when he beat her, but he always stopped at that. These men were capable of much worse.

She'd realized immediately what was going on when the doors had slammed shut behind her and Guptar had thrust the twenty-pound note into her face, demanding to know where she'd got it from. She'd tried to deny knowing anything, but they'd crowded around her, pushing and shoving, all screaming into her face at once.

'My uncle made those marks!' Guptar had screeched at her, pointing wildly at the smudged marks in the Queen's eyes.

Suzie was shocked, and very, very frightened. None of Mal's crew had noticed the marks. The only indication they'd had that night that the separate bundle was somehow different from the rest had been on the bag itself. It had borne the initials 'S. M.'

'You murdered our uncle!' the brothers had accused her angrily.

'I didn't!' she'd protested. 'I swear to God, I didn't!'

But they hadn't believed her. How else would she have the money, unless she'd done it – or knew who had? And why else would the police have been in here with her photograph? Either way, the brothers were going to find out. And if that meant beating her until she told them what she knew – then so be it.

They had dragged her kicking and screaming into the stock room where Guptar had conducted his strip-search. When they had found the other marked twenty in her pocket, they had decided it was time to call in The Man.

Ranjit waited at the back door as Guptar tied Suzie's hands behind her back. He saw the Jag turn onto the road and held the door open as The Man and Jake pulled into the yard, hissing at them to hurry up.

The Man came in first, striding into the small room like a boxer going into the ring. 'This her?' he asked, looking down on the terrified girl perched on the desk with her hands tied behind her back.

'Murdering bitch!' Guptar snarled, handing the two twenties to The Man. 'She had these!'

The Man took the notes and turned to Suzie. 'Where did you get these?' he demanded.

Suzie's mind was racing. She knew this was really heavy and debated telling them about Mal and Lee. But, remembering that Ged and Sam were at the flat, she decided against it. She couldn't put them in danger. And surely this man wouldn't do anything bad to her?

'I said, where did you get it?' The Man repeated.

When she didn't answer, he motioned to Jake with his head. Grinning, Jake stepped up to her and grabbed her hair in his hand, forcing her head back until she was staring up at The Man.

'Where?' The Man said.

'At the p-post office,' she said, gritting her teeth against the pain. 'I got it at the post office when I cashed my giro this morning.'

Still holding her hair, Jake brought his other hand up and slapped her hard.

'Where?' The Man said again.

'The p-post office!' she sobbed, her mind reeling from the blow.

Slap!

'Try again!'

'I did! I swear I did!'

The Man curled his lip and sneered at her. 'I ain't playin' games wi'choo, bitch! Now tell me, or I'm gonna let my man here—' he gestured towards Jake '—take you for a long ride in the country!'

Suzie glanced at Jake and the smile she saw on his face chilled her to her soul. Her heart began to rattle and the breath constricted in her throat. Jake leaned over, staring into her eyes with his strange green ones. He smiled at her terror.

'I'll take her now, boss!' he whispered evilly.

'NO!' Suzie yelped, imploring The Man with her eyes. 'Please, no!'

Ranjit reached out and touched The Man's arm. 'We can't keep her here. The police were round earlier, asking a load of questions. And they had a picture of her.' He nodded towards Suzie. 'Asked if we knew her name and address.'

The Man motioned Jake to let go of Suzie's hair and checked his watch. It was only four o'clock. It would be an hour before it started to go dark. They couldn't stay here if the police were sniffing around – they had to get her to a safe place. But where? They couldn't take her to his flat because Patrice was due back in the morning. And they couldn't take her to Jake's in case they had to go out again. If she was alone, she might get free and raise the alarm.

Then he thought of the ideal place.

'Right, we're out of here!' he said, grabbing Suzie by the front of her coat and dragging her from the desk. He glared down into her face. 'We're walking out into the yard now, bitch, and if you know what's good for you, you won't draw attention to us, yeah?'

Suzie nodded quickly, too terrified to speak. She flicked a glance at Jake and saw the disappointment on his face. She knew that whatever happened next, she'd escaped something terrible just now. She could see as clear as day what had been running through Jake's mind, and knew she would be lucky to see another day if he managed to get her out into the countryside.

Her whole body shook with terror as The Man had a hushed conversation with the Singh brothers. Then he hauled her outside and shoved her onto the back seat of the Jag.

'Suzie's been an awful long time,' Ged commented, glancing at his watch.

'Tell me about it!' Mal snapped. 'Bitch! I only asked her to get something to stop me bleeding shits. It's a good job it's stopping by itself, or she'd be in for a right good slapping! Anyway, fuck her!' He got to his feet, rubbing at his sore stomach as he went for his mirror. 'I'm having another line. Who wants one?'

'Me!' chorused Lee and Elaine.

'I knew *you* greedy gits would,' Mal said. 'I was asking Ged and Sam.'

'No, thanks, man.' Sam shook his head. 'I'd better get back to mine and see what kind of mood Wendy's in now.'

'Yeah, and I want to go and see Caroline, see if she's had any word from Linda,' Ged said. 'She's been in a right state.'

'Thought we was going looking for that Simon bloke?' Mal said, pulling his bag of coke out of the drawer.

'Bloody Hell!' he exclaimed loudly, holding it up to the light. 'That's gone down quick!' He shot a look of suspicion around the room. 'Have one of you thieving bastards been at this?'

'Behave yourself!' Ged pushed himself up from the chair. 'You've necked it all!'

Mal shook the bag, peering suspiciously at the half-inch of powder lining the bottom. 'Bollocks! I've never done all that by myself!'

Ged laughed. 'Come off it, man. Every time I see you you've got a tube stuck up your schnoz – you and the other two Musketeers there!' He flipped a thumb at Lee and Elaine. Shaking his head, he turned to Sam. 'You coming?'

'Yeah,' Sam said, jumping to his feet. 'Have you got your car, or do you want a lift?'

'You can give us a lift,' Ged said.

'You're coming back to go and sort that pervy bastard out, aren't you?' Mal asked again.

'Yeah. When it's dark,' Ged said. 'See you later.'

Caroline still had no news, and she'd worked herself into a state by the time Ged got there. He tried his best to reassure her that everything would turn out all right, but she burst into tears and said she had an awful feeling she was never going to see Linda again.

'She must have been so unhappy,' she sobbed as Ged fussed around her, making her take a cup of sweet tea and lighting a cigarette for her. 'All I ever did was yell at her and tell her all the bad things she was doing. How could I have been so selfish?'

'Hey,' Ged grinned softly. 'Selfish is my line, isn't it? Now, come on, stop blaming yourself. You've done everything you could. If this is anyone's fault it's mine. I walked out on you. It's me who wasn't here when Linda needed guidance.'

After half an hour, Caroline had cried herself to sleep. Ged covered her with a quilt and sat watching her while he waited for Sam to pick him up. She was becoming so thin, almost withering away by the day, it seemed, and he wondered if she was eating. If he wasn't so worried about Linda, he'd give her a bloody good hiding when he found her, for what she was doing to her mum.

Before he knew it, Sam was honking his horn outside. Ged wrote a quick note telling Caroline he'd see her later and propped it up on the coffee table before quietly letting himself out.

Ged asked Sam to take him back to his own flat before they went to Mal's. He desperately needed to eat. Sam was very quiet on the drive, and Ged asked how it had gone with Wendy. Sam said she'd been strange when he got home. She looked like she'd been crying, and she hadn't given him any grief, even when he said he'd be going out again. He'd expected ructions, but she'd accepted it without a word, and now he was suspicious.

'What do you think she's up to?' he said. 'You don't think she's planning to take off with the kids while I'm out, do you?'

'She wouldn't be that cruel,' Ged said. 'Anyway, she loves that house. She's not going to walk out because you've had a row, is she?'

'I don't know,' Sam said. 'I don't know what she's capable of at the moment.'

'She won't,' Ged said with quiet certainty. He peered

across at Sam's worried face. 'It's really getting to you, isn't it? Not just Wendy – all this Pasha stuff.'

'It's everything,' Sam admitted. 'Mal and Lee acting like they've done nothing wrong. Suzie being weird. And now Wendy. I can't take it. It's all getting out of control. And it was bad enough that it happened, but it's really spooked me, them telling Elaine. God! If they could tell a big mouth like that, they're capable of anything!'

Ged nodded. 'It's put the wind up me, too. The only good thing is we didn't actually do it. And that's about the only thing we'll have going for us if this blows up, so just keep reminding yourself. As for Elaine – the way she's necking the coke, with any luck she'll do herself in before too long. Maybe someone should suggest she tries mainlining?' Sam shot a worried look at him. 'Just wishful thinking!' Ged assured him.

'And as for Suzie,' he went on. 'I reckon those three have upset her. Have you noticed the way she looks at them?'

'That's Mal,' Sam said. 'She's terrified of him.'

'Yeah,' Ged agreed, frowning. 'But I'm sure it's not just him. She really hates Elaine. I've seen the way she looks at her. And look at all that business with the laxatives. Why would she give it to Lee and Elaine if she wasn't upset with them as well?'

Sam smiled and shook his head. 'Funny, though, wasn't it? She's got a right little vicious streak in her!'

'Good for her!' Ged said. 'It's about time Mal got some of his own medicine! Anyhow, don't worry about Suzie. She can obviously take care of herself if it comes to the crunch. The thing you need to sort out is this business with Wendy. It's not good for you, her or the kids.'

'That's what's bothering me,' Sam muttered.

'Well, the way I see it,' Ged said, 'Wendy's doing her best to give her kids a decent future. Think about it, Sam. She's stuck by you through everything. Even now, with all this shit with Mal and Lee. And yeah, she nags, but she's only trying to help you. Hassling the council for that house, doing her damnedest to keep people like Lee away. And what do you go and do? You invite him in, and let him think it's only Wendy who's got a problem with him. Anyway, do you think she'd have gone to all this trouble to keep you if she didn't love you? Don't make the same mistake I made.'

Sam turned to look at him. 'Do you regret leaving Caroline?'

Ged shrugged. 'I've spent the last year telling myself that it was the right move. But, if I'm honest, I've missed her. Oh, I know I've slagged her off, but I suppose I was just shifting the blame away from myself. These past few days have shown me what I've thrown away. I look at her and see the girl she was – especially now she's so vulnerable. But she looks awful, Sam. I'm worried about her.'

'Enough to go back?'

Ged bit his lip and stared out of the window. 'I've been thinking about it, but I don't even know if she wants me back. It's not exactly a good time to ask, is it?'

'It could be exactly the right time,' Sam said quietly.

'I envy you,' Ged said. 'Seeing you with your kids and your wife, at home – having dinner, watching telly. Normal family stuff. I really wish you could see it through my eyes. You don't know how good you've got it. Don't lose it. I mean, what's the alternative? Hanging around with tossers like Mal and Lee?

'Anyway, enough of the lecture. Let's get something to eat, then we can pick up the tossers and go sort out the bastard who's got my Linda!'

'Do me a favour,' Sam said as he turned onto the road that would take them past Greenheys. 'Put your seat belt on. They can fine me now for not making you.'

Ged pulled the belt on and glanced at the station. 'Maybe we should go and grass them up, eh? Get them collared before it all goes pear-shaped?'

'You don't think they'd go down without taking us with them, do you?' Sam snorted. 'No, Ged. The further we stay away from the police the better.'

As Sam and Ged passed by just feet away, Paul Dalton was tapping away at a computer in a secluded office, painstakingly trying to access the recorded owners of BMWs in the Manchester area. It was a painfully slow process, given that he could only type with one finger and he had very limited time because his shift was due to finish in ten minutes. He jumped when the door opened, but was relieved to see that it was just Eddie.

'What you up to?' Eddie asked, coming in and closing the door behind him.

'Looking for a needle in a haystack,' Paul said, rubbing a hand across his eyes.

'You want to get Diane to do it,' Eddie suggested. 'She's a little whiz on that thing. What you looking for, anyway?' He leaned over Paul's shoulder and peered at the screen. 'Looking to buy a motor? BMW, eh? Bit upmarket for you. Got someone special to impress? Your little nurse friend – Jane, for example?'

Paul elbowed him in the ribs. 'Jane's a mate, that's all.

Anyway, I don't think you should be joking about *my* nurse friend, do you?'

Eddie raised his hands and took a step back. 'Whoa! Let's not go there. I won't mention Jane again if you forget all about that other . . . *thing*! Deal?'

'Deal,' Paul laughed. 'Anyhow, I'm not trying to get rid of you, but I want to get on with this. I've only got ten minutes and I'm nowhere near finding what I want.'

'Here, let me have a go,' Eddie said, nudging Paul aside. 'You'll be here for ever with your one-finger shit. Now me – I've got skill, I have! You're doing it wrong, anyway, just asking for the make. You want the CC and colour too. Let's see now . . .'

Paul shook his head in amazement as Eddie's fingers flew around the keyboard. In seconds he'd accessed a list of all registered owners of silver 325s and 318s in the Greater Manchester area. Hundreds of them!

'I'll never find it in that lot,' he moaned. 'I'm finishing in a minute.'

'The magic doesn't end there!' Eddie winked. Pressing 'print', he sat back as the machine spewed out its information.

'There you go,' he said, taking the folded sheets and handing them to Paul. 'Now you can study them at your leisure, can't you? Word of advice, though. Don't let the sarge catch you taking it out or you'll get a right roll-icking. Coming to The George tonight?'

'No, I want to go through this,' Paul said, rolling the sheets up and sticking them inside his jacket. 'Looks like it'll take all night.'

'I'll bring some cans over and help if you want?' Eddie offered.

Paul considered it. DCI Jackson had told him to stay

shtum, but would it really hurt? Anyway, he was sure he could trust Eddie.

'Okay, yeah,' he said at last. 'Thanks, mate. Only thing is, it's got to stay strictly between us for now, otherwise DCI Jackson will have my balls!'

'Say no more,' Eddie nodded. 'Must be something hot if your new buddy's in on it! So, you gonna tell me about it?'

'Later,' Paul said, looking at his watch. 'Right, I'm off. See you this evening – and don't forget those cans!'

Paul passed Jackson's office just as the man himself was leaving.

'Good evening, sir,' he said. 'Have we got anything new yet?'

Jackson glanced over his shoulder as he bent to lock the door. 'Oh, hello, lad. Not much, but I'm working on it.' Straightening up, he began to walk down the corridor, still talking quietly.

'The blonde our Mrs Lilley ID'd. Seems we've had the pleasure of her company a few times already. Shoplifting, a couple of drunk-and-disorderlies, and a GBH she managed to wangle her way out of. Not too nice. I'm going to pay her a visit tomorrow and have a little word. See if she comes up with anything interesting, and find out who her red-headed friend is while I'm at it. Which reminds me, pencil me in for a ride tomorrow. And I want to call in at the Singhs' other shop.' He stopped and glanced at his watch. 'You off duty now?'

'Yes, sir,' Paul said. 'I'm just going home, to check out a list of BMW owners . . .' He let the words trail from his lips, then blushed.

Jackson shook his head with a wry grin. 'Trouble with you kids, you can't keep your gobs shut. Never mind. I'll pretend I didn't hear you. See you in the morning – and don't be late: we've got a lot of travelling to do.'

23

Max wasn't pleased when he opened his door to The Man, Jake and a girl he'd never seen before. All the grief The Man had given him about never bringing pussy to his flat, and here he was, doing exactly that to him!

'Wha'pp'n?' he asked, eyeing Suzie suspiciously.

'Need a favour,' The Man said. 'Let's get her out of sight, and I'll explain.' Without waiting for consent, he shoved Suzie before him into the hall.

'Why's her hands tied up?' Max hissed, looking out quickly to check if they'd been seen before closing the door.

'We need to get some answers out of her about these,' The Man said, taking the notes the Singh brothers had given him from his pocket. 'She was caught with them at Pasha's.'

'Raas!' Max exclaimed, taking the notes and looking at the marks. 'Where'd she get them?'

'That's what I want to find out,' The Man said. 'You got somewhere nice and quiet we can take her?'

'Down the cellar,' Max said. 'Just let me get my keys.'

In the cellar, they sat Suzie on a chair and tied her ankles to the legs. This done, they went upstairs to have a drink and a smoke, leaving her to sweat. They figured the more frightened she was, the quicker she'd tell them what she knew – and, with luck, they wouldn't have to get too rough. It was hard to tell how much damage you were doing to women when you slapped them. The last thing they wanted to do was make it so she couldn't tell them!

They left her for an hour before going back down.

Suzie's eyes had become accustomed to the dark and she winced painfully when the light suddenly came on. The unshaded bulb blazed viciously, making the men appear too stark – too real. She peered up at them nervously as they advanced on her. They were all big men, and their size intimidated her. She was used to Mal leaning over her, threatening and bullying, but he seemed like a petulant child by comparison.

The Man was enormous, his clean-shaven head glistening with the sweat of irritation and his eyes so dark they almost seemed alien. But the thing Suzie noticed above everything else were his hands. Huge square hands covered in heavy gold rings. Hands that could do a lot of damage with very little effort.

The second man – Jake, The Man had called him – was a bit smaller and lighter than the others, but there was something about him that turned Suzie's stomach to water. He was incredibly handsome, his face only slightly marred by an angry-looking scratch across his cheek. His nose and lips were finely shaped, and his eyes were a very strange but beautiful shade of green. But beyond the perfect features lay a cruelty – a violence that Suzie could almost taste. He seemed to hate her, and even though she knew they *all* hated her for being part of the Pasha thing and for having that money, none of the others were giving off such strong vibes of malevolence.

The third man, the one whose house this was, was as tall as The Man, but not as broad or muscular. And of the three, he seemed the most ill at ease with having her there. She wondered how far he was prepared to allow them to go with her – here in his house, his cellar. Surely he wouldn't let them kill her? Surely he wouldn't be stupid enough to put himself on the line just as a favour for his friends?

'Right then, Red,' The Man said when they were all standing around her. 'Tell me where you got my money.'

Suzie looked up at him wide-eyed. 'The post office,' she whispered.

He leaned forward with his hands on his knees, his face just inches from hers. 'Don't fuck with me,' he said, his voice low and menacing. 'I ain't letting you go until you tell me the truth, so you'd better start talking. That money is mine, and there's no way you could have got your bleached-out hands on it unless you had something t'do with Pasha getting killed. Do you understand what I'm saying? I know you had something to do with it, and if you don't start talkin', I'm gonna get real mad! Now I'll ask you once more. *Where . . . did . . . you . . . get it?*'

Suzie understood, all right. It wouldn't help her to carry on lying about the post office. So she opted for saying nothing – which only fuelled the flame.

The slap knocked her head into the wall with a sickening thud. She was stunned for a moment, then nauseous and dizzy. Her eyes rolled as she tried to focus, and her ears seemed to explode in a rushing, hissing cacophony of noise – so loud that she almost couldn't hear what the men were saying as they discussed what to do with her.

Then, suddenly, the room became a vacuum devoid of all sound as she saw Max open his strongbox and take out a gun. He handed it to The Man, who then pointed it at her face. Opening her mouth to scream, she felt the cold steel ramming between her lips. Gagging wildly, she stared at him.

'That's better,' he said, pulling the gun out and brushing it slowly along her lip. 'Now, where were we? Oh, yeah . . . Where did you get my money? And if you don't tell me I'll start tekkin' little bits off you. Let's see, now . . . Where should I start?'

'Hands and feet,' Jake suggested. 'Very painful, but no danger of her dying!'

'Good idea.' The Man grinned. 'Hands it is, then!'

Jake took a dangerous-looking flick knife from his pocket and sliced through the twine binding Suzie's hands. He drew the flat of the blade slowly across her cheek before flicking it shut, then grabbed her wrist and slammed it flat against the wall, holding her firmly so The Man had a clear shot at the hand.

'Last chance,' The Man hissed.

Suzie's eyes swam. She felt the numbness rush up her cheeks as darkness swept across her vision. There was a rushing in her head and she was dimly aware of the warm trickle running down her legs as her bladder gave way to the fear. Then, mercifully . . . Nothing.

'She's fainted.' Jake grinned. 'And look. She's pissed herself!'

'Good,' The Man said, pulling a chair from the corner of the cellar and sitting down to wait for her to wake up. 'She's good and scared, so this shouldn't take long. And if she still doesn't give it up when she comes round, I'll take her little finger off. That does it every time!'

'And the rest!' Max said, pointing at the gun. 'You'll take half her arm and part of the wall out if you shoot her with that!'

The Man turned the gun over in his hand, admiring its

sleek lines. 'That good, eh?' he said. 'It's a nice piece, man. What do you want for it?'

Max shook his head. 'Sorry, man. It ain't on the market. Hey.' He nodded towards the girl. 'She's coming round.'

Suzie opened her eyes, hoping against hope that it was just a horrible nightmare. But it was all too real. The Man was sitting in front of her now, leaning forward with his elbows on his knees and the gun still in his hand – still pointing at her. She was aware of the cold wetness between her legs and blushed with shame. This was more humiliating than anything she'd ever experienced, and she almost wished The Man *had* shot her. At least it would all be over now.

'What's your name?' The Man asked her quietly.

'Su-Suzie,' she stuttered.

'How old are you Suzie?'

'Seventeen. N-nearly eighteen.'

'And where you live?'

'In the Crescents.'

'Wid your folks?'

'N-no. My b-boyfriend, Mal.'

Max's ears instantly pricked up. 'Just a minute. You say *Mal*? An' you live in the Crescents?'

Suzie nodded.

''S up?' The Man asked. 'You know this dude?'

'Nah,' Max shook his head. 'It's just the name rings a bell.' He turned back to the girl. 'You know Stevo?'

Suzie frowned, trying to remember. 'I don't know. I think I've heard the name somewhere.'

'Scottish bloke,' Max went on. 'Black hair. Dealer.'

Suzie thought hard. 'Oh, yeah,' she said after a moment. 'He knows Mal. Does he sell coke?'

Max slapped a hand on his thigh and turned to The Man. 'That's it, star! It wasn't *Millie*, it was *Mal*! I told you Stevo said a name an' I couldn't remember it proper, yeah? I thought it sounded like Millie or Melly or sump'n. Remember? Well, it was Mal! *He*'s the dude who took your money round to Stevo!'

'Well, well!' The Man said. 'Looks like we found our bwoy! What number you live at, Suzie?'

Suzie started to cry. 'Oh please . . .' she sobbed. 'What are you going to do?'

'First thing I'm gonna do is find out what you know about all this,' The Man said. 'You help me now, an' I promise I won't hurt you. But you start playin' fuckeries with me, I'll punish you. Understand, Suzie?' Suzie nodded. 'Good girl,' he said, smiling. 'Now let's start with the money. Your man give you this?'

'Yes,' Suzie whispered.

'Where he get it?'

'From Pasha.'

'He kill Pasha?'

She shook her head. 'No. His friend did it. But it was an accident.'

'What d'y' mean, *accident*?' The Man snorted disbelievingly.

'Well, I wasn't there,' Suzie said. 'But they said Pasha shot at them first, and Lee just panicked and shot back.'

Max nodded. 'There were two guns. That one,' he nodded to the one The Man was holding, 'an' another I've got in the box.'

'Raas!' The Man shouted, throwing the gun to Max and wiping his hands down his legs. 'You got me holdin' the fuckin' claat gun that kill't the dude? You stupid? Wipe my raas prints off of it, man!'

'Nah, man,' Max said, carefully wiping the gun down and laying it back in the box. 'That ain't the one! That's the one Pasha had hold of. The one what killed him is in the box.'

The Man rolled his eyes. 'Don't fuckin' do that to me again, right!'

'Sorry, man,' Max muttered. 'I didn't think.'

The Man gave him a dirty look, then turned back to continue questioning Suzie.

'Now then, Suzie. What about the money? They know that was mine?'

Suzie shook her head. 'They just thought it was the takings from the shop.'

'How much was there?'

'I don't really know.'

'Suzie . . .?' He spoke softly, peering hard into her eyes. 'Don't fuck up on me now we've come this far.'

She looked down. 'About seventy thousand.'

Max whistled between his teeth. 'Man!'

'Seventy grand!' The Man spat at her. 'And they thought it was the shop's takings? You think I'm stupid or sump'n, eh? They must have known it wasn't shop money! They must have known it was mine. Which means—' his voice was ice '—they planned to rip me off!'

'They didn't,' Suzie said. 'Honest, they didn't! Lee planned it. He said Pasha always took the takings home on a Sunday night to take to the bank first thing Monday. They didn't think anything else about it, and the shooting was an accident, really it was.'

'Yeah, well, never mind that now,' The Man said. 'Where's the rest of the money?'

'They shared it out,' Suzie told him. 'But I think they've spent quite a lot of it already. That Stevo—' she turned to

Max '—he came round the other morning with a big bag of coke. Mal bought it off him.'

'My fuckin' ounce!' Max snorted. 'He never even paid me for that!'

Suzie shook her head. 'Oh, no. I'm sure it was only half an ounce. And Mal paid him for it, honest! He's good when it comes to paying his debts!'

'Yeah! When it's not his money he's spendin'!' Jake sneered. 'Where is he now? This Mal?'

'At home,' Suzie whispered, unable to meet Jake's piercing eyes. 'He was there when I left.'

'With?'

'Lee, and Lee's girlfriend, Elaine. And two friends, Ged and Sam.'

'They know about it?' The Man asked.

Suzie hesitated, then nodded reluctantly. 'But it was nothing to do with them,' she blurted out. 'They just agreed to go along with Mal and Lee. They freaked out when they found out Lee had a gun. They didn't want anything to do with it after that, but it was too late 'cos they were already there. They didn't even go in the yard, 'cos Lee had already shot Pasha before they went over the wall.'

'You a good friend of this Ged and Sam, then, are you?' The Man asked.

'It's not that,' Suzie looked up at him, a worried frown on her face. 'I just don't think it's fair for them to get the blame for something they didn't do.'

The Man looked at her hard for a few moments, then nodded. 'Loyalty,' he said quietly, casting a sly glance at Jake. 'I like that.'

He stood up suddenly, pushing the chair back and bending to untie Suzie's ankles. 'You've been a big help, and I said you wouldn't get hurt if you helped so I'm gonna let you go. But not just yet. You'll have to stay down here till we've sorted out what we're doing.' He turned to Max, motioning to the stairs with a nod. 'Jake can stay and watch you.'

'NO! Don't leave me,' Suzie called after him, her eyes shining with naked fear as she flicked a glance at Jake. 'Please!'

'Yo, Jake,' The Man called with a laugh in his voice. 'You're frightening the little lady. Tell you what, why don't you go an' mek us all a brew, spar. We can trust you on your own for a bit, can't we, Suzie?'

'Yes, but can . . . can I go to the bathroom, please?' Suzie asked, getting shakily to her feet.

'Sure,' The Man smiled, stepping aside to wave her up the stairs.

While she was in the bathroom cleaning herself up, the men sat around the kitchen table discussing what to do now they knew where the money was. The first thing they needed to sort out was what to do with Suzie. They couldn't let her go yet in case she warned her boyfriend before they got to him – and that would be the last they ever saw of the money. They also didn't want to leave her alone in case she managed to escape. They needed to put her somewhere safe until they'd sorted it out.

'How about Marie's?' Jake suggested.

'Don't forget she's got that Linda there already,' The Man said.

'Oh, yeah,' Max said. 'What about the bloke with the wallet – the one who came axing about you an' that Linda?'

'What? The Babylon claat?' Jake snorted.

Max shot a look at him. 'I hope you're not gonna start that shit up again?'

Jake held his hands up. 'Chill, man, I'm jokin'! Look, I'm prepared to admit I got it wrong. With what we've just found out, I guess you've been on the level, an' I'm sorry. Okay?'

'All right,' Max said. 'But I didn't appreciate the things you said, Jake. We're supposed to be brothers, ain't we? Don't do nutt'n like that again, seen?'

'Seen,' Jake agreed, holding his fist out to touch Max's.

'While we're on it,' The Man said, giving Jake a cool look. 'You've been out of order with me too, dread. You wanna tell me what's goin' on in your head?'

Jake shrugged uneasily. 'I just don't understand why you wanna be so lenient wid all these scallies. I mean, man . . . that Millie. Why you have to *talk* to him?'

'It was good I didn't do nutt'n else, seein' as it wasn't him,' The Man said levelly. 'He was the wrong dude, man. What if I'd done him like you wanted?'

Jake didn't say anything.

'This is why I started thinking a while back that we should consider all the facts before we mek a move,' The Man went on seriously. 'That way we got a better chance of not fucking up, and the more I do it, the more I know I'm right. It don't mean I'm going soft. It just means I always know where I'm at. Mistakes are too easy, and just one can bring us down. That's what we've got over all the other posses right now. Logic. Sense enough to keep ourselves out of the shit until we got roses to grow.'

Jake dipped his head. He knew The Man was right, and wondered again if he'd guessed what he'd had in mind about taking over his businesses. He hoped not.

'Anyway,' The Man said, pushing his chair back. 'It's

time to get moving. Max, call Suzie down an' we'll get off.'

Max went to call her down. When he came back with her he was grinning.

'You said I'd get a bonus if the money turned up, yeah?'

The Man nodded. 'Yeah. And another if you're in on this.'

'Sound,' Max said. 'You want me to bring one of the guns?'

'Yeah. The one the dude used on Pasha. That should freak them out!'

'I'll have to meet you at the Crescents,' Max said. 'Only I've got a couple of things to do first.'

'No, come to my yard,' The Man said. 'But give us a couple of hours. I want to get the girl over to Marie's, an' get something to eat.'

He stood up and walked to the door, taking Suzie's arm. Turning back to Max, he said, 'Don't forget to load it, spar. These roses are definitely for pruning!'

Suzie didn't make a fuss as The Man led her from the house with a firm hand on her arm. She tried to memorize the door number in case she needed it later. Then she tried to get a look at the registration of the Jag, but only managed to get the letter 'S' and the number '1'.

Max went back down to the cellar when they'd gone, rubbing his hands together in anticipation of his share of seventy grand. He deserved it for all the crap The Man and Jake had put him through over the last few days. Losing his ounce when Stevo took off had just been the start. He'd then lost money that was rightfully his, and nearly been set up over the Millie business. Now he could add his part in kidnapping the girl to the list, and that wouldn't be good. The Man owed him a lot more than the other hundred of his own money and a poxy bonus! And Max would make sure he got it.

But first things first. He had to get his house in order, to minimize his risks.

Reaching for an industrial-size tin of Jeye's Fluid, he set about cleaning away all trace of the girl – starting with the chair and the floor where the poor cow had pissed herself. If it all came on top, there must be nothing left to say she'd ever been here. There was no way he was getting done for kidnapping!

24

Paul had written out a list of possibles by the time Eddie arrived.

'Do you know any of these?' he asked, handing it across in exchange for the pack of beers Eddie was carrying.

Eddie scanned through the names, then pointed out two. They were both local.

'This one, Ali Akram from Whalley Range, he's straight as a die. Owns a cash-and-carry, got burgled a couple of months ago. But this Winston Dennison from Moss Side, he's totally *not* straight. He's a right gangster.' Handing the list back, he ripped the tab off a can and took a long drink. 'So what's it all about?' he asked.

'Before I tell you,' Paul said. 'DCI Jackson doesn't want this to get out at the station, so you've got to keep shtum.'

'Why?' Eddie asked. 'It's a live case.'

'It's delicate,' Paul explained. 'Remember that call we took from Iggy's? Well, it was from an old woman who'd witnessed it, and the DCI wants to sit on her name to protect her.'

Eddie frowned. 'I thought we already had an eye-witness?'

'Do me a favour!' Paul laughed. 'Did you read her statement? It was bollocks. But this old girl's kosher, and she's given us everything – times, descriptions, cars.'

Eddie smiled. 'I get it. So she's ID'd this Beemer you're looking for? How old is she?' he asked. 'She all there?'

'Oh, she's all there, all right,' Paul said. 'Jackson's well impressed with her.'

'So why the secrecy?'

'Because she reckons there were at least four men at the yard that night, and she's scared what'll happen if anyone finds out she saw them before we get hold of them. Anyway, back to these names. We can cross this Akram off for a start. All the men our lady saw were white. Except the BM driver. He was black, with dreads.'

'Could be Winston Dennison,' Eddie said. 'And this is just his style. Your old girl see who did it?'

'She only heard it,' Paul said. 'But the black guy came later. It was three white guys she saw running out straight after. They took off in an Escort, and a couple of hours later, the BM turns up. There was a girl as well. She came between the two cars, went into the yard and brought someone out. It was just after that when the BM turned up.'

'That's one bored old woman!' Eddie laughed, shaking his head. 'Sure her name's not Barbara Cartland?'

Paul smiled. 'I know what you mean, but she's okay. Now, this Dennison. You say this is his style?'

'Yeah,' Eddie snorted. 'He's bang into his shooters, him. We've nicked him a few times, but he's got this red-hot brief, always manages to get the evidence discredited. He even sued us once – and won! Sly bastard! Said we were harassing him, and with all the racism shit going on, the judge favoured his version. Got a massive pay-out . . . probably how he can afford the Beemer. He certainly didn't work for it.'

'Sounds likely,' Paul said, circling the name. 'But I don't get why he only turned up after the shooting?'

Eddie raised a brow. 'Like I said, he's sly. I wouldn't put it past him to pay these other guys to do the job. Likes to keep his hands clean, does Winston. So what about this other car – the Escort?'

'It was dark – blue, or black,' Paul said. 'It had blacked-out windows, and probably some sort of kit – fin on the back, that sort of thing. She only saw it for a second when they drove past, but the BM parked right outside her window. The Escort must have been parked up further down the road, possibly in the flats' car park. I thought it'd be easier to trace the BM first.'

'Sounds like it's the Escort you want for the shooting,' Eddie said. 'Trouble is, all the scallies use them, and they're hardly ever registered. Still, blacked-out windows aren't exactly standard. It might be easy if it's still local.'

Paul sighed. 'Yeah, but what's the chance of that? Still, we'll get 'em in the end.'

Eddie laughed. 'You can tell you've not been here long. Don't hold your breath, eh? Give us a look at the list.'

The phone rang. Paul answered it, spoke for a moment, then hung up, smiling sheepishly. 'Er – that was Jane. She's coming over.'

Eddie blanched. 'Alone?'

Paul shook his head.

'Tell me it's not that freak or I'm out of here!' Eddie said, throwing the list down on the table.

Paul laughed. 'Chill out! It's Vanda.'

Eddie tutted. 'The ugly sisters! Thanks, mate!' He waved a hand around the small room. 'Think that Jane'll get her fat arse in?'

'She's not that big,' Paul grinned. 'And she's sound when you get talking to her.'

'Mmmm,' Eddie murmured. 'So long as talking's all she's after! Well, we'd better get a move on,' he said then, picking up the list. 'So you can devote all your attention to your girlfriend when she gets here!'

Half an hour later, they had another fourteen names of local BMW owners. All black men living within a ten-mile radius of the supermarket.

Including Winston Dennison, Eddie knew five of them. He ruled one out straight away – he'd been in Strangeways for at least three months. That left Lenny Wilde, Benjamin Cooke and Max King, and Eddie said they were all capable of being involved in something like this.

Paul circled their names alongside Dennison's and said he'd check these first.

They'd just finished when Jane and Vanda arrived. Paul made Eddie promise to behave himself before letting them in.

Jane had brought a couple of videos, and Vanda had a couple of bottles of wine. Eddie decided he wanted something to eat before they settled down to watch the films, which reminded Paul that he hadn't eaten yet either. Vanda offered to drive them to her favourite Chinese takeaway in Moss Side.

As they turned off the Parkway a short while later and drove past the fire station, Paul happened to glance out of the window in time to see the back end of a car turning onto the road leading to the flats. Something stirred in his gut. It couldn't be – could it?

Probably not, but he had nothing to lose by checking it out.

'Pull over!' he said.

'What is it?' Vanda asked, swerving in to the side of the kerb and braking hard.

'What's up, mate?' Eddie turned to look back at Paul who was desperately trying to open the back door.

'Let me out, will you?' Paul said. 'It's a bloody child lock!'

Eddie jumped out and opened the door. Getting out, Paul leaned back in and said to the two nurses, 'Just wait here, we won't be a minute.'

Eddie followed as Paul ran across the road to the wall running alongside the approach road to the flats. Ducking down, he waved Eddie to get down too.

'What is it?' Eddie asked, crouching beside him.

'Not sure yet.' Paul hopped along until he found a section where the wall was missing some bricks. Peering through, he had a perfect view of the car park. And there it was, reversing into a space behind a Jag. 'Look,' he said, pointing through the gap in the wall.

Eddie moved up to the gap to look. He couldn't see anything amiss. 'What?' he asked.

'It's on the other side of the Jag,' Paul hissed excitedly. 'A Mark Two Escort – with a full body kit and blacked-out windows!'

Eddie peered hard, but still couldn't see it. 'You're imagining things,' he jeered.

'I'm bloody not!' Paul said. 'I saw it reversing in. You can't see it now, but I'm sure.'

'What are you two whispering about?'

They both jumped at the sound of Jane's voice.

'Jeezus!' Paul hissed. 'You frightened the bloody life out of me!'

'Sorry!' she giggled. 'Let's have a look.' She pushed her face into the gap. 'I can't see anything.'

'Sshhh!' Paul shifted her aside as the car door suddenly opened. 'We're checking something out.'

'This is great!' Jane whispered excitedly. 'Is police work always like this?'

Before Paul had a chance to shush her again, a man climbed out of the car, laughing as he hopped about pulling his underpants from his bum.

'Bloody Hell!' Jane yelped. 'That's him!'

Paul threw a hand across her mouth. 'Who's *him*?'

Jane pulled his hand down. 'That man in Cas the other night. The one who stuck his hand up my skirt!'

Ignoring Eddie's incredulous look, Paul said, 'Are you sure?'

Jane snorted softly. 'I'll never forget that filthy laugh!'

'What's this?' Eddie was puzzled.

'I'll tell you in a minute, mate,' Paul said. Then, turning back to Jane, he asked, 'Now, you're absolutely sure?'

'Positive!'

He pinched her cheek playfully. 'You beauty! I could kiss you!'

He almost laughed aloud at Eddie's look of horror. But he managed to keep his face straight as he sent Jane back to the car, telling her, 'Wait five minutes, and if we're not back, go home. I'll ring you tomorrow, okay?'

'Okay,' she agreed reluctantly.

'She isn't half good at creeping about, for a big lass!' Eddie said when she'd gone. 'Now, what's going on?'

Paul told him Jane's experience with the man at the hospital, emphasizing the implication of the timing of the incident – in the early hours of Sunday morning!

'Don't you see?' he said, gabbling furiously as the story took shape in his head. 'Our eyewitness sees an Escort – and there it is. There was one injured, who the girl went back for later. Then Jane treats a bloke at Casualty and says that's him in the car – the same type of car as that used in the job! The witness says one of the men was big, and Jane says the man who brought her pervy patient in was big. And get this! Jane thought her bloke had been shot when she first saw him!'

'And had he been?' Eddie asked.

'Well, he reckoned he cut himself climbing park railings.' Paul shrugged. 'But he would say that, wouldn't he?'

Eddie shook his head. 'It's a bit far-fetched, mate.'

'You'd have to have been there,' Paul said. 'It makes sense to me.'

'You reckon we should call for back-up?'

'No!' Paul hissed. 'We've got to get something more solid!'

'Like what?' Eddie asked. 'A solid bullet through your head?'

'Let's just watch for a bit,' Paul said. 'See what they're doing. Come on.'

They shuffled along the wall until they were almost in line with the men in the car. Then they settled down to watch.

'What we gonna do, then?' Lee asked, back in the car now.

'Wait and watch,' Ged said, shifting uncomfortably in the cramped back seat. 'God! Why did we have to come in this rust bucket?'

'Oi! I'm doing you a favour,' Lee said. 'It's better than

sitting in your car, innit? What if that bloke who pulled the gun on you turns up? I don't fancy getting shot 'cos he remembers your clapped-out piece of shit!'

'All right!' Ged held his hands up. 'Point taken! Someone make a spliff.'

'What we waiting for?' Mal asked, getting his skins out. 'I don't wanna just sit here all night. I thought we were going door-kicking?'

'We've got to get inside first,' Ged reminded him.

Just then the beam of headlights turning onto the road lit up the interior of the car.

'Shit, that's bright!' Ged said, wincing at the approaching light. 'Stupid git's got his full beam on!' Squinting at the car, he felt a sudden jolt in his chest. 'That's him!' he yelled.

'Who?' Lee bobbed his head up and down, trying to see past Mal.

'The shithead with the gun!' Ged snarled.

They all turned to watch as the silver BMW came to a stop on the other side of the Jag. The man who climbed out was exactly as Ged had described him.

'Let's spark him!' Mal said, sneering at the man through the darkened window. 'Look at him . . . Wanker!'

'Good job he can't hear you,' Ged muttered.

Mal twisted around to glare back at him. 'What's that supposed to mean?'

'Fuckin' 'ell, Mal!' Lee hissed, whacking him on the shoulder and nodding nervously towards the man. 'Don't start yelling, he'll hear you!'

'Well, tell *him* not to make out like I'm some sort of tosser!' Mal snarled, still glaring at Ged.

'I only meant because he's got a gun,' Ged said. 'I'm

not calling you a coward. Why do you take everything so personally?'

'I ain't scared of him,' Mal snorted. 'Even if he has got a gun!'

'Be scared of the bullets, then,' Sam said seriously.

'What we doing then?' Lee asked. 'He's going in. We gonna follow him, or what?'

Ged shook his head. 'We'd never get over in time.'

'So what are we gonna do?' Mal asked, lighting his spliff.

Ged didn't know what to say. He'd been set on finding Linda tonight, and hadn't considered what would happen if this man turned up at the same time. This just complicated things. They couldn't risk going in unarmed, but he didn't want to leave, either.

'Let's just wait,' he said after a minute. 'See if anyone else comes.'

'I bet he's gone to see that Simeon,' Lee said.

Mal shook his head. 'Nah, I reckon he probably lives here.'

'Either way, he must know him,' Sam said quietly. 'If he's in the guy's flat and we go steaming in, we'll get our heads blown off. And if he just lives here and hears a door going in, he's likely to do the same.'

'That's why I think we should wait,' Ged said. 'I only need to know if she's here. I can work out what to do if I know that.'

'Yeah,' Mal agreed. 'We can just suss out if she's here, then come back when the dickhead's out and snatch her.'

'She won't like it,' Lee sniggered. 'She's been here for days now. He must be doing something she likes!'

Reaching over the seat with lightning speed, Ged

grabbed Lee's hair and pulled his head back, snarling into his face, 'Shut your filthy fucking mouth!'

'All right, all right! I'm sorry!' Lee yelped. 'Owwww – mind me stitches, man!'

Ged let go and slumped back in his seat. 'Don't ever talk about Linda like that again!' he hissed, wiping the grease from his fingers. ''Cos I'm warning you, man, one of these days I won't be able to stop myself!'

Lee patted his hair down and turned away, pulling a comical face at Mal.

'Here,' Mal said, passing the spliff over the seat to Ged. 'Have a puff on that and calm down. And you . . .' He kicked Lee's leg. 'Stop going on about Linda, before you get your head kicked in!'

'Why hasn't anyone gone in after him?' Eddie asked.

Paul frowned. 'I don't know. I can't work it out. What the hell are they doing?'

They shifted along a few more inches, hoping to get into a better viewing position. But they still couldn't see into the Escort.

They'd thought it must be a meet when the BMW suddenly turned up, and had expected at least one of those from the other car to go inside with the driver. But he hadn't so much as glanced their way, and they weren't making a move. It didn't make any sense.

Ten minutes passed, then the door of the flats suddenly opened and Max came out. Holding the door open, he looked all around, then motioned to someone inside.

In the Escort, everyone lurched forward in their seats to see who he was waiting for. Seconds later, two more men appeared, leading a girl between them.

'That's not Linda, is it?' Sam asked.

'I don't think so,' Ged said, peering hard through the window. 'But I can't see too good from here.'

'Holy fucking shit!' Mal yelled as the group passed beneath a dim light. 'It's not Linda – it's Suzie!'

'What?' they all chorused, straining forward with disbelief.

'It is, as well!' Sam said, his voice high with surprise. 'What's *she* doing here?'

'The two-timing little slag!' Mal snarled. 'No fuckin' wonder she never come back from the shops, the fuckin' little whore! She's been hiding out here all fuckin' day! Bitch! I'll kill her!'

Ged leaned across and grabbed Mal's shoulders, hauling him halfway into the back seat.

'Shut your fuckin' mouth!' he hissed as the men and Suzie neared the BMW. 'Look at her face, man! She's scared out of her mind!'

'She fuckin' will be when I get my hands on her!' Mal spluttered. 'Slag!'

Ged threw his hand across Mal's mouth. 'Will you listen to me, you bloody idiot! She's scared! There's something weird going on here. Think about it! I find out Linda's here, and get a gun pulled on me for asking. And the next thing, we see the same man with Suzie. It's not right, man!'

'He's right,' Sam said. 'Look how they're gripping her arms. She's in trouble!'

Mal looked around, his fury at Suzie turning to outrage at the men. 'Bastards!' he spat. 'What do they think they're playing at? They got no bleedin' right. I'll pan the bleedin' lot of 'em if they hurt her!'

'Shut up!' Ged hissed. 'They've got a bloody gun!'

'So what am I supposed to do? Sit here and watch them take my Suzie away?'

'You'll fucking calm down,' Ged said. 'Now shut up before you give us away! Lee. Don't start the car until they pull out, but as soon as they do, get after them. And for God's sake, keep a bit of distance between us!'

Paul Dalton couldn't believe his luck. First he'd found the Escort, then the silver BMW. Now the red-haired girl from the photo – and she did not look at all happy. In fact, she looked like she was being taken somewhere against her will. Something big was in the offing here. He could feel it in his gut.

He fidgeted excitedly as the BMW drove out of the car park, followed a full half-minute later by the Escort. As soon as they'd both disappeared around the corner, heading for the Parkway, he jumped up, dragging Eddie with him onto the road. Looking around in the vain hope that Jane and Vanda had waited, he was disappointed to see that they hadn't. Pulling his mobile phone from his pocket, he tapped in the station number with shaking fingers.

'Back-up?' Eddie asked.

Paul shook his head. 'I just need to speak to DCI Jackson.'

'I hope for your sake you're right about all this,' Eddie said. 'You've got to admit it was a bit easy, mate. A bit too convenient, like.'

'Yeah, I know,' Paul muttered. 'But if I don't follow it through I could be blowing the best chance of nailing the whole lot in one go.'

'I think you're in grave danger of making a complete prat of yourself,' Eddie snorted. 'Just keep my name out of it, eh?'

Paul grimaced, feeling queasy at the prospect of Eddie being right. But just as he began to contemplate hanging up, the phone was answered.

It was Sergeant Daly. Paul didn't really know him, but had heard he was up the Super's backside. He decided it'd be better not to tell him what he was doing, saying instead that he needed DCI Jackson's mobile number to change an arrangement they had for the following day. If he was wrong about all this, he didn't need to drag Jackson down with him.

Eddie turned to look as a car came up behind them, beeping its horn in short bursts. Seeing who it was, he tugged on Paul's sleeve.

Paul turned with his finger in his ear and his face creased in concentration as he tried to memorize the number Sergeant Daly was reluctantly giving him. His face lit up when he saw Jane and Vanda.

'Now that's what I call brilliant timing!' he grinned, snapping his phone shut after thanking Sergeant Daly. Jumping in the back with Eddie, he said, 'Anyone got a pen? I need to write this number down quick.'

'And follow those cars!' Eddie added dramatically as Jane handed a pen across to Paul.

'What?' Vanda turned with a smile. 'You serious?'

'Too right!' Paul said, writing the number on his hand. 'Just turn right onto the Parkway and drive straight on. I'll tell you what to do when I see what I'm looking for!'

Jane and Vanda looked at each other and gave a squeal of delight. Then Vanda threw the car into gear and roared onto the Parkway.

Paul phoned Jackson's mobile number and waited impatiently for him to answer. 'Come on . . . come on!'

'It's a good job we came back the same way,' Jane said,

beaming over the back of the seat. 'I had a feeling we'd see you again tonight.'

Eddie grinned back at her. 'Ladies, you are truly a gift from the gods!'

Jane turned to Vanda and winked. 'I could get to like him!'

'Hello?' Paul barked into his phone. 'DCI Jackson? It's PC Dalton, sir. I've, er, got something you might find interesting.'

Praying he was right, he explained as best he could about the cars, then listened as Jackson told him what to do. They were to follow the cars until they reached their destination, then he was to call Jackson again and let him know where they were. But under no circumstance whatsoever was he to approach them, or let them see him.

Jane passed a tray of chicken chow mein and a little plastic fork into the back. 'Here you go, lads, you must be starving. I'll share Vanda's.'

'Make sure you remember that!' Vanda said. 'I don't want to find you polishing my half off as well. I know what you're like!'

'I won't!' Jane promised, shovelling a sloppy forkful into her mouth. 'Oh, this is great!' she said around the food. 'I've always wanted to do this! Oi, Starsky,' she laughed, nudging Vanda. 'Give this mutha some gas!'

25

Jackson downed his pint in one, then jumped to his feet like a man half his age. Mac watched with an incredulous look on his face.

'By 'eck, Ted,' he chortled. 'That's the fastest I've ever seen you move! Where's the fire?'

'Up your backside, if you don't get yourself off that stool!' Jackson said, pulling his overcoat on. 'Come on!'

Mac managed half his drink, splashing a good amount down his moustache. Slamming his glass down, he struggled out from behind the table as Jackson steamed off towards the door. 'Hold up, Ted!' he shouted, almost breaking into a trot to catch up.

'Bloody hell!' he gasped, finally falling into step with his speedy friend halfway down the street. 'What's going on?'

Jackson finished tapping out the station number without breaking step. 'That lad, Dalton – that was him on the phone. He's following an Escort following a silver BMW up the Parkway. I told him to call me again when they get where they're going, and I want to get something sorted, in case.

'Hello, yes,' he barked into the phone. 'Get me Superintendent Clarke. Don't prat about, man! It's DCI Jackson and I want the Super – NOW!

'Goddamned night staff!' he grumbled, still marching as he gripped the phone to his ear. 'Superintendent? DCI Jackson, sir. I'm on my way in with DS Macintosh. I'll explain when we get there, but we need a car, a driver, and back-up – preferably armed response! No, sir, I'm not joking. This could be a major incident. Okay, sir. We'll be there in two minutes.'

He snapped his phone shut and put a spurt on, almost breaking into a hop-and-skip run as he hurtled around the corner.

Mac valiantly stayed with him, his face purpling with exertion as sweat rolled down from his armpits by the bucketful. But he didn't care. If Jackson had a gut feeling, there was definitely something to chase.

Sergeant Daly looked up sharply as they burst in and steamed straight through the internal door heading for the Super's office.

Superintendent Clarke gestured at them to close the door and sit. Jackson plonked himself down and drummed his fingers on the desk.

'What's the urgency?' Clarke asked, clasping his hands together and with his elbows on the desk. 'And why, may I ask, do you need an ARU?'

'There's a good chance the men we want for the Singh shooting last week are heading down the Princess Parkway right now in two cars of the types positively ID'd by an eyewitness, sir,' Jackson explained hurriedly. 'There's a PC following in a civvy car, sir, and I've good reason to believe there may be a major incident when they reach their destination.'

'Involving the PC?' Clarke asked, clearly alarmed.

'No, sir. I've ordered him not to approach under any circumstances, but to call me as soon as they stop.'

'You still haven't convinced me you need an ARU,' said Clarke. 'You know I'll have to justify whatever decision I make, so make it good.'

'Sir, with respect, the longer we take, the further they're going to get,' Jackson said, impatiently glancing at his watch. 'It's going on fifteen minutes since I spoke to PC Dalton, and he was already on the move. Now, the men he's following have a girl with them, and according to Dalton, she might well be being held against her will. That's a potential kidnapping, sir. I know how it sounds, but I urge you to humour me on this. If I'm wrong, I'll hand in my resignation first thing in the morning – later tonight, if you like! But if I'm right, we could pick up the whole gang in one go!'

Superintendent Clarke pursed his mouth as he contemplated the possible consequences of making the wrong decision. Finally, he nodded. 'All right, Ted. But please be right about this because I don't want to have to accept your resignation.'

Rising, he gestured them to the door. 'Sort out your car and driver with Sergeant Daly. I'll organize the ARU.'

'Thanks, sir!' Jackson released a sharp breath. 'You won't regret it.'

'I hope not,' Clarke said, dropping back into his seat and picking up his phone. 'Oh, and Ted – get yourselves some bulletproofs, and take one for PC Dalton!'

'Yes, sir. Thanks.'

26

Max turned off the Parkway and eased down the slip road heading for Wythenshawe.

'I don't see why you couldn't bring her earlier,' he grumbled at The Man who was in the back with Suzie. 'I don't like bringing my car down this end.'

The Man frowned at him in the rear-view. 'I already told you, Marie was busy. You remember to bring the rose pruner?' he asked.

Max patted his jacket pocket. 'Yeah! And I hope none of these dirty white scally bastards down here touch my wheels, or I'll be using it on them! So what's the plan?'

The Man smiled at Suzie before answering. He'd taken a bit of a shine to her. He'd always liked real redheads, and beneath the fading bruises this one was a little beauty. But he especially admired the loyalty she'd displayed back there. That had earned his respect.

'We're gonna drop Red with Marie,' he said. 'Then we'll go pay her boyfriend a visit.' He slipped his arm along the back ledge, letting his fingers brush against Suzie's thick hair. 'Teach him a little lesson.'

'You sure he'll still be in?' Jake asked, turning to look at Suzie with his strange eyes. He looked so evil in the half-light that she shuddered with fear.

'He should be,' she answered quietly, averting her eyes.

Looking out of the window, she tried to figure out

everything that had happened since she'd been caught with the money. The Man's behaviour was odd. They'd spent the past hour and a half in his flat waiting for someone called Marie to give them the all-clear. And he'd been the perfect host – lighting cigarettes for her and making her cups of coffee. She was very disorientated by it all: she certainly hadn't expected considerate treatment like this from the man who had earlier kidnapped her and threatened her with a gun.

She began to wonder what he'd do with Mal when he found him and realized, with a brief stab of guilt, that she didn't care as much as she should. She'd given everything to Mal, and all she'd asked in return was his loyalty – his love. Then he'd started all that with Elaine and didn't even seem to care how much he'd hurt her, Suzie. For two years she'd put up with the beatings and verbal abuse. Well, now it was his turn! She looked forward to seeing how he coped when these men got their hands on him!

'Which way is it?' Max was asking.

'Get to the lights, turn right off the roundabout and follow the first road off to the left,' The Man told him, leaning forward to point. 'It's only two minutes from there. There's a park on the left. Marie's is opposite the gates halfway down.'

'Where the bloody hell are they going now?' Lee moaned for the fifth time in as many minutes. He turned onto the slip road, scowling petulantly and complaining loudly about the wild-goose chase.

'And I need petrol!' he went on, glaring around at everyone. 'So youse had better get your dosh out 'cos I left mine with Elaine. Anyhow, I don't see why I should have to pay. It's not my bird we're chasing!'

'Will you stop fuckin' whining!' Mal yelled, pulling a handful of notes from his pocket and throwing them at Lee. 'Here, y' tight-fisted cunt! Now stop doin' me head in!'

Lee swerved exaggeratedly, swiping at the money as it landed on his lap. 'What y' do that for, man! I coulda crashed!'

'Will you just shut it, the pair of you!' Ged yelled from the back. 'Keep your damn' eyes on the road, Lee, and stop pissing about or they're gonna suss us! Jeezus!' He hissed through gritted teeth. 'What the fuck's wrong with you two? You've been bickering like a pair of schoolgirls since we set off!'

'Well, no one told us we'd be out this long, did they?' Mal said, flicking an accusing glance at Ged. 'I'd have brought me Charlie if I knew!'

'Oh, so that's what it's all about?' Ged snorted in disgust. 'You're coming down? Well, that's just great, that is! You're nothing but a pair of junkies!'

'Piss off!' Mal retorted angrily. 'I ain't no bleedin' junkie! Anyway, it's your bleedin' fault we're here. I was only doing you a favour in the first place, so I don't know where you get off callin' me a junkie, y' cheeky cunt!'

'Have you forgotten who we're following?' Ged yelled back at him.

Sam rubbed his throbbing head. 'Shut *up*!' he moaned. 'I should have stayed at bloody home.'

'Yeah, well – you might end up walking back if this petrol goes any lower!' Lee moaned, banging on the gauge.

'Oh, belt up about the fucking petrol,' Mal snapped. 'There's probably a bleedin' tankful! That gauge probably ain't working, anyhow, knowing this heap of crap!'

Ged threw his hands up in despair. 'Right, that does it! If you're just gonna carry on with yourselves, you'd better pull over and let me out!'

Lee immediately swerved towards the kerb. 'Right, then! I will!'

'What the fuck d'y' think you're doing?' Mal screamed at him, grabbing the wheel and forcing him back onto the road. 'My Suzie's in that car . . . Now move it!'

'Oh, it's "my Suzie" now, is it?' Lee sneered. 'Well, I'm— Ooowwww!'

'Fuck was that?' Mal yelped.

Ged had shot his hand out between their faces, catching Lee with the back and rebounding with a sharp smack onto Mal's cheek with the palm.

'What d'y' do that for?' Mal's voice was high with indignation.

'You're doing my fuckin' head in!' Ged screamed down his ear. 'Now just *SHUT THE FUCK UP!*'

They drove on in silence, slowing as the BMW, which was three cars ahead of them now, veered right off the roundabout. But just as they reached the lights, they changed to red, and Lee was forced to stop as a huge lorry trundled across his path.

He cursed under his breath as the BMW disappeared. The second the lights changed, he rammed his foot down and shot out onto the roundabout.

He spotted a flash of silver as the BMW took a sharp left, immediately disappearing from view again. He needed to put his foot down to catch up, but the car in front was doing a steady twenty-five and didn't seem to want to speed up. Pulling right up to its bumper, Lee honked his horn, waving at the driver to get a move on. The driver glared at him in his rear-view and carried on as before. Lee slammed his hand down on the horn, giving a continuous blast as he flashed his lights. It was only when the other driver saw how many men were in the car that he decided to pull in to the side, and Lee roared past, throwing the car around the left turn as he wound his window down to flip a furious 'V' back at the car.

He couldn't see the BMW at first and thumped the wheel angrily. Then he saw its brake lights in the distance.

'They're stopping,' he said, nodding down the road to where the other car was manoeuvring into a parking space outside a pair of closed park gates.

'Pull in!' Ged said. 'Back here where we can still see them.'

Lee quickly pulled into a space about ten cars behind and turned off the lights. All they could do now was wait for the men who had Suzie to make their next move.

In Vanda's car, now parked four spaces back from the Escort, Paul was calling DCI Jackson. He told him where they were and listened as Jackson explained what he was organizing – reiterating again that Paul was not to approach them or attempt to do anything heroic.

'What's happening?' Jane asked when he'd finished his call.

'We're just to watch, and let him know if anything else happens,' Paul told her, adding despondently, 'And we're not to move out of the car.'

'Oh, so you fancied getting shot, did you?' Eddie asked, raising an eyebrow. Knowing how seriously DCI Jackson was taking this, he was beginning to realize the potential danger they were in.

'What?' Jane squeaked, twisting around in her seat. 'Have they got guns?'

'And you got me to follow them?' Vanda's eyes were wide with shock. 'Well, thanks a lot!'

'Don't worry,' Paul reassured them. 'They haven't spotted us or we'd know about it by now. Just stay calm, it'll be all right.' He glanced at his watch, wondering how long it would take Jackson and the ARU to get here – and, more importantly, what would happen when they did.

'Wonder what the Dragon Master's got up his sleeve?' Eddie said, as if reading his thoughts. Rubbing the condensation from his window, he said, 'Do you think we should get in the front?'

Paul nodded. 'Good idea. We'd see better from there. And if anything did happen . . .' He let the words trail off.

'Like what?' Vanda barked at him.

'I'm just saying if – *if* – anything happens, we'll be first in line,' Paul explained. 'Not that I think it will,' he added quickly. Turning to Jane, he said, 'Mind swapping?'

'I suppose not,' she said. 'But how d'y' suggest we do it? It's not exactly the biggest car in the world!'

'And your backside ain't exactly the smallest!' Vanda flipped back good-naturedly.

'Funnee!'

'Take it in turns,' Paul said, shifting across to the door to make room. 'You come through here, Jane, then I'll go over there.'

The exchange took place with a lot of difficulty and giggling. When they were in the front, Paul and Eddie leaned forward on the dash to watch the other cars.

They couldn't see the BMW as it was too far ahead,

but they could see the blacked-out windows of the Escort. So far, no one seemed to be making a move.

'What d'y' reckon they're up to?' Eddie asked.

Paul shrugged. 'Maybe they're waiting it out to make sure they're not being watched. They can't just sit in their cars all night, though, whatever they're doing.'

'Hang about,' Eddie said, pointing down the road. 'They're on the move.'

Max got out of the BMW first and scanned the road as Jake climbed out the other side. Then The Man got out and offered his hand to help Suzie. She hesitated for a second, then decided it was best not to offend him by refusing.

She was still uneasy, but she was also beginning to feel a little flattered. It was an odd sensation – almost perverse, she thought. But he was treating her so nicely, as though she was a lady – and she was beginning to quite enjoy it.

Mal had never treated her like this in all the time she'd been with him. His idea of being nice was calling her 'doll' and making crude remarks about their sex life in front of his friends. He only ever said he loved her if they'd had a fight – and only then to soothe his conscience and make sure he got his dinner on time. Mal wasn't much of a man at all, she decided, putting her hand into The Man's.

He gave her a knowing look as she stepped out of the car, and she blushed – ashamed to be letting her imagination run away with her. Especially given the circumstances. They *had* kidnapped her!

The men stood together on the pavement, having a quick discussion about what they would do once they got to Hulme. Suzie stuck closely to The Man's side throughout – keeping as much distance between herself and Jake as possible.

'Did you see that?' Mal screeched, bouncing about dementedly in the Escort's front seat. 'In danger, my bleedin' arse! The slutty little fucking whore bitch! She was holding his fucking hand! I'll kill her!'

No one said anything. They were all confused now. It certainly looked as though Suzie was all right – she didn't look half as frightened now as they'd initially thought. And she hadn't been forced or dragged out of the car. And she was sticking pretty close to the big guy.

Ged still wasn't altogether convinced that everything was as it seemed. He couldn't put his finger on it, but he knew there was no way that Suzie would have been carrying on with this man in secret. She never left the flat for any great length of time, so how could she have got into a relationship with anyone? And bad as Mal was, Suzie adored him. Ged couldn't work it out right now, but he was prepared to keep an open mind until it was sorted out.

Mal wasn't so convinced, and he went into a blind rage as he watched Suzie brush against The Man's arm.

'Right! That does it!' he yelled, grabbing the door handle. 'I'm gonna find out what's going on. I can't just sit here and watch the back-stabbing little whore slagging about with that goon! I'm gonna make her tell me what she's playing at!'

'Sit fucking still!' Ged told him. 'No one's going anywhere till we think this through!'

*   *   *

'There's someone hiding round the corner back there,' Jane squawked, pointing through the back window to the end of the park fence.

'Where?' Paul and Eddie asked, turning to see what she was pointing at.

At first they couldn't see anything in the dark, but then Eddie spotted the faint glow of a cigarette.

'She's right,' he said quietly, trying not to alarm the women further. 'It could be nothing, but we'd better keep our eyes open. It could be one of that lot on the lookout.'

'You don't think they've spotted us, do you?' Vanda whispered fearfully. What had started off as a good laugh was quickly becoming a potentially life-threatening situation – and she was trapped in this car!

The theme tune from *Rocky* suddenly began to play.

'What the fuck is that?' Eddie yelped. He almost laughed when Paul took his phone from his pocket with a sheepish grin. 'Shit! You nearly gave me a bleeding heart attack!'

'Hello?' Paul answered, trying to keep an eye on both directions at once. 'Yes, sir. Mmmm. Mmmm. Right.'

Snapping the phone shut, he breathed a sigh of relief. 'He's one of ours.' He nodded towards the shadowy figure on the corner. 'There's an ARU around the corner, and DCI Jackson says we're to get Jane and Vanda out of here.'

Eddie nodded, his whole tone becoming noticeably more serious as he quickly motioned to Vanda. 'Swap places with Paul, love.'

'What are we doing?' she asked, shaking visibly as she moved to let Paul climb through into the back.

Eddie reached across and patted her shoulder as she took the driving seat. 'First thing you're going to do is stop worrying,' he told her. 'You're not in any danger, I assure you. Even if we were spotted now, there's a skilled Armed Response Unit sitting not thirty feet away from us who'd take them out like *that*!' He snapped his fingers. 'Now, sweetheart, I'll tell you exactly what to do, so don't worry. I'll be right here on the floor next to you.'

Vanda tried to start the car as Eddie had instructed her, but she was so nervous, she stalled three times. She was almost crying when she felt Eddie's strong hand cover hers on the wheel.

'Just take it easy,' he said, smiling up at her reassuringly. 'Start it up, nice and calm . . . That's right. Now, move out slowly and take that turning.' He pointed towards a right turn just a few feet ahead. 'Turn in, then reverse out and drive back up the road towards the end. When you get there, turn right and don't stop until you're at the back of the police vehicles. Okay?'

Vanda's eyes were wide with fear. 'But if I go that way, I'll have to drive past that car!'

'Don't worry about that,' he told her. 'They're watching the others – they probably won't even notice you. If they do, they'll only see two women. They're not going to think anything of it. Believe me, Vanda, you're safe. But the sooner we get you out of here, the sooner our boys can deal with whatever's going on. Now, just take it easy, that's right . . .'

'Someone's coming,' Lee said, turning to look at the car that had pulled out of a space some way behind them.

'So?' Mal snarled. 'People *do* live round here, you

know. Anyhow, I've got more important things to think about – like what I'm gonna do to that little bitch when I get my hands on her!'

'There's a car coming,' Max said, turning his face away from the road and kicking at a stone.

'Don't freak out,' The Man chuckled. 'Bwoy – you are jumpy! This ain't where the action is, dude! Anyhow, it's going the other way now.' He turned to Suzie. 'You on the phone at home, Red?'

'Er, yes,' she said.

He took out his mobile and opened it before handing it to her. 'Give your man a ring. Make sure he's in.'

'What should I say if he is?' Suzie asked, not relishing the idea of talking to Mal.

'Just find out if he is, and tell him you'll be home soon so he should stay in, yeah?'

'All right,' she whispered, tapping out the number.

'An' mek sure y' don't say nutt'n else!' Jake hissed at her. 'Y' don' wan' lose dat pretty face, eh?'

Suzie shuddered, but The Man silenced Jake with a warning glare and he didn't say anything else.

'It's engaged,' she said a second later as the tone beeped down her ear.

'That's cool,' The Man said, taking the phone from her. 'At least we know he's in. You can try again in a bit, just to make sure he stays in, yeah?'

Suzie nodded, edging closer to him as Jake looked at her with narrowed eyes.

Back at the flat, Elaine was having a great time by herself. Lying on the rug, with the fire turned up full and the phone stuck between her shoulder and her chin, she chattered on, oblivious to the fact that Suzie was trying to get through.

Earlier, she'd made a neat pile of Lee's money on the coffee table and had then counted it – over and over, whooping with delight each time. The things she would do with this money! She had Lee wrapped around her little finger – whatever she asked for, he was sure to give. But just in case he decided to be stingy, she'd peeled off several hundred for herself, stashing it at the bottom of her bag.

As she was counting it for the fifth time, she'd decided to help herself to a bit of Mal's coke from the bag she'd seen him put in the sideboard drawer earlier. The generous line she gave herself lifted her spirits massively, but it also left her with a raging desire to tell someone about her good fortune.

So, fetching the phone from the table, she'd dialled, feeling ridiculously pleased when Tommy had answered – although he hadn't sounded overly pleased to hear her voice.

He'd soon cheered up when she'd told him about her money.

The Armed Response vehicles were in place, the men huddled around their commanding officer as Jackson explained the situation.

Mac politely interrupted to inform Jackson that PC Dalton's car had just turned the corner. Jackson excused himself for a moment and followed Mac to the car.

'Oh, oh!' Eddie hissed as they struggled up from the floor. 'He doesn't look best pleased!'

Paul lifted his head and climbed out just as DCI Jackson reached them. 'Sir—' he began, but Jackson stuck a hand up, silencing him.

'What the bloody hell did you think you were playing at?' he barked. 'You put your own life in danger, that of one of your fellow officers, *and* the lives of these ladies!' With flaring nostrils, he nodded curtly at Jane and Vanda, who were standing beside the car, clutching at each other in mute terror.

'Well?' he barked, still glaring at Paul.

'I, er, thought I was doing the right thing,' Paul stuttered.

'Well, you bloody weren't!' Jackson blasted him. 'There are procedures to follow in cases like this, and doing a Starsky and bloody Hutch is definitely not part of that procedure. Do I make myself clear?'

'Yes, sir!'

'Good! Now get these ladies out of harm's way,

then get your arse back over here and tell me what's going on.'

Turning, he marched over to the unmarked car he'd come in and radioed in to the station to inform Superintendent Clarke that the PCs were present and unharmed.

'That's why they call him the Dragon Master,' Eddie muttered to Paul under his breath. 'See the flames?'

Paul let out a shaky breath. 'I can understand why, though,' he said quietly. 'It was a pretty stupid thing to do.'

They led the women over to another unmarked car and left them with the driver, then went back to DCI Jackson with dread in their hearts.

Paul immediately apologized for his rashness, explaining that it was the only thing he could think of doing since he hadn't wanted to let the cars disappear from view. Jackson told him they would discuss that later. For now, he wanted a complete rundown of everything that had happened.

Paul explained all about seeing the two cars together, and the men bringing out the redhead Mrs Lilley had ID'd. Then he told him Jane's story about the driver of the Escort.

'So you see, sir,' he concluded, 'it all matches what we know of that night.'

Jackson digested the story, and contemplated the likelihood of these being the right men. He had to agree that it was far too coincidental for there not to be some connection, but they had a problem now. They couldn't just arrest anyone without some sort of hard evidence to substantiate the suspicion.

As he considered it, one of the men from the ARU

sprinted across to tell him that something was happening and Commander Oliver wanted to speak with him.

'I'll be right there,' Jackson told him. Then, turning back to Paul, he threw him the bulletproof he'd brought along for him.

'Put that on and stay out of the way,' he said. 'And you'd better ask one of the unit boys if they've got a spare for Hutch, here!' He thumbed towards Eddie Walker, then walked away, shaking his head.

'Spark's worse than his flame!' Mac whispered to the PCs before trotting off after him.

Jackson approached Commander Oliver. 'What have we got?'

Oliver led him to the edge of the park fence. 'Not quite sure yet,' he said. 'But there's been movement. I've got some of my men inside the park heading in that direction. We should get word back soon if it looks like we'll have to go over.'

A light suddenly started to flash on his radio receiver. 'Yes?' he hissed into the tiny mouthpiece.

Jackson couldn't hear what was being said as the message was relayed to the Commander via an earpiece. He waited patiently, feeling a tingle of relief that something was happening – with luck, something that would justify his request for the ARU.

'Seems one of your men from the second car has approached the others, and they're having an argument,' Oliver told him at last. 'Looks like it's getting heated, so we're going to get into position in case there are any weapons involved.' With that, he turned and ran – Jackson was impressed how silently – along the fence to a gap, where he ducked through and disappeared.

'I wish we could get a bit closer and see what's going on,' Mac said.

'We'll know soon enough,' Jackson said, rooting through his pockets for the cigarettes he'd left on the table at The George. 'Damn!' he said when he realized. 'Give us a fag, Mac.'

Mac flipped his pack open and tutted. 'Four left. It's gonna be a long night!'

'Stop moaning!' Jackson said, reaching over to take one. 'I'll buy you a pack when we get back to the station. In fact, I'll buy you a whole carton if we pull this off!'

28

Incensed by the proof of Suzie's betrayal, Mal had managed to get the car door open. Dodging past Ged's grabbing hands, he had jumped out and stormed towards the group on the pavement, screaming Suzie's name.

'Oh my God!' was all Ged could say, as Lee's mouth fell open and Sam dropped his head into his hands.

None of them moved an inch as Mal ran towards the group, seeming even smaller than usual the closer he got to the taller, broader men.

'Raas!' Max said, putting his hand into his pocket for the gun.

'Max!' The Man hissed. 'Not here!' He turned to Suzie. 'Who's this, Red?'

Suzie's face had drained of all colour. 'It's M-Mal,' she stuttered, completely confused to see him here.

'Your boyfriend?' Jake asked with a sneer.

Suzie nodded, too shocked by Mal's unexpected appearance to say anything. She flinched as Mal threw himself at her, but The Man quickly blocked his path, knocking Mal down to the ground and advancing on him as he struggled to his feet, looking all around to make sure there were no witnesses.

'How did you get here?' The Man hissed down at him. 'Eh? You follow me, claat?'

'Yeah, I fuckin' followed you!' Mal spluttered, crazed

by paranoia and too strung out by coming down from his coke high to realize the danger he was in. 'That's my girlfriend!' Jumping to his feet, he pointed an accusing finger at Suzie. 'I got every right to follow me own bleedin' girlfriend when she's slaggin' about! You dirty bleedin' WHORE!' he screeched at Suzie, struggling to force his way past The Man.

The Man easily held him at bay, laughing at his futile fury. 'So you think your girl's been chattin' with me, eh?' he asked. 'Raas, you're a dumb fucker! An' y' got no respect for your lady, dude! That's a special little lady you got there, an' what do you do, eh? You treat her like a ho', disrespecting her in the street! You got no shame?'

'Don't tell me about my girl!' Mal squawked. 'She's mine! Not yours!'

The Man shook his head, grinning at Jake and Max. 'What we gonna do with him?'

'Saved us a journey,' Jake sneered. 'Let's tek 'im somewhere quiet, eh?'

'You're not taking me nowhere,' Mal snorted indignantly, totally unaware that they'd been about to come looking for him. 'I'm taking *her* – home!'

'That so?' The Man laughed again, amused by the little squirt's feeble struggling. 'Listen up, junkie bwoy—'

'I'm not a bleedin' junkie!' Mal yelled. 'You bleedin' arsehole!'

The Man reached out and grabbed Mal's throat in his huge hand. 'Don't cuss me, bwoy!' he snarled menacingly, shaking Mal like a doll. 'See, the trouble with you junkie dickheads, you don't got no respect for your betters! I seen how you think you is a big man.' He pointed at the slowly fading bruises on Suzie's face. 'But that don't mek you a hard man. That jus' mek you a piece a shit!'

As The Man's voice got louder, it reached the others in the car. Lee started to freak out.

'We've got to do something,' he groaned, looking to Ged and Sam frantically. 'We can't just leave him on his own out there! They'll kill him!'

Ged shook his head. 'He deserves everything he gets, the bloody idiot!'

Sam sighed heavily. 'I agree. What good's it going to do if we go out there now? If he's lucky, they'll just give him a kicking and let him go.'

'What if they don't?' Lee moaned.

'It'll be worse if we go over,' Ged said. 'We know they've got a gun. If they think we're coming after them, they'll probably use it on us all.'

Inside her flat, Marie was watching TV. Hearing raised voices out on the street, she flipped the volume down and went over to the window to see what was happening. When she saw who it was, she called Linda over.

'Here, Linda! Come an' look at this! Simeon's got some little farty bloke by the scruff of the neck, ragging him like a dog!'

'Simeon!' Linda squeaked delightedly. 'Where?'

She ran to the window, squeezing in beside Marie and pulling the net curtain up over her head. It had been days since she'd seen Simeon, and she was desperate to put things right with him. Spotting him, she started waving like a lunatic. Marie laughed, pulling her hands down.

'He can't see you, luv, and you're blocking my view! Anyhow, shut up, 'cos I can't hear what they're arguing about, you giddy moo!'

As they watched, The Man suddenly threw the little man aside and put his arm around the girl who was standing beside him with her back to them. Linda's excited grin dissolved in an instant.

'Who's that tart?' she screeched indignantly.

Marie pulled her head back, giving Linda an amused look. 'Whoa there, green eyes! What's all this about?'

'That – that . . .!' Linda spluttered, pointing out of the window furiously. 'I'll rip her flaming head off, the bitch! Where's my shoes?'

She ran from the window like a mad woman, throwing things aside as she searched for her shoes, muttering and cursing as she found them and dragged them on.

'He won't thank you, luv,' Marie told her, watching the jealous display with amusement.

'I don't care!' Linda yelped, jumping to her feet and rushing for the door.

'Wait, Linda – wait till he comes up!' Marie shouted. But it was too late. Linda had wrenched the door open and was already racing down the stairs.

Marie shook her head and turned back to the window. Seconds later she saw Linda hurtle out of the downstairs door and fly across the road, screaming: '*Simeooooon!*'

'That's Linda!' Ged said, shocked to his core to see his daughter tearing across the road and launching herself at The Man. 'What the hell is she doing here? And what the bloody hell does he think he's doing to her?' he added, growling.

Tearing the door open as he saw The Man roughly grab Linda by the arms, he heaved himself out of the car, yelling at the top of his voice: '*LINDAAA!*'

Hearing his voice, Linda stopped dead in her tracks.

'Oh my God! My dad!' she whispered, looking around, her face white with shock.

'*Dad*?' The Man said, holding her at arm's length. 'What d'y' mean, *dad*?'

'Yo! That's the dude with the wallet!' Max said as he recognized the man hurtling towards them.

'Where?' The Man asked, becoming more confused by the second. 'What you talkin' about? What the fuck is goin' on here?'

Ged reached them at a run, crashing into The Man, almost knocking him down as he himself fell. 'Get your filthy hands off my daughter!' he yelled, rolling over and struggling to his feet.

'Dad!' Linda screamed. 'Don't!'

'Yo! Yo!' Max shouted, pulling the gun from his pocket and pointing it at Ged's head. 'Hold it right there!'

Ged stopped dead with his hands raised to strike, and for a second, the road became deathly quiet. Then they all heard the shout coming from the bushes behind them.

'Go! Go! Go!'

The Man spun around. 'What the—'

Jake turned on his heel and tried to run, colliding with Mal, who'd had exactly the same idea. They were instantly pounced upon and thrown to the floor.

In seconds, the pavement and road were teeming with armed police. Surrounding the group, they trained their guns on them as yet more officers swarmed through the gates of the park, barking at them all to put their hands on their heads and drop to the floor, face down.

Max felt the world close in around him as he raised his hands, the gun dangling from his finger. A second later he was face down on the ground alongside Jake, The

Man, Ged and Mal. His hands were wrenched sharply up behind his back as three armed officers pounced on him and handcuffed him.

Linda screamed as an officer grabbed her arms, pulling them back behind her to clap the handcuffs on.

Ged twisted his head around, bucking at the men kneeling on his back. 'Leave her alone!' he yelled at the men holding his daughter. 'She's only fifteen!'

The Man cursed loudly. '*Fifteen*? Raas!'

'Yeah, you stinking piece of scum!' Ged growled at him sideways. '*Fifteen*!'

In the car, Lee and Sam had sunk to the floor, trying their best to hide as the police swarmed all over their friends. They both jumped, cracking their heads together, when the door was suddenly wrenched open.

'Well, well!' DCI Jackson crooned, looking down on them, and smirking gleefully.

Lee groaned. 'Oh, no. Wacko!'

'One and the same!' Jackson grinned evilly. 'Out you come!' He stepped back, exaggeratedly waving them from the car.

'I didn't do nothin'!' Lee said, climbing out, an arrogant sneer on his face. 'You ain't got nothin' on me!'

'We'll see about that, me laddo,' Jackson grinned. 'Now, if you wouldn't mind . . .?'

Lee was convinced he could worm his way out of this because he hadn't set foot out of the car during the disturbance. He became cocky as he turned to face the car, putting his hands back behind himself, ready for the cuffs.

'I'm gonna love seein' your mush when you have to let me go, Wacko,' he jeered. 'I'll sue the bollocks off you for wrongful arrest! You just watch me!'

'That right?' Jackson snorted scornfully, snapping the cuffs on and turning Lee around by the shoulders. 'You might think you're out of this one, sonny – but what about that little job you pulled off last Sunday, eh? Reckon you'll walk away from that, do you?'

Lee blanched visibly, then quickly pulled himself together. 'I don't know what you're talking about,' he said, sniffing casually. 'I ain't done nothin'!'

'Well, I hope you've got a good alibi for Sunday night,' Jackson said. 'Not that it'll do you any good when our eyewitness pulls you out of the line-up!'

'What you talkin' about?' Lee sneered disbelievingly. 'You ain't got no eyewitness! No one saw—'

'Lee!' Sam muttered sickly.

'No one saw what?' Jackson asked, grinning jubilantly. 'Didn't see you down at the supermarket at approximately twelve thirty-five on Sunday night?'

'I ain't saying nothin'!' Lee blurted out, only too aware of the blunder he'd made. 'I want my brief!'

Jackson snorted with amusement. 'Of course. You're entitled to a solicitor. You'll be able to call one when we get you to the station.'

'What about me?' Sam asked.

'No doubt you'll be wanting a solicitor too,' Jackson said. 'And the same thing applies – you can call one when we get you down to the station.' He peered at Sam hard. 'I don't think I know you, do I?'

Sam shook his head. 'No.'

Jackson shook his head. 'Well, if you will keep company with this little villain, we were bound to meet at some point, weren't we?' Turning back to Lee, he smiled sarcastically. 'Here we go again, eh?

'Lee Francis Naylor, I am arresting you . . .'

29

It was almost three in the morning before they had all their prisoners booked in. Jackson, Mac, Paul and Eddie travelled back together, and stayed to the bitter end, determined not to miss one second of the action.

Too shaken to drive, Vanda and Jane were driven to the station in Vanda's car by a uniform. They gave their statements, then Jane gave a separate one about Lee's visit to the casualty department – although she refused to make a formal complaint about the indecent assault, wanting to get the ordeal over with in one go rather than face the prospect of a separate court case. Apart from anything else, both women were due to start their shifts at the hospital in just three hours, and they wanted to get home for a bit of sleep.

Paul walked them out to the car and thanked them for their help, promising to ring Jane the next day to let her know what happened.

Back in Jackson's office, the mood was one of elated exhaustion.

'Well, that's what I call a good result,' Jackson said. Then he turned to scold Paul once more for his foolishness. 'Which is not to say I endorse your methods, lad. You should have put your and your friends' safety first. But all's well that ends well, I suppose. We've got some good stuff here, and a belting chance of making it stick.'

Mac yawned noisily. 'What exactly have we got?'

Jackson read from the printed sheet on his desk.

'Maximilian King we've got by the proverbial short and curlies! Armed and endangering life. And when we get the results from the lab, we'll know if the shooter we caught him with was the murder weapon. We've still got him for possession of firearms if not, and we'll be searching his house first thing – see what else turns up.

'Lee Francis Naylor,' he went on, grinning. 'Scummy little sod! We'll have him and his mates in a line-up tomorrow, see if our Mrs Lilley can't put them at the scene.'

'I thought she only saw three men?' Mac reminded him. 'He might worm his way out of it.'

'You think his mates are going to let him walk away scot-free?' Jackson asked, smiling. 'I don't think so! I reckon when we get them positively ID'd, they'll all start talking. Anyway, we've got that blood we took from the scene. If that matches Naylor, we'll have all the evidence we need to place him.'

'What about the girls?' Paul asked.

Jackson looked back to his notes. 'Linda Grant's been released to her mother, and we'll be interviewing her tomorrow. Her dad's staying in, and we'll see if he's the big one Mrs Lilley saw running to the car that night.

'The other one, Suzanne Edwards. Obviously not involved in the murder, but she did go later. We'll see what she's got to say about that. Threaten her with conspiracy, see if we can't get her to finger the others, eh?

'Now then, Samuel Donaldson and Malcolm Kenny. Donaldson I don't know, but Kenny's a regular little villain. Petty stuff: drugs, burglary, an assault and battery – young girl, dropped the charges.'

'Obviously a favourite pastime of his,' Mac muttered. 'You see the bruises on Edwards's face?'

'Mmmm.' Jackson frowned. 'We'll see if we can get her to press charges, eh? I don't want him getting off. The arrogant little bastard winds me up.'

'He needs slapping down!' Mac said. 'I'd love to wipe that smug look off his face!'

Jackson nodded. 'Anyway, that leaves Jake Costello and Simeon Marchant. Marchant's been released already. He's totally clean. No weapon, wasn't at the murder scene, isn't wanted. Claims to know nothing about the disturbance tonight and, to be honest, we can't prove otherwise. Says he was visiting Marie Sinclair when the others kicked off, and she's confirmed, so that's the end of that. We'll wait and see what his mates are saying, but I doubt it'll make any difference.'

'What about Grant's allegation that Marchant had a sexual relationship with his daughter?' Mac asked. 'Sex with a minor. We can have him for that!'

'She's denying it,' Jackson said. 'Can't try him on suspicion, can we? But don't worry, I'll be keeping a close eye on him.'

Putting the paper down on the desk, he pulled his drawer open. 'Well, I think we've got enough for the time being. How about a celebratory drink?' Pulling a bottle of Scotch from the drawer, he sent Eddie Walker to the canteen for some plastic cups.

'What about Jake Costello?' Paul asked while they were waiting for the cups. 'Has he been released?'

'Not yet,' Jackson said. 'I'm just having something checked out.' He tapped the side of his nose. 'You'll just have to wait and see.'

Eddie came back with the cups and handed them to

Jackson. He told him, 'The Super wants you to go down to the interview room, sir. Suzanne Edwards volunteered to give a statement, and he thinks you might be interested to have a listen. Apparently she's – and I quote – "singing like a lark"!'

Jackson poured the drinks and took a tiny swig from his own before jumping to his feet. 'I don't want to miss this! Stay and finish your drinks, gents,' he said to Paul and Eddie. 'Mac, you coming?'

Paul and Eddie waited until the senior officers had left the office, before jubilantly yelling: 'YES!' Clashing their cups together, they toasted their successful night.

30

Clutching her bail note tightly in her hand, Suzie ran from the station as fast as her legs would carry her. She was so relieved to be released – relieved it was nearly all over.

She felt sick with guilt about grassing Mal up, but the old policeman had frightened her. Sixteen years he'd said she'd get if she covered up for them. Sixteen! She couldn't do that – she'd die! Anyway, he'd been right when he said it was too late to play the loyalty game. Mal was doomed no matter how hard she tried to help him. She realized that now. He was his own worst enemy, and lying for him now wouldn't help him – or her.

Jackson watched from the doorway as she ran hell for leather down the road. He felt truly case-hardened for frightening a statement out of the poor kid. And that's what she was, after all – a kid. Just seventeen years old – and look at the losers she'd got herself tangled up with. He shook his head sadly. Men like Malcolm Kenny really got his goat.

When she'd run out of sight around the bend, he went back inside and slapped a very tired Mac on the back. 'What a night, Mac! What a bloody night!'

'What a result!' Mac yawned, grinning happily.

Suzie had told them everything they needed to know about Sunday night, putting Mal Kenny and Lee Naylor firmly in the frame. She'd explained all about being sent back for the mask, and then again to see if Lee was all right, and Jackson had no reason to believe she was lying. She'd been scared shitless. Her statement, along with Ivy Lilley's, and the blood sample – as long as it was a match, and he had no doubt that it would be – would go a long, long way towards securing a sound conviction.

It was highly unlikely Suzie would be prosecuted, as he'd eventually explained to her – much to her relief. Because of her co-operation, she would probably walk away from the whole experience unscathed – if a lot more careful about the type of man she got herself involved with!

Strangely enough, she'd flatly denied being with Simeon Marchant against her will. He obviously had quite a way with women, Jackson supposed, which was presumably why they all felt driven to defend him.

She was also adamant that Gerald Grant and Samuel Donaldson had played almost no part in the robbery – and none whatsoever in the shooting. Jackson hadn't been able to relieve her fears for them, but had told her he thought it unlikely that they would receive long sentences for such minor roles. His instincts told him they were pretty clean and basically decent blokes, and he didn't think a jury would view them in quite the same light as Naylor and Kenny. Grant and Donaldson might get lucky – this time.

It was going on for six when Suzie stopped at a phone box and called Wendy. By then, she was practically hysterical with guilt and regret, but Wendy was very calm. She said she would sort out a good solicitor for Sam and Ged at nine – but refused to even consider helping Mal and Lee. They would have to take whatever the courts allotted them. She then told Suzie to go home and collect her things and jump in a taxi. She could stay with Wendy for as long as she wanted. And she wasn't to worry, because she'd done exactly the right thing in telling everything she knew. It was time to start living her own life now.

Putting the phone down, Wendy looked down at Melissa and smiled.

'Where were we?' she cooed softly. 'Oh, that's right. Mummy was telling you how precious you are, wasn't she, sweetheart? How very, very much she loves you. And how very sorry she is for being so horrible to you. But Mummy's going to make it up to you. And she's going to make sure Daddy comes home safe and sound. Oh yes, she is . . .'

Melissa snuffled contentedly, reaching tiny fingers to her mother's lips as she spoke.

When Suzie reached the flat, she was disgusted to find Elaine fast asleep in her bed. She debated whether to wake her and kick her skanky backside out there and then, but decided to wait until she'd gathered together what she'd come for.

Making her way silently around the flat, she rooted out not only Mal's share of the money, but Lee's too. Stashing it safely in the bottom of her overnight case, she added the few things she wanted to take, then zipped it up.

Taking a last look around, she spotted Elaine's bags sitting by the door. Out of interest, she tipped them up onto the floor. Amongst Elaine's junk, out fell Suzie's favourite lipstick, a necklace Mal had bought her when they first got together, a small photo of Mal she'd thought she'd mislaid – and a carefully stashed wad of Lee's money. Ripping the photo to shreds, she left it there with Elaine's junk. The rest of the stuff she put into her own bag.

Walking into the bedroom with Mal's bag of coke in her hand, she poured it into Elaine's sleep-gaping mouth. Elaine woke immediately, choking and spluttering as she tried to spit the powder out.

'What the hell are you doing?' she screeched, seeing Suzie standing over her with a livid expression on her face. 'You could have fuckin' killed me, you stupid bitch!'

Suzie shrugged. 'Thought if you liked it so much, you might as well finish it,' she said. 'And it's the last thing you're getting out of me! Now get your fucking filthy arse out of my bed and piss off out of my flat before I rip your fucking face off!'

Elaine hesitated for just a second, then jumped up and dodged past Suzie and out of the door. She knew better than to argue with a psychopath. And judging by the look on Suzie's face, that's what she had to be. It took less than a minute to stuff her things back into her bags and leave.

She just hoped that Tommy would take her back without the money.

31

Going back to the office later that morning, Jackson and Mac found the last piece of the puzzle waiting for them on the desk.

The dossier of unsolved rapes with the same MO, reported over the last two years.

Jackson sat down quickly and threw the thick folder open. The photofit pictures made up from the victims' descriptions were all there at the top.

'I knew it!' he said, slamming the photofits down on his desk and spreading them out. 'Look at that, Mac!'

Mac came round and studied the pictures. 'Bloody hell!' He hissed out a breath between his teeth. 'Another result!'

'Better than that,' Jackson said, grinning. 'Read the descriptions. What's the most obvious thing?'

'Weird green eyes,' Mac read aloud. He looked up and smiled. 'That's our boy! Never seen such strange eyes. And look at the rest. Exceptionally good-looking, neat dreadlocks, light-skinned, freckles on the nose . . . It's him, all right!'

'We've finally got the fucker!' Jackson winked, beaming broadly. 'Want to come and give him the good news?'

'Wouldn't miss it!' Mac said. 'Boy, that *was* a good night! I reckon we might well be in line for a nice bit of promotion – well, you, anyway!'

'Fingers crossed!' Jackson said. 'But I'd take *de*motion if it meant getting this one banged up. Let's hope the evil little shit's prepared to take what he's been giving, eh? Life is a long, long time to play prison wife!'

Mac shuddered exaggeratedly. 'Ooh, it doesn't bear thinking about, Ted! Come on. Let's go and wake him up!'

'Why not?' said Jackson, heading for the door. 'He might as well get used to the early-morning rude awakenings! Like I always say,' he grinned, opening the door and stepping out. 'What goes around . . .'

'Comes around!' Mac finished, closing the door behind them.

If you enjoyed *The Front*,

why not read Mandasue Heller's next novel,

Forget Me Not.

Coming soon from New English Library.

Prologue

She looked at her watch and decided to make a move. It was four in the morning and thus highly unlikely that there'd be any more passing trade. Just in case, she stepped forward into the dim pool of light at the pavement's edge and checked up and down the Lane one last time. It was dead. Silent. No cars passing by at either end, and no drunken stragglers to tempt out of their last tenner. Still, she had the thirty quid she needed for her morning hit and a bag of nappies for the nipper. There was no reason to stand here freezing her tits off any longer.

Turning, she climbed over the trodden-down section of fence into the field. She didn't usually take the short cut alone but as there was no one about she figured she'd be safe enough. It only took five minutes to cut across to Stanley Road this way, whereas walking around took at least twenty. No contest.

Little more than fifteen feet in she was plunged into pitch darkness, the street lamp she'd left behind too weak to cast even a glimmer of light into the tall grass she was wading through. The sensation of blindness unnerved her and for a moment she thought of turning back. But tiredness won out and she carried on, stumbling in the numerous small pits and rabbit holes that seemed to have sprung up all around her.

Halfway across, her heel caught in the mangled wheel

of a long-abandoned bicycle. Cursing as her ankle twisted painfully, she wrenched her foot free of her shoe, then dipped down to wrestle the heel clear. That was when she heard a rustling in the bushes behind her. Her heart leaped into her throat. Was it the breeze? A startled rabbit?

A *rat*?

Ripping the shoe clear, mindless now of the new patent leather, she rammed it back onto her aching foot, all the time peering fearfully around in the darkness. If it was a rat, it would be from the sewers at the far end of the field. It would be big and dirt – and *hungry*.

Seeing nothing, she half hopped, half trotted on, dreading with every step the sharp yellow poisoned rat-teeth sinking into the back of her legs.

And she had no doubt it had seen her – whatever it was. She could feel its eyes following her. And the more she was aware of this, the more she panicked, sure it would smell her fear and know exactly where she was – exactly where to bite.

And it was definitely following her. She could hear it rustling through the grass. Stalking her.

'Saaandraaa. . . . '

She stopped dead, not breathing, unsure if she'd actually heard the voice or only imagined it. Straining to hear above the whooshing of her own blood rushing through her ears, she heard the breeze whispering through the undergrowth, and the distant rumble of traffic on the Mancunian Way. But nothing more.

'Stupid cow!' she muttered to herself, trying to stop the shaking in her legs by chiding herself. 'Freaked out by the bleedin' wind! Get a grip, girl!'

Pulling her jacket tighter around herself she set off again. She hadn't taken three steps when she heard it again.

'Saaandraaa . . . '

There was no mistaking it this time. It had whispered her name. Its tone was low – male. Mocking. Hissing through a smile. She could hear it in the sing-song inflection.

'Who is it?' she called out, peering blindly into the pitch dark. 'I know you're there, I can hear you!'

'Remember me, Sandra?' The voice was close behind her now.

She spun around but there was no one there. Then, behind her again, a twig snapped and she was sure she heard a tiny laugh. Whoever it was, he knew her name, she thought, slightly relieved. It was probably one of her regulars, playing games.

'Who is it?' she called again, her voice stronger now. 'You can stop messin' about 'cos I—'

He moved so quickly that she saw nothing but a blur in the darkness. She was too surprised to defend herself as his arms enveloped her in a vicelike embrace, his breath hot and heavy on her face. And then she was flung around so that her back was against his chest, her arms pinned to her sides by his grip.

She had just about recovered her wits and begun to struggle when she felt the tip of a blade piercing her stomach. Icy fear mixed with scorching, searing pain as he wrenched it upwards, slicing easily through the material of her jacket, her dress and the flesh beneath.

As her flesh gaped and her guts began to spill from her abdomen, she gave way to unconsciousness, only vaguely aware of the knife withdrawing, then re-entering – cutting horizontally now.

Then nothing at all.

Jeff was ten minutes late, as per. Mike lit another roll-up and shifted his heavy work-bag onto his other shoulder. He wished he'd stuck to nights now: it was a pain in the arse leaving the house at half-five in the morning. Especially on days like this – struggling to make it to dawn and ball-numbingly cold.

'Oi! That you, you tosser?'

Mike turned in the direction of the voice. In the half-light, he could just about make Jeff out. ''Bout bleedin' time!' he called back. 'I've been waitin' ages.'

Jeff laughed. 'Aw, shaddup! You're worse than Yvonne for naggin'! Subject of . . . ' he went on, coming alongside and giving Mike a playful punch on the arm. 'Should have seen the gob on it last night!'

'What you done now?' Mike grinned, following him through the gap in the fence into the field.

'Wouldn't go to bleedin' bed, would she?' Jeff flipped back over his shoulder. 'Thought we was gonna get all cosy-cosy on the sofa. But I soon sorted that little game out.'

'Yeah?'

'Yeah. Shoved the bluey on, didn't I? Does the trick every time that. She gets well narky.'

'You're a right wind-up merchant.'

'S'right, though, innit? Should have heard her kicking off. I said don't bleedin' watch it, then, if you don't like it! Jeezus! It ain't like I got it for her benefit, the dozy bitch! Like I'd splash out forty quid to look at her pulling her mush!'

Mike laughed at his friend's indignant expression. 'So what's she say?'

Jeff gave him a lopsided grin. 'Exactly what I knew she would. Told me to go fuck meself, then pissed off to bed with two sleepers. Well sorted! Snuck that little Hannah one in the back door and shagged her rigid.' He yawned exaggeratedly. 'Didn't get a wink of kip all night.'

Mike shook his head. 'I don't know how you keep it up, mate. I'm too knackered to give Sharon one half the time, never mind taking on another one.'

'The secret's in variety,' Jeff told him quite seriously. 'You get bored with the same old same old. I mean, I've been with Yvonne for – what – six years? I'd get less for bleedin' murder!'

Mike laughed. 'You want to watch yourself, mate, or it'll be *you* getting murdered!'

Jeff opened his mouth to answer, then let out a howl of surprise as he tripped. Mike laughed as his friend fell flat on his face in the rubbish-strewn grass, but he soon stopped when Jeff immediately leaped to his feet, his face white with shock.

'What is it, mate? What's up?'

Jeff pointed to a bush. 'That! Shit . . . Shit!'

Mike peered down to where he was pointing and felt the blood leave his own face as he made out the shape of a foot sticking out from beneath a bush. It was wearing a shoe – a patent-leather stiletto, half on, half off, its gleam dulled by streaks of dried blood.

'What is it?' Mike muttered stupidly.

'It's a bird,' Jeff croaked. 'Oh my God, Mike! It's a bird, and she's dead to fuck!' Turning away, he threw up violently.

Mike watched his heaving shoulders for a moment.

Then, overtaken by a sudden morbid urge, he dipped his head to have a look for himself.

He immediately wished he hadn't.

'Better call the dibble,' Jeff said when he had recovered. He dry heaved as Mike emptied his stomach beside him. 'Make sure you don't splash none of that on . . . on the shoe, mate.'

Digging his mobile out of his pocket with wildly shaking hands, it took Jeff four attempts to tap in the three digits.

Detective Inspector Seddon closed his notepad and looked down at the two men huddled together on the tree stump. Big and scrappy as they looked, he pitied them. They were shocked now, but there was worse to come. Nightmares. Flashbacks. They would never forget what they had seen beneath that bush. Seddon himself found it hard enough to shake off the brutal images of death and destruction he saw day after day, but a case like this stayed in the minds of even the most hardened operators for the longest time. And these men, who right now looked more like frightened little boys, weren't equipped to deal with it at all.

'Look, lads, the café's open down the end of the Lane,' he told them kindly. 'Why don't you go and get yourselves a cup of tea, eh? I've got your details, so I'll contact you later to make a full statement at the station. Okay?'

'Yeah, sure. Thanks.'

Getting to their feet, Mike and Jeff picked up their work-bags and headed for the gap in the fence, grateful to be escaping the now-crowded field.

Seddon watched them go, then walked back into the field to the bush. Dipping beneath the scene-of-crime tape posted all around it, he sidestepped the white-suited forensics team and made his way over to the pathologist, Lynne Wilde, who was on her knees beside the body, making notes.

'The same?' he asked, knowing full well what the answer would be.

She peered up at him and nodded, saying quietly, 'And neater – again. Look.'

Seddon crouched beside her, shifting slightly to make way for the official photographer. The flash of the camera in the dawn light accentuated the blood that seemed to have drenched every inch of the area. It also highlighted perfectly the vertical and horizontal slashes to the victim's stomach that Lynne was pointing out to him. He immediately saw what she meant.

This was the fourth killing of its kind in the past two months. But these incisions were almost professional in comparison with the jagged, frenzied cuts that Lynne and Seddon had first encountered.

'Seems our friendly neighbourhood whore-slayer has honed his skills somewhat,' Lynne said grimly. 'Makes me wonder if there aren't more we haven't discovered yet.'

'You don't think it could be a different guy?'

She shook her head, pursing her lips emphatically. 'No chance. Even if someone had managed to get info on the exact cutting method, they couldn't possibly have known about his gift.'

Seddon leaned forward slightly and peered at the inner organs protruding from the ruined stomach. Lacerated beyond repair and drained of all blood, they reminded him of the chicken giblets his wife boiled for the cat. He quickly shook the disturbing image off and looked deeper.

And there it was, its delicate petals barely visible. The trade-mark forget-me-not, nestling innocently in the wreckage of Sandra Foggarty's remains.

'Why does he do it?' Seddon muttered, saddened by the incongruity of it all.

Lynne shrugged. 'No good artist leaves his work unsigned.'

Finished with her examination, she stood and motioned Seddon aside as the team moved in to bag the body.

'Raped?' Seddon asked, lighting a cigarette and pulling on it hard, releasing a great stream of smoke from his nose, making his eyes water – his way of erasing from them the sight of the mutilated body.

'Yep . . . and before you ask, no, there's no semen deposit. This guy covers himself so well he could be one of my team.'

'Don't suppose you've any freaks with a fetish for cross-cuts and flowers?' Seddon asked jokingly.

Lynne smiled. 'Not that I know of, but I'll keep my eyes open.' She checked her watch. 'Look, I've got to go, Ken. I've four autos to get through before I'll get a chance to look at Lady Bush. I'll call you if I find anything, okay?'

'But don't hold my breath, yeah?'

'Not unless you get a kick out of self-asphyxiation.'

Seddon grinned, then said seriously, 'He'll slip up sooner or later, Lynne. And when he does, I'll be waiting for the bastard.'

'Me too,' Lynne said. 'Nice sharp scalpel in hand! Speak to you later.'

'Yeah, bye.'

Seddon waved Lynne off, then turned to look back at

the bush. He stared at it for a moment, then let his gaze wander over the surrounding area. It was fully light now and the field looked exactly what it was – a rubbish-strewn piece of wasteland, with next to no chance of it holding clues to this latest murder.

But he'd meant what he had said. He would find his man – hopefully sooner rather than later. Especially now that the bastard seemed to be getting so good. There was no telling what he'd turn his hand to once he'd perfected his art. This kind of killer rarely stayed satisfied for long. The ones who felt a compunction to sign their work craved recognition and would vary their style to achieve it.

And Seddon just hoped that the fucker would slip up before he moved on to bigger and better things.